Duck

Rebel Wayfarers MC
Book #8

MariaLisa deMora

Edited by Hot Tree Editing

Cover image by Michael Meadows Studios

Cover model: James Xavier

Cover design: Debera Kuntz

First Published 2016

ISBN 13: 978-0-9863562-9-2

DEDICATION

Everyone has three lives: a public life, a private life, and a secret life. ~ Gabriel Garcia Marquez

Public or private...or secret, sometimes the right decisions are the hardest ones to make. This book is for all the extraordinary people I know who keep carrying on with those honorable and true decisions, and then building on that, regardless of popular opinion. You're righteous. Rock on.

Contents

ACKNOWLEDGMENTS

Can I be honest with you? I still don't know exactly how Duck came to be in my head. There's no one person or moment that defined the character, but rather this was a story that revealed itself to me in bits and pieces, fits and starts. It's a tale plundered from dream observations, misheard and overheard conversations, and the brilliance of human imperfections.

From the beginning, back when Mica began coming to me as I slept, I liked the idea that she brought along her friends. It was cool to see the people she surrounded herself with. I noticed along the way that there was this one guy who worked in the background to keep her safe. Who tried to steer bad things away from her. An undefined man who often accompanied her, but edged through the shadows.

For a chick who hadn't much good in her life, it made me happy to know this mysterious character cared enough to give her that and, over time, I found something there I could work with. An echoing kaleidoscope of beauty that helped cement the man, taking him from the shadows and into the light, bringing Reuben Nelms out where we all can benefit from knowing him.

The story spinner in me wanted to know: What would it take to become that person? What could drive a man or woman to devote their life to keeping another being safe when there is no benefit, and in fact, a significant sacrifice required in order to do so? What would have to happen in order for them to become that person doing right, holding on to that charter? And once there...what would motivate them to stay the course?

Life would be good for the person under that kind of protection. What a boon it would be to have someone to count on like that. Someone who we'd know would do right for right's sake. A guardian who dealt in justice from a position of strength; who would shield and keep us safe at any cost.

This book is about finding that within yourself. Digging deep and discovering the bones to build yourself into that person. That hero. About learning how to heal from what might have seemed a crippling blow. An injury, not on the outside, where people can see the struggle, but on the inside, where things fester. That hollow inside us where bad things have the darkness and isolation needed to grow and take root. Infestations of fear and guilt brought about by betrayal, beaten back when we find a way to shine light on them. Take away their power to hurt, and scar. Becoming righteous. Heros.

Becoming...a man like our *Duck*.

As always, the book you're reading is a product of much love and hours of hard work. Here's where I get to express appreciation to the folks who've helped along the way!

I want to say thank you to Hot Tree Editing for a phenomenal job. As ever, your editorial and beta-reading efforts are much appreciated!

The cover photo of James Xavier by Michael Meadows Studios is one of my all-time favorites. To me, James makes a perfect Reuben Nelms, and his secret smile in this image holds so much mystery. Makes me want to get in there and see what I can learn about his story. Get in his head, find out about the character...the man. Love the shot, love the man, love the fotog who made it all possible. Thank you both!

Debera Kuntz, thank you for being willing to tackle this project with me, I adore the cover! You rock, chickie!

My alpha readers: Individually, you each deserve more thanks than I can fit in a single book. Collectively, you've helped me distill the story down to a place that allows the characters to shine through, and I love you for it! Kristen, MirandaPanda, and LeeAnn – your feedback helped me find the ways and means to give Duck his voice. Thank you for your efforts to keep me, and Duck, on track.

My friends and family: You are all my heros.

Muuwah. Love alla y'all. <3

Woofully yours,

~ML

No sanctuary

Lamesa, Texas

Reuben stood stock-still in the mouth of the short upstairs hallway leading to the bedrooms. He had his eyes closed tight to shut out the sight greeting him, but couldn't deafen his ears to the sounds coming from the room to his left—his father's bedroom.

The sound of his father's playtime surrounded him. Door standing wide open so anyone walking past could see, but the woman standing at the foot of the bed would never know, *thank God*, with her eyes bound by tape as they were. The air was thick with effort-filled grunts, sounds of leather slapping bare flesh, and openmouthed vocalizations accompanying intentionally inflicted pain, all working to twist a knot in his stomach. The brief glimpse was enough to stay with him for a long time. He reached out to find the wall, using touch and his knowledge of the house's layout to ease past the nightmare room towards his own.

"Rue." He heard his younger brother call out loudly and Reuben knew his full-body flinch had to be visible. His reaction extreme because he also knew the single word would capture his father's attention. Two quick strides carried him past the doorway and he opened his eyes to find Raymond blocking the hall.

"You runnin, bro? Why you runnin' blind, Rue? Why you runnin'?" The questions came in a singsong because Ray knew why he didn't want to stay in the hallway, why he didn't want to see...or stay around and watch. It looked as if Ray had just come from the shower and was naked except for his jeans. Reuben flicked a glance down to see the buttons on his fly only halfway done up, a clear indication Ray intended to join their father in his evening's entertainment.

A pause in the sounds emanating from his father's room, then he heard, "Reuben...*boy.*" A long pause, followed by the sound of an open palm against flesh, then, "You better get your ass back over here." That order came from David Nelms, patriarch of their family, and not someone he could safely ignore.

"Damn it," Reuben muttered, glaring down at Ray. At fourteen, his brother was barely five feet tall, while Reuben had topped six already, only a year older. It didn't matter. Over the past two years, they had learned size had nothing to do with having the stomach for their father's playtimes, because Ray could—and would—match their old man moment-by-moment for cruelty, cultivating a capacity to deal out pain exceeding anything Reuben could ever imagine.

Ray was rigid hardness, having no give in him anywhere, while Reuben, according to Ray and his father, was the soft one. He felt every pain, lived his life flooded with guilt and shame. Pathetic and weak in his father's eyes, he was the son who helped their women clean up at the end of the night. Gently tending their bruises and wounds, he would urge them to get medical attention if, as often happened in the Nelms' house, things had gotten intense. With the summons from the open door behind him, he had to return to the entryway at least, would have to witness again the extreme demands being placed on the too-willing woman.

His brother nimbly dodged around him and sauntered up the hallway, turning and entering a room ringing with stifled sobs. Reuben took a breath and then followed him, stopping short at the doorframe.

She was tied to the footboard of the four-poster bed, white knuckles on desperate hands clenching around the ropes binding her wrists, legs spread wide with already-bruising ankles secured to the foot of the bed, her own feet suspended off the floor. Since his initial glance inside as he'd passed by, his father had stuffed the woman's panties into her mouth, creating a makeshift gag to muffle her cries.

There were ropes wound around her upper body, tightly binding her breasts into protruding, discolored lumps of flesh. From the bright red striping on her titties, it looked as if his father had been whipping her, probably with the leather straps resting on the floor at her feet. Broken and discarded reins put to a use never imagined by their maker.

Clothespins were fastened to intimate parts of the woman's body, lines of them jutting out from her skin like alien wooden appendages. Reuben knew each would leave their own tiny bruise, and from the interlocking nature of the lines, he wondered what his father had spelled out on her body this time. Whore was one of his favorites, but slut and fuckhole were also go-to phrases in Nelms' arsenal.

She jerked against her bonds, giving a muted squeal. Ray's arm stretched out, his fingers brutally clenching around one of her painfully swollen and purple breasts. "You eat supper, boy?" The question surprised him, and he swayed in place, pulling his attention back so he could focus on his father, hearing him impatiently ask again, "Well? Did you eat?"

"Yes, sir," Reuben responded, desperately trying to keep his eyes averted when the woman wailed again, higher pitched this time, pain bleeding through her tone in spite of the fabric in her mouth.

"All right." David Nelms shook his head in what appeared to be disgust, and Reuben knew the look on his own face must be sickened. Horrified. Weak. His father's next words underscored that knowledge, reinforcing the belief that in this area, as in most, Ray held their father's approval while Reuben did not. "Close the door, boy. Go on to your room now. This is men's work."

Reuben did as he was told, pulling the door shut, muting the sounds of hard thuds made by hands slapping flesh, those sharp noises punctuated by broken sobs. He stood in the hallway for a moment, sucked in a harsh breath, turned, and went to his own room at the end of the hall. He couldn't wait until he was old enough—to be on his own, to leave. For good. Just walk off the ranch and never look back. That wasn't now, though, so he would just have to get as far away as he could. It was never far enough to escape the sounds coming from that room. He knew from experience there was no place in the house where he could go to find peace. No sanctuary to be found.

Nothing changes

Goddamn it.

Reuben stood across from their parking space on the contestants' lot and watched as Ray led a cute—but obviously tipsy—redhead into the living quarters of their trailer. She was new to the circuit, a promising young barrel racer and pole bender, stumbling along, giggling and giddy at the attention paid her by the reigning champion bull rider.

Reuben knew if he stayed, there would be no sleep for him tonight. The skin on a redhead like that would mark up in ways which would make Ray creative, and he knew his brother would keep at her long past the point where she would have had enough. Ray's evenings ran late when he had company, and even if he wouldn't go as hard on her as he could one of the gals he had already broken in, Reuben did not want to listen to her cry as Ray took her dry and rough. Or hear her gag and vomit around Ray's cock when he thrust it down her throat. Or listen to the girl scream, if Ray had occasion to show her the sharp blade of his displeasure.

Untying his horse from the side of the trailer, he led the mare towards the barns. He would rent a stall for her, saving the horse from having to deal with the stench of terror that would surround their equipment by morning. *Then I'll take my happy ass to the fucking motel yet a-fucking-gain*, he thought, deliberately slowing his quick retreat to a swaying saunter. It wouldn't do for anyone to wonder why he was fleeing his own rig, and he had long ago learned not to risk bringing attention to Ray's proclivities. Not if he wanted to keep getting invitations to meets and rodeos with good paydays.

Part of his avoidance was fear. Since turning eighteen, Reuben expected if things went bad, by him leaving the gal in Ray's clutches he would be counted as an accomplice. Part of it was embarrassment, because if people knew what kind of animal his brother was, if they knew what their father had raised Ray to be, he knew they would wonder about him, too. Already their nosiness and distrust of his family was brought home by sidelong glances, or whispered conversations that trailed off when he got near. The townsfolk weren't above talking about the Nelms men. God knew he already had a full measure of that type of talk, just from the rumors flitting around the rodeo grounds when Ray held court. His brother didn't have it in him to be quiet about what he liked, frequently boasting about the quantity and quality of the buckle bunnies he scored, along with the kind of hard riding he liked best.

Two more rodeos. Two more, then I'm bailing on him, Reuben decided as he walked. Enough was enough. With what he had in the bank now, two more rodeos gave him a chance of earning enough money to keep him going for a while. He could stomach two more, then leave Ray to his own devices, let him dig his own hole with the rest of the competitors on the circuit. Reuben could stay on the ranch, work for the stock company, and deal with his father. A third-generation business, DN Rodeo was a stock contracting outfit, supplying all sorts of livestock for both the close-to-home southwest circuit, as well as several further afield. If a wrangler or event organizer wanted to locate hard-to-ride bulls, rank bucking broncs, fresh-from-pasture roping calves, or steers ready to be wrestled, DN was known as the go-to company. As shitty as it would be back in Lamesa, it was still a lot better than continuing to try to cover for Ray.

He walked through the open archway into the shed row and nodded to the barn manager. Five minutes later, on his way out with his stall assignment, he caught sight of another of the circuit's talented barrel racers. Mica Scott.

His mare pulled up lame at a rodeo a couple weeks earlier. Out of options, he had been ready to scratch from his events when Mica came up and talked to him about the injury. She had a massage treatment she wanted to try, and by that point, he didn't have anything to lose. So he'd bought her dinner, then watched as she worked some kind of voodoo magic to unkink pinched nerves in the horse's hip, her strong hands sure and confident as they pressed and stroked.

She had done an excellent job on the mare, enabling him to compete, and he had gone on to win big that weekend. He wanted to see if she thought the horse could use another one of her tune-ups. A side benefit of this interaction was since she was sweet, sassy, and cute, Mica was everyone's favorite on the circuit, including him, so talking to her was no hardship. She was sorting gear near where her horse was stabled across the way, so after settling his mare, he walked over to talk to the girl.

Keep her safe

CHICAGO, ILLINOIS

"No, Prez," Reuben said in response to the clipped question. "She's not my woman. She's..." He shook his head. "Jesus. My brother hurt her. It's been years ago now, but I just gotta..."

Frustrated, he trailed off, looking down at the bar in front of Davis Mason, national president of the Rebel Wayfarers, a motorcycle club he had recently patched into as a prospect. He was trying and failing to explain why he needed to head out of town tomorrow, which would mean he had to bail on a club party this weekend. As a prospect, that kind of thing just wasn't done. A prospect's life was the club, and he was expected to be in attendance at all events.

Lifting his head, he looked Mason in the eye, trying to convey the depth of his commitment to this woman. "My brother hurt her. I could have stopped it, should have, but I didn't. I ran like a coward, leaving her to pull her own fat out of the fire. Friday night, tomorrow...he will be heading into her town, down where she's going to college. After everything he put her through, she's just getting her life back on track, barely starting to make her own way again. He's a hell of a threat from a distance, now he's rolling into town and she doesn't have a clue. I can't let her down again.

Sucking in a deep breath, Reuben continued, "I have...I *need* to make sure he doesn't catch sight that she's within reach, Mason. That means I need to get down there and see the lay of the land once the trucks show up, figure out how to keep her...safe." His words were rushed, tumbling over themselves as he said, "Means I can't do the gig here, man. I'm sorry, but this is—"

With a nod and a chin lift, Mason wordlessly interrupted, giving him permission. Reuben sucked in a harsh breath of relief, knowing he would have been going anyway, but this way, Mason made it easy for him. Easy for him to keep his solemn—if unspoken—promise to make up for his cowardice. For walking away, for closing his ears to the tortured screams coming from the rig. For letting his brother touch something that was sassy, sweet, cute, and loved, breaking that beauty in ways Reuben knew would never be healed.

He couldn't undo the past, no matter how much he wanted...needed, even prayed for a chance to walk a different path. He couldn't change history, but he could hold tightly to the future. And he would. He had promised himself he would. For the rest of her life, Mica Scott would be safe from Ray. Reuben would make sure of it. She wouldn't see Ray, didn't have to think about him, and—*please, God, someday*—she wouldn't have to remember time spent with him and what he'd done to her. No skeletons in her closets to bring her grief. Not as long as Reuben could keep her safe.

***

Three nights later, leaning a shoulder against the wall behind the clubhouse, Reuben took the first untroubled breath he had drawn in days. The first free-feeling lungful of air since learning his family had won the bid for the college rodeo at UI in Springfield. Tension had coiled around him as soon as he knew their trucks would be rolling into Mica's town, bringing the chance of Ray with them, because once he'd lost Mica, Ray had dropped from the circuit. He had gone home to help run the business, taking over when their old man died.

At least that was the official line presented to the public.

Reuben knew differently, which was why Ray coming to Springfield scared the absolute shit out of him. Because the unofficial, back-door talk said Ray was looking hard. Obsessively going through his contacts trying to find the one woman he never thought would walk away from him, using the business to hide his inquiries.

Finally, after a weekend which seemed as if it lasted for-fucking-ever, everyone was safely at home. A none-the-wiser Mica tucked back into her on-campus apartment, and him standing just outside the club's base in Chicago. Since patching into the Rebels, he chose to keep a room at the clubhouse instead of renting a place. This had the dual benefit of giving him access to the few amenities he needed, as well as making sure he stayed deep in his brothers' pockets, keeping him in the middle of things within the club. As a prospect, he still worked to prove himself every day, and this situation immersed him in the club in a way he found he liked.

He shifted, tipped his head back, and closed his eyes, resting and relaxing for a moment. Still filled with nervous tension from the weekend, he was trying to unwind before heading to bed. By himself. He knew if he were looking for company, he could have it at the drop of a hat. There were plenty of girls inside who would be happy to help him. Party dolls, prospects of a different sort, proving themselves, ready and willing to do whatever any member wanted.

He could have his pick of them, but as always, not one of them drew any interest from him. Even now, when the emotional response to a satisfying day was to want to master something, not a single one of those women were what he wanted in his bed. None of them were his dream woman, the one girl who ruled his thoughts. Most would think it was the girl he kept safe, but they'd be wrong.

"Bee," he breathed and his cock swelled in response. Just her name enough to make him hard, his thick dick straining the buttons on his jeans. *My hometown beauty.* In the West Texas countryside, where ranches could be miles apart, neighbors were separated by pastures, surrounded with barbed wire fences and dangerous ravines. In those situations, you took the time to build relationships with the ones who lived closest to you. For Reuben, Brenda McCoy had been the only kid within fifteen miles, which meant they were automatic playmates and became good friends growing up.

She was now Brenda Calloway, and the proverbial girl-next-door had been helping out with DN since before his father's death. He hadn't seen her in more than five years, not since his last night in Lamesa, when he left to begin his search for Mica. Brenda had built a life, a family, something he would never allow himself to have, deciding long ago the risk of his father's blood too much to take on. He hadn't seen her since he'd walked away from where she lay sleeping in the bed they had shared, his retreating footsteps echoing in his ears, a decision he regretted every day.

Bee.

With a guttural groan, he slipped one hand down, cupping himself through the fabric of his jeans. Stomach muscles tense, his cock twitched and jerked in response, the heat from his hand adding to the growing need to feel something...anything around him.

His mind briefly returned to the women inside the clubhouse, but he pushed those thoughts away. They weren't what he wanted. He wanted Bee.

Fingers working at his waistband, he unfastened the first two buttons. Corded muscles in his arm tightened as he pushed a hand into his pants, the urgency to *feel* trumping any concern he might have over potential discovery by his brothers.

Cupping his palm around the shaft of his erect cock, his fingers ringed the base with a brutal grip and he hissed, feeling the blood pulse and throb in the engorged head as he tightened down a second time. *Fuck. Bee.*

With his other hand, he shoved his pants down and open in the front, bringing his cock out into the heat of the Chicago summer night. Humid, unlike the nights in Lamesa, but his mind painted over the empty clubhouse courtyard with an image of the room shared with Brenda, memories lending the air an acrid, desert tang.

"Reuben," she whispered through a delighted giggle, her mouth slipping down his jaw to his neck, teeth delicately nibbling on his skin, lifting her mouth to his for a sweet kiss.

Her hand moved down his stomach, fingers delving under the covers she had pulled over them, her sweet modesty making the contact even more gratifying. Two years earlier, with tightly clenched teeth he had listened to her high school boyfriend brag about his backseat conquest, torturing Reuben with inept pictures painted by crude words.

At the time it had upset him, thinking about the asshole wedging his hips between her legs. Aggrieved him even more knowing the bastard hadn't held her in enough regard to keep his mouth shut about what they had done. Reuben had provided a lesson about respecting a woman, making it an unforgettable and bloody one for the boy.

Now, lying beside her, the knowledge she had been with someone else didn't bother him as much. Knowing she wasn't a virgin would make their coming together easier. He would have liked to be her first, had wanted that for himself, but life conspired against them. He wasn't a virgin either, but he hoped his experience in this arena would be an advantage tonight. He wanted to make it good for her, make it memorable. Make her love him.

He groaned into her mouth when she touched him, her palm stroking the underside of his rigid cock. Twisting on the bed, he rolled her onto her back and slipped a knee between her legs. The soft pillows of her breasts pushed at his chest, flattening against him, peaked nipples teasingly rough as they rubbed across his pectoral muscles. Pushing a hand into the panties she'd left on while disrobing, he found her wet—soaked. Her pussy lips swollen and hot when he slid his fingers between them, the tip of his middle finger teasing, slowly circling her entrance.

Her hand jacked him, moving up and down his shaft, fingers wrapped around with a firm hold, not tentative. Pausing to cup her palm over the head, she rolled her thumb across the sensitive spot just under the rim, jerking a curse out of him as he jolted and shivered in response to her touch. He pulled a similar reaction from her when he pushed his finger deep, gliding steadily inside until his knuckles were pressed against her body, then he crooked his finger, curving and stroking before pulling out and thrusting back inside. "Bee, I wanna be in there."

She gasped a breath and her head moved, nodding. Rolling away, he pulled his cock out of her hand and grabbed his wallet from his pants. Three years ago, he had put a condom in there, hoping for a time like this with her. His lucky condom. Rolling it on, he moved and stretched out over her body, supporting his weight on his forearms. Looking down, he held her gaze as he pushed slowly, gliding inside on one long stroke, feeling her all around him. He watched as her deep blue eyes filled with a light he had never seen, chest swelling with pride as her lips moved, breathing out his name. His *name on her lips, "Reuben."* His Brenda, *finally.*

With a groan that echoed through the night, he flung his head back, semen splashing onto the grass at his feet. Swaying shadows of supple, wind-blown trees danced across the evidence of his desire for a woman thousands of miles away. Still, after all this time, she could take him there with only a memory. "Bee," he breathed again, his tone filled with sadness and loss. When he stopped trembling, he tucked himself away. Buttoning up his pants, he turned, striding into the clubhouse and his home.

Going home

SIX YEARS LATER

He leaned his head against the curved wall and stared out the window. The pre-dawn view remained unchanging for a moment, lights twinkling in the distance while nearer lay motionless shapes. Then a growing, growling roar filled the space around him and his head lifted as a jet flashed past, hearing the bark of its big wheels on the runway as it landed.

The speakers crackled and he heard the first officer's smooth voice. "We are next in line for takeoff, folks. Flight attendants..." He stopped listening at that point, feeling the chassis of the plane jerk and sway beneath him as they taxied onto the runway.

He felt the familiar kick of the engines revving, the coiled potential of the plane waiting impatiently for the pilot's guiding hand. Thrust backwards into his seat, he watched out the window as the cement and buildings surrounding the complex pattern of roads built for wide wingspans fled from them, faster and faster until, with a jerk and a bounce, they were airborne. Headed home.

For the first time in eleven years, Reuben was on his way back to Lamesa, Texas, where his family had owned land since 1879. The town where the legacy of his grandfather's stock contracting business had flourished; and, where, once he arrived, he would be the sole surviving member of the Nelms clan.

Home.

Eyes turned back to the window, but he didn't see the bank of gray clouds visible over the edge of the slowly flexing wing. Instead, the image filling his head was a picture saved for months on his phone. The stark black-and-white image showed a flat stretch of land, trailing out into the distance as far as the eye could see. Dotted with mesquite brush, the foreground of the photograph held the sharply slanting edge of a ditch. Dumped into that ditch as if it were last week's trash was a body.

It lay in a heap, twisted, one arm caught underneath the torso so the elbow stuck up like the broken slat in a fence, awkwardly angled over the rest of the figure visible in the shot. Sand and dirt had drifted across the face, but he would know that compact, powerful body anywhere, having seen it in too many places and across too many years to count.

Familiar, known, hated...Ray, his brother. Killed due to his own actions because Reuben had never been successful at stopping him from being the jackass their father had raised them both to be. Try as he might, he hadn't been able to prevent his brother from traveling such a wellworn path.

Gaze still absently tracing the horizon through the tiny airplane window, he sighed, shifting slightly as his shoulder rubbed against the man seated next to him. Right about now he was sorry he hadn't taken advantage of the upgrade offer from Digger, the club's resident travel expert, but he hadn't wanted to chance any delays. He needed to be in Lamesa yesterday because it sounded like he had already ignored things for too long as it was. A little unpleasantness along the way would just get him more in the mood to deal with all the uncomfortable things waiting for him at the journey's end. A short detour in his life.

His plans were to be on the first fucking plane out of there the moment he dealt with the things that needed his attention. He'd pull a U-turn, gladly leaving the shithole of a dust-covered town in his rearview for the last time. He sighed again, then grinned humorlessly when the guy moved away, giving him a few additional inches of space. Either his own considerable and intimidating size, or a belated respect for his leather cut caused the movement. He found himself uncaring which, simply thankful for whichever it was. For years now, Reuben had been a fully-patched member of the Rebel Wayfarers, based out of the Chicago chapter, and during this time, he found when most people realized the affiliation, they gave him, or any of the Rebels, a wide berth.

Reuben, or Duck, as he had become known in the club, was finally headed home nearly three years after his brother's death, because he had received a troubling message. He rubbed his forehead with finger and thumb, trying to ignore the headache he got every time he tried to figure this out. Brenda had left a confusing message on his phone; maybe more than one. He shook his head. *Definitely more than one.*

Duck scoffed at himself, twisting to find a comfortable position in the tight seat, thinking about the dozen or more messages she had left over the past few months. Simply hearing her voice still had the ability to cause him pain. Each message a raw reminder that the longing for Brenda hadn't diminished with time. *My Bee.* After torturing himself with the first few messages, he first started archiving, then deleting them. Until the most recent one.

Without meaning to, he drew the memory of her last message into his mind, again hearing the trembling tone of her voice as she spoke. *"Reuben, you either come home before the weekend, or I'm calling the auction company. Not foolin' around here, big man. I've given you ample time to make this right, and you've been putting me off, but no more."* The steel in her voice showed itself, and she had finished with, *"I'm done. Come home, or lose it all."*

'Come home, or lose it all' was a joke, because he had already lost it all. Lost his father to his brother's treachery, and then lost his brother to the bastard's own stupidity. Lost his other dream to another rodeo king.

A rasping snore broke into his thoughts and he looked left to find his annoying seatmate had dozed off, chin resting heavily on his chest. *Yeah, I shoulda listened to Digger*, he thought. *Probably shoulda listened to Bee, too.* He leaned back, tipping his chin down, hoping to make the trip go by faster by trying to sleep.

They landed in Midland, the closest connection Digger could find to Lamesa, and Duck prepared to deplane. Stepping out from the seat, he yanked his duffel bag from the confines of the overhead bin, hooking the strap over his shoulder. That accomplished, he then stood in the motionless line, head and shoulders bent awkwardly in the aisle of a plane sized for normal people. As the passengers slowly cleared from in front of him, he made his way off the aircraft and up the jetway, digging out his phone.

A brief message from Digger announced he had arranged ground transport and with laughter underscoring his words said Duck would undoubtedly recognize the driver. The humor in his voice didn't bode well for Duck, and he listened to the voicemail a second time, frowning at the abbreviated message.

Stalking through the terminal and into the parking lot, he carefully scanned the trucks idling at the curb, trying to pick out which should be the so-called familiar face. He saw a beat-up, black four-by-four pickup with the company logo on the door sitting in the line of vehicles, and a moment later saw the petite face peering out at him from behind large round sunglasses, finely-drawn features half-hidden in the glare of the windshield.

The face and fall of dark hair from underneath the cowgirl hat settled his memories and his head tipped back on a groan. Feet stuttering to a stop, he stared upwards for a moment, shaking his head and muttering,

"Digger's gotta be fucking *kidding* me." Duck pushed his feet into action again, continuing on his way as he shrugged the duffle's strap higher on his shoulder.

The driver opened the door and moved to stand on the running board, tipping her hat backwards on her head. Leaning her elbows on the doorframe so she could excitedly wave with both hands, she wore a broad grin on her face, those sunglasses under that cocked-back hat managing to somehow look both stylish and ridiculous.

"Fucking shit," he muttered, tossing his bag into the bed of the truck and reaching for the frame of the driver's door. "Slide the fuck over," he growled and slapped the top of the truck in frustration when her response was to stick out her tongue and giggle. *Goddammit*, he thought, *I do not need this brand of fuckery today.*

"Happy to see you again, too, grumpy." She laughed as she slid across the bench seat, settling on the passenger side and buckling her seatbelt. "No, really. All jokes aside, I've missed you, Reuben," she said, reaching over to lay one small hand on his forearm, laughing aloud as he shook it off with a growl. "Digger didn't tell me who I was picking up, just said I'd recognize my passenger. It really is good to see you. You comin' back home? Thinkin' of comin' back to the circuit?"

He sighed, looking over at the girl sitting across from him. "Essa," he greeted her, ignoring her questions. "You wanna tell me what the hell you're doing in Midland, girl?" Without waiting for her response, he put the truck in gear and pulled away from the curb, easing into traffic as he prepared to drive the still-familiar patterns away from the airport and out into the country towards the ranch. Back home. Away from his found family, surrounded everywhere by painful memories. *Fuck.*

"Y'all's annual rodeo is only a few weeks away. I came out to help Brenda deal with all the vendors. There's a slew of 'em, and they all have different demands. It's a lot for her to keep up with, so I said I'd help out. I showed, and she put me to work." She said this quickly, aiming her shades out the window and he interrupted his survey of the changes in the city to glance her way, studying her for a moment.

"Since when do you work for DN Rodeo?" he asked, and watched in surprise as she twisted her hands in her lap. Essa, or Esmeralda Waldon, was a long-time rodeo competitor. A successful one, too. Talented, she rode barrels and raced poles, honing her remarkable aptitude and competing professionally for the past several years.

Reuben had known her for a while. She had been a young and flighty eighteen the last time he'd seen her. Immature, but damned determined to make her mark in the world, she had a solid focus on what she wanted. Eyes on the prize. Now, he could see she was maturing, thought he could glimpse what would be in store for them when she finished growing into her own. A beautiful, poised young woman.

Her wanting to help Brenda out didn't surprise him. The stories told through the grapevine said she was still the same caring and giving person—at least when she wasn't snarky and snide. His surprise at her presence had more to do with his second association with the woman and her family than anything else. Essa was a cousin of two women important to him in ways which carried both a responsibility and burden alongside their friendships.

Mica and Molly, the Scott sisters. His hidden protection of Mica had wound up involving the entire Rebel membership, and now both women had the protection of the extended family of Rebel Wayfarers. Through a series of events unrelated to Duck, Mica had come to the attention of Mason. The man had given her a unique title, one granting her a highly respected status few women achieved within an all-male club. So, while it was expected Essa would know Brenda given they ran in the same rodeo circles for much of the year, both her presence here and being related to who she was certainly made things interesting.

"Not really working for ya, just helping Brenda." She bit the words out, her tone sharp and from the corner of his eye, he watched as she smoothed down her legs with her hands, palms to her thighs. He noticed the fingers of the right one dug in a bit, thumb rubbing circles on the area just above her kneecap. He glanced at her again, taking in the dark smudges under her eyes, and the wrinkled creases in her forehead. She was hurting, and in a way that kept her from restful sleep.

"How'd you get hurt?" he asked and she jerked, swinging her gaze to him. Her incredulity was so apparent he had a hard time suppressing a grin at her response.

"What makes you think I'm hurt?" She huffed air out through her nose, frowning at him, tipping down her chin and staring at him over those absurd shades.

"Can't deny it, honey." He continued to gaze out the front windshield of the truck, keeping her in his peripheral vision.

"How'd you know I was hurt?" She fired back with a question of her own and he didn't even try to hold back the grin, because this time she hadn't bothered denying the injury.

"Just do." He let the two words hang out there without any trappings, giving her nothing to go on other than that and he watched as her hands nervously twisted in her lap again.

"Wasn't Breezy's fault. My pony did good," she muttered, and he grunted in response, not sure what her horse's performance had to do with anything. "Boscol Rodeo." She sighed, her frustration clear. "I should have scratched when I saw what the arena looked like." She lifted one shoulder in a shrug, skirting the edges of elegant while still retaining a bit of the coltish awkwardness he remembered. "He can do deep and loose, but slick is hard."

She was referring to the condition of the ground on which the competitions were run. Deep meant there was ample depth of lightly packed dirt in the arena. Loose would indicate it was less than ideally packed, but still workable. Slick, well, that added an entirely different level of complexity to an already tough sport. If the surface was slippery, it made it difficult for the horses to successfully complete the kind of hard, abrupt turns and quick, explosive accelerations necessary to compete at the national level in the timed event of barrel racing.

She continued, "He went down on two and the dang horn gave me a whack." Her fingers dug into the muscles above her knee again. When her horse fell on the second barrel in the cloverleaf pattern, the hard, leather-covered wooden horn of the saddle must have gouged her leg, which would usually just result in a bruise or some sore muscles, but this seemed different.

"Breezy okay?" Summer Breeze was her go-to horse for competition. He knew from conversations with Molly that Essa had been in the stall the day the colt first dropped to the straw, and the two had grown up side-by-side. Molly competed professionally for several years, too, but now lived in Chicago with her son, Tomas, and her husband, J.J. Rupert.

"He went all the way down." He saw her mouth twist sideways. "Pulled tendon," she said and shook her head, and he didn't know if it meant she didn't agree with the veterinarian's opinion, or something else.

"How long ago was Boscol?" If it had just happened, then her apparent soreness made sense.

She huffed out a heavy sigh, blowing her bangs back off her face. "Three weeks," she finally said, quietly, face turned to the window.

"Oh, man," he muttered, turning the wheel to steer the truck onto the heavily rutted road leading to the ranch. Three weeks was a long time for her horse to still be injured. Suddenly aware of where they were, he blew out a breath, frustrated because he wasn't prepared for what was coming next. Their conversation had made the trip go by much faster than he would have liked, a distraction which meant he wasn't ready to deal with Brenda at the end of the drive.

Essa didn't respond and he allowed the conversation to die, focusing instead on the state of the road, which looked as if it hadn't been graded for some time. The pothole craters combined with the washboard surface made the driveway a challenge to navigate, even in the sturdy pickup. He knew it would be worse with a semi, and worse still on any stock transported in the big trailers they pulled.

Up ahead, the main homestead slowly came into view and he saw the house, too, had not been maintained as well as it should have been. Even from the distance, he could see the eaves and window frames needed sanding and painting, and there was a sag to the porch roof over the front door that made him frown. There were several trucks parked between the buildings, all but one just as beat-up as the vehicle he was currently driving. He suspected the newest truck belonged to Essa, which meant the rest belonged to the stock company. *Fuck*. At least the barns, corrals, and catch pens looked to be in good shape.

Okay, first order of business will be to look at the books, see where we are financially. He could pull in the Rebels' money guy to look things over if needed. He shook his head, thinking, *I'm glad Myron is always up for a challenge*.

Parking the truck, he stepped out and stretched, hearing Essa move around inside the vehicle. There was shouting from the house, and taking the three steps up to the back porch in a single stride, he pulled open the screen door exactly as he had a thousand times each summer of his youth and stepped into the kitchen.

State of things

Brenda ducked her head, wincing as heavy thumps sounded from the second floor. "Elias Calloway," she yelled in the direction of the stairs, "you wanna take a little more care with my walls, honey?"

"Sorry, Mom." She got a muffled yell in response, and grinned, turning back to the task at hand, putting up the bags and boxes of groceries scattered across the floor. Thank goodness the ranch house had a huge pantry, because that amenity, paired with the gigantic refrigerator and freezer, meant she didn't have to go shopping more than once every few weeks, even when feeding a dozen men three meals a day.

She had just sunk to a squat in the middle of the kitchen floor, efficiently sorting canned goods into one of the boxes when she heard the door behind her open without a knock. Shaking her head because there was only one person on the place who would just waltz in without announcing themselves, she put the last can in the box and called, "Essa, honey, can you help me carry this box over to the pantry? I find myself overambitious in packaging, but lazy in execution, and now it's too heavy."

From outside, she heard Essa's answering voice, and startled, she spun in place, putting a knee on the floor as she looked up into the face of someone she never really expected to see again. Without a word, he stalked towards her—no other descriptive phrase came to mind, the man was definitely stalking—bent over, and picked up the box. He strode to the pantry, put it on the small table in the middle of the room and glanced around for a moment.

All of this action was conducted in complete silence. Closing the pantry door behind him, he turned and looked at her, still without saying anything. Not saying anything with his mouth, at least, because his eyes and the expression on his face were shouting at her, and they didn't have anything nice to say. Not at all. He was pissed as hell to be here.

Tall. Dark. Gorgeous. Broad shoulders filled out his shirt in a way more than hinting at the muscles she knew were hiding underneath the fabric. Reuben Nelms was all of that. Then again, he always had been, for as long as she had known him, and she had known him a long time. Nearly all her life. At least since she moved to Lamesa as a child. So many years ago.

"You came." Even to her own ears, her voice sounded small and frightened in the stillness of the room, but he didn't respond or react to her words, just stood there and stared at her. It was as if she never spoke at all, almost as if she didn't exist, didn't ripple the fabric of his world or register in any way. Small and disposable, forgettable. Just as she had felt around him all the time while growing up. All the time, except for one night. *Oh well*, she thought, *there's my confirmation nothing ever actually changes.*

It was at that moment she heard booted feet galloping down the stairs, sounding far larger than their decade of years warranted. Her eyes flicked anxiously towards the doorway. *Crap.* Elias hit the bottom of the stairs at a run, rounded the kitchen counter and slid to a stop in front of her. Excited eyes bright, hat in hand, his dark hair was sticking up all over his head. *Holy crap.* "I finished. I swear. So, General? Please, Mom. General? Can I?"

Impatient eyes only for her, he hadn't noticed the man standing across the room.

"General still kicking around then?" When Reuben spoke, Eli jumped at the strange voice, turning around quickly to face him.

She reached out for Eli's shoulders, pulling him to stand in front of her as she straightened to her full height, not even aware she was using her son to shield her from their visitor. "Elias Calloway, I'd like you to meet Reuben...Mister Nelms."

With good manners drilled into him from the time he could form words, her son stepped forwards, pulling out from under her hold. He reached out one hand, head tilted back so he could look the tall man in the face. "Pleasedtameetcha, Mister Nelms." His words were jammed together as Reuben's hand engulfed his, because he was trying to get the required politeness out of the way so he could again make his plea.

Hand still locked in Reuben's grip, her son turned back to her, hat dangling from his fingers. The way they stood caused her breath to hitch in her chest. Because like this, connected as they were, the stance seemed familiar instead of a required greeting, and the two faces, bearing more than a passing resemblance, stared at her with nearly identical questioning expressions.

How did I never see this? she thought in despair. That was followed quickly by, *How will I ever tell Reuben?* Her ill-conceived plan to get Reuben to come home in the hopes he would see Elias and simply *know* seemed to have fallen apart, and right now, she couldn't say she was sorry. As angry as he looked to simply be here, she couldn't imagine the eruption of rage which was going to follow the revelations she knew she couldn't put off for long.

Pushing aside her thoughts, she took a breath and told her son, "Yes, you can ride General, but you watch out. Just because he's old doesn't mean he can't scrape you off on a fence if he wanted to. That gelding has tricks you've never had to learn. You pay attention, and make sure you're back home in time for chores, okay?" Those words were for Eli, whose face broke into a broad grin at the words granting him permission to engage in an entire afternoon of his favorite activity: ride his beloved horse. Lifting her gaze to Reuben, she confirmed, "Yeah, General's still around. Still teaching kids to ride and the dang beast is still opening gates."

Because her gaze was fixed on him, she saw what she thought was a moment when Reuben might have begun to question things, when he looked down at the smile on her son's face, frowning. Then the expression was buried because Essa breezed into the room, distracting him from whatever he had been about to ask. "I ain't carrying your bag in, Reuben." She huffed as she flung herself into one of the kitchen chairs. "Elly-belly, come gimme a hug. I'm in desperate need of a kiddy hug today."

Dutifully, Elias moved towards her, dropping his hand from Reuben's as he did, breaking the tableau. Brenda took in a relieved breath, hoping she had dodged the bullet on any questions, at least while they had an audience. She needed to tell Reuben; that was the plan all along. Get him back here, tell him, and figure out how they moved forward. But because of Eli, she needed to be careful. She allowed herself a long, furtive look at Reuben, marking the changes his life had produced in him over the years. Eleven years. That's how long it had been since she'd seen him last. His face held more lines, but they seemed formed by laughter, not anger, and added astounding character to an already striking countenance. *God, I hope he's had a good life*, she thought.

Standing motionless as he was now, he seemed relaxed. At ease. His complexion a rich olive, of course that gift from his Mexican mother wouldn't change. His hair still raven dark, untouched by gray, at least what she could see of it underneath his baseball cap. The damned goatee still on his chin. Sexy and strong, he was, as he had always been, all man.

His eyes were still dark, too, liquid and warm, and she felt the full weight of his stare when she walked across the kitchen towards the countertop. "Thank you, Reuben," she said, feeling suddenly clumsy and stiff. Her face heated as she thought about the last time they had been in a room together. There hadn't been anything awkward between them that night. Glancing over at him, she reached up to grab two mugs from the cabinet, and asked, "Coffee?" He nodded. "You take it the same way?" He nodded again. Silence, his go-to buffer to keep people at bay.

She watched him, mesmerized when he reached up, took off his cap to ruffle his hair, and then replaced it on his head. Everything about him seemed so familiar, the same boy she had known all her life, but then when she took him in...he was so different, foreign. This man was hard in ways she hadn't expected, beautiful in ways her body would never forget.

Vaguely, she heard Essa and Eli chatting in the background but jumped, startled when Essa called out, "I'm going to take one of the boarded horses out for a ride with Eli and General. Blow the cobwebs out of my head." Brenda nodded with a jerk, dragging her gaze away from Reuben with some effort, staring down at the mugs as she filled them with hot, black coffee. The kitchen door closed and she startled again as the door slammed shut.

She jolted yet again, spilling hot coffee on her hand when the heat of Reuben hit her back, his arm appearing beside her, reaching out for his own mug. "Crap," she muttered, moving sideways towards the sink and away from him, putting space between them as she turned on the cold water and plunged her hand underneath the flow.

"Sorry," he said, appearing beside her again and gripping her wrist with one big palm. The feel and sight of his hand against her skin stirred long-suppressed memories, and she struggled not to react to his nearness. Clearly he didn't have the same thoughts, because he was all business when he pulled her hand from under the water, looked at it a second and then placed it back into the stream. "First aid box still in the mudroom?"

She nodded and opened her mouth to tell him not to bother, but before she could get the words out he had already moved away. Rolling her eyes at his reaction to a little burn, she pulled her hand out of the water to look at it just as she heard him call, "Leave it under the water, Bee." With a slanted grin at his bossy use of her childhood nickname, she rolled her eyes at him again, placing the rapidly numbing appendage back beneath the cold flow of water.

"Let's see it," he said, startling her for the fourth time as he showed up right beside her.

"How the hell do you do that?" The question was rhetorical because for all his size, Reuben had always been light on his feet, nimble on the football field as well as in the rodeo arena. Some of his records in both venues still stood in this county, and a couple of the ones for calf roping were even at the state level.

"Do what?" He turned off the faucet and used a clean, soft dishtowel to blot the dampness from her skin. The reddened patch had grown and she glanced back over at her mug, realizing she had managed to spill about half of it on her hand. "I think some salve will do for you." He released her, pressing the cloth into her other hand as he turned towards the first aid kit on the counter. Rummaging around in it, he came up with the burn ointment. Opening the tube, he carefully rubbed a generous amount onto the burn. "How do I do what?" He reminded her of the question and she waved it off with her other hand.

"Nothing." Biting her lip, she stood in silence for a moment, lost in the feel of his hands on hers, pleasurable even in this clinical fashion, and then blurted, "I didn't think you'd actually come."

"You didn't give me much of a choice, did you?" His immediate response held a note of accusation, and she winced at the implication that she had forced his hand. Which she had, but it was for a good reason. Now she just had to find the right way to explain everything to him. Explain something she was still struggling to wrap her own head around. *Right. Like that'll go well*, she thought.

"You wouldn't pick up the freakin' phone when I called. What was I supposed to do? Even the registered letters got signed for and accepted, but you never responded. Fell off the face of the freakin' earth where this place was concerned." Her breathing hitched. *Where I was concerned*. That thought nearly did her in, and she tried without success to hide her emotional reaction. Turning her head away, her voice dropped to a whisper, a betraying tremble in her tone as she asked, "What was I supposed to do?"

She glanced back to find Reuben had straightened from where he had leaned against the countertop, a tension running through him that hadn't been there before. Motionless, he stared at her for a long minute before he shook his head slowly, side to side. "I don't know, Brenda." He sighed as he asked, "Are you set on doing this right now, or can it wait until after I shower? I stink from the plane."

"It can wait," she said instantly, her soft words latching onto the opportunity to delay, even for another few minutes. She didn't know what his reaction would be, couldn't predict how angry he would be at the news. She didn't know him anymore, and wasn't sure she would survive if he... "Of course it can."

An hour later, he had finished with his shower, but the conversation she planned would have to be postponed, as the ranch foreman and hands crowded into the house to meet Reuben and welcome him home.

Caught off guard

"What's on the agenda for today, boss?" Brenda heard Gill ask the question, knowing without looking up it was directed at Reuben. After only three days, everyone except her seemed to have fallen into a comfortable routine of having him around the ranch. Even the men, like Gill, who hadn't met or worked with him before. Last week this particular question would have been directed at her, and she and Gill would have been standing comfortably in the kitchen, having the conversation over mugs of hot coffee instead of hat in hand, stuck in the official office out in the barn.

Her entire routine was askew and in the days since Reuben walked through the kitchen door, she hadn't found a private opportunity to talk to him. Hadn't talked to him at all except in passing. She tried in vain, every day.

Beginning each morning in the bathroom, she stood staring into the mirror, giving herself a pep talk. With no idea how long he would be in town, she knew she had to move it along, but he had proven himself adept at avoiding her. Every morning he rose early and then isolated himself in the office for the remainder of the day. Knowing where he was didn't matter, because he was never alone. She'd stood on the porch for the past three days and watched a never-ending stream of visitors in the form of ranch hands, suppliers, and vendors head into the barn, all eager to meet the Nelms behind the name.

At Reuben's request, Brenda had provided his accountant access to the business' bookkeeping software. She filled that man's inbox with information and records for the past few years, and then found he left her pretty much alone, too.

Reuben was definitely avoiding her, burying himself in the tedium of an everyday routine completely unfamiliar to him. Something he had never really been involved in, and all, it seemed, so he didn't have to see or talk to her. She wasn't sure where his head was, if he had been struck with a sudden desire to understand the business, or—and this thought cut her to the quick—if he didn't trust her to run things anymore.

Gill wasn't making things easier by going around her, and she decided to attack this issue head on. Making a scoffing noise in the back of her throat so both men's eyes swung to her, she saw Reuben's dark ones assessing and Gill's light blue ones questioning.

"The agenda today is to check all the hay shed roofs. We can't risk leaks like last winter ruining half our bales. Then, the agenda includes checking on the two dozen heifers penned near the main barn; see how close they are to calving. Then, if there is time left in the day, we'll amend the agenda to include maintenance items. Because, as we all know, there's always fence to run, and stalls to check." Gill made a wry face and nodded, acknowledging her unspoken point about still being the boss and he turned to leave the room.

"Brenda," Reuben's deep voice filled the room, "a word, if you don't mind. Thanks, Gill." With two short sentences, he effectively both put her in her place and released Gill, wresting control back from her with such ease she thought her head would spin.

Gill nodded, and as he stepped outside, gave Brenda an apologetic glance, pulling the door to the office closed behind him. She and Reuben waited in silence until they heard the outer barn door slide shut, which meant she was fuming by the time Reuben stood, planting his knuckles on the desktop as he leaned over and barked his question irritably, "What the hell was that?"

"What's what?" She shrugged one shoulder. "Oh, you mean me making sure the boys all know when you waltz back out of town, it's still me they need to answer to? Is that what you're referring to?" Her own frustration sounded clearly in her tone. Over the past three days, he had refused to interact with her, and now he wanted to call her to task for doing what he had been paying her to do for years?

"I don't plan on waltzing out of town, as you put it. At least not until I know what was so damned important you had to threaten me to get me to come home." He had straightened and hands on his hips, stood behind the desk, glaring at her.

"Well if you'd talk to me, you'd know, wouldn't you?" She shook her head, leaning her shoulders against the wall, arms crossed beneath her breasts. "But, you've either been out and about, or holed up in here, so we haven't talked, even though you're finally in the same freakin' time zone as me." Drawing what she hoped was a calming breath, she deliberately lowered her voice to continue, trying hard to sound reasonable. "Reuben, I didn't mean to step on your toes just now. But, I can't lose my authority with these guys and expect to be an effective manager. And you know I'm right, so if you want me to stay on, then you have to let me do my job."

His jaw tightened as he gritted his teeth, turning his head to look at the pictures thumbtacked to the bulletin board beside the door. Following his gaze, she clenched her own jaw when she realized which picture he was looking at. Taken five years ago, Tommy stood with his arms around her and Eli's shoulders, holding them close to his sides, a broad grin on his face. In the photo, she and Tommy appeared nearly the same height, with Elias already more than half as tall as Tommy. The picture was a little deceiving because she was actually taller than Tommy by nearly five inches, and a then five-year-old Elias had been in the middle of one of many growth spurts.

They were posed in front of closed and quiet chutes with a big cardboard check positioned in front of them, still in the picture but she and Elias held it low enough so you could see the gigantic belt buckle Tommy had just won. Tommy with his dark complexion and dark hair, looking like he could be a larger version of the boy who had his head tilted up, somberly staring at the man he knew as his father.

That had been one month before Tommy's diagnosis of amyotrophic lateral sclerosis, ALS. Four years and ten months before her world came crashing down around her ears, carried there by a brief, clinically-worded report in a plain white envelope.

She saw movement from the corner of her eye and turned to face Reuben as he stepped close, catching the end of his nod towards the picture. "That Elias' father?" *Oh, man, is that ever a loaded question*, she thought, not wanting to lie to him but not wanting to have this discussion right now, especially not like this, when he was already more than half-angry at her.

Neither denying or confirming, she simply said, "Tommy Calloway." She paused and took a breath, verbally sidestepping even more with, "My husband."

His gaze swung back to her face, and he asked, "Where is he? That was a present tense response, so the husband part is still in effect, yeah? Haven't seen him around. Why's that, Brenda? Is he out on the circuit?"

As it sometimes did, the pain and grief of their loss swept over her, followed by what felt like a traitorous relief, her dismay that rode along with the last emotion nearly buckling her knees. If it hadn't been for the supportive wall behind her, she knew she would have collapsed to the floor. Biting her lips hard, struggling for self-control, she lowered her gaze to the floor as she said, "He died five months ago."

"Oh, darlin', I'm so sorry," Reuben murmured, and his hands were on her shoulders even before she knew he had moved. He pulled her into his arms and held her against his chest as she melted into him, her body remembering too well how this felt, how good this could be. This was who she knew him to be, the Reuben she had watched all her life. The boy who stood strong for everyone around him, the man who was a fierce friend...and generous lover.

For a moment, she considered just letting go, thinking about how good it would feel to be free to accept this unspoken offer to take some of the grief from her. In the end, the walls she had built over the years and months were too high, those paths too well worn, hard to deviate from. The thought of opening herself up to rejection from Reuben again filled her with paralyzing fear, and without giving herself a chance to change her mind, she shut down the impulse. With dry eyes, she leaned back to look up in his face, his arms still wrapped securely around her waist, holding her tightly. "Thanks, Reuben. You give good hug."

Ignoring her unspoken desire to move away, he stared down into her face, concern written on his features. Gently, he asked, "What happened, Brenda?"

"ALS. Flat stole him away, took everything he loved, except Elias and me." She glanced back at the bulletin board, but her mind was seeing Tommy in the hospital bed positioned in the living room, where he had spent his last days. Shaking free from the bitterness of those memories, she smiled at the picture on the board. "That was the first prize money he had taken in about a year." She sighed. "And it was the last time he competed. He knew something was wrong. Went and saw the doc. A few weeks later, we knew, knew for sure. From then on, it was a waiting game, but the disease progressed fast." She pushed against Reuben's chest again, blowing out a huff of air when he didn't release her. "Reuben, let me go."

In response, he didn't loosen his grip, but instead, snaked a hand up her back and into her hair, turning her head to press her cheek against his chest. "I'm so sorry, darlin'." He repeated his words from before, but now she felt as much as heard them. "I shoulda picked up the fuckin' phone. Lost and caught up in my own shit, but that isn't any kind of excuse. I shoulda picked up the phone and I shoulda been here for you."

"It's okay, Reuben. It still hurts, but it was a release for him. By the end, he was trapped inside his own body, and...for a man like Tommy, that's worse than death, really. I know he wanted to stay for Eli, but...well, everything happens for a reason, right?" If it hadn't been for ALS, she would never have done the gene testing on Elias, would never have seen the words on the paper denying Tommy's paternity of their son. Would never have had to remember the single night spent with Reuben, before he'd left Lamesa, and her, for good. The beautiful night branded into her memory, something she never dared think about while Tommy lived, because the what-ifs could overwhelm her if she did.

She pushed back against his hand, forcing him to loosen his hold as she looked up into his face, seeing his expression was shuttered, closed off. Closing her eyes, she swallowed hard when his hand gently cupped her cheek, the scorching heat from his palm welcome against her face. Feeling the fiery puffs of his breath against her lips, she waited for a moment, half-hoping he would kiss her, but then his lips touched her temple instead, pressing and holding for several seconds. His voice was low and smooth when he asked, "He your bull rider? The one you talked about that night?"

That night. So, he remembered their encounter too, because it was certainly the first time she had ever mentioned Tommy to anyone. Talking about him to Reuben made her infatuation for the athletic, good-looking man seem real. But their conversation took place only hours before they had been drunk enough to fall into bed together—a bed where there weren't many words, just talking with their bodies. The way she felt that night, with him, the rich wealth of emotions swirling through her when they were together made her schoolgirl crush on

Tommy laughable, and in those hours, she came to realize she had always been in love with Reuben.

Then, when morning came and she woke, her heart full of hope, he had been gone. A brief goodbye note on the nightstand the only thing left behind. *Not quite the only thing*, she thought, her eyes flicking again to the picture. "Yeah, that was Tommy."

"So, you guys hooked up. That's good. It's what you wanted, right?" His voice rumbled in his chest, and she wondered if she imagined the wistful tone she heard in his voice.

"Yeah, it was good. We were together nearly eleven years." She smiled, thinking about those first years, her working the stock contracting business, him chasing buckles and checks across the western half of the United States.

She would take Eli with her to visit Tommy when he was off on trips. Often, all three of them would stay in the living quarters of the bull-hauling trailer she used to transport stock to rodeos. She and Tommy got along well enough back then and learned to give each other the space they needed to become the people they wanted to be. Things changed later, but she clamped a lid on those memories, ruthlessly shutting down her mind from those pathways.

"You loved him." This was a statement, but she answered him anyway.

"It was a decent relationship." She nodded, a smile curving up the corners of her mouth. "He was a good partner, and good with Eli." Her chest hitched, because at least he had that. He never knew he wasn't Eli's father, and had died believing he was leaving part of himself behind. She pulled in a shuddering breath, then another one which came a little easier. "Now, you gotta let me go before I blubber all over you." Stepping back, his arms loosened and dropped away, leaving her longing for a return of the secure feeling his embrace provided.

"Is this why you called, Brenda? You need to focus on Elias instead of the business?" His quiet question pulled her attention back, and she nodded, but then just as quickly shook her head.

"I don't mind the work, and I can generally take off when I need to. I just...more than anything, I wanted...needed to talk to you." She shook her head, laughing softly. "My tactics might seem a bit...extreme to me now. I knew I didn't have any right to ask you to come home, but I did. Couldn't stop myself, Reuben. I'm sorry."

Her chin was gripped in his palm and he lifted her face so their gazes locked. "I'm not," was all he said, but his thumb grazed across her lips. "I'm here for as long as you want me, darlin'. As long as is needed."

"Hmmm." She sighed, pulling back, missing the heat of his hand as it dropped away. "Want and need are two entirely different things." She tried to lighten the conversation with a joke. "While I have you, I'll work you, though. I warn you, I'm a slave driver." She paused, but his expression didn't change, so she continued, "We can settle some questions I have on the direction you want to take the breeding program, make sure I've done the right things. There's some land I'd like you to look at with me. I think we could use some additional acreage given the head of stock we're carrying these days, but I want to make sure it's an investment you're okay with." *Maybe now is right*, she thought. She took a step backwards, creating more distance between them. "It would be good to have a Nelms at the rodeo, too. Do you think you can stay that long?"

"As long as you want me," he said, leaving off the qualifying words this time, his message even less clear than before. Was it possible he meant what she thought he did?

Closing her eyes, she took in a shuddering breath, and then released it, looking at him. *This is the time, right now. This is right*, she thought. "Reuben," she began and the phone on the desk rang. *Shit*. Shaking her head, she pointed at it as she stepped towards the door. "Better get that, boss man. Time to earn your keep."

***

Duck watched the door close quietly behind the woman he had loved for as long as he had known her. *That's a puzzle*, he thought. Her family, torn apart by disease. She had been with the bull rider for eleven years, the man had given her a beautiful son, then died, and she characterized their relationship as only *decent*. Something there didn't smell right.

He had been purposely keeping himself separate, even going so far as to eat his lunch in the office, working on various projects until well after dinnertime, trying to maintain distance. Calling home to Chicago, talking to his brothers in the evenings, keeping his finger on the club's pulse as best he could from here. He found himself even keeping Mason at arm's length, holding back about anything except club or the contracting business while he tried to sort out his feelings for Brenda. Until five minutes ago, he wasn't certain she even remembered their night, but now...his hand reached out to scoop the handset. "Du—" he began and then swiftly corrected himself. "Nelms," he said with a headshake. *This going back and forth was going to take some getting used to*, he thought.

"Reuben." Memory danced along the edges of his mind, elusive, as a voice he should know called his name. "Damn, boy. Welcome back. I heard you were back in town. Wasn't sure whether to believe the guys or not."

"Yeah, got in a couple days ago." Hopefully, his evasive answer didn't expose his lack of recognition for someone who apparently expected to be remembered from just a voice on the phone.

"Hey, me and Donny are going to Mitchell's tonight for a couple of beers. Want to join us?" The reference finally identified the person for him. This was Steve Simmons and he was going to a local bar with

38

Donald Lewellen. Reuben had played football with them all through high school, and then they had traveled together to rodeos for a couple of seasons, competing in different events for the most part.

"Steve, the last time I drank with you, I was too hungover to stand on my own two feet the next morning and had to scratch from my event." He laughed, receiving a chuckle in return, and followed up with, "I'll come have an iced tea, but I am not drinkin' with you, dude."

"You do remember," Steve said with satisfaction, then shouted at someone away from the phone. "Reuben's in, we'll meet up about five. Don't be late, Donny."

"Tell Don I said hey," Reuben said, shaking his head and grinning. "I'll see you at five, man." He had an idea and acted on it without thought, asking, "Is it okay if I bring Brenda along?"

"Seriously? You and Brenda, already? Hell, Reuben, you don't let grass grow underneath your boots, do ya?" Steve laughed slyly and Reuben found himself frowning. "She's kept pretty. I'll give you that. She any good in the sack?"

Suddenly furious, Duck clipped out a brusque, "Fuck you, Steven," in response, and his tone of voice expressed his disapproval of Steve's words.

He knew the other man got the message when he said, "Sorry, man. Of course, yeah. Yeah, bring Brenda if you want. Will be good to see her, too. Haven't seen her since Tommy passed."

"Yeah." Reuben paused, then repeated, "See you at five."

Hanging up the phone, he turned to stare at the picture on the bulletin board again. He had done this often over the past three days, looking at Brenda's face, head tilted so she could see her son, who was staring up at Tommy. It was the only picture on the board of the three of them together, and she wasn't looking at her husband. Elias was her

39

whole world, and the devotion she gave was apparent from the expression of love captured on her face.

For a moment...the barest moment when he had first seen Elias bounding to a stop in front of her, he'd thought...had hoped perhaps he and Brenda had a connection deeper than he had known. Then when he'd seen this picture of Tommy, he'd known it couldn't be. He and Brenda had only been together the one time, and sweet as it was, even before he'd touched her skin, he had believed that given his family's history, she was better off with anyone other than him.

That night had begun innocently enough. Hesitantly, she'd talked about the bull rider with a shy, wondering tone and he'd known the man was it for her. But, as they had so many times, they'd spent hours together, sitting, playing pool, dancing...talking and joking...touching and teasing. Innocent teasing, at first. They had been drinking. Throughout the years between then and now, when he'd tortured himself by looking back on that night, no matter how he tried to twist it in his head, he still knew the beer was the only reason she'd fallen into his arms. Had to be, because she wasn't into him. The whole encounter from her side was just things getting out of hand after a casual touch blazed between them, stripping his control.

Waking early the next morning, he'd laid quietly in the bed beside her, content for a time simply to watch her sleep. He'd stayed like that, stretched out alongside her naked form, running her words from the night before through his head, trying to make sense of his feelings. She had detailed everything about this other man, and in the end, the memory of her excitement about the bull rider was what had settled things in his mind.

He'd had to go. Had to, because he wouldn't be able to stay and watch her hook up with her guy, knowing what he knew. How she tasted, what she felt like underneath him. The feel of every curve of her body and how they fit next to him. The way her neck arched when she came hard while riding his cock. No, staying would have been worse than leaving her sleeping in bed alone, because if he'd had to watch her with someone else again...had to see a man woo and win her, he didn't know if he could have stood it.

Before they'd hit the dance that night, he had already made up his mind to leave home and find his brother, had planned to tell her of his decision, those words derailed by the evening. Then, lying there beside her, heat from her skin bleeding into him where they touched all along the length of his body, he'd decided he would simply continue with his plans, making the pain-filled decision to let Brenda go without a fight.

She hadn't been his to begin with. Reuben had always been just a buddy for her, their shared childhood making it so he was firmly stuck forever in the friend zone, knowing she would never look at him the way he suspected she looked at Tommy. So he'd gotten up and dressed quietly, had written her a brief note expressing his affection and explaining where he was going, and then he'd left. He'd stood in the doorway for a long time, watching her sleep, impressing the memory so deep he knew he would never lose the feeling of love and loss. Then he'd left, walking away, his path not returning him home until now.

He let his gaze travel over the rest of the pictures on the board, as well as the ones in frames on the wall. There were a bunch of Elias, a few of Elias and Tommy, but the bulk of the pictures were of Brenda and Elias together. They were shown riding horses side-by-side, Elias up on General. The corners of Reuben's mouth turned up when he looked at the image which had quickly become his favorite, one of her wielding the business end of a water hose, using her thumb to create a powerful spray of water she'd turned on Eli. The shock on his face at behavior he didn't expect from his mom was plain, as was the self-satisfied smirk on hers.

Looking across the display, he tracked the boy's growth in those pictures with his mother. Guessing the boy was about ten now, it was knowledge that hurt in a way he didn't like. Eli's age meant she and Tommy had moved fast, the two of them quickly becoming serious enough to create their family. Moving fast...moving on. Now Tommy was gone, and she was alone. Shaking his head, Duck reached out to touch the edge of the water fight picture, then stepped to the side and opened the door, walking through and closing it tightly behind him.

Looking around the buildings within sight of the barn, he cataloged the work that still needed to be done, as he had every day since coming home. Not the normal list of chores, but the maintenance parts, which got pushed aside all too easily. They were chipping away at his mental list, had been making steady inroads in the past few days. His other mental list, the one to do with Brenda, in contrast had been growing every day. He needed to either let her say her piece so he could leave, or decide he was going to dig in, try to find something he had been craving for years. He could begin by talking to her, he decided, turning his steps to the house.

Back inside, he hoped to find Brenda, but the entire structure felt empty, the silence conveying a sense of solitude. Not sure where she would have disappeared to, he decided to wait and strolled to the mantle. Taking his time, he surveyed the pictures of the Calloway family displayed there. At the second image, Reuben stopped in his tracks, startled. It was Tommy and Brenda's wedding picture. She looked much taller than Tommy, which was surprising. But what really startled him was recognizing her maid of honor, Chelsie Transom.

He knew from talking to Slate, the Rebel's president in Fort Wayne, that when he'd traveled through Lamesa years ago, he'd hooked up with Chelsie. That was when Duck first met the man, back before they were club members, well before either of them were in the life. Before Duck had walked away from the best thing he'd ever had. Slate, whose citizen name was Andy Jones, had been working at the Transom ranch repairing fence for some fast cash when Reuben had ridden up to say hello.

They'd hit it off quickly and even after Slate had moved on down the road, they'd kept track of each other for a time, until circumstances brought them back into close contact. Both of them joining the Rebel Wayfarers had not been planned. Andy patched into the club first, earning his road name of Slate long before Reuben darkened the door of the club's bar, Jackson's. Him knowing Slate had made his entry into the club smoother, had gained him important indulgences from Mason, the club's national president. Those favors had allowed him to track and watch over Mica Scott, now Mica Rupert.

What a twisted web my life has been, he thought, remembering the times he and other members had ridden down to Springfield to check up on Mica, back when she was in college. She was the reason his brother, Ray, wound up dead, but it was no fault of hers. That shit sat firmly on Ray's plate. The result of feeding the twisted desires their father had left in him.

Reuben had left the circuit earlier that year, rather than watch the slow destruction of the beautiful young girl at his brother's hands. But, once he was home, he'd struggled with guilt and second thoughts, heading back out only to find she had already fled. That was when his brother became obsessed with her. Dangerously fixated on finding her, Ray's intent had been to return her to his bed as if she were a possession that could be owned and retrieved at will.

With a driving need to keep her safe from Ray, for months Reuben had looked for Mica across the southern and western states. Every circuit town found him scouring the locals for information and each one saw him coming up dry. Finally, he'd gotten wind of a lead, then another, and ultimately received a solid tip from an old ER doc in Oklahoma, pointing him towards Chicago.

Strolling the streets of that city hadn't turned up any clues as to her location. Frustrated, he had nearly given up entirely when he'd found himself in Jackson's for the first time. He'd walked in and met Mason, not knowing his world was on the cusp of change. A single meeting which would set the course for the rest of his life, bringing him to the man he was today. Without thinking, he muttered, "Rebels forever, forever Rebels."

"What does that mean?" The first soft syllable had him spinning on reflex, half-crouched in a defensive move before he realized it was Elias. Extending the movement to stretch back to his full height, he looked down at the boy without saying anything, his heart racing in his chest. Warm, dark brown eyes met his and they stood there for a minute staring at each other before Elias asked again, "What does 'Rebels forever' mean?"

Reuben shifted his shoulders, missing the weight of his leather vest. The absence of his cut left him feeling exposed. Like a raw nerve, the lack was a constant, painful reminder he wasn't home, had no backup, and was entirely on his own down here in Texas. The garment bearing the club's patches hung in the guestroom closet—Mason having agreed for the short time he would be here, it would be best to be anonymous.

"It's a pact. I belong to a motorcycle club. It's a promise to my brothers that there will always be a club, because men like me will always be loyal to it. 'Rebel Wayfarers forever,' that's the club being true to me, then the last part is 'forever Rebels,' and that's me. It's a different way of saying once a Rebel, always a Rebel." Nodding to the boy, he turned to look at the pictures on the mantle again.

He didn't hear the kid move, but Eli's voice came from beside him when he said, "That's Dad and Mom."

Eyes fixed on the bride in the picture, Reuben quietly said, "Brenda told me about your dad earlier. I'm sorry. It's hard to lose someone you love."

"Yeah," Eli muttered, his voice thick with emotion. "Even when everyone tells you to get ready, to expect it...even when the pastor talked to both Dad and me about it, it still..." He trailed off mid-sentence. Reuben looked down to see Eli's eyes were wet, looking at a picture of him and his mom: A proud Eli sitting on General, spine straight and grinning, while a beaming Brenda reached up to hand him a ribbon. "Sometimes things just go bad. Mom's had it hard, so I don't..." His voice trailed off again, then he picked back up the thought, "You can see it hit her, sometimes."

"I don't know if you could ever be ready for something like that. Like a gopher hole, it'll catch you off guard, throw you off balance," Reuben offered, and the kid's gaze swung to him. Lips pursed tightly, he gave Reuben a solemn nod, then stared at the picture for another minute before turning to walk out. Reuben stopped him with a gentle, "Eli, if you need or want to talk to me? You can. Anytime, kiddo." Without looking back, Eli nodded, then slipped quietly outside, the screen door's wooden frame absorbing all sound as it closed softly behind him.

As Reuben turned to look at the pictures again, the room faded away and he had eyes only for Bee's face. After everything she had been through, she deserved some goodness in her life. He would make her go with him tonight, see to it that she had a chance to laugh.

Hidden blessings

Boots discarded in the mudroom, Brenda stood in her sock feet and stared up at Reuben for a minute, unable to decide if there was a joke behind the question. Finally, she asked, "I'm sorry. What does that mean?"

"It means I want you to come with me to Mitchell's." Reuben shook his head at her, staring into her face with an intensity he didn't try to hide. "Not a hard idea to fathom, Bee."

"But you're meeting your friends." She allowed her confusion to shadow her voice, and he looked annoyed.

"They're your friends, too," he countered, but she quickly shook her head.

"Nope, they're yours, Reuben. Steve's married to my friend, but it doesn't sound like Chelsie is going. So that will make it one awkward evening I'd really rather skip. Thanks for the invite, but no thanks. Will you be eating at Mitchell's or with us?" She turned to the sink, reaching for a glass from the drain board. She filled it with water from the tap, drinking about half the liquid before she realized he hadn't answered her. Twisting back to look at him, she saw his eyes had narrowed on her. "What?"

"If Chelsie comes, would you go with me?" He was being persistent about this, and she wasn't sure why he was digging in this way.

"No, I have to cook for the ranch hands. It's part of the manager gig, making sure everyone has food in their bellies. Then there's the evening feeding of the bottle calves, and I'm pretty sure I saw a half dozen invoices in today's mail that need to be entered into the computer, along with the breeding results for those new heifers." Shrugging, she quipped, "Normal for a Tuesday," before drawing back slightly at the dark scowl her words seemed to provoke.

"Hands can cook for themselves for once," he offered, but she silently shook her head, still not sure why he was chasing this so hard. "Well, then, they can do the bottle feeding for you." She snorted at the thought, shaking her head again and his features darkened even more, brows lowering over narrowed eyes. "Invoices can wait for tomorrow morning."

"Reuben, it's not a big deal. There's always work and chores that need doing. Today isn't any different from the last thousand days." She shrugged, pulling the pan of marinating pork chops out of the refrigerator, setting it on the countertop. Shuffling around the kitchen, she gathered the rest of the things needed for supper before realizing he had left, as soundlessly as ever. The way he moved was graceful and quiet. "He's not a Mexican...he's a Ninjacan," she muttered with a smothered giggle.

Thirty minutes later, the meal prep was done and supper was in the oven with the timer set. Resting for a moment on the mudroom's built-in bench, she pulled her boots back on with a groan, yelling up the stairs, "Elias, come help with the calves, honey." She waited until she heard what sounded like an agreement, before standing and walking outside. Halfway to the pen where they kept the calves, she heard a commotion and picked up her pace, hitting a quick trot. There had been trouble with predators in the past, but it would be unlike them to come up this close to human activity in broad daylight. *Unlikely, but not impossible*, she thought, heart rate spiking with a sudden push of fear, *which is why I'm running*.

Rounding the barn, she stumbled to a halt, a surprised shout of laughter escaping her lips at the sight greeting her. Reuben, Gill, and a half dozen of the ranch hands were in the pen, each wielding a bottle in either hand. Which was all well and good, but there were fifteen calves more than the men had hands between them, leading to a free-for-all melee among the hungry calves not currently attached to the nipple of a bottle.

Slowly walking the remaining few feet to the fence, she propped one foot on the bottom board, silent laughter still shaking her shoulders. Brenda was trying hard to hold it together, and was succeeding until one of the calves became more impatient than its pals, walked up to Reuben and butted him with its head. She knew from experience how hard those bovine noggins were, and given the location the calf was aiming at, the pained grunt from Reuben wasn't unexpected. She lost control over her laughter when she heard him mutter, "Jesus. God. Stop it. You could still be called veal, you turd calf."

At the sound of her amusement, he twisted and looked over at her, a hopeful look on his now light green face. "Help," he pleaded, and she laughed again at his desperate expression.

Moving to the gate separating the pen from one of several smaller ones next to it, she dragged it open and whistled, calling one of the dogs from the barn to her. She and the dog put a half-dozen calves in that pen, and then repeated the process for the next two enclosures, effectively separating the hungry calves from the ones being fed. This left the ones already on a bottle in the larger pen and no longer having to fight for their hold, they made quick work of the bottles.

She lined bottle holders along rungs of the gates for the small pens, and began loading the rest of the pre-mixed bottles into them, creating an assembly line of food for the divided groups of self-sufficient calves. By the time Reuben walked over to her with an embarrassed grin on his face, she had already moved back to the first pen to release the fed calves back into the larger one.

"Hilarious, Reuben. Best show I've seen in a while. What were you thinking would happen?" She grinned at him and caught up in the moment, acted without thinking, reaching up to wipe a streak of dirt off his cheek with the pad of her thumb. Brenda wasn't prepared for the look of passion that filled his eyes at her touch.

He quickly lifted his hand to cup her palm against his cheek, holding it in place before she could pull back. She glanced away, having to press her lips together, pushing down a responding heat of her own at the look on his face. They stood like that a moment, their bodies close enough for her to feel an exposed intimacy. His voice held a sheepish note when he spoke softly. "I forgot how demanding the little boogers can be." Tone deepening, his voice was rough when he continued, "I just...want you to come with me tonight, so I thought if I took care of feeding the calves, you'd be able to find the time." Releasing her, he reached out, resting a hand on either side of her waist. "Brenda—"

"Calves are already done, Mom? Why'd you call me then?" Reuben's words were interrupted by Eli's irritated questions and she looked down to see her son's eyes narrowly focused on her middle, where Reuben's hands were touching her.

"They weren't done when I called you," she explained. "It's just *someone* took his sweet time getting ready for chores." Eli rolled his eyes and she snorted, turning and twisting out of Reuben's hold. "No worries, the job's not finished. You can help me wash bottles." Her son sighed, lifting his still-narrowed gaze to Reuben when the man blew out a frustrated sounding breath.

"Brenda, stop it." Reuben reached out, flattening his palm at the small of her back, the heat of the contact warming her skin through her clothing. "Gill, get the hands to wash the bottles." He shouted across the pen towards the men, who had all begun to walk away, and she heard a collective groan from them as they turned to slog back to where she had tossed the bottles on the grass outside the pen. "Brenda's working on dinner. I'll be in the office for a half hour, and then meet y'all up at the house, yeah?" Reuben looked down at her with a grin. "I'll have invoices entered before supper. Then there are no excuses left, Bee."

Shaking her head, she frowned at him before asking, "It matters that much to you?" She watched as he pulled in a deep breath, his chest rising and falling as he blew it back out with a silent nod. Staring into his eyes for a moment, she saw the hope rising in them, and gave in with a soft, "Okay, then. Okay, I'll go." She looked down at Elias and smiled at her son, "I guess I'm going out tonight, Eli. You'll need to clean up the dishes after the men get finished." He groaned as loudly as the ranch hands had a moment ago, pulling another laugh from her. "If you can rinse them and load the dishwasher, I'll take care of everything else when I get home. Essa will be just down the hallway, so you'll have company if you want it."

As she spoke, he cut his eyes towards Reuben, frowning. Without looking back at her, he muttered, "Yeah, whatever."

"Elias Thomas Calloway, is that any way to speak to your mother?" His attitude surprised her because he wasn't a sullen child. His moods were generally easy, even right after his fa—her brain stuttered for a minute, and she realized what was wrong. *Reuben. Eli has to be upset about him being here*, she thought.

Before she could say anything else, he responded with a contrite sounding, "Sorry, Mom. I can handle the dishes." He paused and the sound of his swallow was loud. "You...you'll be back before I go to sleep?"

"Yeah." With one soft word, she promised him he wouldn't go to sleep without her telling him goodnight. It was a ritual they'd started back when Tommy's condition had worsened to the point he couldn't be part of their daily lives. She thought of it as droplets of normality, a few stolen ordinary moments out of the day when it could be just him and her. The predictable routine meant he always had a chance to talk to her about his dreams or fears, or just the funny things that happened to him throughout the day. Or, as often transpired, they could say nothing at all, sitting in companionable silence while he fell asleep, head on her thigh, her fingers running through his hair. "Wouldn't miss it, Eli."

Nodding, he turned away and she jolted when the hand at her back flexed, fingers digging into her skin, closing around her shirt and tugging her sideways. Twisting, she saw Reuben looking down at her, having stood silently throughout the exchange. He released his grip and snaked an arm around her waist, pulling her tight against his side. Gruffly, he said, "He's a tough kid." Turning back to watch Eli walk towards the house, she nodded, knowing Reuben was right.

***

Leaning back in his seat, Reuben shook his head in disgust. *I shoulda listened to Brenda*, he thought. Steve had already been a few beers in when they got to the bar, and over the past forty-five minutes, his assholeness had grown to such proportions, it was impossible to ignore. Chelsie hadn't been able to accompany him out tonight, and he didn't know if Steve's behavior was because he was an unhappily married man, or just an ass, but Reuben had suffered through about all he could stand of the man's obnoxious flirting, hitting on every woman around. Including Brenda.

He placed his mouth near Brenda's ear, inhaling a hint of her perfume as he whispered, "I'm ready to go if you are, honey." Drawing back in time to see her relieved smile and nod, he laughed quietly. Catching the waitress' eye, he offered her a couple of bills and got a sweet grin in response to his apologetic, "Thanks, darlin'. Sorry."

"It's just Steve," the waitress muttered, underscoring for Reuben that Steve was an ass. She leaned around him and, her tone friendly, said, "Good to see you out, Brenda."

"Good to be seen," Brenda responded with a fond smile as she stood.

When Reuben stood as well, Steve and Donny complained a bit, but they let it go fairly quickly, saying their goodbyes. Mostly because Reuben had just bought another pitcher for the table, and if he and Brenda were leaving, it meant more beer for the two men.

Hand possessively pressed to the small of Brenda's back, he steered her out of Mitchell's and into the parking lot, both of them sighing loudly as the noise and heat of the bar receded. Curving his fingers around her waist, he steadied her against his side as they walked to the truck, shortening his strides to match hers. "Sorry that wasn't more fun, Bee." He sighed. "Those guys were jackasses in high school, too, weren't they? I just didn't see it."

She laughed good-naturedly and tilted her head up to look at him. "Yeah, they were, but it's okay. I still had fun tonight with you." Her gaze dropped back to the gravel at her feet, focusing on careful navigation of the uneven surface in the short heels she had paired with a sleeveless sundress.

He liked seeing the expanse of skin when she came down the stairs at the house, her shoulders, arms, and legs on display. Sideways glances on the short drive into town gave him opportunity to appreciate it even more. But, once realization hit that every man in the bar would be enjoying the same view, he had been surprised at a sudden jealous anger that burned through him. She was so beautiful, and his greedy reaction underscored how much he wanted her for himself.

Dragging his attention back to the conversation, he grinned and shook his head, saying, "Liar." *God, I like her*, he thought, not surprised to find he wasn't ready for the evening to end. Reuben thought for a moment before asking, "What time does Eli go to bed?"

"Nine o'clock," she said, glancing up at him again with a questioning crook of an eyebrow. That expression fled her face as she stumbled, but his arm around her waist kept her from falling. Without taking her eyes from where they had locked with his, she found her footing and softly said, "Thanks."

"Let's go see what's showing at the drive-in. It's still open, right?" This would be another experience from high school, but not something he and Brenda had ever done together. At what he hoped was an eager nod, he moved them a little faster towards the truck, reaching out to open the door for her. Helping her into the seat, he watched as she tucked the full skirt closely around her thighs, feet primly lined up side-by-side on the floor of the truck, eyes fixed on her knees. "What do you say, Bee? Want to go see what's playing?"

Without looking at him, still silent, she nodded again and he frowned at her lack of response. "Honey, if you don't want to, it's okay. We don't—"

"I do want," she said softly, interrupting him as she glanced up at his face. Her soft expression of confused hope and desire stunned him and he couldn't say anything, simply nodded and closed her door. He stood for a moment, looking at her through the window, their gazes still on each other. He thought about their one night together and how right it felt to move from friends to lovers. How often he had pulled out those memories over the years, the thought of her enough to arouse him. Now, staring into her face, he wondered, *Why couldn't she have loved me?*

With that painful thought, he turned away, walked around the hood of the truck and climbed into the driver's seat. Without looking in her direction, he navigated the parking lot, pulling out into the busy street filled with traffic from local folks and tourists in town for the annual rodeo. Based on the no-vacancy signs on several of the motels, he expected there would be a near-record turnout for the shows. Driving through town, he looked around curiously. This was the first time he had left the ranch since coming in with Essa and he recognized more differences than similarity this time through.

"Y'all had much trouble with new folks in town?" he asked as they drove past a bar positioned on a corner in the center of town, only a couple blocks from Mitchell's. There were more than two dozen bikes parked along the front of the building and he wondered what patches would be on display inside.

He hadn't asked Mason to reach out to any local clubs yet, and since he didn't have approval to be in town flying Rebel colors, wanted to be respectful of their territory. So, tonight he had on a blue jean vest, leaving his cut hanging in the closet. *I don't even know which clubs call Lamesa home*, he thought, somewhat surprised at his lack of concern. A week ago, the club had been in his every waking thought; but since returning home, being near Brenda for the first time in more than a decade consumed him. That and the sheer weight of daily chores were enough to sweep club politics and drama right out of his head.

"Coyotes, more than anything," Brenda said, staring out the window.

He grunted, following her gaze, seeing the flat, brown landscape that was West Texas. She didn't mean animals. He knew the kind of coyotes she was talking about were of the two-legged variety, running illegals up the backroads to avoid border patrols, one of the things he never missed about home. Musing, he started talking, not sure where he was going with his words. "You know, when I first moved, everything up north looked so different. Illinois is flat, too, at least where I live. I've spent quite a bit of time in Indiana where it's even more so, especially up by Fort Wayne where I'm at now. But, the differences were stark. It felt like a different country.

"The first time I went from Lamesa to Chicago, it was like I was a kid in the movie theater again, watching as the colors on the screen changed from black and white to the beautiful jewel shades of a dream. The crops up there were emerald green, endless across the landscape. In the fall, the tree leaves turn every color you could imagine, and the sparkling white of a winter snow is nearly impossible to describe.

"Even the buildings there are different, multi-level townhouses mixed in with old rambling two-story farmhouses, tall office buildings and stately courthouses. Steep, angled roofs intended to slough off the weight of snow. Beauty everywhere I looked, different and striking."

She turned to look at him, a musing expression on her face as he continued. "But now I'm back? I see the beauty here, too. I'd nearly forgotten how things look. The way the land races far out to the skyline, the shifting pastel shades of sunrise bleeding out to a blue so bright it hurts your eyes. Here the palette is shifting tones of brown, and the buildings are flat-roofed structures designed to work with the harsh climate, nearly all a single story leaving the sky clear to be seen, horizon to horizon. Even the people, the way they talk? I didn't know I'd missed it until I found myself surrounded by the music of their voices again, but I did."

He twisted, looking over his shoulder to check traffic before changing lanes to turn into the drive-in theater, easing to a stop in the line. "I left because of family, stayed gone because of family, and now I'm back because I don't have a family. Everything seems so big, Brenda. There. Here. Everywhere. So big it's hard to describe how small it makes me." There was heat and pressure on his leg and he glanced down to find her small hand resting on his thigh, her attempt to comfort and reassure him.

Shaking his head, he pulled on the steering wheel to lean forward, taking his wallet out of the back pocket of his jeans. Paying for their tickets, he tossed the leather wallet onto the dashboard and drove to a nearly empty field of metal posts, their tethered speakers hanging tidily from a holder on either side of each pole.

Laughing, he reached down and covered her hand with his palm, readily wrapping his fingers around it. "So you want close to the front, in the middle, or back by the snack shack?" Glancing around, without waiting for a response, he picked a parking space near the back, telling her, "They'll start the show just after sundown. Lean back and relax. We'll make sure you're home in plenty of time to tell Eli good night, yeah? Half a movie is good enough for me." She nodded and smiled her thanks at him, then kicked off her shoes and leaned back in the seat.

When she put her bare feet on the dashboard, that damn skirt of hers slipped up her thighs and he groaned silently. Turning her head, she looked at him and smiled again, "This is nice, Reuben. Thanks."

"Much better than Mitchell's with Steve getting his drunk on." He shook his head in disgust. "I don't know what I was thinking, asking you to go with me." When a look of hurt and uncertainty washed over her face, he mentally reviewed what he'd said, then shook his head.

"No, honey. I didn't mean it that way. What I was trying to say is I should have taken you out for dinner and a real movie, not pretzels and beer in a rowdy bar, followed by half of a two-year-old drive-in show." Gently squeezing her hand, softly he said, "I should have asked you on a real date. Wined and dined you. Done it up right. You're worth it." His throat tightened, dropping his voice to a whisper. "*God*. Sweeter and even more beautiful than I remembered. You take my breath away."

"Oh." The exclamation was soft, coming as she wrapped her fingers more tightly around his. Holding on.

Surprised at how his mouth was running on by itself tonight, he heard himself ask, "Do you ever think about that night, Bee?" His spontaneous question hung in the air for a moment while he waited, holding his breath in suspense. Then, when he saw her flush, bright pink embarrassment climbing into her face, he had his answer. Before she had a chance to respond, he told her, "I do, too. All the time. Never forgot a moment. Not a whisper...not a kiss." He wondered suddenly, *What would she do if I kissed her right now?* Eyes locked on hers, he slowly shifted towards her on the bench seat of the truck, the weight of an eleven-year-old longing driving him on. "Took you with me everywhere I went, Bee. Everything I saw, I wanted to share with you."

Finally close enough to touch her, he reached up and did just that, cupping his palm around her cheek, tilting her head towards his. *Her skin's every bit as silky as I remember.* "Every word, every sound, all of you...branded in my brain," he whispered, lowering his face. "Every touch, every taste, the feeling of your skin sliding against mine. Soft. Sweet. Beautiful." Her blue eyes were bright, looking up at him, wide in what he prayed was wonder. "Is it wrong of me to want that again? Because I do, Bee. I want you. I never stopped."

Covering her mouth with his, the kiss began soft and slow, a questing of lips alone, brushing and grazing tenderly, tasting the lip gloss she wore with a soft hum that she returned. Unhurried, he carefully built it, giving her every opportunity to pull back. He tried not to give in to the fear swelling inside him that she might not want him, but with every touch, he begged for a chance to take this farther, to prove what she meant to him. *Trust me, Bee.*

Slipping his thumb up along her jawline, he traced the corner of her mouth, moving to follow the soft caress with the tip of his tongue. Kissing across her cheek to her temple, he pressed his mouth there, whispering, "My memory failed me, Bee. What I've been holding onto wasn't this. This is so much more—exquisite." He kissed her again. "Exceptional." Caressing her cheek, he brushed his knuckles across her skin. "Far superior to my memories. *God*, Bee. What else is waiting for me on memory lane? What do you have waiting for me, honey?"

Placing his mouth next to her ear, he traced the shell with the tip of his tongue, then pulled her earlobe into his mouth, tenderly nibbling, listening to her breath catch and then speed up. *She wants this*, he thought, *wants me*. Gliding his hand down her neck to her shoulder on one side, he matched the movements with his mouth on the other, kissing across her collarbone to the point of her shoulder, then back to her neck. He groaned his approval when she arched into him, tilting her head to grant him greater access and he worked his mouth across her skin, gratified to hear the soft noises she made.

"Bee." His voice was rough, the urgency of his need laid bare when he whispered her name. Bringing his mouth back to hers, he kissed her deeply, demanding a response. Leaning forward, he dipped into her mouth, finding her more than ready to work with him. Her tongue sliding along his, hungrily fighting for contact as her moan filled the cab of the truck. He swept his tongue across her lower lip, biting and nibbling softly, slowly pressing deeper as she opened to him.

With a groan, he slanted his head, control slipping for a moment and he feverishly kissed her, sucking on her tongue and eating at her as if he had been starving since the last time she'd given him this, given herself to him. Her soft whimpers and frantic movements under his touch brought him back to himself, even as he struggled for a moment to reel it in, wanting more. So much more. *Fuck. Slow it down*, he thought. Releasing her, he brought both of his hands up, cradling her face and using that trembling grip to break the kiss. Breathing hard, he tucked his chin towards his chest, resting his forehead against hers.

Fuck.

When his eyes opened, she looked dazed, staring at him and he dropped down to kiss her again. This time, he took it slower, keeping his eyes wide to gauge her reactions. He groaned again when he saw profound desire in her expression, as dilated pupils and panting breaths showed the need surfacing in her, too. His whispering voice was hoarse with passion when he said, "No secret here, Bee. I want you. Never stopped wanting."

She inhaled shakily and whispered, "Me, too."

Surprised, he froze for a moment, then one corner of his mouth crooked up into what he knew was a grateful smile. Playfully wrinkling his nose at her, he sought confirmation of what he hoped was happening. "Does this mean our memory lane is a two-way street?" She nodded again, lips first pursing then flattening as she drew them into her mouth. "Okay, Bee," he said, brushing his lips across hers, gently pursuing her before drawing back.

"You're my pace car in this, and it isn't a race. I'm not rushing to get to the finish line. I'm way more interested in going the extra mile. You tell me what you're ready for, and I'm good with that. You want more, or I'm not moving fast enough? Tell me. You need me to slow down and back off the throttle? All you have to do is say so."

He kissed her again, lovingly this time, lips questing across hers, tasting and exploring. Promising himself a lifetime of the same, he teased responses from her in the form of more soft whimpers in the back of her throat. Pulling back, he sucked in another deep breath, looking into her eyes. He liked what he saw there, her confidence and excitement, mixing with a deep arousal. *She needs to know what she means to me.* Leaning towards her, he trailed gentle kisses across her cheek, whispering, "Took you everywhere with me. Decided you're worth the wait."

Her mouth was so close to his ear, he felt as well as heard her take in a breath. As he kissed along her jawline, she moved and he was about to ask her what she wanted to say when a knock came at his window.

***

Reuben's arms tightened around her as Brenda silently groaned. *Seriously? Every freaking time?* She had just been about to say she had something she needed to tell him. She tilted her head to look around Reuben to find Gill peering in the driver's window, wearing a broad grin. Standing right there beside him with the darkest frown she had ever seen on his face was Eli. *Crap.* During their kiss, Reuben had slid across the width of the bench seat until he'd pressed her against the passenger door of the truck. A quick glance reaffirmed at least his hands had stayed above the waist, and her skirt still covered her modestly.

"Are you *fuck*ing kidding me?" Reuben's gruff voice sounded angry in the cab of the truck and she winced, knowing their audience could hear his reaction. She pushed at his chest and he moved away, settling behind the wheel while she sat up and tried to compose herself. With short, angry movements he yanked at the handle to open the door, forcing the duo outside to take one long step backwards.

A moment later, without saying a word, Eli was climbing across Reuben and into the truck, a knee in Reuben's lap pulling a pained grunt from him as her son crawled in, flopping his butt onto the seat between them. Without looking at her, he glared at Reuben, loudly stating, "I didn't know you were coming to the movies, Mom."

"Last-minute decision," she said, frowning down at the top of his head, trying to decide how upset he really was. "I didn't know I'd given you permission to come to the movies, Eli." She cut her gaze up to Gill, who had the good sense to look contrite. "It's okay, but a call would have been good."

"We tried calling, Mom. But you left your phone at home when you went *out*." Eli forced a hard emphasis on that last word, tipping his head back and staring out the windshield at the flickering screen where ads for local businesses were beginning to play, the pre-roll before they got to the previews. *Oh, yeah, he's pissed*, she thought.

Gill chimed in, clearly unsure of the feelings emanating from the truck. "I planned on having him home before bedtime. Essa needed to haul Breezy over to the vet's so they can get him doped up in the morning before they do his x-rays." *Crap*. Breezy was still lame, so the new veterinarian wanted to rule out a fracture before continuing treatment. She had forgotten about the appointment in the excitement of Reuben asking her out.

"It's okay, Gill. Did you bring Anthony with you?" Gill cut his eyes to Reuben as he nodded, and she wondered if he had outed himself to the ranch's owner yet. Anthony was the son he had with his partner, the two men having adopted the child nearly five years ago. He and Samuel had been together for fifteen years, but he had only worked on the ranch for nine or so, coming on board after Reuben had left the last time.

She asked, "Eli, you want to sit with Tony or stay here?"

"Doesn't matter to me." He shrugged, his thin shoulders moving up and down jerkily. "I'm here now. I can just stay here." His words carried a curt tone, eyes still fixed on the distant screen, studiously not looking at her. "Right here."

"Okie dokies. No worries, Gill. We'll see you tomorrow. Eli looks to be riding home with us." Reuben's head had turned towards Gill as he began to say his goodbyes, but at her words, he whipped back around, his features flooded with a disappointment which thrilled her. Their eyes locked for a moment before he smiled sheepishly and mouthed the words, reminding them both, *Not a race.*

Having Eli with them meant they were free to stay for the entire feature. They crowded close together for the first half of the movie, Eli sandwiched between them as they shared popcorn Reuben bought. She tried to talk to Eli while Reuben had gone to buy snacks, but after receiving only terse responses, she decided to let him nurse his snit. It had only been a few months since Tommy had died, and seeing her out with another man had to be a shock.

When he got back with his purchases, Reuben passed the goodies out, earning a small smile from Eli when he spun a crazy story about the teenagers manning the concession stand. Over the next hour he worked hard to draw Eli out of his funk, finally rewarded with light giggles at Reuben's comments about the comedy on the screen. The mood lifting meant laughter from all of them came more often, but she had hooted the loudest when Reuben impulsively tossed a popcorn kernel at Eli, prompting a brief but competitive popcorn fight which ended when Reuben pretended to get salt in his eye.

Elias immediately got to his knees on the seat to check on Reuben, concern etched on his features. Reuben had wrapped his arms around the boy, pulling him into his lap and tickling him fiercely for a couple of seconds. When they finally stopped wrestling, breathless with laughter, popcorn was all over the cab of the truck. But, the bright look on her son's happy face was worth every moment it would take to clean up.

After repeated but half-hearted denials of sleepiness followed by jaw-cracking yawns, Elias had fallen asleep about halfway through the movie, slumped sideways and leaning into her. When he realized Elias was finally sleeping, Reuben smiled at her from across the space that held the boy between them. Reaching down, he gently pulled Eli's feet from the floor, tugging her loose-limbed child into a more comfortable looking position, head in her lap and legs in his.

Reuben's hand captured hers and they watched the rest of the movie with their clasped hands resting on Eli's hip. The connection between the three of them brought tears to her eyes when she thought about what she had to tell Reuben, what she had been about to lead into when Gill knocked on the window. *Every single time I start to say something, I get interrupted*, she thought with a frown. Taking the cowardly way out and not disclosing her secret had crossed her mind several times, but she wouldn't do that to Reuben. Knew she couldn't live with herself if she tried to hide from the facts. He needed to know, to have the choice of what he wanted to do. She had to believe he would eventually understand and prayed he wouldn't hate her. At least the interaction tonight gave her hope that in time he would be able to bring himself to love Eli.

When she'd discovered she was pregnant, there had been no question in her mind whose child was in her belly. Reuben had used protection, and the condom broke with Tommy their first time. Simple deduction left her with one answer, and Tommy had stepped up as soon as she'd told him. There was never any reason to wonder, even when Elias was born with skin and hair darker than hers, looking as much like the man who'd stood in the delivery room as he did the one now seated at her side.

Those were the good days, when she thought they would be able to make a go of it together. Before he'd changed, becoming surly and angry, resenting the limitations having a family so young put on them. Before Ray befriended him, twisting him. It was a blessing Tommy never knew he didn't father Eli, because she was sure his rage at what he would see as a deliberate deception would have reached epic levels.

It seemed like every day she noted another way Reuben was so different from Tommy, patient where her husband had always rushed her. Kind and teasing with Elias, whose own father seldom had time for him, even when Tommy was healthy. She glanced towards Reuben as she settled sideways into the door, resting the back of her head against the doorframe. Reuben was good, through and through. Always had been, the only hurt he ever dealt her was not his fault. Her gaze fell to Eli, sleeping quietly between them, and she thought, *Pain be damned. I came out the winner here. Wouldn't change a thing.*

Dreaming

Slowly pulling into the driveway, careful not to jostle his passengers, Reuben looked across the cab of the truck, smiling softly. Elias was still between him and Brenda, buckled into place. Seated and leaning heavily into his mother's side, the deeply sleeping boy's head was tipped back, mouth hanging slightly open, an occasional sharp snore sounding loudly in the truck's cab, each followed by a soft, sighing exhalation.

On the other side of Elias, sagging against the passenger door was Brenda. She had one elbow propped on the armrest, her cheek resting in her palm. Eyes closed, her head tipped and bounced as the truck's springs complained about the roughness of the drive and Reuben made another mental note to organize one of the ranch hands to use the road grader on the span before it got any worse. He knew all it would take was a single downpour and they would be driving through trenches instead of ruts.

He pulled into the side yard, smoothly gliding the truck to a halt. Turning off the engine, he twisted in the seat and stared at the two of them, something akin to homesickness taking root. It was her, Brenda.

She was his home. All his life he had dreamed of having her again, making her his in truth.

And tonight, their outing—beginning as a date but ending up more like a family event—stirred something deep inside him. Pairing that with the trust she gave him, her humbling belief he would bring her and her son home safely, staggered him. He felt lost, not knowing what to do with these feelings threatening to overwhelm him.

Even now, just sitting here and watching them quietly sleeping, his chest clenched. *Brenda.* This was something he'd wanted for so long, the ghost of their single shared night chasing him throughout his life. After tonight, even more than her in his bed, he wanted this gorgeous life all around him. Brenda, laughing as he teased Eli, eyes flashing with love and humor when she watched them wrestling and playing around. The smile creases in her cheeks taking up permanent residence at their antics. Her hand in his, eyes to the screen, fingers responding with a squeeze when he shifted, not wanting to let him go.

This.

Her, with him.

Through the years, nearly every time his eyes closed in sleep, it was with a prayer for visions of her. He wanted it so much, wanted her so he wouldn't be walking alone, at least in his dreams. Now, he had *this* and it was as if he had been given the greatest of riches, precious gems piled in his hands.

With a happy sigh, he stepped out of the truck, turning back to unbuckle and pick up the sleeping boy. He carried Elias in and up to his bedroom where he bent over, placing him on the narrow bed. Carefully, he tugged the boy's boots off and dragged a lightweight blanket up to cover him, standing for a moment watching to make certain he didn't wake.

Back out at the truck, he carefully opened the door on which Brenda rested, unbuckling and catching her before she dropped out, still she woke up with a start. Shifting her, he picked her up with an arm behind her back, the other underneath her knees. He suppressed a groan when he realized her skirt had ridden up her legs and he was clasping bare skin. "I can walk," she murmured, cheek rubbing softly against his shoulder.

Bumping the truck door closed with a hip, he walked up the path to the house. "I know you can, Bee. But I already got you." She sighed and shifted her head, nestling against him, sleep claiming her once again.

He carried her upstairs, gently setting her in the middle of her bed. Slipping off her shoes, he set them aside, fingers lingering for a moment to caress her instep and heel. Sliding his hands underneath her, he found the zipper for her dress, lowering it by feel, careful not to pinch her tender skin as he removed it.

The sight of her in a strapless bra and matching panty set caused his cock to fatten and grow, tenting the front of his jeans. She was so beautiful, skin glowing in the dim light seeping in from the hallway, and he lifted a hand, slowly stroking across her shoulder. He swallowed and his throat felt knotted and raw all at the same time. Shaking his head at his reaction, he gently tucked a blanket around her shoulders, his fingertips trailing along her skin for a moment, relishing the touch. He turned to drape her dress over a chair and then looked back down at her. Rich, thick sandy blonde hair spread across the pillow, features flawless, she looked relaxed and at ease, claimed by a deep sleep.

Beautiful, just as he remembered.

Glancing around her room, a framed photo on the dresser caught his eye. Bending to get a closer look, he sucked in a breath of surprise and picked it up. It was a picture of him and Brenda, taken the night before he'd left town. The night they were together. Out on the floor at a barn dance, the photographer captured them in the middle of a fast two-step. Brenda's face tilted up to look at him, a broad smile stretching her lips, joy unmistakable in her expression.

In contrast, Reuben's face held a look of pain and longing. He remembered that dance. The previous half hour had been spent sitting at one of the small tables listening to her talk about her bull rider for the first time. The interest she showed in the other man made it clear she wouldn't be giving Reuben the green light for any play he might have wanted to make. Their conversation throughout the evening was why, when the opportunity presented itself, he had taken a chance to spend the night with her.

He set the frame back on the dresser and paced towards the door, mind still awash with memories. He was almost there when she called his name. Looking over his shoulder, he saw she had twisted in the bed, turning to face him, eyes half open. "Thank you," she said softly, reaching out and patting the covers, her words and actions giving him a confused invitation.

He shook his head, glancing at the picture displayed out in the open where she could see his pain every day. Not sure what to make of it, he looked at her and quietly said, "No worries, Bee. See you in the morning." Then he turned and walked out of the room, gently shutting the door behind him.

***

His fingers trailed gently across her mouth, back and forth, hypnotically stroking along the bow of her lips. He embraced her. Threaded his fingers through her hair, cupped his palm to the back of her head and cradled her tight to his shoulder for a moment more, knowing he would soon need to get up and leave. Tipping his chin down, he lightly kissed the top of her head and held his lips pressed to her hair, drawing in her scent.

Leaving Brenda was always the worst part of this dream, and as always, he was already struggling against the inevitable, trying to change the path ahead of him. Wishing and hoping with everything inside him he would get to hold to this feeling for a little longer, at least in his dream.

She was sleeping so sweetly. Calm, resting. Beautiful. God, she was so beautiful it hurt his heart, a hard band constricting and tightening around his chest. No, no, he thought, feeling his body begin the sideways slide that would take him from her bed. Give me just a few more minutes. Let me hold her. Please. Not yet. Merciless as always, the dream marched on around him, dragging him through. He stood at the side of the bed, looking down at her sleeping. Bending at the waist, he brought the covers up and tucked them carefully around her. Longing for the silk of her skin, his fingertips skimmed the softness of her bare shoulder.

She stirred in her sleep, dreaming in his dream and he soothed her with a breathless, "Shhhh. Little Bee. Shhhh." Twisting to the side, he looked for paper, finding nothing on the motel desk. Standing at the dresser where he'd tossed his bag last night, he pulled out the Polaroid the photographer had handed him of them dancing, and saw the paper napkin tucked next to his shirts. Pen in hand, he stared at the blank paper for a moment, composing his thoughts.

Brenda, he wrote and paused, finally adding in my little Bee. *Even knowing exactly what he would write, he paused again, then continued slowly, begrudging every sibilant stroke of the pen,* I know this won't make sense to you, but there is something I have to do. Something I left unfinished when I came back to Lamesa, and now I have to go take care of it. I'll always treasure you, Bee, and I hope you know how much you mean to me.

His fingers itched to write the truth, to close the note with a declaration of love, but he knew it would be a disservice to Brenda, because he learned tonight that she loved another, her bull rider. So, instead of begging her to wait on him, instead of promising to return as soon as possible, instead of declaring he would be hers forever if she only wanted him, *he simply wrote,* Always, Reuben.

He dressed quickly but quietly and stood for another moment in the doorway watching her sleep. He had pulled the door shut and was turning to walk away from the room as he always did, heading to the truck to drive away when he felt it. Things had shifted. His feet still moved towards his pickup, but he did it with his head turned towards the room, seeing the door easing back open and a shadow filling the open space. "Why you runnin', Rue?"

At that voice coming from so near his Bee, he tried to freeze, attempted unsuccessfully to halt his steps. His body climbed into the cab of the truck, fingers wrapping tightly around the wheel as he saw Ray's silhouette retreat from the doorway, hand reaching out to push the door closed, teeth glinting in what he knew had to be a wicked smile. "Why you runnin', bro? Got you a sweet piece of ass here. Finally tagged that pussy and now you're walking away? Loser. Just a loser, like always."

Key to the ignition, his hand twisted it viciously, the truck's engine roaring to life. "You walk away, you leave me no choice." *Sweat broke out on his face and shoulders as he fought against the pull of the dream. He felt the sheet underneath him dragging against his damp skin, that physical sensation anchored in reality.* It's just a dream.

"I'll own her, brother. Rest of her life, she'll remember you were the one that lead me to her." *The truck reversed out of the parking space and pulled into traffic, accelerating quickly while he stared out the back window at the shadow moving through the room behind the sheer curtains, heading towards the bed where his Brenda lay.* Just a dream.

"No choice. We are what he made us into. What we were made to be." *The voice hissed,* "I am what I am." *The motel receded into the distance, but Ray's voice was still loud, sounding as if it came from right beside him, maybe even from inside his head.* "And, you are what you are, Rue. Blind and weak. Always were, always will be. I own her now."

With a jerk, Reuben sat up in bed, palms scrubbing against his face, wiping the sweat away along with the last vestiges of the nightmare. He stood, leaving the dream sodden bed and walked into the hallway, pausing for a moment to listen to the sounds of restless sleep coming from Eli's room.

Turning, he padded to Brenda's door, soundlessly opening it, sucking in a breath when he saw her lying there, bare shoulders illuminated by moonlight streaming through the window. Peaceful. Resting. Ray never got his hooks into her, never found out how much she meant to Reuben. *Thank God, I saved her from that, at least.*

Making amends

Walking into the town's main feed store the next morning, where the ranch had done business since he was a kid, Reuben entered a space so filled with tension it was palpable. He couldn't be certain, but as he approached the counter, he thought some of what he was sensing was anger, and that anger was definitely directed towards him. He stopped near the register and nodded at a dark-haired woman standing behind the counter. She was on the phone and didn't respond, but he didn't think it would have mattered, because five seconds before she gave him her back, she had thrown him a blistering look of profound contempt.

Turning to an older man he recognized as the owner, Reuben smiled a greeting. "Mister Kennwort, good to see you, sir. How are you?" That got him a grunted response and he frowned, not understanding what he had walked into, but not liking it at all. He decided to get straight to business. "I need to order some feed," he tried, and found an order pad wordlessly tossed towards him from the side.

"Write down what you want. I'll give Brenda a call and verify." These terse words came from the woman and he turned to look at her again. The woman—who he wasn't sure he had ever met—was off the phone, glaring at him as if she hated him with every fiber of her being.

71

"Yeah," he drawled out the word, annoyed, "if you're gonna call Brenda, then clearly you know who I am. So, why don't I just place the order." Shaking his head, he reached out to pull the pad closer, looking up and down the counter for a pen. One skittered noisily towards him from the other direction. He stopped it with the palm of one hand and tilted his head up to look at the woman, waiting for her reaction.

"If it's all the same to you, I'll just call Brenda," she repeated herself, words slightly different, her accent even more pronounced in her anger and he frowned. That was not the right answer, and it just wasn't in him to let it go today. Not after his restless night and that fucking dream.

"Actually, it's not all the same. So, since I own the spread and pay the invoices, why don't I just save myself the stamp and pay this delivery in advance. In fact, I'll just take the feed. Load it up today. Just so there isn't a misunderstanding." He bit off the words, his tone curt and short because her attitude was pissing him off and while he'd been nice up to now, he wasn't sure he could maintain 'nice' for much longer if she kept pushing on that bitch switch. "If it's all the same to you." He offered her words back to her in a snide tone, mocking her, watching with some satisfaction as her head whipped backwards in reaction.

"Nelms." The call came from behind him and Reuben turned to see an older rancher standing close, weathered face drawn into stern lines of disapproval. Recognition came after a moment, and Reuben smiled, trying to shake off his anger as he held out his hand. This was Chelsie's father, Amos Transom.

"Mister Transom," he said, hoping his pleasure was evident in his voice. That only lasted a moment though, because neither his smile nor his hand were met with the same, so he stood there awkwardly for a second before allowing his arm to fall. "Saw Steve last night, he said Chelsie is doing well."

"Why are you in here, Nelms?" The older man asked this question as if it made all the sense in the world, and Reuben frowned, feeling like he was out of step with whatever was happening.

"It's a feed store." He paused, trying to decide if it needed clarification, and added, "I'm buyin' feed." Frowning, he looked around the room to see there were three other men glaring at him. He stepped closer, asking in a low tone, "Is there something I'm missing here, Mister Transom?"

"Write down your order. Let's take a walk, Reuben." Transom's face softened slightly, allowing pain to creep in around the edges. "We'll have us a chat."

Several hours later, Reuben backed the truck up in front of the barn and sat waiting for the ranch hands to unload the feed he'd brought home. He sat, leaning his head against his hands on the wheel, overwhelmed by feelings and emotions suppressed for so long.

Hatred and anger, betrayal and pain. It all swept through him, carrying him along and battering him like rocks in a raging river. Weighty wings of shadowed shame rested on his shoulders, because of blood.

The picture Transom's words painted was harsh, agonizing to hear, and Reuben was devastated by what the tale revealed. The woman behind the counter was Lisa Kennwort. She was the only daughter of the man who owned the feed store, and a classmate of Ray's back in high school. She had competed on the circuit, running timed events and winning more often than losing. Just like Mica.

Mica. His mind took him back to the last time he'd stood outside his brother's trailer. The slamming of the door echoing across the lot even while he listened to cries of pain and humiliation. Agony given voice as her body took blow after blow from the flank rope of Ray's bull-riding rig.

She was the first girl Ray took that Reuben had *known*. Known and liked. Laughed with. Shared meals with. It was impossible for him to reconcile the giggling, beautiful, green-eyed young woman who dipped her fries in gravy with the mascara-smeared, sobbing play toy of Ray's. That was the night Reuben had left the circuit for good and went home, running away from what he had heard and seen, trying to put it out of his mind.

For a time, he'd convinced himself leaving was the right thing to do. That she was a big girl. Told himself it was her choice to stay with the sadistic bastard his brother had become. After all, she could have always left.

His firm conviction had wavered, however, when he'd met and talked to Andy Jones. Thinking through it, talking it over, he'd come to the realization that it was his own fear holding him back. Fear that Mica would view him the same as his brother. Fear he would *become* the same. That somehow he would wake up and find himself just as twisted and depraved. Fear that the monster lived inside him, biding its time. Waiting.

He knew Mica wasn't equipped to deal with Ray, none of the girls he'd played with were, so Reuben had gone out hunting his brother. Years after closing the door on that skeleton in his closet, it was boney and rattling, a shadow come home to roost in a painful way.

When he'd caught up to Ray, Reuben discovered Mica had left. Running; hiding from the demon populating her living nightmare. She'd gotten away, *thank God*, but not before it got worse. Reuben found her, protected her. Got her on the club's radar and organized safety for her. Since then, he'd been protecting her, even before Mason loved her. But he knew her time with Ray was so much worse than what he had seen. In the beginning, Reuben might have run like a coward, but at least he had sucked up enough courage to circle back around and make sure she was okay.

No one had done that for Lisa.

It wasn't until she'd miscarried and had to be hospitalized that anyone knew what Ray was doing to her.

The local ER doc called her father as soon as he got an inkling of what was going on. Her daddy was a good man, one who had to stand by and witness what was done to her. Had to look every day at the scars she bore. A good man who'd held her hand as she lost her baby.

Reuben's thoughts turned to Molly, Mica's little sister. She was another woman he knew Ray had raped and gotten pregnant. Molly's outcome was far sweeter than Lisa's, because her child was loved by her husband, J.J. Rupert, as if Tomas was his own son. Precious mother and son both loved and protected by every Rebel member, because she was Mica's, which made her theirs.

Lisa didn't have that. She didn't have anything like that. She had a widowed father, who struggled on his own to deal with what happened, never quite finding his way to help her.

What Lisa did have was a small town, which enjoyed gossiping entirely too much, and a Nelms' sized skeleton in her closet attracting the chatter.

Chelsie and Lisa were best friends, so Transom, Chelsie's father, knew the story from that side of the equation. He knew how Chelsie's heart hurt for her friend, watched and listened from the hospital room door as she'd cried with Lisa for the loss of so much.

But, Transom was also friends with Kennwort, so he knew the story from that side, too.

Transom had sat with a sorrowful, raging, drunken father, holding Kennwort up as he seethed in impotent fury. Listening to his wrath and anger against the way the high and mighty Nelms men acted, and how they had treated his baby girl.

Like father, like son.

Apple don't fall far from that wicked tree.

Those boys will always be trouble.

Transom recounted Kennwort's furious rants, and Reuben learned his father's appetites had not gone unremarked in their not-large hometown. Where they were widely known as *the Nelms*, a family of bastards who seemed to ruin everything they touched.

Memories flooded him, things he hadn't thought about in years. Women, paraded up and down the stairs of the house Brenda now lived in with Eli. The walls of the house soaking up the pain and humiliation delivered by his father. And then, by Ray. Next generation of evil. Growing up, some of the women he recognized around town. Some he didn't, but he knew they saw him. Distressed and disturbed, his skin crawled with the fear that he might have stumbled on them like he had Lisa today, never knowing how his presence might be affecting them.

All of that, Reuben got from his chat with Transom. Now...*God*...now, he knew his walking into that store today had cost Lisa and her father something. Those emotions as painful as the day it happened, barely-healed scabs torn off by his boot falls through the door, exposing their still raw wounds to the caustic atmosphere being a Nelms brought with it. The cost to them might be intangible, but it was *real*. And he knew the something it cost them didn't stop there, because he knew it could cost him...everything.

Ray had done that.

Apple don't fall far from that wicked tree.

His father had done that.

Like father, like son.

His blood.

Those boys will always be trouble.

Took you with me

Reuben leaned forwards in the chair, resting his elbows on the kitchen table, head in his hands. He had been sitting in this position for a while, running things through his head, over and over. *Ray. Lisa. Mica.* Everything swirling round and round with no resolution.

He heard Brenda walking in from the yard, her voice preceding her and he watched as she moved through the room, graceful motion as natural to her as breathing. There she was, everything he had ever wanted from life. Right there, within reach, but so far away.

He had been home for hours and still didn't know what he was going to say. So many possibilities, he was sick from contemplating them. Every one of them broke down to two things.

Go.

Stay.

So many ways this could have worked out between them, but now, he was lost. Reuben Nelms was nowhere to be found. Tangled up in his own mind, thoughts spinning around in his head like on a carnival ride.

Be the man his brother wasn't. The one he knew he could be. Be the club member the Rebels demanded, the brother Mason expected. Be whatever it was Brenda wanted from him, twist himself to be anything she would let him give her.

Could he let himself stay in town, knowing what he now knew? Always wondering how many other women were out there that Ray hurt as he had Mica and Lisa? Fears running rampant that each woman met on the sidewalk had been another of Ray's victims? Looking into each face, wondering if his brother preyed on them as he had Molly. Mica's baby sister, who—*thank God*—had only suffered at his hands a single night, but been given a reminder of him that she smiled at every day. Would this question ricochet through his mind every time he saw a hometown gal, wondering what his blood had done?

"Supper will be about an hour, Reuben. Eli's with Gill and Tony, the boys decreed it was movie night," Brenda said, walking towards him. When he didn't lift his head, he heard her footsteps slow and halt, the soles of her boots scuffing the floor. With a breathless note in her voice, she cried, "Oh, no. What's happened? Is it Breezy?"

"No, no, honey." He was quick to reassure her. "The horse is fine. Everyone's okay." He picked up his head, letting his hands fall to the table as he looked at her. "Everything's fine, Bee. I'm just...in a mood," he said by way of weak explanation but she shook her head, rejecting his pat answer.

"No, something happened today. I can tell. Something bad. What is it, Reuben?" She came closer, tugging a chair out from underneath the table and shifting it so that when she sat, it was directly beside him, her thigh pressed tight against his. "What happened?"

"Nothing," he said, and moved in the chair, twisting his neck to keep from having to look at her. If he glanced at her, it meant she could see him, and he didn't want to give her a chance to spot the lie in his face. Everything was too close to the surface and he didn't know if he could hide his pain, not from her. Pain that came from knowing so much, but being helpless to make a difference.

All his life it seemed as if he had been a day late and a dollar short. Dealing with his father, and the man's failures. Coming along after the fact with the women, with the stock, hell, even with the ranch. Then, following behind Ray, cleaning up each mess as best he could. Ineffectual at soothing the pain that remained long after his brother was finished with his play. Today wasn't any different, just the length of time between actions and responses was drawn out. The pain was the same, for Lisa, and for him.

He felt the weight of Brenda's gaze and swallowed hard, looking down. The heat from her leg seared him, and he saw her hands clenched into tight fists, balanced on top of her thighs. Reuben waited, because she seemed on the edge of something, some reaction, and he wondered which way she would fall.

Seeming to make a decision, she stood, drawing his gaze up to her face. Slowly she reached out, palm up, fingers curled invitingly. He saw the set of her jaw, and stared at her outstretched hand for a long moment, weighing his options. He could accept the solace she offered, understanding it would be fleeting because he didn't believe he could bear to stay in town knowing what he now did—wondering if every female face he looked into held ghosts of Ray. Or he could set aside the need building in him, the desire to hold on to something good, and right. Turn her away, play it off with a joke, let her down easy.

He knew what he should do, but his desire for her was so strong.

That need was all Duck, not Reuben.

Gone from Lamesa for a long, long time, he had been busily making his own way. Building a good life, one filled with friends who pushed him to reach for more, friends who worked to make him better. Friends and a found family who built him up and didn't tear him down. That life he made, it meant his world was in Chicago, Fort Wayne, or any of a

79

dozen other cities where the Rebels had a chapter. The club had become his life. A good life, one where the legacy of his blood would never again define him.

He was not his blood. Not his father. Could never be. He could dig deep and would never find his father's brand of evil. It wasn't buried inside him; he wasn't a monster. *Duck* was not the product of his father's raising. Duck belonged to Mason and the Rebels, and they had forged him into the worthy man he knew himself to be.

Duck closed his eyes, swallowing hard, because he could feel himself wavering. Right and wrong were so clear, but still he wanted. *God*, he wanted Brenda. *I've loved her for so long.*

He knew he could have this with her right now, the possibility of expanding his horizons in a different yet familiar way. Create a changed definition for Reuben Nelms, one outside of what his father and Ray tried to twist to wrongness, this man balancing the one the club had built inside him. Duck. Wanting.

Reaching up, he placed his palm against hers, stroking against her skin, allowing those strong fingers to wrap around his hand, letting her tug and pull him to his feet. She was strong, so strong, and he could lean on her for now. Follow her lead. Her initiative; his willing cooperation. Without a word, she led him up the stairs to her bedroom, turning to lock the door once they were inside. Silently, she looked up at him and then he saw a smile light her face, bright as the sun's reflection on a river.

"I know it's not a race," she repeated his words from last night softly, reaching with her hand to trace her fingertips across his cheek, gently covering his lips when he would have spoken. "But I think it's time to get some skin in the game." She grinned and whispered, "After all, I've always heard racin' ain't racin' without rubbin', right?"

He pursed his lips, kissing her fingertips, staring at her when she said, "Let me love you, Reuben. Then we can talk. Something we should have done as soon as you got home, but I want this first. Give me this. Let me love you." He didn't understand her words, but the tone was clear; she wanted him. After all this time, she still wanted him. Strength and beauty standing before him.

Reaching up, he clasped her fingers in his, bringing the back of her hand to his lips, caressing it softly. "I want this too, Bee." He kissed her knuckles, bringing them to his mouth and biting lightly, keeping his fingers wrapped around her hand. When she gasped, he said, "I want you." Using his grip to pull her close, he slipped his arm around her waist, bending her backwards as he kissed down the column of her throat.

With every touch of her skin against his, the darkness threatening to swallow him edged back a bit. All the fears and pain caused by his brother's long-reaching actions, receding just a little more. Just by breathing, by existing, she helped him. *So strong.* Helped him beat back the demons that had pursued him for years. He knew, had known forever that he could never be worthy of her, of her love. But, today he would take what she offered, accepting the gift as it was meant, an statement of affection and fondness, and yes, love.

Reverently, he undressed her, skimming along her bare skin with the backs of his fingers just to see her shiver in response. He stroked across the curves to which her bra clung, watching goosebumps chase his touch until she gasped, letting her head fall back in reaction.

Unveiling her bit by bit, he took his time with each article of clothing until she stood before him nearly bare. He leaned in to kiss her, hands working at his own belt and jeans, mouth sliding and catching at hers as he discarded his clothes and knelt before her naked. Cock rigid with need, it curved upward from his groin as he ran gentle hands over her thighs. He stilled, feeling her legs tremble under his touch and he gazed up.

Cheeks flushed, tendrils of her gleaming blonde hair hung loose around her face. Her deep blue eyes were luminous and heavy-lidded with passionate anticipation. Lips parting slightly on an indrawn breath, he watched as she caught the lower one in her teeth, worrying at it for a moment. *Beautiful.* Honest and candid, her expression gave away everything, telling him what this meant to her.

Giving, she was still giving to him, even now, with him on his knees before her. God, he would worship her every day if she allowed it, giving back to her in all the ways he knew. *My Bee.*

She reached down, threading her fingers through his hair, grasping and tugging upwards gently. The touch pulled him out of his thoughts, and he smiled and shook his head, leaning forwards. Nipping gently at the tender flesh of her inner thigh, he drew another hushed gasp from her. Memories of the nights spent reliving their single encounter ripped through his mind, and in an instant he moved from quiet need to a raging desire, desperate to pleasure her.

"Gotta taste you, baby," he said in a voice gone rough, hooking a finger underneath her panties on each side of her hips. He slid the fabric down her legs with shaking hands, letting them fall in a tumble to the floor while he nuzzled into her, drawing in a breath rich with her scent, feeling the blood pounding through his cock in response. *This*, he thought, *this is what I need.*

Licking and lapping at her, he glided his hands up between her legs, using the pads of his thumbs to hold her open for his advance. She quivered and trembled, anticipation seeming to make her knees weak. *Draw it out, make it last,* he thought. Slow and easy, he took his time, patiently waiting for her response to each touch, each stroke of his tongue, listening as her breathing quickened, the muscles in her legs straining and tightening. Sucking her clit between his lips, he teased and tugged at the bundle of nerves. Then added his tongue down between her lips, delicately stroking and tracing around her entrance before again focusing on her clit. He hummed deep in his throat, and felt her squirm against his face. *Giving this to her, she's giving herself to me.*

His Little Bee was like honey and expensive wine on his tongue. Dark and rich. Uniquely delicious. *I could have this in my bed every night*, and with that thought...in that single moment, his life's path altered.

The shift was nearly physical as things changed, twisting in space...his mind transforming dreams into possibilities.

Everything changed because he knew he wanted this—*her*—in a way he had never wanted anything before. Craved her, wanted this...wanted there to be a *them* he could hold onto. Something that mattered, something real. *An us we can build from where we are today into something bigger and better than we can ever be on our own.* Together. His Brenda, his life. Consequences be damned, he wouldn't back down from this. She was his, now and forever. *I'm not going anywhere*, he thought, *no matter what, this is where I'm meant to be.*

Her legs trembled and he knew she was close. Frantic hands stroking his cheeks, she called his name on a sobbing breath. *Gonna take her there, give her this.* Pressing outward on her thighs, he spread her legs wider. *Give her me if she'll have me.* Spearing into her with his tongue again and again, he thrummed across her stiffened clit with his thumb until she spasmed, falling apart, and he watched her as the climax hit her hard. *All of it. Everything.* He cupped the cheeks of her ass in his palms, lending her his strength, holding her tightly, making love to her with his mouth as she came. Slowing his caresses, he stared up, waiting as her breathing slowed and evened out, those sexy-as-fuck little hitches coming less frequently.

Rising to his feet, he lifted her, and she wrapped her legs around his waist. Draped across him, she leaned heavily against his chest, arms loosely clasped around his shoulders. He carried her to the bed and carefully settled over the top of her. The condom in his wallet was too far away, and he couldn't wait. Wouldn't. *I'll take anything I can get with her*, he thought. A vision of her nursing an infant flitted across his thoughts and he groaned.

Knees and forearms pressed deep into the mattress, he moved until her legs cradled his hips, the tip of his engorged cock poised at her entrance. Shifting slightly, he thrust the first few inches inside, mouth falling open on a groan, then pulled back to still again. "Bee." *God, I've waited so long.*

He paused, arms trembling as he held tight to his control, waiting as her eyes fluttered and opened. Waited until her breath came deep and unshuddering. Waited, and when, eyes hooded, mouth soft, she looked at him with an expression he would give his life to see every day, he rocked into her, the slickness of her inner walls welcomed him. *Home.*

He pushed to the root, seating himself completely, holding there while his cock throbbed and twitched, stomach muscles jerking. He nearly lost control when a relentless round of waves and shudders from her climax fluttered around and underneath him, and her body twisted on the bed as she called his name on a whisper.

"Bee," he said, voice sounding foreign even to himself, low and gravel-filled. Forcing himself again to hold still, he waited. *Gonna take her where I need her to go.* "Are you with me, honey?"

She nodded, her neck arching back, pressing into the pillow and he licked his lips, again tasting the richness she offered. *Fuck, she tastes so good... feels so good. Mine.* He dipped his mouth to her neck, teasing her skin with soft touches, feathering kisses up and along her throat until she made an impatient noise. He repeated his question, teeth gritted with the effort of holding back, waiting. "Are you with me?"

"Reuben," she said softly, "I'm here, baby. Right here with you."

When he lifted his head, she took him by surprise, stretching up and pressing her mouth to his, the tip of her tongue stroking slowly along the seam of his lips. With a groan, he fell into the kiss, their mouths working against each other as he moved inside her, thrusting slowly, angling and rocking his hips, grinding himself as far as he could get into her pussy. *Make it last; make it good.*

Her heat surrounded his shaft, inner walls clenching tightly and filled completely by his cock. He was hard, engorged, and so sensitive her heartbeat thudded through him, through that connection. That beat pounding hard, leading him forward. Movements broken down into moments; drowning in sensation, all thoughts fleeing as he made love to her. *Waited on this half my life.*

Urgency built in him, low over his spine, the need driving him to stroke harder, deeper. *All my life.* Heavy with want, his sac swinging and slapping against her ass with every rough thrust, he felt the slipperiness of their sweat as his belly slid across hers. Teeth gritted, he fought to regain control. *Give her what she needs; I'll get mine. Fucking perfect.*

Push inside, fast and hard.

Pull back, an unhurried, slow withdrawal.

Thrust forwards recklessly fast, rocking deep.

Sounds of their breathing filled the room, with rasping indrawn gulps and heated air blown out hard on a groan.

Dipping his head, Reuben captured her breast in his mouth, sucking deep, thrilled when she moaned, her voice low, body arching up into his. Her nipple hardened against his tongue and he sucked harder, dragging fast reactions from her. "Fuck, Bee, you're so perfect. Suck these titties all day. Follow you around my mouth on you, head under your shirt, titty on my tongue," he murmured, moving to her other breast, wrapping his lips around the pebbled peak, drawing it into his mouth.

At his words, she tightened around him and he paused mid-stroke, awed at the reaction. "Fuck me, darlin'. Come on, fuck me back, let me ride you, baby." She gasped and clenched around him again, and he nipped at the side of her breast, lips curving up into a wicked smile as he recognized what was going on. "You feel so fucking good, wrapped around me. Your pretty cunt taking all of me. Loved eating you, darlin'. Feasting on your pretty pussy. Never had better pussy than yours." With every dirty word, she jolted and jerked, and he lifted his head to look into her face.

"Bee, baby, you fuck so good. Feel so right under me, where you belong. This is my home, between your legs, buried inside you. My cock rooted deep inside your pussy." He watched as her lips parted on a moan. Then her teeth clamped down on her bottom lip. Sucking it into his mouth, he rescued it from her control, nibbling on it and groaning when her tongue dipped out to slide across his lips again.

He fucked her hard, hips twisting and pushing, and mouth next to her ear, whispered, "You like that, baby? Like me talking to you? Like me telling you how much I like your pretty pussy? Your hot, tight, 'so fucking good I can't believe it' pussy? My pussy." Her head nodded and when she drew in a stunned gasp of air, he grinned. "Yeah? You like that? Little bit of dirty talk in bed revs your engine?" She nodded again and then clenched tight around him, holding him inside, muscles all over her body tense with desire.

He thrust deep and held, grinding into her. "You like me deep, like taking all of me? Every fucking inch I have for you? I want you to like it, want you to need me in your bed every night, Bee. I want to be able to roll over and fuck you in the morning, want your sleepy eyes on me. Want my face to be the first thing you see every morning, see me loving you right before you come. The last thing you see at night, before you go to sleep at my side." She was twisting and moving beneath him as he slowed and eased back, pulling out almost entirely. Hips moving, she chased the sensation, and her lusty movements nearly undid him.

"Want you to want me, want for me to keep you. Want this, baby. Want you." Hips still, he lifted up on his elbows, cupping a hand to either side of her head, threading his fingers through her hair and tilting her mouth to meet his as he crashed down. Tasting her, tangling their tongues together, slanting his mouth across hers again and again, he was desperate for every reaction he could wring out of her.

Breathing hard, sucking air in audible pants, she grew more frantic underneath him, her voice murmuring his name, hips lifting and pumping, trying to draw his rigid length deeper inside her pussy. "Need you in my life, Bee. Open your eyes, darlin'. Look at me." When she did, locking on him with half-hooded eyes filled with arousal, he began a slow glide in, taking his time until he was buried, then withdrawing to the tip and pushing back forward, working hard to maintain a sensuous rhythm with his thrusts. Her eyes fluttered and began to close, and he reminded her, "Look at me."

God, she feels so good, right...all mine. The way her pussy tightened and fluttered around him, he knew she was on the brink, waiting on something to push her over. Rearing up on his arms, he locked his elbows and lifted his torso off hers. Looking down to where they were joined, he watched his glistening cock slide in and out of her pussy, the blood-engorged shaft and darker veins a sharp contrast to the dusky rose of her much paler skin.

"So wet for me. Fucking ready to take me, ready for my cock." Her hands clenched in the sheets, knuckles white with the strain of holding on, and he realized he hadn't felt her touch since he laid her on the bed. Once he sensed their absence, he was desperate to feel her hands on him. Wanted the silk of that skin-on-skin from her. "Bee, baby, touch me. Put your hand on my hip, feel me move into you."

One arm rose at his command; when she rested her hand on the curve of his ass, he drove into her harder, loving the helpless little noise she made at the back of her throat. "Touch me, baby." Her other hand rose, curving around his bicep, sliding up and over his shoulder. "My baby, God, yes. Touch me. So fucking beautiful, so ready for me. Mine. Taking every inch. Look at how greedy your pussy is for my cock." He was able to see her jolt at his words this time, the reaction causing her head to go back and nearly closing her eyes. "Look at me," he gritted out, because he was beginning to close in on his own orgasm, having to savagely push it back in order to wait for her.

"Bee, baby, what do you need to get there with me? I'm close, darlin'. So fucking close, I want to take you with me." His arms shook with the strain of holding himself off her, but he wanted to watch her come. *Need to see her, take time to appreciate what she gives me.* Wordlessly, she shook her head back and forth, and he knew she was trying to wave him off. "Ain't happenin', baby. Want to bring you with me. What do you need?"

She shook her head again in short, sharp movements and he groaned. "It ain't selfless, Bee. I want to feel your pussy clamp down on me hard, trying to hold my cock inside you while you come. I want to feel the heat inside you draw me in, pull me deep."

He sped up, the sound of their bellies slapping together coming faster. "Love fucking you, goddamn perfect pussy *all* around me." Tilting his hips, he ground against her clit, watching the expression on her face change even as he felt the reaction deep inside her to that pressure. "Perfect woman under me." No way would she touch herself, not if she could hardly bring herself to touch him as he worked over the top of her. *I'll have to be inventive*, he thought.

"Put your hand on my cock, baby. Wanna feel you." He watched as her eyes widened, but damned if she didn't obediently move her hand off his hip and put it between them. "Yeah, reach down, stroke me. Touch me, feel me sliding in and out of your pussy. Me inside you, *fuck*, finally in there. You under me. *My Bee*."

The first tentative touch of her fingertips on his cock nearly undid his control, but he worked hard to maintain the steady pace, rocking into her hard and deep with each plunge. "Feel how wet my cock is, Bee?

How slick? That's how much you want this, baby. Want me. Love that you want me, baby."

Her mouth opened, the pink tip of her tongue sliding along her top lip. "Touch your clit for me, honey, slide a finger across it. Feel how bad you need to come? Let me watch you play with yourself while I fuck you. Nothing hotter than you in this bed under me, your hand on your pussy while we fuck."

He knew the moment she found that nub of nerves, because the walls of her pussy clamped hard around him. "Aww, yeah, baby. God." Words were nearly beyond him now, and for a moment, he was afraid if she didn't come soon, he wouldn't be able to wait for her, but gritting his teeth, he pushed past it, and decided that leaving her behind wasn't going to happen. "*Jesus*. Bee."

He moved faster, harder, watching her tits shake and bounce with every thrust. The curve of her arm forced one breast high and proud, so he tipped his head down and kissed the erect nipple. Plucking with his lips, he pulled it into his mouth and rolled his teeth across, biting down gently but firmly. He knew the exact moment when the sharp edge of pleasure-driven pain finally pushed her over the brink and into a hard climax. He sank his teeth into her again, still gently but a little harder. He was rewarded when she groaned out his name, the end raising on a cut-off wail as the feeling swelled in her again.

Raising back up on his arms, he watched as she moved through the orgasm, watched the waves of emotion and pleasure wash across her features, her mouth opening and closing soundlessly, the one utterance of his name the only sound she made.

Elbows to the bed, he covered her, picking up the pace again as he moved. Fucking her hard and fast, hips pistoning, Reuben had to chase her only a moment before he was there. Balls drawing up to his body, the tingle in his spine expanding out hotly, tightening his ass and driving him in deep where he held, his cock jerking inside her as he came hard.

"Brenda, baby," he groaned, mouth to her ear. "Jesus. Fuck, darlin', so fucking good."

Her hand was on his side, fingers holding tightly, nails dragging, teasing along his skin, causing him to buck his hips forward, finding another half-inch inside her when he thought he was already as deep as he could go. "Fuck, baby. *Goddamn.* So hot and good, Brenda. Loved this, love being home, inside you."

Head shoved into the pillow beside hers, he wasn't in control. At all. Not of his reactions, and certainly not of his mouth. It was running away with him, whispers writing promises, stringing together sounds and words drawn from his soul. She took an audible breath, gasping when he said, "Love you, baby. Loved you all my life. Took you with me everywhere, but nowhere in my mind was it this good. As much as I dreamed about you, thought about you, never imagined you'd want me back here. Love you, Brenda."

***

Brenda sat on the floor of her little bedroom, her back wedged into a corner, settled far down into the space between the mattress and the wall. Arms wrapped tightly around her bent legs, her forehead rested against her knees. She was trying not to listen, waiting for the shouting to stop. Her aunt and uncle had started earlier than normal tonight, right after dinner, and as she always tried to do, she retreated as soon as the first voice was raised.

It wasn't an unusual occurrence. After she'd moved in, she'd found that unlike her mother and father, her aunt and uncle seldom went long without fighting. Recently, their arguments had gotten more frequent, shouted words turning mean in a way they had never been before. At ten years old, Brenda had lived with them for the past four years, ever since the accident on a Kentucky mountain road stripped her of her family.

Sitting quietly, waiting, she turned her head and looked up and out the window, watching as the last colors bled from the sky. It's so pretty at night here, she thought. She had few memories from before, didn't remember much other than living with her aunt and uncle, but even so, she still thought it was beautiful.

Her only real memories from before were unfocused, hard to hold. One was of her mother's face hovering over her, soft words threading echoes together in a lullaby. Brenda Bug, called in her sweet mother's voice. Another memory, more a feeling than a picture, was the way it felt when her father lifted her up over his head, tickling and shaking her gently, bringing her down and arranging it so her cheek rested on his strong shoulder. The scent of his aftershave, spicy and fragrant. Loved. Protected.

A final memory was tied up in pain and the overwhelming stench of burning plastic, the shrill whine of hot air escaping from captivity, the deadening silence of the woods after their car had crashed into the trees. A stranger's voice saying, "Oh, God," over and over. That memory most often came to visit in her dreams. From her position on the floor, she reached up, slipped her hand between the mattress and pillow, and allowed her fingertips to gently wander among the treasures there: a crow's feather, a pink-dyed rabbit's foot, and her mother's locket. Her dreamcatchers.

She heard a noise and rocked up on her knees, balancing with her palms on the windowsill to look outside. Shapes moved through the darkness beside the horse barn, and fear trilled through her veins, making everything tingle. If the horses had gotten out of the barn, Uncle Albert would be even angrier than he was now.

Brenda couldn't imagine how bad things could be if that happened, and instantly, she decided to see if she could fix whatever this was, hopefully even before he knew anything was wrong. She quickly pulled jeans and a sweatshirt from her dresser, changing from her nightgown to the clothes, dressing as rapidly as possible.

Sliding the window open, she levered herself headfirst over the sill, balancing for a moment on her belly and reaching down to break her fall to the ground. Once outside, she heard the unmistakable pounding of horse hooves. They were measured, controlled, holding a steady pace, not accompanied by sounds of distress she would expect if the horses were running loose. Crouching beside a bush near the outside wall of the house, she took a moment to survey the area around the barn.

From the movement and shadows cast by the security light on the far corner of the barn, it looked to be just a single horse. The animal wasn't running free, but galloping easily, being worked on a long line. She frowned. There was no easy way she could see anything from her position beside the house. She needed to get closer.

Darting from the sheltering shadows, she ran across the open space to one corner of the wooden corral. Flinging herself at a post, she quickly climbed the weathered boards, one bare foot wedged into place on either side of the sturdy support. From this fresh vantage point, she got the impression the person in the center of the circle, the one controlling the massive horse, was a kid not much older than she was.

The boy's calm voice spoke ceaselessly to the horse, encouraging him, soothing him. Almost hypnotic in nature, the tone he used was far more important than what his words meant. Peace. Through the minutes, as the horse made circuit after circuit around that anchoring pivot in the center of his world, the words came. Promises. Soft and sweet, he spoke gently, making her shiver in the still-hot night air. Comfort. That thrill of fear or something like it was back, washing over her, making her throat tighten with an unnamed emotion.

The outside lights came on, shining from poles around the house and barn, startling her and the horse. The bright glare illuminated the boy, revealing he was solidly built, topped with an unruly shock of thick, dark hair. Immediately, she knew it was Reuben. Cute Reuben Nelms.

The oldest son of a neighboring rancher, Reuben was tall and strong for his age, nearly four years older than Brenda. More than good looking, he was sweet and kind. Like most of the girls in town, she'd noticed him, her gaze silently following him between each class as he walked the hallways of the school. Unaware of her interest, unaware of her...surrounded by his gang of friends.

His brother was good looking too, but everyone knew Ray held an edge of mean. She'd never seen him do anything bad, but he watched her sometimes, and that watching made her uneasy. He was the kind of boy she instinctively knew would pull wings off flies, kick dogs for walking too close, or grab a girl's arm tightly just to watch pain cross her features.

She could see Reuben's face in the lights. See well enough to recognize he knew things were about to hit the fan because fear was deeply branded there, but he didn't abandon the animal. Instead of running, he called the horse to him, securely gripping one side of the halter he stroked the horse's neck with long, slow sweeps of his hand. She watched the horse settle, head dropping as it relaxed. She imagined for a moment it was her Reuben was holding, that touch telling her she was protected, certainty washing through her that his strength and confidence would make her safe.

Her uncle strode into view, and it was clear from his scowling face Reuben's fear was warranted. He snatched the lead rope from the boy, growling at him not to move. He was to stay put and wait. Uncle Albert turned to lead the horse into the barn, and Brenda pressed herself into the corner of the corral, hiding as best she could behind the post. She watched Reuben and saw he was waiting, standing tall even as her uncle stalked back towards him.

"Boy," her uncle shouted, "what in the hell did you think you were doing, taking my horse out of my barn in the middle of the dadgum night?" He reached out a hand to grasp Reuben's shirt collar, but the boy jerked backwards, staying just out of reach, the motion to avoid capture

clearly one he frequently practiced. Her uncle froze at the motion, and she wondered what Reuben's home life was like, if he hid too, maybe to avoid more than raised voices.

"Daddy said he forgot to come work your colt," Reuben told her uncle. "I didn't want you to be mad at him, and I knew the horse needed the work. I thought I would put a half session into him tonight. Then I could come back tomorrow morning for another half session. Then he would be back on track."

"How long have you been out here, boy?" Her uncle's tone was different, much calmer when he asked this question.

"Only about a half hour." When he spoke, Reuben's head made a move as if he was going to turn and look at her, but then his neck twisted and he faced her uncle again. "I was about ready to cool him off and put him up."

Her uncle breathed out a heavy sigh and shook his head. "Boy," he said, and then paused. He seemed to be considering his words. "Don't let me catch you back out here working my animals without telling somebody. You come to the house and knock, no matter the time of day. It's light enough here by the barn so we can work horses after dark if need be, but it ain't safe to do that all by yourself. You find me, or my wife; we'll come outside and sit with you while you do your work."

Reuben's head turned again, face shadowed as he turned her way and she was sure he'd seen her, that he was aware she was there. Later, she would realize this was when she'd fallen in love with him, when he'd kept her secret and didn't tell, simply responding to her uncle with a muttered, "Yes, sir."

Brenda rose to consciousness slowly. Drifting awake, the dream still wrapped around her made those long ago days of uncertainty seem not far behind her. She hadn't dreamed of that young Reuben in forever, and thought she barely remembered those days and nights spent watching him work her uncle's horses. Eyes barely cracked, she saw the bedroom was dark, only a little light coming in through the curtains over the window. The house was silent in a way which spoke to being filled with sleeping occupants, attesting to the late hour.

She was hot. So incredibly hot, all wound up in the sheets and blankets. She wanted to cool off, but when she tried to toss the covers off, she found they were weighted, held in place. Tilting her head, her gaze fell on a massive, brown arm curving around her waist, muscles bulging even at rest. With a shiver, it all came back to her. *Everything* came back, and she remembered.

Remembered him touching her, loving her, making love to her...everything they had done in her bed. Then, her brain flashed to what he had said and her core clenched, a soft, gentle ache blooming between her legs. Comfortable and welcome, the pain was a quiet, private reminder of their lovemaking.

She had evidently gone to sleep after he'd finished with her. After they'd finished with each other, he'd settled in, lying curved around her, spooning. It wasn't until then that she'd realized they hadn't used protection, quickly counting days in her head as she felt the wetness between her legs. *Safe as it can be, I guess*, she remembered thinking.

Not able to help herself, not even really trying, she flattened her palm, slowly smoothing down the soft skin of his arm, extending the touch and curling her fingers around one large wrist. When he was standing or moving, working or even just leaning against the counter in the kitchen, it could be hard to remember he was so big and fit, but she remembered the view as he covered her last night. The muscles in his stomach and chest moving fluidly underneath his dark skin as his hips rolled, that exotic coloring courtesy of his mother.

She let her eyelids sink closed again at the heat rising with the memory and then jerked partially upright, waking Reuben. "Oh, shit. I didn't do supper," she blurted, wiggling to free herself from underneath his arm.

"Nu-huh, Bee. 'S okay," he reassured her sleepily, words coming slowly. "I got Essa to take care of it. She made sure Eli got home from Gill's, too." He tightened his arm, pulling her back down into the bed and against him with a contented sigh. "I told them you weren't feeling well; went to bed early." He nuzzled into the back of her neck, pressing his lips against her skin, soft and warm. "Go back to sleep. Rest, darlin'," he whispered, already more than halfway there himself from the sound of things.

She relaxed into his hold, feeling him wrap himself around her a little tighter, slide a little closer. Tommy would never have done that, made it so she had time to sleep. He would have woken her, and then been pissed he had to do even that much. She'd never had someone to make it easy for her. *All that he is, and then he does something like this, making him so much more*. Then, just before she dropped off into sleep, she heard his whispered words, "Sleep, baby. Love you, my Little Bee."

***

Hands on his hips, Reuben looked at the sagging roof over the porch, mentally reviewing what needed to be done. Nail a header board into place along the eaves; wedge a support post under that header. Remove the warped board, replacing any others that needed it; put in the new permanent header. Remove the temporary pieces and then paint the whole shebang. *No problemo*, he thought with a grin.

"Need any help?" Eli's question came from behind, startling him because he hadn't heard the boy walk up. He grinned, amused. Over the past week the kid had started emulating Reuben's way of moving, and Eli slipping up on him now was a far cry from his loud running the first day.

"Can always use a hand," he responded. "We're going to fix the porch first, and then see about that dang chicken coop. Smells like it needs shoveling out." Turning, he laughed when he saw Eli's face scrunch up. "Yeah, that's gonna be a stinky job. Nothing for it, though. Just another job that's gotta be gotten through."

"Porch first?" Eli asked cheerfully, and Reuben saw he already had a hammer in hand. *Good boy*, he thought, *came prepared to back up his words with actions.*

"Yeah, I picked up the boards from town. They're in the back of the truck." Before he was even finished speaking, Eli had set his hammer on the edge of the porch, showing he had common sense by placing it next to a post where it was unlikely to trip anyone, and was trotting towards the truck. His eagerness to please shone through the boy, and Reuben wondered for a moment about Eli's relationship with his deceased father. *Had it been good? Did he miss Tommy, miss the man?* Shaking his head, Reuben followed towards the truck, trying to hide a grin as he watched Eli wrestling with the longest and heaviest of the wood pieces stacked in the bed.

Four hours later, Reuben declared, "Lunchtime." Straightening his back with a wince, he leaned his forearms on the handle of his shovel, gloved hands dangling. "I think we've got enough chicken shit cleared out. I'll get Gill to drop some shavings in here this afternoon. Eli, my boy, good work. Nice job. Hard job, but well done."

Eli looked up at him, brown eyes dancing as they peered over the bandana tied around the bottom of his face, dirt and sweat streaking his forehead. "Finally," he muttered, a joking tone in his voice. The boy had done a hell of a lot of work, turning his hand to anything asked of him, including helping to shovel what looked to be nearly a half-ton of chicken manure, the smell of ammonia thick in the air around them, stinky dust settling on their sweaty bodies.

After putting up all the tools, they were walking side-by-side back towards the house when Reuben stopped for a moment and cocked his head, looking at the cattle tank. He had some good memories from the ranch, helping to balance out the bad, at least a little. A lot of those memories were tied up in the horses, because they gave him something to focus on, take him out of himself. The other ones surrounded water. Swimming hole or cattle tank, water had provided an escape that wasn't present elsewhere. A slow grin spread across his face as he stared down at the boy and asked, "You got any stuff in your pockets? Paper, phone, that kind of thing?"

Scoffing, Elias laughed. "Uh, no, sir. I don't got no phone."

Nodding, Reuben rubbed across his chin with the palm of one hand, covering up his smile. "You sure?"

"Yes, sir, I'm sure. I should know if I got a phone, shouldn't I?" Eli grinned up at him.

"Good," he said as he swooped Elias up in one arm and stripped off the boy's boots before he tossed him, screaming, into the large, round cattle tank, filled to the brim with water pumped out of the deep aquifer by the windmill. Fresh, cold water. Frigid. The water cut off the sound mid-yell and Reuben grinned at the sudden silence. He kicked off his own boots and cleared his pockets of things that wouldn't be best pleased with a drenching, tossing his phone and wallet to the side before he leaped in himself, splashing a just-surfacing Eli, making him sputter in surprise.

The cold water closed over his head, washing away the sweat and grime of their day, isolating him in near silence. As a kid, he'd spent some of nearly every summer day in the water, either swimming the creek or a tank like this, so for him, it was another moment of coming home, this time in a good way.

"I was hot," he explained when he surfaced, seeing the shock still in place on Eli's features change to a pleased grin. "Thought you probably were, too." He reached out a long arm, settled his hand on top of Eli's head and pushed, dunking him under the water. An again sputtering Eli surfaced and kicked towards him, climbing Reuben's shoulders like a monkey in an attempt to return the favor. He failed, and went sailing over Reuben's head to land in the water, fingers pinching his nose closed, delight on his face.

They played in the water for twenty minutes, feet sliding on the slick metal bottom of the tank as they pretended to fight. Dunking each other under the water again and again until the laughter of the ranch hands registered. Gathered nearby on their way in for the midday meal, the men were standing close, but out of the splash zone. Reuben stood, the water nearly reaching his waist, feeling the liquid sluicing from his body. He turned to see Brenda standing on the newly repaired and painted porch, a broad smile on her face.

"Watch this," he mock-whispered to Eli as he climbed over the edge of the trough, saturated socks slapping against the dusty path leading to the porch. Taking the steps two at a time, he reached out and grabbed Brenda before she realized what he was about to do, throwing her over his shoulder and walking back towards the tank. Her pounding fists against his back were far from painful, and he was aware of her rounded ass right beside his head. "Bee," he called, making sure she could hear him over her protests. "You got anything in your pockets that can't get wet?"

"Don't you dare. *No!* You put me down, Reuben. Don't do this!" she yelled at him, and he turned his head, nipping at her ass and drawing an indignant-sounding squeak from her. "Don't!"

"Last chance to salvage anything that can't get wet," he warned her, bringing her down from his shoulder and into his arms as he stood next to the tank. Glancing down, looking her over, he didn't see any bulges in her pockets, and fortunately, her feet were already bare. "You ain't got anything on ya, do ya, Bee?" While he waited for her response, he used his heels, alternately trapping the toes of his muddy socks, tugging the encasing cotton from his feet, leaving the soiled proof of his travels lying in the dirt.

"Don't," she said again, twisting to try and free herself but he tightened down, holding her firmly in place against his chest. He hiked up his ass, putting it on the edge of the tank, balancing there for a moment. She yelled at him, her voice rising an octave. "Don't, Reuben! I'm warning you!"

Swinging his legs into the tank, he walked one slow step at a time through the water and over to where Eli was floating on his back. The boy's eyes were closed, face upturned, ears riding just below the surface blocking out most of the noises. Reuben grinned, this way the boy could always claim ignorance later if he caught grief for not helping his momma out.

"One," Reuben counted and her muscles tensed all over her body, hands clutching at his soaked shirt, her wordless shriek sounding loud over the laughter of the ranch hands.

"Two," he said, and she made a different noise, turning and pressing her head into his chest.

"Three," he called, and threw himself over backwards, taking her with him, plunging them both underneath the heated layer of water and into the chill nearer the bottom.

With Brenda still in his arms, he got his legs underneath him and crouched, bringing their heads and shoulders out of the water. "I hate you," she whispered, reaching up to push her wet hair out of her face.

He glanced over, seeing Eli watching from the corner of his eye. "I love you," he whispered back, dipping his mouth briefly to hers, the kiss tender and sweet.

Good together once

"Go out to dinner with me." Reuben's tone was wheedling and sweet, coming from behind her as she stood by the kitchen sink, rinsing the lunch dishes. "I'll take you into Midland. We'll have a nice meal. We could go dancing or take in a sit-down movie. Does that sound good, Bee?"

Without turning around, she smiled, dipping her chin towards her chest. *Hell, yes, it sounds good,* she thought, but before she could respond, he stepped close behind her, fitting his front to her back and wrapping his arms around her waist. Chin on her shoulder, he nuzzled into the side of her neck, restating his plea on a whisper. "Please."

Still smiling, she nodded, and he gave her a tight squeeze. "Go get ready, Bee. I'll finish up in here." In his arms, she turned and lifted to press her mouth to his, marveling at the sure knowledge he wouldn't turn her away, would kiss her back. That he wanted this as much as she did. He groaned against her lips, and there was a sharp sting as his palm dropped hard on her ass. "Woman," he growled, nipping at her bottom lip, "go get ready. Stop makin' trouble for yourself."

"What kind of trouble am I making?" With a grin, she raised to her toes and kissed him again.

It had been like this for the last few days, ever since she'd found him nearly broken, and then together, they'd put the pieces back into place. Eli had quickly become accustomed to how possessive Reuben was, and while he still watched their exchanges with a considering eye, his smiles and interactions with Reuben were becoming more natural every day.

His voice had changed to rough and needy when he said, "The best kind of trouble if you want me buried deep inside you in about two minutes." Gently nibbling up the side of her neck, he swatted her butt again, and she moved sideways, coming to a stop against his strong arm. He slipped it around her waist, holding her in place so his mouth never left her skin. Glancing at the refrigerator, she focused for a moment on the calendar pinned there with magnets and then groaned.

"We can't do either," she said, tipping her head back to look up at him. "The event vet is supposed to be on site tonight to inspect the arena and treatment areas. We have to be there." Shaking her head, she snorted a laugh. "I can't believe the rodeo is nearly here already."

"Home after the inspection then?" He leaned close, brushing his lips delicately across hers as his hand slipped down her back, cupping her ass cheek, and pulling her against him, letting her feel the hardness of his erection. Whispering, he said, "You're all I want to eat, anyway," grinning as she gasped, his words causing heat to flare in her belly. "But after the rodeo, I'm taking you out on a proper date, Bee."

Stepping back on unsteady legs, she tipped her chin down and nodded. "Home with you sounds phenomenal. Let me finish up in here, and we can head out."

The heat from his hands covered her shoulders for a moment, then his palms slid up her neck as he cupped his hands around her, running a thumb softly along her jawline. He stared into her eyes searchingly, tipping her chin up. She didn't know what he found there, but after a moment, he bent down and kissed her with a small, satisfied sound. Stroking her tongue with his, delving deep into her mouth, not stopping until her breath came ragged and she felt drugged, sinking against his chest with a sigh. His mouth pressed to the top of her head, and he said, "Love you, Bee."

Sounds outside were rapidly approaching the house and Brenda recognized the excitement in her son's voice as he called for her. "Mom, *Mom!*" She stepped slightly away from Reuben and was facing the door when it slammed open. The screen door slapped against the end of the spring and banged shut behind Eli as he sprinted inside, boots sliding for purchase on the wooden floor. "Mom! Gill said the new vet worked magic and Breezy is ready to ride! Essa's good to go for the rodeo!" Eli's joy was contagious and she found herself returning his grin as he ricocheted across the room, arms pinwheeling for balance.

"Excellent news," she said, reaching out to steady him as he slid to a stop in front of her. "She's due for a break in her luck. This could be exactly what she needs."

Eli nodded, head moving up and down quickly as he stood, looking up at her. Bottom lip clenched firmly between his teeth, a half-smile curled the edges of his mouth up in an expression she recognized. She had seen that exact look on Reuben's face not five minutes ago, just before he'd kissed her. *You have got to tell the man*, she scolded herself, feeling the dark cloud of worry settle over her. She knew with every passing day it became harder to come up with a rational reason to delay. She wanted to tell him, needed to, but the timing never seemed right.

"Want to come with us to the grounds? We're meeting the vet in a little while. Ice cream afterwards?" Reuben offered this casually and Eli's face lit with pleasure as he peered around her and up at the big man.

"Heck, yeah," he yelled, spinning and running flat out at the door, hitting the surface with his palms and shoving it wide to crash back into the frame behind him. His voice trailed, "I'll be in the truck."

Before she could turn around, Reuben had pressed up against her back, arms wrapping around her to hold tight. Nuzzling against the side of her head, he peppered soft kisses on her cheek, up her temple and into her hairline. "He's a good little man," he murmured and she stiffened. His next words told her he had noticed and had mistaken her reaction for something it wasn't.

"Don't do that, Bee. Don't be mad. I wouldn't ever try to take his dad's place, but I love how good that boy is. You've done such a good job with him, and he's so tough and sweet. Protective of his momma, wanting only to do right." He nibbled on her earlobe, gently pulling it into his mouth and sucking softly. "You, however, are purely sweet and delicious." Nipping harder, he growled, "Makes me want to eat you right up. Lap at your honey, my Little Bee."

Relaxing into his arms, she twisted her head and offered her lips. "I'm all yours," she said in between kisses and smiled to hear the hum of pleasure deep in his throat.

***

Reuben glanced across the cab of the truck, laughing at the cacophony of sound coming from the passenger side as Brenda and Elias competed for the lead part in some country western ballad. The boy mischievously put his palm across his mother's mouth to quiet her, and she just as mischievously pretended to bite him.

When he laughed and continued to try to prevent her from singing, it looked as if she had licked his hand because Elias quickly drew it back with a disgusted, "Gross, Mom," as he wiped it on his pants leg. His antics pulled uncontrolled laughter from Brenda and Reuben frowned for a moment, loving the sound but wishing she did it more often. Laughing, carefree. It transformed her face, making her natural beauty something stunning, but more than that, the exuberant merriment was filled with such joy and a freedom he loved to hear from her.

Glancing ahead, he saw the bar where he had seen bikes before coming up on the right, and realized with a shock there were probably more than a hundred on the lot now. *Fuck. That's a lot of fucking bikes.* Men stood around in groups, looking at the bikes, talking and comparing rides, as bikers do, and this gave him a chance to get a good look at the cuts they wore. Each had a central patch with an American flag, set alongside empty boots and a gun. He knew that patch, knew it well. These men were Southern Soldiers.

Jerking the truck off the road and into the far corner of the lot, he parked, setting the brake as he muttered, "Need a minute, Bee," when she asked a question, but he didn't pay much attention to her words. He had seen a face he recognized in one of the groups, and needed to pay his respects. "Wait in the truck."

As he climbed out of the vehicle, he saw three groups of men were already moving towards him, converging on the corner where he had parked, and he didn't want that. There was no need for Bee and Eli to hear anything citizens didn't need to know, so he quickly moved away from the truck, walking towards one of the groups. The lead man in the crowd called out a casual sounding question, "You in the right place, man?"

With a nod, he walked past them, using his agility to maneuver through and around each man who reached out to halt his progress. He quickly found himself behind them, listening to curses and shouts rising from all sides. He stopped in place and put his balled fists on his hips, shocked for a moment there wasn't leather underneath his hands, and then he threw his head back and roared, "Fucking shit, Watcher. The hell you doin' in my hometown?"

His shout called down silence around him, drawing the stare of every man on the lot. At his name, the head of the man he had seen jerked up and twisted to look at him. The dark stare would have unnerved most men, but the smile that followed it warmed his heart. "Duck," Watcher called, his long strides eating up the distance between them. "I think the question is what the fuck are you doin' in *my* town?"

First clasping wrists, then drawn into a back-thudding one-armed embrace, the two men wordlessly greeted each other. Watcher, a longtime friend and national president of the Southern Soldiers, pulled back first, having apparently noticed the lack of a patch underneath his fist, because his next question was a hushed, "What the fuck, man? Where are your goddamned colors?"

"I'm not here officially," Duck reassured him. "I didn't want to stir shit, so I told Mason I'd respect with removal. They're hanging in my closet out on the ranch."

"Ranch? You're really from here, then? No shit? Hometown boy?" Watcher shook his head in surprised disbelief, motioning several men forward. "Good to see you, regardless, Duck. While you're here, want you to meet some of my local men."

For the next fifteen minutes, he was introduced and reintroduced to men who wore the Soldiers' patch. Some of the men were from Lamesa and he knew their family connections, if not the individuals, but most had been assigned to the chapter here in town, relocated from other chapters across the southern United States and northern Mexico.

Watcher was talking through some things he was working with another club to put into place, when his gaze moved to over Duck's shoulder, and he nodded towards whatever he saw. "Brother, your old lady got tired of waitin'.'"

Fuck, Duck thought, turning to see Brenda walking towards him, her stride uncertain as she gave each group of men a wide berth, skirting the edges of the ones she couldn't avoid entirely. Seeing she had his attention, she picked up her pace, a tentative smile on her lips that did not come close to reaching her eyes. "Brenda," he called, holding out an arm invitingly. He frowned when she didn't step into his embrace, but gripped his hand instead, staying a couple of feet away.

"Watcher, this is Brenda Calloway. She's been running my stock contracting business for years." He tugged on her hand, pulling her closer so he could slip an arm around her waist. She stiffened, every muscle rigid, and he gave her a reassuring squeeze as he said, "She's with me."

Watcher inclined his head in a slow nod, but his eyes didn't leave Duck's face as he said, "Pleased, Brenda. We'll be done with your old man here in a minute." At his dismissive words, she jerked and Duck looked down to see a dark cloud of anger settle on her features.

Not acknowledging the thin greeting from Watcher, she fixed her gaze on Duck. "Vet's waiting, Reuben." He winced at her use of his government name and heard a few snorts of laughter from the men in the group. "We have an appointment."

Looking down at her, he nodded in response, and then looked back at Watcher, because the business she had interrupted was something they had to get sorted soon. "Watch, I got some shit to take care of right now, but can meet you tonight. Nine okay?" He returned Watcher's nod, saying, "See you then. You cool with my colors?"

"Disturbed to see you without them now, brother," Watcher told him somberly, conveying that while he grasped the reasoning behind the actions, he did not appreciate Duck slipping into their territory for nearly two weeks without placing a call to inform the local chapter.

"Understood," he responded, letting go of a silent Brenda to reach out for a warrior's shake with Watcher. Turning to leave, he nodded at every man who said his name in farewell or met his eye, then walked away, returning his arm to its position around her waist. Peering towards the truck, he saw Elias standing in the back, having crawled out the sliding back window of the cab, probably in order to keep an eye on his mother. Brenda split from Duck when they got to the truck and he let her go, reaching up to pluck Eli from the bed, setting him on the ground and watching as the boy ran around to where Brenda waited by the passenger door.

Back in the truck, the lighthearted atmosphere from earlier had entirely bled away, leaving a tense hush that told him Brenda was waiting for an explanation. Shaking his head, he glanced at her, noting the thin line her lips made as she stared forward. Neither of them spoke, and he finally reached out and turned the radio up, filling the silence with music they all ignored.

Stopping beside the office on the rodeo grounds, he parked the truck and sat still for a moment as both Brenda and Elias climbed out the passenger side. Staring around at the setting, he was rattled, feeling a strange disconnection from where he'd been only a half an hour before. In the brief conversation with Watcher, Duck had gotten so deep into club headspace he found he needed a minute to pull out his Reuben persona.

Putting it back on, he found places it chafed more acutely, felt the uncomfortable pinch of the citizen world where it no longer fit. With a snort at his mental imagery, he opened the door and swung out of the truck, tugging the smile Reuben frequently wore onto his face. That last piece of the puzzle slipped back out of place immediately when he saw Brenda waiting for him at the front of the truck, her hand resting on the hot hood as she watched him.

"How do you know those men, that gang?" She asked the question quietly, but his head snapped back at her language. An affront she didn't even know she gave, still seemed like a direct attack against him.

"It's not a gang," he responded, feeling that pinch again as portions of his rancher role stretched thin. Not something he'd ever wanted to be, not what he identified with. "The Southern Soldiers are a club that's friendly with the one I belong to. Those men are my friends."

"First Steve, now this gang." Muscles all over his body tensed. It seemed as if she were deliberately persisting in her use of a word she should have already realized was guaranteed to piss him off. "Looks like your taste in friends has remained true."

"Bee," he said warningly, not wanting to have this discussion now, when he already felt off balance. "Don't push me."

Turning on her heel without another word, she strode away from the truck, anger radiating from her form. Her dismissal of him more cutting than any words she could say. He looked around, that foreign feeling displacing any ease he had built up. She belonged here, though.

Uncomfortable, Duck shifted his shoulders to settle his cut into place, scowling heavily when he realized what he felt was an absence. The loss of the leather's weight, unnoticed in recent days, now seemed acute. His loyalty should be present, borne on his skin to show the association with the Rebels was as much a part of him as anything. The loss, now recognized, was painful. *Wrong.*

Playing house over the past few days, he hadn't felt naked like he did the first week. So wrapped up in Brenda and what was blooming between them, he had hardly spared a thought for the club. A hard ache of disappointment in himself settled into his chest, because the club had saved his life, given him something to hold on to. Something to be proud of, when his own family provided nothing good. A life filled with honor, versus nothing but shame.

***

Stalking away from Reuben, Brenda felt hot tears pressing at the back of her eyes. Blinking rapidly, she refused to allow them to fall. Compared to some of the men her high school friends had hooked up with, Tommy had been a good partner, for the most part. Sure he could get angry, but what man didn't? Before he got sick, he had been a decent husband, but from the beginning, there were whole segments of his life he defended fiercely against all comers, including her. The bull riders were a closed, exclusive group. Elite athletes, they were blessed with a surgeon's ego, paired with a preacher's certainty they could do no wrong.

Being told to stay in the truck sounded too close to what Tommy would tell her when she and Eli would go to his events. "Stay in the motel," he would say as he pulled his boots on, dusting his hat against his jeans-covered thigh. Then Tommy would walk out and leave without a backwards glance, his wordless dismissal of their company a tacit reminder she would never be able to breach the tight pact with his friends. Never understood the bonds holding them together.

She had seen that same rejection in Reuben's face today when he turned to watch her walk to him. His attention only returned to her because the man he was speaking to had called her out. The unpleasant introduction to a single man in the group of twenty underscored the fact they were his friends, and her presence not only wasn't needed, but appeared unwelcome. The man beside her in the crowd of bikers didn't seem like the same man who'd held her less than an hour before in the ranch kitchen, a promise of love on his lips, dirty talk making them both hot.

"Mom, I found the doc." She heard Eli's voice coming from the largest exhibition barn to her right, and shifted her trajectory to head that way. Stepping into the cool darkness of the barn from the glaring late summer sun, Brenda paused a moment to let her eyes adjust. She saw Elias about halfway up the shed row, standing in front of a stall. "Mom," he called, "Doc Winters is in here."

Brenda took a moment to draw in a calming breath. It wouldn't do to make a bad first impression on the event vet, because he held a lot of power over the rodeo. If he determined the environment unsafe, or a contestant's horse unsound, he could, and should, go to whatever lengths were necessary to correct the issue. As the organizer and stock contractor, it was in her best interests to get on his good side. Hopefully, this wasn't one of the old school vets, the kind of man who couldn't accept a woman's involvement in an event such as this one.

With steady steps, she walked up the shed row, smiling at Eli when he looked at her with wide eyes and a too-pale face. She held the smile until she smelled the rancid scent wafting from the stall. The odor made her wince, because it did not bode well for whoever's animal this was. Turning to look into the enclosure, she first saw the bent back of a man she suspected would be tall when he was upright. His denim jeans wrapped around his ass and legs tightly, the confining, form-fitting fabric exposing the firm lines of his muscles. *Definitely not one of the old school vets*, she thought, watching as his hands worked down the horse's leg, effortlessly lifting the hoof and bending the knee to give him the best view of the problem.

"Badly abscessed?" She saw the flash of a blade and the horse grunted, shifting restlessly and then settling back into place as the infection flowed out of the incision created in the frog of the hoof, the painful pressure lessening with every moment.

"Yes," the faceless man responded curtly, still bent over the horse's lifted hoof. "Hand me that soaking boot, would you?"

Glancing around, she saw his equipment nearby, the boot already set up with a soapy drench in which to soak the foot. A treatment designed to draw any remaining infection out rapidly, hopeful of ensuring a full recovery. Quietly, she slid the stall door open a third of the way and leaned in with the boot in hand, intending to set it within reach of the vet. He turned his head, looking up at her with a stern expression. "This your horse?" God, no wonder Essa had spent so much time at the vet hospital since this guy got into town. She hadn't said anything, but he was good-looking, with dark eyes and a strong jaw.

Shaking her head to dislodge those thoughts, she muttered, "Nope." Looking up at the animal, she recognized the gelding immediately and sighed heavily. "He belongs to one of the local boys. I'll give him a call and let him know he's scratched unless he can surface another horse to use." Wrinkling her nose, she said, "That hoof is stinky enough he should have caught on. I'll make sure I let his daddy know, too."

The example of quick small town justice seemed to surprise Winters and he barked a laugh, which in turn startled the horse. She watched as he gentled the gelding, lowering the foot into the boot and securing it in place. The vet stood, unfolding, and stretched to his full height. He held out a hand before grimacing and pulling it back, preventing her from grasping ahold of him. With a grin, he explained, "No need for both of us to take the stench home." She nodded and he stared at her for a moment, his attention flicking to the shed row behind her, and then back to her face. She felt a heavy presence at her back and knew it was Reuben's stare, the substantial weight of his anger filling the air. She sighed but didn't turn, her irritation having not yet flared out.

"Thanks, Doc." She pushed past the awkward feeling, intending to take control of this meeting one way or another. "I'm Brenda Calloway, of DN Rodeo. While I am pleased to meet you, on your professional recommendation, I do believe I'll pass on the shake." She smiled and nodded, tipping her head sideways. "The growing food vacuum behind me is my son, Elias." A quick glance showed she had been right about Reuben's approach. "And this gentleman is Reuben Nelms, owner of DN."

"Mr. Nelms." He nodded coolly at Reuben, flashing a grin at Eli before returning his gaze to her. "Missus Calloway," he said her name softly, seeming to relish the feel of it in his mouth. "I'm Doc Winters, and I'm very pleased to meet you."

Resentment at Reuben still flooding through her system, she knew it wasn't a mature decision, but still she tilted her head and nodded at the handsome man smiling at her, knowing exactly how it would sound as she responded, just as softly, "Likewise."

***

What the fuck does she think she's doing? Duck's thoughts were chaotic. Just minutes ago, he had been furious with her for making him remember the differences in his lives between Chicago and Lamesa, and now he was raging at her for something entirely different. He had been upset because she had shoved Lamesa down his throat, her words shining a spotlight on his fears.

Lamesa. He'd been unwilling to come back to town, begrudging the time. This entire visit started as involuntary because, with her call, she'd forced his hand. But in doing so, he'd found his way back to her, the beauty she gave him. He'd come home. Now, she stood here flirting with the vet right in front of him, flaunting it in his face, as if he hadn't been embracing her not an hour ago, promising what their night would hold.

Stepping forwards into the opening the stall door made, he snapped, "Was there an agenda for this meeting today?" His action seemed to startle both of the human occupants of the stall, and Bee jerked her gaze to him, guilt staining her cheeks beautifully pink. "Not to rush anyone, but if we're inspecting things, it could take a while." He gestured towards Elias, "Promised Eli some ice cream. Can't welsh on a deal with my best boy."

For the next hour and a half, they walked the grounds, looking over and reviewing all aspects of the operation. Winters didn't find anything wrong, but offered a dozen suggestions for safety or comfort of the equine and bovine competitors Brenda noted on her phone. The first time she had it out, the doc had boldly asked for her number. "In case there were any issues or emergencies." His excuse so reasonable Duck couldn't argue.

Twice he'd tried to capture and hold Bee's hand, and twice she'd cut him a look so full of anger and sadness, he hadn't made the attempt again. By the time they finished and were walking out to the truck, the evening, which had begun with such joy and laughter, had turned to ashes, the taste of his failure bitter in his mouth.

Wanting too much

"Reuben," she said, keeping her gaze flat and level, "I need to tell you something." She stopped and swallowed, her head shaking back and forth involuntarily. Reaching up she opened the medicine cabinet, losing her reflection for a moment, gaze catching on her diaphragm container, absurdly thinking it had gotten more use in the past few days than the previous five years. Hands trembling, she shut the cabinet, again looking at herself in the mirror.

"Reuben," she began again, voice quavering. "There's something I need to say to you." Tipping her chin down, wet streamers of hair fell in curtains on either side of her face. "This is harder than anything I've ever done in my life," she whispered, lifting her gaze back to the mirror. *He deserves to know*. With a deep breath, she said, "Reuben, we need to talk."

Her shirt had pulled on crooked, sticking to her, and as she attempted to straighten it the fabric slid in jerky movements over her still damp body. *Nothing's easy*. Turning, she opened the door, gasping in surprise to see Reuben there. Leaning against the opposite wall, his arms were tightly folded across his chest. He made an imposing figure, standing there immobile, staring at her. His voice cold and toneless, he barked, "You got something to say to me, Brenda?"

Mouth open, she stared at him, unable to speak. Her practiced words failing at the evidence of his anger. He let the silence build between them for a moment before he said, "Never mind, just save it. I get it. You saw a side of me you didn't care for today, then saw something you could like better. This won't work between us, Brenda. Good thing we learned it early on." His words made it impossible for her to suck in breath, hitting her in ways that felt physical.

"We can both go back to our lives. I'll stick around until after the rodeo, make sure you have help in place. It's why you called me, right? Just for the business. Nothing else going on here, right? Nothing else on your mind. Nothing to say to me." He paused, tipping his chin down, gaze raking along her form, lips twisting in a sneer that froze the blood in her veins. "Means there isn't any reason for me to stay beyond that." He straightened and unfolded his arms, hands hanging in heavy balls of clenched muscle at his sides. "Just like before, there isn't anything here for me. Nothing but goddamned stupid pipe dreams."

When the last word fell from his lips, he turned and stalked up the hallway to the bedroom he had been occupying until they'd come together. Since the first time they'd made love, neither had slept alone, the bed in his childhood room going unused. She heard the door whisper shut behind him, the soft sound of the latch seating in the frame much more final than a slam. Her breath came in ragged, hard gasps, painfully rasping in and out of her throat, as she tried to hold onto any hint of control. The smooth closing of that door tipped the balance, releasing the tears to fall in silent sheets down her face.

She wasn't worth the energy of anger.

She was still standing there, body hitching with unvoiced sobs when he came back out. The leather vest, which had hung in his closet since arriving on his back, now rode his shoulders like a second skin. His movements tense, yet fluid, he walked with the sense of power and silent strength she had always witnessed from him.

Took you everywhere with me.

The memory of his lies ripped through the last vestiges of her self-control, and she covered her mouth with both palms, trying ineffectually to hold in the anguished cries of pain. He didn't react at all. Without looking to where she stood, without even glancing at her, he strode past, headed for the stairs.

Loved you all my life.

Wordless and motionless, she listened for the sound of his boots on the steps, but there was no noise to accompany his departure. Not until the truck engine started outside, the mechanical racket rapidly dwindling as it moved away from the ranch, down the drive, and away towards town.

Need you in my life.

Her heart broke as the silence settled around her, heavy and thick, pressing against her skin. Sagging to the floor, she curved and wrapped her arms around her bent knees, angling her legs and curling into herself. Trying to protect herself. Trying to hold back the pain. Trying, and failing. Just as when he'd left her the first time, she wasn't worth the effort of goodbye.

***

"When did Mason get back from out west?" Watcher lifted his beer to his mouth, taking a slow swallow, measuring the amount in an unconscious acknowledgement that, as always, he needed to remain in control. The man had been a friend of the club for decades. Had known Mason since they were both pre-teens in an eastern Kentucky mining town. Word had it that Watcher had tried to recruit Mason a dozen times before the Rebels were formed, and now the men's clubs shared a multistate partnership built on an unshakable trust, nearly unheard of among clubs.

"He wasn't home yet when I flew down. On his way, but hadn't made it back. Should be in either Chi-town or the Fort by now," Duck responded. "Man seems to have found his woman, finally. Thank God." Willa Shipman, the chestnut-haired beauty from Fort Wayne, had drawn Mason's interest in what looked to be a permanent way. They had taken off on an extended bike ride nearly two months ago and the club's chapters had eagerly tracked the couple's cross-country progress. Members and officers exchanging notes and comments about the steadily growing ease filling their president's voice with every mile his woman rode wrapped around him. Peerless relaxation through road therapy.

"Willa's something else," Watcher snorted a laugh. "Met her at Slate's shindig. Woman had a thousand questions about a thousand different things. I was flat wrung out when she got done with me. She should work for the government, be an interrogator. Start her own Gitmo."

Duck laughed. "She works in a school full of lying little teenaged bastards. She probably picked up the skills in a need-to-deal environment. Learn as you go."

There was silence between them for a moment. Then Watcher quietly asked, "She doing okay since Utah? That was some shit, man. Never seen a set-up like that one. Someone put money and time into their play. Y'all get a read on who and what yet?"

Utah was all about Mason. It was where Judge, Mason's own blood, had imprisoned four women, each with a different piece of the Rebel president's history in their heart and hands. Mica, the woman he had first loved, now married and a mother. His baby sister had been at the compound, too, isolated in her own cell. Carrie Sosa, mother to his son, had taken a final trip before being dismembered in an effort to intimidate the man. Then there was Willa, the woman he had grown to love more than life itself, stolen from him and nearly destroyed by Judge. Watcher and Duck had been part of the group that made the journey to Utah at Mason's side, retrieving three of the women, some more damaged than others.

Duck shook his head, not in a 'no,' but in a necessary denial of what he had seen, what he knew had happened in the compound in Utah. "She's doing as well as can be expected, I think. That's the main reason he took her on the run. Give her a chance to settle with him without eyes studying, watching…knowing. He never spilled it, but every man who was there that day knows what Bones saw on the video. Sometimes at night, I can still hear it…can't get the sound of her voice out of my head. Shit like that sticks with you. Sticks deep and dark. I cannot fucking imagine what it must have been like to live it."

He sucked in a breath, thinking and remembering his first time with Brenda. How sweet and giving she had been, tipsy enthusiasm making up for the limited experience her younger self had. Then he compared it to their reunion, thinking about how quiet and still she was. That stillness and so many other careful behaviors drummed into her by someone…her husband? He knew not even a marriage bed was proof against the same kind of abuse Willa suffered at the hands of a madman.

"Tell me about the beauty you had in your cage today." Watcher grinned slyly at him and tipped his bottle. "Woman was pissed, but cool about it. She know she's your property?"

Duck's heart stuttered; this pain was too fresh for humor. He'd watched Brenda with the vet today. A man without a history in the town. Winters was someone she could be proud to be with, regardless of the audience. A man who'd made it clear he was interested. Who seemed to intuitively sense there were no claims on her heart, because he pushed the charm hard, even with her kid and a man walking beside them. A man worthy of Brenda. Worthy in ways Duck could never be since he didn't have a magic wand, and couldn't change his blood.

Once they got home, Duck had been determined to talk to her. Hash things out and find a way forward, because while he could see Winters would be a smart choice for her, he was not going to give in without a fight. He'd needed to see her, talk to her, and understand what had changed. Talk it through like adults, because it was more than just the two of them tied into this knot. Eli sat right there with them both, and his confusion today at the rodeo grounds had been painful to watch.

Then, on his way up the hallway to Brenda's bedroom, he overheard his name and stopped to listen. Her voice coming from the bathroom had given him an earful, far more than he'd been prepared for as he listened to the false starts and stammered practice at giving him the boot.

Even as hurt as he was, when she opened the door, his cock evidently hadn't gotten the message her body was no longer welcoming. The little fucker had stood at half-mast upon him sighting that mass of tousled hair, delicate strands clinging to the sweep of her cheek, skin still damp after her shower. The thin shirt she wore clung to her in other places, outlining the curves of her breasts, the slope of her collarbones. Beautiful. His.

Waiting for her words had been agonizing, but he had given her a moment to launch into her prepared speech, and then another. When she didn't, it seemed she wasn't able to follow through, couldn't bring herself to say the words. He had felt stuck, but knowing what he'd heard, wrenched himself out of it, and took it all on. Took the words he'd listened to through the door and carried them to the obvious conclusion. In the space of two minutes, he'd killed his dream. Made it easy for her by being the first to step away, the sounds she made tearing at his chest, ripping his heart in two. A necessary pain. His no longer. Not his Bee.

Now, Watcher wanted to talk about her, find out who she was, what she meant to Duck. Wanted to try and determine the best way to understand this addition to his mental profile of Duck, the man. Watcher wanted to ask about the statement he'd made today, telling them all she was with him, not knowing later events would pull those words into confused disarray. *Time to deflect*, he thought, *bring the conversation back to club*.

"How are you faring with the lack of Diamante in your territory?" Diamante was a fairly new one-percent club that had been dogging the Rebel's heels across four states for the past couple of years. Not long ago, Mason and the Rebels had assisted in the dismantling of a two Diamante chapters by absorbing two different clubs in Chicago.

They might not have been Diamante, but the removal of those rivals proved enough to distract the Diamante chapter in Chicago until the Skeptics could shut them down. In a coordinated effort, at the same time things were going down in Chicago, Watcher's men in Las Cruces were taking care of their Diamante nuisance. The two takeovers left dozens of homeless club members to migrate east, looking for another Diamante chapter to settle into.

Then the Rebels in Memphis had a hand in pushing the Diamante chapter there to abandon their territory. Not a shutdown, not a takeover, but an extremely effective blow to the club. To make things even more frenzied, about the same time as the Memphis deal, the Fort Wayne Rebel chapter had absorbed the men from a Diamante chapter there, which had shut down of their own accord, voluntarily relinquishing their charter. So much change in the power dynamics in four different regions had left many clubs feeling off balance, eyeballing the Rebels with concern at what looked to be a growing ambition for domination at a national level.

This did not leave any of them with an atmosphere conducive to trust and peace, so all Rebels were on high alert for any sign of retaliation or war. All their members had come to a place of paranoia, seeing enemies behind every bush, which was honestly the only way to stay upright and breathing. They had lost a few men to an ambush, and in addition, there had been several single-bike accidents that cost lives, seeming to happen without rhyme or reason. Each accident reviewed by the club's officers with an eye towards cause. Maybe operator error, sliding out on the greasy wet of a rained-on street. Or, maybe a tapout from a cage, the assassin's car bumping the bike out of control, off the road. Difficult to say with each case happening in isolation. So much to consider, to think about.

Watcher gave him a look that told him the diversionary tactic was noted but accepted as he laughed. "Fuck absence making the heart grow fonder." He grinned broadly. "Diamante's absence makes my fucking dick hard. Glad as hell they aren't an issue any longer. I know Bones feels the same." Bones was the president of the Skeptics, and had been a Rebel friend for decades. Been a friend of Mason's since before there was a club.

From there, Duck and Watcher traversed a dozen topics, their conversation sticking to club business. Duck was thankful to leave his life off the table for the balance of the meeting.

***

Brenda had forced herself to stay awake and was waiting for Reuben when he got back to the ranch. As far as she was concerned, there were no other choices, because she wouldn't let it happen again. He didn't get to just walk away, not like he had before. She needed him to tell her what had happened, not just snap phrases in her direction, riding roughshod over her own words. Over the past two hours, she had moved restlessly from seat to seat, trying to find a comfortable position, eventually coming to realize there would be no comfort for her this night, not while things were left unsaid.

The truck growled up the drive, headlights continuing to move for a moment after the engine cut off, gravel crunching underneath the still gliding vehicle until the squeak of the brakes signaled it pulling to a stop. The ka-chunk of the driver's door closing caused her to draw a sharp breath, because he would be coming through the door any minute now.

Perched on one end of the kitchen table, she stilled her nervously swinging feet, bare toes curling tight until the muscles in her legs threatened a sharp cramp, uncurling slowly when, by her counted breaths, he should have already been inside. Quietly, she shifted on the hard surface, then heard the sound of booted footsteps outside. Gaze trained on the door, she waited. And waited, hearing her son turn over in his sleep overhead, the squeak of his bedframe witness to the restlessness of his rest.

She waited until the footsteps again trailed away in the distance, realizing he would not be coming inside. *Stupid man*, she thought, sliding off the table and striding towards the door. Just as she reached it, the screen door opened and she sucked in a surprised breath when underneath her hand, the inside door opened effortlessly, pushed from outside. Reuben stood there, face blank, his expression impassive, backlit by the security lights outside.

"I thought you'd gone to the barn," she said softly.

He shook his head, gesturing over his shoulder. "Been standing on the porch, needed to think for a minute."

"Can we...can we talk?" This wasn't how she intended things to go. All the conversation preparation done in her head had flown right out the moment she'd seen him standing there on the porch. "I'd like to talk."

Chin tipping to his chest, he gave a slow shake of his head, and then raised his gaze to meet hers head on, his dark brown eyes somber. "Brenda." He paused and shook his head again. "There's not much to talk about."

"Not much to talk about?" Maybe she had misunderstood these past days, misheard his words. *I love you.* Lies. "Not much to talk about?"

Now her voice was shrill even to her ears and she struggled for composure, fought with herself against anger in her pain. "We can't have a conversation?"

"About the ranch or the business, yeah. We can talk about those things tomorrow, in the office. Unless there's some catastrophe I don't know about, we don't need to have that conversation now, here in the doorway." Jaw set, he stared at her, the tension in his body unmistakable. He wanted to be anywhere but here, would rather be doing anything other than speaking to her.

"What happened?" Tears had found their way close to the surface again, and she knew the sound of them was in her voice because he flinched from her words. "What did I do?"

"We're just two different people, Brenda. No going back to when we were kids, holding on to dreams of coulda, woulda, shoulda. Life"—he gestured with both hands—"moves on." Her throat closed at his repeated use of her name. Not Bee, not honey, nothing special in his words. With a fluid shift of his shoulders, he shrugged and she heard the leather of his vest creak in protest. "You built a life here in spite of the people you chose to work for. A good life, and I won't stay and fuck that up for you. The Nelms' name is shit in this town, always will be."

Brenda tried to interrupt because once again, he wasn't letting her talk. She couldn't get her words out past the dam of pain. *Eli's your son*, her brain shouted. *I love you*, her heart whispered. Standing frozen, her lips and mouth were silent, pretending they were locked tight, letting her emotions take the beating.

"I got a life outside of Lamesa. A life where folks look up to me." He touched a piece of fabric on the front of the vest. "A name I'm proud of when I hear it in the mouths of the people around me." His fingers clutched the side of the leather, crumpling and shaking it as he said, "This is my life. I've worked hard to make the club a place of prosperity. But, it's not the place for a woman like you. Never would be a fit for you. Pipe dream to think otherwise."

123

"No, Reuben." Her mouth was finally working, and her faltering voice edged into the silence between his words. "We had an argument. People do. It happens all the time in relationships. Then they talk and make up, understanding better what makes the other tick. It was just an argument."

"No." He dropped the word with the finality of the timeclock's buzzer stopping a ride. It didn't matter if the outcome was positive or not. It was a done deal once that sound hit the air.

"Tell me what's going on? Please, Reuben, talk to me."

"Rodeo's in a few days. I'll be here three beyond the event, then I'm in the wind." He moved slightly and she smelled him, soap clean, spiked with the faint scent of yeast speaking to the beer he'd been drinking. "Your life goes back to what it was before. Goes back to what you want."

"What if I don't want that anymore?" She held her breath, fingers clutching tightly at the edge of the doorframe and knob, tension holding her in place and keeping her from flinging herself at him.

"Beds were made years ago, Brenda," he said, disappointment and bitterness heavy in his tone. "Too hard to change course now."

"So that's it? Your friends come to town and you get reminded I'm nothing but a small town girl willing to stay in place for years, liking that place, and it's not anything you want? Not anything you ever wanted? I'm not?" She panted, taking in short, sharp breaths, the sound piercing the quiet night. "You said you loved me. Took me everywhere with you." On a whisper, she reminded him, "Said being inside me was coming home. Your home. Pretty words for a small town girl?"

He stared at her for a long minute, expressions running across his face too fast to identify, not settling into place until his features tightened. In the next moment, she fell headlong into the coldness and distance created by his words. "Nice to have a warm and willing woman when you're going to be around for a while. Eases the mind to please the body."

***

He watched as his words hit her, saw the hard punch in the movement of her chest when she gasped for air as if her heart was seizing. Her arms slowly dropped from where they propped her between the door and the wall of the house, hands losing their grip only to find a new one when her arms wrapped around her body.

He stared as her fingernails dug viciously into her skin, saw the welling tears in her eyes recede, pulled back under control by deliberate infliction of pain. The fact this was a go-to response said a lot about what her life had been like, but he couldn't back down now. He had to drive that wedge in deeply, pushing her far, far away.

Eyes on his, she took a step back and then paused, knee bent, leg lifted, foot suspended, a broken music box dancer halted in mid-pirouette. Her mouth opened a time or two without sound, and then she drew in a shaking breath through her nose, lips pressed tightly together.

"Is that all it was to you?" The hoarse question caught him off guard, and he very nearly shook his head, rejecting the idea, before he remembered her overheard rehearsals earlier in the day. Before he summoned up the picture of her walking alongside Winters. Before he remembered what a terrible fit they would make, here in this town where his family had caused so much pain and havoc. A town where him simply going into a store to buy feed brought hard pain to good people.

Instead, he shrugged, feeling his cut shift and move, accommodating his motion, accepting of whatever decision he made, as long as it was permitted to stay in place. Silent in his dismissal of everything they shared.

125

Without another sound, she whirled, foot finally coming down in a running stride straight away from him. Up the stairs and down the hall, short steps overhead ending with the complaining shift of her bed. Followed by the gut-wrenching sounds of her scarcely muffled sobs.

Giving space

Elias stared at him from across the room, not saying anything with his mouth, letting his eyes do all the talking for him. *I hate you*, they glared and Duck took a pained breath. *You hurt my mom*, he read the implicit message and dropped his chin to his chest, breaking the connection. In less than ten seconds, the screen door slapped shut, Eli having made his point and then his escape.

Staring at the floor, he sat and waited patiently. She hadn't come down this morning. Essa delivered a blunt message Brenda wasn't feeling well as she shoved eggs and bacon across the countertop towards him, making sure he got the 'asshole' message loud and clear, before she strode out the door. The men filed in fifteen minutes later, and Essa's mouth had evidently been running because none of them would meet his eyes, and Gill didn't ask him for any assignments, handing out chores as if Duck weren't even in the room.

Essa, the men, now Elias—it seemed everyone on the ranch hated him just as much as the folks in town did. *Good enough*, he thought, *since I'm not sticking around past the rodeo*. Brenda's voice floated from the second floor. He listened closely, unable to make out the words. The house phone hadn't rung, so she must have been on her cell phone. Twenty minutes later, she came running down the stairs, hair up in a twisted ponytail. She spared him a single glance, and he caught a glimpse of her eyes, swollen and raw, then her gaze was firmly on the floor as she hurried past him to the mudroom.

"Brenda," he said, and then stopped because he had no idea what he had intended, where he wanted a conversation to go. It didn't matter anyway. She didn't react or respond, just tugged on her boots and practically raced out the door. A minute later, he heard an engine start and he went to the door, watching as she backed one of the trucks out, turning and driving down the recently graded road. Gone.

An hour later, the truck came back up the drive, pulling a small horse trailer. Essa was on the passenger side, Brenda in the driver's seat as she drove past the barn and backed the trailer up to a small dirt ramp with practiced skill. The women piled out of the vehicle and he could hear their obviously continued conversation as they stopped and leaned against either side of the truck.

Essa asked, "What are you going to wear?" She tipped her head back and laughed. "Never mind, I already know. Jeans and a shirt, boots and a hat, just a regular everyday cowgirl."

Brenda responded, "It's business, not a date. Jeans and boots are work clothes for me, so yeah, that's what I plan on wearing. Don't make it more than it is, Essa."

"Not a date, my sweet ass." Essa chortled, and he moved closer to the door in order to hear better. "I knew as soon as I saw him I should tell you. Winters is hot, woman. You should tap that."

Brenda didn't respond, just turned to walk to the back of the trailer. Her gaze swung to the house and he watched her stride pause when she saw him, then the moment was past and she was lowering the back ramp, Essa moving into the trailer and backing Breezy out, the big chestnut stepping carefully.

When she finally came into the house, he was still waiting. She stopped in the mudroom long enough to toe off her boots, then stepped to one side to move around him, her intentions of heading deeper into the house clear. Without meaning to, he reached out with one hand, his palm wrapping around to seize her upper arm, pulling her to a halt. "You're going out?"

The sensation of her skin under his palm made his heart beat faster, pounding out his need. Duck pulled in a breath, thinking the same thing he had every day over the past two weeks, every time he had her with him. *So fucking beautiful.* Dark blonde hair in a tousled ponytail, color in her cheeks, rounded breasts straining the button front of the practical work shirt she wore. She was gorgeous.

Brenda didn't respond to his question right away, just dropped her gaze to his hand where it clutched her arm and he watched as, after several moments, her lids dipped slowly closed. She licked her full bottom lip, and without opening her eyes, she whispered, "Yes." The word was like a kick to the belly and he knew she felt him jerk when he saw her eyes squeeze shut even tighter.

"With Winters?" His voice was gruff and it was all he could do to force it out of his throat. He didn't want it to be true. "Is this what you want, Bee?"

At his use of her nickname, her eyes flew to his and he saw the pain and hurt he had caused her, saw the raw emotion she tried to hide and if possible, his throat closed even tighter. Her breath came faster and faster the longer they stood staring, and by the time he released her, lowering his hand, she was panting in short, sharp bursts of air. This was not her moving on, but backed into a corner by events she couldn't control. Like she told Essa, meeting Winters was part of the job. Sucking in a hard, shuddering deep breath, she lowered her eyes and walked past him, up the stairs.

Duck moved through the rest of his day by rote, not accomplishing much. He stared at the top of the desk when he was meant to be sorting paperwork, took three tries to successfully straighten a pile of tools in the tractor barn, and finally gave up reviewing breeding proposals for the stock. He did all of this while still doing his level best to ignore the pain in his chest. Several times he caught himself rubbing his sternum with the pad of his thumb, pushing hard against the bone to get at the pain underneath.

Headed to the house for supper, he noticed one of the trucks was gone. His suspicions were confirmed when he saw Essa in the kitchen. Duck stared at her for long minutes, until she looked up at him and with heavy sarcasm asked, "What?" With that, he clamped his lips shut and headed upstairs, ignoring her shout about needing help setting the table. Rushing through a shower, he dressed quickly and slung on his cut. Rattling down the stairs in his socked feet, he headed to the mudroom. "Fucking bike'd be good about now," he muttered, shoving his feet into his boots.

"You aren't staying for dinner?" Essa asked and he nearly jumped, her voice came from beside him. He had been so caught up in his internal planning, he hadn't even noticed her walking across the room. Responding with a shake of his head, he stood and turned to walk out the door. A gentle hand on his arm stopped him and he tipped his head to look at her. "They'll be at the steakhouse, and then probably head to Mitchell's."

"What makes you think I'm going lookin' for Brenda?" He downplayed his heartache as he asked the question.

"Because I know what pain looks like," she responded softly. "Don't push her away, Reuben. Y'all are too good together. Don't let something small come between you."

"If it were small, it wouldn't be a problem," he told her. "Our lives are very different. She never wanted to leave Lamesa and I couldn't wait to get out of town. Nothing's changed from eleven years ago."

"Stupid, bull-headed men." Essa snorted a laugh and shook her head. "She hates this town. She only stayed because of you and this ranch."

Duck went still, every noise in the room magnified until he could hear the grease popping in the frying pan on the stovetop; hear each tick of the dime store wall clock as it churned ahead, spacing out the next second, then the next. "What do you mean?"

"Blind as well as stupid," she said, shaking her head again. "Brenda has loved you since she was a kid, so many years now. She loves you, Reuben. She'd do anything for you. Even stay in a town she hates, just because you needed her."

"Her husband was here, their son." He knew there was a heavy scowl on his face, but he couldn't spare enough attention to try and smooth it away. Everything seemed poised on the cusp of something important.

"Yes, her son was here. In addition, there was that jackwit she married. Did you think to notice she only went out with him after you left town? If things had turned out different, I can't imagine how your lives would look today, but they didn't. She stayed, and you left. She settled, in more than one way." Essa's ponytail swung back and forth like a pendulum. "You need to talk to her, Reuben."

"I left town because she wanted the bull rider. Offered her the job with DN when things lined up because we needed the help." He swept his hand out, indicating the entire ranch. "Her whole life is here. Her aunt and uncle didn't leave her anything and without the ranch, she would have had to leave, go to Midland or somewhere else and start over. I only ever wanted to take care of her, wanted to keep her safe."

"Look at the pictures sometime. See how happy she looks if the focus isn't on Eli, and by that I mean she looks like shit. Miserable and tired...sad, except for Elly-belly. And now, when she looks at you? Same look she turns on Elly-belly. She loves you, Reuben. Always has." She swallowed, then drew in an uneven breath. "Learned long ago, from some smart people we both know, a place isn't what makes a person happy. It's not where you live, it's *who* you share that life with that matters most. The people you bring in to surround yourself with, the ones you trust...those you love." Stepping closer, she pressed one palm against his chest. "Like Mica in Chicago, who found herself a family like no other with Mason and Tug," her voice caught and she cleared her throat before she continued, "and Slate. It's who you love that makes everything work."

***

Duck entered Mitchell's through the side door, grabbing a beer from the short bar at the back of the room and finding a section of wall to lean against. With the rodeo only days away, the place was crowded with cowboys and cowgirls, competitors by the looks of them. Most dressed in well-worn boots and jeans, hat brims creased from sweaty hands, and belt leather broken in just right. Mixed in with that group were the tourists, here just for the spectacle of the rodeo. It was easy to see the difference in the groups because the wannabes mixed designer shoes with their jeans, or had on stiff felt hats which had never seen a day's worth of sun to wilt the starch.

From his position, he had a clear view of the dance floor as well as the main bar, and within moments had spotted Brenda. She and Winters were seated at a square hightop table on the far side of the smooth, wooden floor filled with couples shuffling and swinging along. He watched for a moment, scarcely registering the dancers; women twirling out to the end of their partner's arm and then back again, fluid movements giving witness to the hours spent in locales such as this.

With only a corner of the table between them, she and Winters were engaged in what looked to be animated conversation regardless of the volume of noise in the bar tonight. He was leaned close, his mouth near her ear and Duck watched as her head tipped back with laughter at something Winters said.

Duck frowned and then tensed even more, looking at her face. She might be laughing, but she wasn't enjoying herself. There were lines of strain across her forehead and alongside her eyes, and he gripped the bottle in his hand tighter, his fingers aching to rub those worries away.

***

Winters placed his hand on Brenda's forearm near her elbow and then slid it down to cup around her hand. Squeezing her fingers, he leaned close again and half-shouted, "Let's dance." Without giving her a chance to decline, he stood and tugged, pulling her along behind him as he moved into the spinning crowd of dancers on the floor, just as the music changed from a bouncy two-step to a slower song. Tugging at her hand again, Winters caused her to stumble and he caught her, swinging her around and pressing her against his chest.

He brought her hand up and placed it palm-down on his shoulder, then wrapped both of his hands around her waist, aligning their bodies for the dance. *This is the last thing I want to be doing right now*, she thought as she brought her other hand up and plucked his off her hip. Using the connection to push back from him by a couple inches, she looked up to see an amused look on his face as they moved to the music.

Dancing in a slow circle, she kept her head upright as she followed his lead. Leaning his upper body close, he placed his mouth near her ear and said, "I thought it might be something like that."

Surprised, she pulled back and looked at him, seeing a smile on his face, the amused look resting easily on his features. "What are you talking about?"

"Nelms," he said, one corner of his mouth quirking regretfully. "The other day I couldn't decide if I had a chance, or if y'all were just in mid-tiff when I saw you. Now, I know."

Lowering her chin, she broke eye contact, dropping her gaze to the vertical lines on his western shirt. With a sigh, she nodded and agreed, "Mid-tiff." She sighed again and began to push back, saying, "Thanks for a lovely—"

"Not so fast." He interrupted, pulling her close again but maintaining the three-inch separation she had forced between their bodies. "You looking to make up with him soon?"

Her gaze snapped up and her body stiffened as she retorted, "I'm not looking for a fling or to fool around."

"Not what I meant, darlin'." He laughed aloud as he said this, a tug on her hand trying to urge her slightly closer. "He's watching us, had eyes on us since before we hit the floor, and it looks like there's about a month's worth of pissed off on his face right now. If you wanted to tweak his nose, we could snuggle up and have a sweet little dance."

Pushing back again, she shook her head. "I'm not a game-player, Doc. Not my style."

"You came out with me tonight," he reminded her. "You sure about your style?"

Brenda snorted and laughed, feeling like she sounded, brittle. "Hate to burst your bubble, Doc, but I came out with you because you're the event vet and new to town, and I'm the boss of the stock company putting on the rodeo." Her back heated as his hand slowly moved up from her waist to a more respectable position just underneath her shoulder blade.

He stiffened and an odd energy radiated from him. Leaning close again, he put his mouth near her ear and in a voice that was only half-joking, warned, "Brace yourself, pretty lady."

A hard hand closed around her bicep. Not painfully tight, but not tentative. There was no demanding tug, no pull to wrench her away, just a soft, gentle, immovable hold she could feel in every part of her body, the sensation racing through her. Welcome, possessive, claiming. *Reuben*, she thought and dropped her hands from where they were touching Doc. Winters' hands fell away, releasing her and she turned towards the man holding her arm. Looking up into Reuben's face, absorbed in him, all sounds in the room receded. Gone. Unimportant. She didn't realize when Winters stepped away, courteously conceding any claim on her. He had ceased to exist for her.

Reuben's face was dark and scowling, his eyes flicking over her features and coming back to drill into hers with a smoldering stare. Brenda's breath quickened as Reuben tugged on her arm, pulling her in close as Winters had tried to do. Closer, even. An intimate hold. One speaking to a familiarity with her body Winters would never have.

With Reuben, she didn't step back or avoid contact. Instead, she leaned into him, feeling strong arms wrap around her, as hers lifted to wind around his neck. His eyes drifted closed at her touch, and she watched the anger fall away from his features in response. He liked her touching him, liked her hands on him, lips lifting at the corners into a quiet smile. Private. Intimate. Hers.

One hand glided up her back and then his fingers were in her hair, turning her head and pushing her cheek towards his shoulder. She rested against the hard wall of his chest, nuzzling into his shirt and relaxing. Pressed tight together from knee to chest, they danced in a single, small circle for the duration of that song, and then the next. Not speaking, just feeling the rightness of their connection.

"Bee," he murmured and she heard his voice break on the lone syllable of her nickname. "So fucking sorry. I can't even tell you. Got no words." She tightened her arms around him and shook her head slightly, her cheek scraping across his shirt and leather vest. "Some days my stupid gets in my way, trips me up so I can't see how to right things. I said things...I can't even believe the shit that spewed from my mouth.

So fucking sorry." He drew in a hard, deep breath. "I want to right this. Work with me to fix us?"

She nodded in response to his question and heard him blow out a slow whoosh of relief. "One argument doesn't change my feelings," she told him and he tensed again. "Can't change my heart with words. You can break it"—he shuddered under her hands—"but not change it." Rocking her head back and forth, she allowed it to come to rest, forehead pressed against his chest. "I love you, Reuben."

"Duck," he responded and she jerked, looking up at the ceiling as he laughed aloud. "Not like that." A grin sounded in his voice and she twisted so she could see him. "My name," he said, and sure enough, his lips had curved up at the corners into a smile. "Duck."

Tilting her head, she raised an eyebrow in question. He glanced down at the front of his vest and she followed his gaze to a fabric patch with the word *Duck* embroidered on it. "No one calls me Reuben. My name is Duck."

"Like a duck? Quack, quack?" They had stopped moving, standing on the dance floor while the other couples flowed around them, a steadfast island in a sea swimming with bright colors and twirling bodies. "Who calls you that?"

"My brothers. The men in my club." He shrugged. "My friends. The men you saw yesterday. Almost everyone who matters in my life calls me by my club name." Leaning down, he rested his forehead against hers. "It's who I am now, Bee. I haven't been Reuben for a long time. I think you're the only one still holding onto that man. The man on the parking lot today, the one you walked towards looking afraid of your own shadow? That's who I am. This is who I am." Raising his head, he looked around the room. "Let's get out of here. There are things I need to tell you, things you need to know before we take another step down this road."

Without waiting for her to agree or argue, he quickly moved them towards the door. They passed close to the table Winters had reclaimed, and her steps slowed for a moment as she acknowledged him with a nod. Winters gave her a sideways smile in response and made a shooing motion with his hand, flicking his fingers at them. Arm around her waist, Reuben's body pressed into her and she felt rather than heard him huff a laugh before pulling her outside.

He guided them towards one of the farm trucks, leading her to the driver's door. It happened in an instant—one second she was walking beside him and then the next, she was forced against the door, his body pressed against her. Her head immobilized by his hands, Brenda stared up into his eyes as he asked with an emotion-roughened voice, "Bee, can I kiss you?" Without conscious thought, her head tilted up and down the slightest amount and even before the motion completed, his mouth crashed down on hers, covering her.

This was not the kiss of someone unsure of his welcome. Reuben took control of her in a way that branded her his, made his intentions clear with the movement of his lips against hers, the thrust of his tongue stroking alongside her own, the taste flooding her mouth. With this kiss, he vowed to never leave her alone, never let her forget her love for him. He gave her assurances and truth with the way he moved against her, the soft gasps of his moans rushing across her lips when he pulled back for a breath. This was love embodied in a kiss, a lifetime promise of faithfulness and dedication.

He played her body ruthlessly, his mouth on hers bringing her to the edge of release and holding her there with ease, suspended over the abyss of desire as he claimed her. Fingers clenching in her hair, he used the hold to angle her head, slanting his mouth over hers, owning her. A car door slamming followed by ringing laughter broke the moment and he pulled back, mouth open and desperately panting for breath, her responses mirroring his. They stood there, his eyes tracking slowly across her face, searching for something. He must have liked what he saw because a small, secret smile slipped on and off his lips, much as the kiss had moments earlier. "Come on," he said softly, reaching past her to open the door. "Hop in, Bee."

Using the steering wheel, she pulled herself into the cab of the truck, her slide to the passenger side stopped by his palm on her thigh, the heat through the fabric of her jeans startling her into stillness. "Sit beside me, baby." She nodded and dug out the seatbelt, keeping her gaze on him as he got in beside her and started the engine. He pulled out and turned towards downtown instead of the country roads that would take them home and she looked up at him, brow lifted questioningly. "Need to talk to you. Thought the park might be a good place."

"Okay," she said, glancing at the clock on the dash. "I think they're open until eleven, but with the rodeo in town, cops won't be worried about running stragglers out anyway." He nodded, keeping his face forwards so she could only see him in profile and that by the dim dashboard lighting. He looked serious and she experienced a twinge of fear, wondering what topic he might want to cover tonight. *So many things we need to say to each other*, she thought, leaning into him, resting her temple against his shoulder.

His hand dropped from the wheel to rest on her thigh, midway between her knee and hip. His fingers curved around and down between her legs, his possessive hold communicating the emotions thrumming just beneath the surface and her core clenched and tightened in anticipation.

***

Duck turned the wheel, steering the truck into a corner of the lot, tucking them back where the shadows were dark and thick, making them nearly invisible from the street. No reason to give the cops cause to drive in if it wasn't part of their regular patrol. He shut off the engine, and in the sudden stillness following, sat quietly for a moment, eyes closed, running conversational openings through his head. His hand slowly stroked up and down Bee's thigh, finding comfort in the heat of her leg underneath the caress of his palm. *Start with the hardest first*, he thought and drew a breath.

"How old were you when Ray tried to dick around with you the first time?" His question dropped into the quiet, causing a ripple as Brenda responded with a quick breath. "I don't doubt you put him in his place. But he pulled some kind of fuckery, of that I'm sure."

He released his seatbelt and twisted in the seat, elbow to the wheel, his other arm draped across the seat back. Looking down into her face, softly illuminated by the silvery moonlight, he waited. The light left swaths of shadows across her features, making her expression hard to read.

"Daddy got what he wanted with one son, the other was a raw disappointment. I'm sure you know which was which, probably heard all about it over the years. I'd never try to excuse a single fucking thing Ray did, but Daddy drove him that direction from the time he could walk. Drove both of us. Hard." He snorted and shook his head. She still hadn't spoken, hadn't even tried to say anything. "I was the weaker one, the son who got the headshakes of frustration. I"—he drew a hard breath and faced front again, cutting his eyes to the side to watch her—"I stopped a lot of shit over the years, but not everything. I couldn't be everywhere and it fucking kills, man. Fucking kills me. Essa ever say anything about Ray?"

A confused expression landed on her face, and she shook her head at what must seem like an abrupt change of direction. He wasn't surprised, not really expecting the girl to have shared her family's history. "She's got two cousins, gals who competed back in the day. Mica and Molly turned into an obsession for Ray. He found the one when she was just a teen, barely out of high school. Stripped her of everything that mattered. Made it so she had to leave home and start over. Left everything behind, just to get away from him. Mica,"—at the name Brenda nodded and he went on—"yeah, she was a competitive spirit he broke so thoroughly I didn't know if she'd ever recover. She got away from him but was so fucking damaged. Tore up, inside and out. Ray did that to her."

He swallowed hard, shame over the night of his cowardice flooding him. "I didn't save her, didn't have the chance. She fucking saved herself. Well, I did have the chance, but didn't take it. I failed her. Fucking failure all around. Ray got her and I bailed. I was outta there. Came home and worked for a couple of months, told Daddy some fucking lie. So wrong. I should have stopped him." Echoes of the ripping cries from the trailer sounded in his ears, and he closed his eyes, shaking his head in an effort to dislodge the memories. "Fucking coward."

"No, you aren't," Brenda said, her hand landing on his forearm, stroking across his skin. "You are not." Opening his eyes, he looked to find he was clenching the steering wheel tightly with his fist. Her hand slipped up his arm to cover the back of his hand, fingers tucking between his. "Never met a man more courageous, Reu"—her correction was nearly seamless, but told him that she understood the importance—"Duck." With a groan, he wrapped his arms around her, dragging her into his lap as he moved to sit in the center of the seat.

"You're wrong. I am. I was. She got hurt so bad, Bee. I can't even tell you. It took a while, but I finally tracked her down. Chicago. That's why I settled there, in Chicago, because it's where she was. I wanted to make sure she was okay, but she wasn't. How could she be after Ray got to her? So, I made it my mission to make sure nothing bad would happen to her again. I vowed I'd at least try this time instead of walking away, leaving her in that hellhole of a hopeless situation like I had. I'd try to keep her safe." A harsh laugh ripped from him. "Best thing I could have done was leave home like I did. The best thing for me because I met a man who showed me the right way to live." He knew she wouldn't understand, not yet. But he had to get it out; had to tell her.

"Mason. Davis Mason. He's my friend...my brother. Day after day he showed me how a real man dealt with things like frustration and anger.

Not by lashing out at weaker folks, which was all I'd ever seen from Daddy, but by finding the problem and helping put a solution in place. Mason made me better, took me from the brink of falling into the monster role Daddy had tried so hard to force down my throat, and he fucking made me a better man. Helped me fucking heal wounds I didn't even know I had. My name came from him." He snorted a laugh.

"I was drunk one night and going on about what a useless piece of shit I was, how I hadn't saved Mica from my brother in the first place. Hadn't saved her at all. She was still in college, doing well, and I was just a prospect in the club. But, I kept watch on her, wanted to make damn sure Ray never got another sniff of her." He ran a hand up Brenda's back, palming the back of her head and tipping it against his shoulder, liking the feel of her pressed against him.

"So I'm drunk and fucked-up in the head, raving mad at myself. Mason listened to it for about a minute, then laughed at me. Stood there, arms folded across his chest and roared with laughter. Told me I had everything wrong. He said, 'You're a good man under it all, Reuben. Can't fake the kind of man you are, which is honorable and loyal to a fucking fault.'

"He told me if it looked like a duck and quacked like a duck, chances were it was a fucking duck. Next day when I finally rolled my hungover ass out of bed, there was a name patch sewn to my vest." He reached down and touched it with one finger, reverently tracing the letters making up his name.

"So now, every time someone calls me 'Duck,' I remember his words. Every single time I see this patch on my vest, I remember his faith in me, remember he saw something I couldn't even see. Duck is a good man, a good brother to my club, a good friend. I work every day to be what he named me."

He tipped his head back and laughed. "Told me later I should be glad the patch guy got it wrong. He wanted one saying 'Fuck a Duck' which would have been funny for about a week." Brenda laughed, the softness of her voice rolling across his skin like satin and he shivered before moving back into the hard topics at hand. "Ray, however...*fuck*, Ray never stopped to look at what he had become. He was so caught up in being that monster. He reveled in shaping himself into those frightening shadows on the wall that gave people the chills. Fucked-up in the head. You know what he did to the gal at the feed store, right? Lisa?" It was her turn to shiver, and he drew her closer, bending to place a kiss on the top of her head as she nodded.

"Wasn't the last time he pulled that kind of shit. He raped Mica's little sister"—at his raw words she gasped, but he pushed through—"left her with a baby too, but hers stuck because he wasn't there to beat it from her body. Fucking killed me seeing her every day. Marking when she started to show, watching her grow. Witness what he had done, knowing she had to live with it every time she looked down at her belly. Knowing her child was the product of a violation, an act so heinous it should be answered by a bullet to the head. No excuses, no appeals." She started to pull back, and he hushed her, holding her still. "Let me get this out, Bee. We can have the give and take in a bit, but let me get this out there, so you know what's what."

When she relaxed into him, he tipped his chin, kissing the top of her head again. "Molls—Molly, Mica's sister—loves her boy." He laughed softly. "Loves him beyond distraction. That child will never doubt her love. Guarantee it. I'd been watching out for her, keeping my distance, not wishing to be another reminder of what she had suffered at Ray's hands. Didn't want to be the thing scraping the scab off at every turn, hoped to give her time to heal, as much as a woman can after something like that." He sighed, his breath coming in broken bursts.

"Molly cornered me one day and lit into me like nobody's business. Told me if I wanted to punish myself for what wasn't my fault then I needed to get out of her sight because seeing me flogging myself was killing her more than anything else ever could. Told me she hated the man who did it to her, but from the first moment she felt the baby move inside her, she had loved it so much. Felt such love and gratitude." He scoffed, shaking his head. "Fucking gratitude she had this blessing in her life."

Brenda started to speak, but he talked over her, needing to get it out. Get it all out. "I was there the night Tomas was born, one of the first people to hold his wet and slippery body, him squallin' like a pissed off cat. Seeing that miracle happen healed something in me. Love her little boy, love him so much." Duck's throat tightened, locking closed for a moment, so that he had to clear it before continuing. "She looked up at me standing there, my arms wrapped around this little bundle. Beautiful baby boy. She stared at me holding her son and she had love and joy in her face. Joy, Brenda. Fucking torture, but such an honor to see, to be there as a witness. Asked me if she could lean on me. Told me it was my responsibility to teach Tomas good things, right things. I look at it as a privilege, because she trusts me. Totally trusts me.

"Lisa," he drew a shuddering breath, "she lives with what happened to her every single fucking day without any joy to draw off that agony. Nothing to drain away the damage done to her, only the pain remains, festering deep inside in a place hard to reach. You should have seen how she looked at me, Bee. Ripped my heart out when Mr. Transom told me what happened. I had no idea. Not a clue what she went through with Ray. Of course I didn't, because I wasn't here to stop it. I was in Chicago trying to protect someone who had a hundred other men who would lay down their lives for her, and Lisa...Lisa didn't have anyone."

"Stop it," Brenda snapped, pushing back and out of his hold as she interrupted him. "Will you just stop it?" He saw the tear tracks running down her cheeks, lips parted as she panted for breath. "You didn't do that to Lisa. You didn't do anything wrong, honey."

Lifting a hand, she roughly raked her hair back from her face. "God, you piss me off so bad sometimes." Shifting to the seat, she rose on her knees, leaning over him, getting in his space to make her point. One hand on the wheel and the other on his shoulder, she shook him, fingers winding tight in the collar of his shirt. "You *are* the man your friend Mason knows, the one he called honorable. All you've ever done is try and make up for the harm your family caused. One of my favorite memories of you was the night you came and worked my uncle's horse. That first time you came, because your dad had been drunk and you were just trying to make things right.

She shook her head. "I got to know your dad, and I knew Ray. I saw them for what they were, baby. Pathetic men who were afraid of giving up any control. Afraid giving up control would expose their weaknesses, show up their shortcomings." Leaning forward, she placed one hand on his chest. "You are not them. Not what they were, baby. Not, never could be. It's not in your DNA. You are what your friend said. A *good* man. And I love you."

She leaned in and kissed him, hard and demanding, teasing with the edges of her teeth, nipping and sucking on his bottom lip until he pushed her back flat on the seat. He stretched her legs out straight and then covered her, holding her in place with his hips and hands, taking control of the kiss in the same moment. Deep and hot, he stroked in between her lips with his tongue, tangling with her as he fucked her mouth. He traced the inside of her mouth, taking everything he craved and she met him movement for movement, giving him back everything he desired...everything she needed.

"Wait, *God*, wait," he muttered, breaking away and pressing his forehead against hers, the tips of their noses brushing together. "I got more to tell you, Bee. I can't...not until you know. You have to know before you take a single fucking step down this road."

"Then, tell me." Her voice was hoarse with need and her hips shifted restlessly underneath him. He moved, pushing his hard cock against her mound, drawing a high keen from her. "Duck," she said and he lunged forward, taking her mouth again roughly, passion inflamed beyond reason at his real name rolling from her lips. Long minutes later he slowed the kiss, realizing she had wrapped her legs around his waist and was pushing back against him as he stroked his cock against her, the rough fabric of their jeans scratching and scrubbing with the friction created, giving a tease of relief with each groaning thrust.

"Fuck," he whispered into her mouth. "You make me reckless, Bee. I love you, but I need to do right." Every muscle tensed tight, he panted, trying to bring himself under control because the urge to strip and sink deep inside her was so strong he could nearly feel her skin, slippery with sweat as she moved with him. "Right by you. *Fuck*." When he felt he could move without risk of coming, he sat up and pulled her with him, wrapping her in his arms again. "Next time we go horizontal, I won't be responsible for what happens, Bee."

She laughed rich and low, teasing as she snuggled closer. "Can't wait, baby," she told him softly, "just give me time to get my diaphragm in."

"Don't care to wait on that, darlin'," he returned, still on a whisper, "so don't be surprised if I won't."

Rubbing her cheek against his shoulder, she didn't respond and he knew she was waiting.

After a moment he said, "Right, then. Let's get the rest of this done and out of the way. No more secrets." He was surprised when she stiffened in his arms and tried to separate herself from him, pushing at his chest, head turned away. "What?" Stunned at her reaction, he tightened his arms. "What's wrong, Bee?"

"You tell your story." He heard her swallow and frowned, wondering what had her so frightened. "And, I'll tell mine." For some reason, the picture of her family on the office wall flashed through his head. The one of her, Tommy, and Eli. Taking a deep, sighing breath, he pushed it aside and nodded.

"Ray's dead." Stated baldly, he waited for a reaction which didn't come. One beat, two...then, "Okay. Not a surprise?"

"No. I've had a feeling for a long time," she said softly.

"I didn't do it, but I would not have tried to stop it even if I'd been right there. Even if I'd been standing beside him." He sighed. "I'm pretty sure he killed Daddy and his own wife. So much damage in his wake. Afterwards, when I went to pick up his rig in Houston, I found a folder of shit in his living quarters. Pictures of women...girls, with tears and fear and snot on their faces...sometimes worse. Bloody pain as souvenirs.

"He had a whole list of the best ways to dispose of a body. Everything I read that day validated his death a hundred times over. Did you know if you bury a person feet first, vertical, and then bury a dead animal on top of them, it is highly unlikely they will ever be found? Even if a cadaver dog alerts at the spot, once they find the animal, the cops will think it's a false positive and move on. Burying them in a small square, upright like that, it also means satellites don't see the obvious outline of a gravesite. Dismembering, putting bodies in septic systems, ocean disposal methods. He had it all in a fucking file. Organized and tidy, like it was something he referred to often. It was a sick fucking read.

"He had fucking pictures and lists, and some of the tools I found in his stash were on those lists, Bee. I expect if I tracked his circuit route and tried to match it with missing persons, I'd find a pattern that would make me sick. Bastard needed to die, and I should have seen it sooner.

"But, what's done is past and he's gone now. Can't hurt anyone, and the only legacy he left is not his. Tomas belongs to Molly and no one else, and you can be damn sure she isn't gonna let who his sperm donor was influence his life. That boy is safe from my blood. Thank God."

He shuddered. "Sick fucker. I asked for proof of his death, just to know I didn't have to worry or watch anymore. Seeing the picture sealed it for me. The nightmare was over. No more monsters. I'm it, and I'm not the man my father was. Not the man my brother was. There will be no more Nelms men fucking over anyone and everyone who had the misfortune to catch their attention." Trailing off into silence, he sat for a minute, and then repeated, "No more monsters."

His arms loosened and she made a noise, shoving her face into his chest. "Bee?" She shook her head. When she hiccupped, he realized she had begun crying so he pulled her close again. "Oh, baby, it's okay. I'm not sad."

"Not true. It's not true," she said with a sob. "I'm…I wish…I should have come right to you when I found out. I'm so sorry." Her body trembled; she was shaking, quivering like a rabbit caught in a trap. Fear pulsed out from her as she pulled away.

Cupping her face in his hands, he swept the tears from her cheeks with the pads of his thumbs, wishing for more light because the weak moonlight hid so much of the expression on her face. Was it fear? It looked like fear. Felt like fear, her trembling in his hands. *Fear for me, or of me*, he wondered.

Then she spoke and the words dropped everything out of focus for a moment. Gentle and strident all at once, a cacophony. It was as if the world rocked on its axis. Once again he would have sworn he felt the earth move underneath the truck, altering in a way it would never go back to what it was before. "Tommy wasn't Eli's dad."

That damn picture flashed through his head again and he saw the general likeness of the boy's face, but the discrepancies were there in so many other ways. *I know. I think I know.* The memory of seeing Eli for the first time, brief moments of confusion and wonder, swallowed whole by painfully dashed hopes he hadn't even known lived inside him.

Now, sitting beside her, he knew what her next words were going to be. He knew. *God*, he knew and waited impatiently to hear her say them. The anticipation drew his arms snug around her, pulling her against him, making her safe, giving her space to find her courage. One single word, one syllable fluttering around his brain, the beat of belief coming stronger as hope grew. *Mine. Mine. MINE.* Determined, he held on like she was the last person in the world. His last hope at happiness. At life. He pulled her tighter, waiting...wanting, his suddenly airless chest burning as he filled with joy.

"You are."

Confirmation. Knowledge he and Brenda had a connection so much deeper than he ever dreamed. Validation of the rightness he held in his arms.

"Mine?" He drew a shaking breath, terrified he'd imagined hearing the word he wanted to be truth spoken aloud. *Tell me again, please.* "He's mine?" The question ricocheted around the truck's cab, a dream come true. His stomach lurched, settling slowly back into place. *Real, this is real. Mine.* "God. Oh, thank God. Thank God he's mine. Oh, Bee. Thank you." She flinched at his first words but then relaxed as he continued to murmur, lips pressed against the side of her head. "Mine, both of you. Mine."

***

Hours later, her churning brain keeping her from rest, Brenda lay next to a sleeping Duck in her bed. Her eyes closed as she slowly stroked her fingertips up and down his arm. *Unbelievable*, she thought. *How could he not be angry?* If the tables were turned, she knew she would be furious at the wasted time, lost opportunities and memories. *I would feel betrayed, blindsided knowing I'd been in town for weeks and still didn't know.*

He was only looking forward, not back, and this was an unexpected gift. To have the chance to build from here with him and Eli, to make them a family—it was so much more than anything she ever dreamed about, beyond everything she could have expected. Not that he didn't have questions, but she did her best to answer everything openly and honestly, putting the puzzle together for him, so he saw what she did at the time.

Now she had to find a way to tell Elias the man he believed his father wasn't. Gently let him know that he bore no ties to the man he'd had to mourn even before they'd buried him. No connection other than the love they shared.

She shifted in bed, exhausted but unable to sleep. Moving again, she felt the difference in his body when he woke. It wasn't because he stirred or made a noise, he just became more...*there*. Every muscle primed for movement. "Bee?" Soft voice so low the question was barely audible, his breath ruffled the hair on the side of her head. "Can't sleep, love?"

"No, my brain won't be quiet. Sorry I woke you." She rolled onto her stomach, away from him and he startled a laugh out of her when he rolled with her, half on her back and half on the mattress, his weight holding her in place.

"Brenda." His voice was rough and intense when he spoke her name. Needy. Firm against her skin, his touch skimmed up the outside of her thigh to her hip where he paused, gripping her tightly as he pushed his already hardened cock against her ass. With a gasp, she rocked back against him, drawing a groan from his mouth. "Does it feel like I'm sorry, Bee?"

He had made slow love to her when they'd arrived home, covering every inch of her skin with kisses and soft strokes of his hands. Telling her so much with his touch, the care he took showing how precious she was to him.

Now, the energy in the room was different from before, charged somehow and she tensed in response. "Asked a question, Bee," he said, voice low and sounding filled with gravel. His hand slid up to cup her breast, finger and thumb meeting in a tight pinch at her nipple, the bright pain sending an electric shock to her core.

"Does it feel like I'm sorry?" He surged against her again, heat from his erection blazing against her bare skin. He had fallen asleep before getting dressed, and with him holding her tightly, she hadn't tried to get out of bed to pull on her nightgown, so he was pressed all along her back and side, skin to skin. Hot, sensual. Naked.

"No, not sorry." Already keyed up, she got the words out between pants, hardly believing how ragged her breathing was in moments. The promise of passion was thick in the air and she wanted...something. "Not sorry."

Slipping his thigh between her legs, he pushed up on one forearm, holding his torso off her. Then he thrust again, his cock sliding up and between the globes of her ass as he groaned. Shoving a hand underneath her, he covered her core with his palm and she moved her legs wider apart, opening to him, knowing what he would find.

Sliding a finger to either side of her clit, he stroked her pussy gently and then moved his hand down, fingers slipping inside. "Oh, Bee. My Bee's *wet* for me." Teeth nipping her shoulder, his laugh was rich and knowing. "Your pussy's soaked, baby." Swirling his fingers in the evidence of her arousal, he spread it over her clit, roughly rubbing side-to-side and she pressed her hips down, pushing hard against his hand, seeking more friction.

"Wet like this? You're wanting, baby. More than your mind keeping you awake." His lips skimmed along the tender skin on the back of her arm, giving her more heat, more sensation. "Bare, lying right here next to me. *Wet.* So fucking wet and wanting." He groaned, his fingers moving faster. "*Fuck*, that's hot, baby."

He pinned her, giving her more of his weight. Mouth next to her ear, breath raising goosebumps along her shoulder and neck, he whispered to her in a voice gone rough with passion. "Be still, Little Bee." Then he moved, shifting slightly until the engorged head of his cock slid just inside, past her already swollen lips, stretching her in delicious ways, but still only barely there. The promise of his possession, poised on the brink of filling her.

Holding back, he waited, his mouth moving on her neck. "Keep still, baby. Let me quiet your mind." She wanted him, desired what he wordlessly offered. Moving restlessly, her legs shifted across the mattress. Holding still and in place, he leaned close to whisper, his voice thick and rough, "Gonna fuck you, Bee. I'm past easy, and so are you. I can smell how ready you are. You're fucking drenched, soaking my hand. I want you, rough and hard, baby. Ready? Ready for me?"

His words caused her heart to stutter and jump in her chest. A tingle-filled tautness settled between her legs as she shivered and nodded in response, and he breathed, "Thank fuck," and moved, slamming deep inside on a long, single, fast—*God, so deep*—stroke. His thumb never stopped moving and she found herself torn between two delicious options, spurred to push back against this welcome movement and pressure, or needing to thrust her mound down against his hand instead, against the mattress.

"Quiet, baby." He groaned again, and she realized the keening sound in the room was coming from her throat. "Hard for you." *God, I love his words*. No one had ever spoken to her with such raw need, and she couldn't get enough of it. "So fucking hard, for you." Rough and passionate, the way he talked through what he was feeling when they made love was such a turn-on.

Without giving her time to think, he moved again and again, plunging in hard and fast, the width and length of his cock stretching her, fulfilling that unspoken need clenching low in her core. "Fuck, Bee. My Little Bee. So fucking tight. So hot. Pussy wrapping around me, taking every inch of me." He groaned and she whimpered when his breath gusted across her skin. "All of me for you. Fucking that pretty pussy, you fucking me back. Quiet your mind; wake your body. Take all of me, fucking...yeah. *God*, baby."

With every word, every phrase uttered in that rough, unmistakable voice, he carried her closer to the edge and her core tightened, pulsing in rhythm. The delicious way he filled her forced a quick breath as she gasped, quaking when the first shocks of her orgasm began to roll through her. Breathing fast and shallow, she chased the slippery, twisting feeling, eyes clenched tightly closed as her neck stretched, arching back. "Duck," she panted, calling his name soft and low. He groaned, grinding into her, pinching her clit lightly in response to the single word.

"Duck," she said again and then felt the heat of his lips, hardness of his teeth grazing the skin of her back. She wondered at his response, and then the pace changed to one guaranteed to give them both pleasure. His movements frenzied and hard, the bed shook underneath them, headboard slapping the wall a half-dozen times before he adjusted the angle. Loving it, she loved everything he did to her, how he controlled her body, her every reaction, driving her closer. Every inch of his cock stroked into her, rigid, hot...*thick*. The delicious drag and slide of his cock inside, crown mushroomed out so large it seemed physically impossible. Pounding deep. Bodies awakened. *My Duck.*

"You're going to fucking come on my cock, Bee. Come for me, darlin'. Come all over my cock, hold me in, pull hard. Tight, *God*, so fucking tight, your pussy so fucking good." He changed the angle slightly and she moaned, shocked at the noises coming from her mouth in response to his words, the pounding evidence of his desire for her. Sounding out of control, and she found she loved that, too, he grunted, "Fuck, yeah. Hot. Feel how hot you make me."

Tipping her hips, she rose to meet him just as he pinched her clit again, the pain jolting through to pleasure and beyond, swelling and filling her. She focused on the wave, riding it as the orgasm rolled through her, pushing up and over the edge as muscles all over her body tensed, legs stiffening and trying to pull together. His words came in short bursts, sounds breathed out with each gasp as he thrust hard. "Feel you going, baby. Feel it. Feel us together. Me and you, baby. Just us, my home." Held open and apart by his knees, his thighs between her legs, her fingers clutched at the sheets, fisting the fabric as she broke for him.

She was lost in the sensations assaulting her from all sides and he kept moving, calling her name, each stroke taking her farther, making it more. Then, as if from a distance, she registered the grip of his hands lifting and helpfully put her elbows on the mattress, resting her forehead on her arms. Behind her now, he had one hand on her shoulder, using the grip to pull her body backwards and onto his cock. His other hand crept around her waist and eased between her legs as she squirmed to avoid the touch. "No, no. Duck, too much. Please. No." The words came out as individual phrases, interrupted by hard breaths and hitching gasps.

Ignoring her pleas, he roughly thrummed his fingers back and forth over her clit and labia, curving them down and around as he pressed hard against her mound with the heel of his hand, fingers splitting to either side of his cock as he entered her. Astonished as the brilliant feeling in her belly caught her unawares, she bowed her neck, coming again, twisting to look back and up at him, wanting desperately to share the moment.

Eyes open wide, he was watching, studying her, gaze flicking up her body to rest on her face and then back down to where he was sliding in and out of her body. "Fucking beautiful, Bee. My cock inside you, my Bee. Mine. My lover." Mouth open, his words interrupted as he paused a moment to suck in a breath, his body never stopping the hard, fast movements, hips snapping forwards and back as he fucked her.

With a roar, he moved, his hand clamping down on her shoulder and pulling her up, lifting her torso so her back was against his chest and his hand slipped around, cupping the column of her throat. Thrusting hard up into her, nearly lifting her off the mattress as he came, he gritted out a single word, communicating a depth and intensity of emotion that stripped her defenses and stole her breath away. "*Mine.*"

They stayed in that position for a minute, and then two as he shuddered repeatedly, his cock jerking hard inside her, pumping heat filling her as his orgasm peaked. Palm still pressed between her thighs, the other wrapped around her throat, he controlled their position effortlessly as the muscles of his stomach rippled and moved with each spasm of his cock. She lifted her hands, cupping them around the wrist of the hand holding her neck, feeling the strength and tension keeping her perfectly in place, the possessive, intimate gesture flawlessly right. *He's mine, and I'm his.*

"*Fuck.*" He took a deep breath, his head dipping so his mouth touched her shoulder. Dropping soft kisses every inch along the way, breath hot on her skin as he worked from her shoulder to her ear, he whispered, "Goddamn, I love you, Bee. My woman."

Sinking back on his haunches, he slipped out of her body, but pulled her with him, keeping a full-body contact, her ass resting on his thick, muscular thighs. "Not sorry," he repeated his words from earlier and she laughed softly, the sound shaky in the nighttime silence settling back into the house. "You want more kids?"

The question came from left field and she shook her head in surprise rather than negation, only realizing how he would take it when he stiffened beneath her. "Not a no, baby. Just an unexpected question," she quickly said with a laugh. "Yeah, I always wanted to have more kids. Tommy and I tried, but no luck. Is that a real question, or an 'oh, shit, I forgot the condom' question?"

"You know me to wear a condom anytime I've been with you, except the first time?" He laughed softly, pride and pleasure warring for dominance in his tone when he said, "And it wasn't a very effective measure that time, was it?"

With rich amazement flowing thickly through his voice, he said, "Eli is mine. Elias. My son." Shifting, he laid her on the mattress, brought the pillow back from where their activities had shoved it and pushed it gently underneath her head. "You. Woman, you are mine."

He stretched out next to her, his arm curving across her belly and chest, legs tangling with hers. She shivered, his fingers trailing up and down her side, hand slipping lower to rest palm down on her softly curved belly just above her mound. Head on the pillow next to hers, he leaned close, pressing his lips to her temple, capturing her mouth when she turned to look at him. He told her, "Yeah, it's a real question because I'm going to want more kids. I want to see you pregnant, knowing I made you that way. I want to go through everything with you. Want it so fucking bad, Bee. Can't wait, honey. Cannot wait."

They lay like that for a time, satiated, sweat drying on their skin. He kissed her again, then as she drifted into a deep, exhausted sleep, she heard him ask her in a drowsy, sexy, highly amused voice, "Did I quiet your mind, baby?"

Shaping up

With satisfaction, Duck looked around at the areas of the ranch visible from the house's front porch. In the short time he had been here, things had changed. The barely-there glow of the sunrise showed the outbuildings standing with fresh coats of the ranch's trademark colors, no longer in need of paint.

The length of the drive had been graded, all potholes backfilled and smoothed. The hands had tackled the closest fences first, replacing sagging posts or boards, and had begun to work outward, ensuring all enclosures on the ranch were in good shape. The differences were small when taken individually, but the overall effect was huge. They now looked like what they were, a successful, thriving stock business.

Lifting his coffee mug to his mouth, he blew across the top of the liquid as he simultaneously heard two noises. One was an engine coming down the long drive, having just turned off the road and onto their track. It didn't quite sound like a truck, but was probably the latest feed delivery, Kennwort's driver getting an early start on the day, trusting there would already be hands at work to help with offloading. The other sound was smaller, much quieter, but so much more important, because he heard Eli breathing hard as he stood in the doorway behind Duck.

"Eli," he called, his voice soft. "Come on out if you want. Plenty of room here on this porch."

"Is there room? You sure about that?" The boy's voice was tense and low, caution edging into the tone along with a bit of anger.

"Yeah, sure as I can be." Duck tensed as he waited to hear the screen door open, then with an inward jolt, he saw the boy silently appear near his elbow. "Mornin'."

"Mornin'." This single clipped word was all he got in return and, from the corner of his eye, he watched as Eli's head swung back and forth, his gaze evidently moving from Duck to a place out in the distance, beyond the barns and horses milling in the corrals. "So you and Mom?" As hard as he must have tried to hold it steady, his voice still betrayed him, allowing a quaver to bleed in on the last word. Clearing his throat, Eli continued, "Y'all back together?"

"Yeah. We patched things up." His tone might be understated, but he knew there was a grin on his face. *A fucking big grin*, he guessed. Pair the quiet of the desert with the thin walls of the old house, and he didn't hold out any hope Eli hadn't heard their noisy lovemaking in the middle of the night. Hell, he expected even in the downstairs bedroom, Essa probably got woken up, too. The grin broadened as he wondered if the hands heard them way out in the bunkhouse. He didn't care who knew. *Brenda so lost in what I gave her that she called my name, claiming me? Claiming us?* Hell yeah, he'd take that every night. And every morning. And any moment in between she gave him a chance.

Eli's head moved up and down, then bobbed to a stop. For a moment, they stood motionless, side-by-side, watching the rim of the sun as it pushed into a cloudless sky along the horizon, soft pinks ripening into brilliant red. "You love her?"

"I do." He stopped there for a second and then decided the boy needed to know how he cherished Bee, had always held her close. "I've loved her since I was fourteen. Waited a long time to get a second chance with her. But, even when you want something as badly as we do this, when you've lived separate lives like we have, there are bound to be things that can get sideways between you. Unexpected misunderstandings at the importance of experiences the other person doesn't even know anything about. Can't have any chance of knowing, unless it's talked about. Talked through.

"Your mom and I talked things through, and we both have an eye on which direction other issues might come from. This is something we both want, me in her life, her in mine. Love her, love that she's willing to go here with me, Eli. So me and your mom, we'll work to head anything off. Stop trouble in its tracks so we don't upset each other again. I love her, Elias. I can't stand to see her hurting. Would cut out my own tongue before I hurt her like that again."

There was silence for a breath, and then, "They used to fight." Out of the blue, the boy offered this detail and Duck wasn't able to control his reaction. No one had come out and told him, but he had his suspicions. "Like…a lot. If she stood there and took it, he got mean." Eli shrugged, thin shoulders lifting the shirt he wore, movement setting the untucked hem swaying against his hips. "Mom never knew how much I saw. You'd cut out your tongue? I wish he'd have cut off his hands."

Fuck. "That mean what I think it does, Elias?" The boy nodded, and then shrugged again, staying silent, chin pointed to the horizon where the sun had lifted from the curve of the earth, suspended in the ever-brightening sky, a space that had always been there suddenly visible to all. "I don't hold with hitting women. Ever. Hard stop on that one. Hell, I don't hit men unless there's no alternative. They pretty much gotta come at me in a way I can't avoid before I'll let loose on 'em."

The sun inched up, gaining room from the curve of the earth. "He wasn't my dad. Did you know?" The whisper filled the porch, pressure from the knowledge the boy held pushing everything away, attempting to keep him isolated in his pain. The gas ball hovering along the edge of the sky cast light that glared on his hurt, no soothing warmth from the bright circle. "He told me. Back before he got bad, before the docs gave up on trying new things. He and Mom wanted more kids, but never got anywhere with it. He found out he couldn't have kids. Hadn't ever been able. That meant…"

Voice trailing off mid-sentence, Eli's shoulders seemed to round down, pulling in, making him small. Filled with sudden rage and pain, not able to stop his actions, Duck reached out, wrapped an arm around the boy and pulled him close, comforting them both. They stood like that for a long time, Eli's cautious hand creeping around Duck's waist in fits and starts, each time testing the waters carefully before heading into fresh territory. This continuing until Eli was wrapped around him, head shifting to press tight against his side. No tears, just an agony the boy had borne alone for too long, and Duck wanted to lighten it in any way he could, so he held the boy, and let himself be held.

The light strengthened, driving shadows back into their place as it slipped into the world, filling every space with bright illumination. The softening brilliance exposed everything, both good and bad. Finally, even when he thought he could speak without anger, Duck still struggled to control his voice as he said, "Not something he should have said to you, Eli. That's the kind of thing you'd think twice before telling a grown man, and you sure shouldn't ponder telling a boy who thinks you hung the moon." He paused when Eli quivered, burrowing closer. "Hate like hell you've carried those words. *Fuck*." *I can't tell him, that's his momma's place.* He squeezed the boy and pulled in a breath, waiting until he was again certain of a steady voice before he asked, "But, with that knowledge in your head, how does it make you feel?"

"I'm glad he wasn't my dad." This admission surprised Duck, because in the pictures, Eli was always looking at Tommy. Taking a sip of his now stone-cold coffee, Duck wondered if it was more watching instead. "He was...you know how you can tell a lot about someone by their friends?" Duck nodded and Eli went on. "He was friends with Mister Nelms."

Fuck. That right there gave voice to everything wrong. Ray had gotten to Brenda after all, just from a sideways angle, through her husband. Now, he had a dozen questions for Bee, would be asking them gently to find the truth. "My brother Ray was a right bastard." He said this softly and the boy's head moved up and down again in agreement, his cheek scrubbing against Duck's shirt, the noise soft in the quiet of the morning.

"I would never have thought you were brothers," Eli said and Duck snorted. The boy's arm tightened around him, holding on in preparation for something. "Not just how different you looked, you know, the size, but...you're nice. Like inside and out." Eli paused for a moment, considering his words as cautiously as he had worked his embrace of Duck around earlier. "He wasn't, and the more time Da—Tommy spent around him, the more he wasn't either. I wasn't sorry when Mister Nelms went away."

"Me either, kid. I've worked my whole life to be a better person than my father and brother. Glad it's apparent enough to notice." Tightening his arm, he gave the boy a squeeze, reassuring Eli physically that badmouthing Duck's son-of–a-bitch brother wasn't going to rile him. He gave an inward snort. It was time to move this conversation on; he wouldn't be saying anything more to Eli without talking to Brenda first, and that was definitely a pillow-talk conversation, not one to have in the harsh light of day. "Sun's up enough to start chores. What's on your list this morning?"

"Move all the tack into trailers, make sure we got enough supplements and vitamins in the big box that goes to the show barn." The answer came swiftly and he knew the change of subject was a relief. It had been a hard conversation for each of them, and Duck was ready to put it behind him for now, too. "Then start mixing bottles for the calves."

"Better get to it then, Eli." He squeezed him again. "I want you to know I heard what you had to say this morning. I'm going to work hard to keep from hurting your mom again. My goal every day will be to make sure she knows she's loved."

Elias still had his arm around Duck's waist and he squeezed him in response, then Duck heard him whisper, "All I can ask."

"No, Eli. You can ask for more, but even if you won't, I'll give it to you." Duck paused a moment, feeling Eli's arm tense. "Here's another goal, just as important as the last. Every day...every single day, I'm going to take care of you, too."

***

Scowling, Duck walked down the drive to where the trailer sat, still hooked to the truck. He snapped, "Gill, what the hell is this?" and then continued without waiting for a response. "We buy stock we didn't talk about?"

Without speaking, Gill stood and waited at the back of the trailer for Duck to reach him. Together, they worked to unlatch the locks and Duck heard an unmistakable squeal from inside the vehicle. He asked, "Stud colt?" and groaned when Gill nodded, eyes fixed on the shadows of the trailer's interior. They had talked about acquiring a new stud for breeding, but none of the ones they had looked at were as young as this animal sounded.

They were pulling the chute wings up to fill the gap between the trailer and the fencing when he heard the ringing racket of hooves on the wooden trailer floor, then the single crash of a kick against the sidewall. Leaning sideways, Duck looked along the length of the trailer and snorted a laugh when he saw the results of the colt's next hard kick, a bulging dent appearing in the metal.

He straightened up just in time to see movement in the shadows, and then a cautious sorrel head snaked out, eyes wideset and intelligent, panicky whites showing all around the edges as the frightened horse examined his new surroundings. The colt looked to be from old stock, the classic lines of his nose and jaw harkening back to the early days of Quarter Horse registration.

The animal jerked his head back into the shadows and Duck heard Gill curse softly under his breath. With a bend of his knees, Duck pushed off, grabbing the top of the rail and swinging his legs and hips over, landing in the middle of the alleyway leading from the trailer to the corral. Quickly, Gill said, "Boss, have a caution. He ain't even green broke. Ain't been around people much."

Duck shook his head at his foreman's advice, faced the ramp and backed into the trailer a couple of steps, hearing the horse behind him move away from the unwelcome intrusion. Duck just stood there patiently, plenty of room on either side for the horse to push past if he wanted out, but he didn't expect that to happen. The colt was curious, his peek a few minutes ago attested to a bold attitude. He just needed to wait the horse out. If he were nosy, and he was, he wouldn't be able to stand not knowing what Duck was doing just standing there.

Sure enough, within a couple of minutes, there were hot gusts of breath against his elbow, then his back, then his other elbow, then a nudge. The nose shoving at him swiftly removed, followed by a tug at his sleeve, teeth precariously near skin making him grin. Moving slowly, Duck took a single step forward, and stopped, waiting for the horse to step up behind him. When the colt moved and he felt the hot breaths against his back again, Duck strode forwards and out from the trailer into the sunshine. He kept walking, and even without looking back, he knew when the colt started moving because the trailer rocked and shifted, and then he heard Gill's soft, "I'll be damned."

He was ready for it and stepped to one side when he heard the tentative hoof beats behind him pick up the pace, becoming a thundering rumble. The colt flashed past him and into the corral, head up, tail flagging high as it raced the wood fencing it in, containing it from running free. Duck watched as the colt's muscles surged beneath the sorrel hide before it slid to a stop, hocks tucked far underneath its body. Ears attentively pointed forward, the horse froze in place for a moment before whirling on its haunches to launch itself in the other direction. Not afraid, not at all afraid. This was pure joy in movement, and instincts like that would make training him a pleasure.

"Pretty colt," was all he said, reaching out to help Gill shut the gate.

"Yup."

He grinned, knowing it would be all the response he would receive from the taciturn ranch foreman.

"Wow!" He heard the breathy exclamation from just outside the corral and turned to see Eli there. The boy's eyes had locked on the eager colt still running circuits along the fence, sliding and turning, effortlessly changing leads on the fly, mane and tail streaming. "He's gorgeous, Duck."

He stood there a minute, studying the boy. Eli had picked up on the name change without anything being said, never questioning, just adapting. He was good around the place, had worked hard alongside Duck on a variety of jobs, but his joy, the one thing he loved more than anything else was the horseflesh he had access to on the ranch. Every time the boy had half a chance, he was on General, saddled or bareback, and Duck had seen the boy stick to the younger horses like a burr, while still handling them like glass. No horse on the place had heard his voice raised in anger, and none of them avoided the boy. Consistent and persistent, he had a natural way of handling the horses that they responded to.

Glancing over at Gill, he caught the man's eye and tipped his head towards Eli, receiving a sideways grin and nod in response. *Right on*, he thought. *Project horse.* This would give Eli something he would not only be good at, but where he could see and measure the results as he excelled. Something to master, but the whole process would require a great deal of compromise, lending itself to good life lessons.

"He is pretty," Duck said, turning back to watch the colt as he stretched out his legs for two or three strides, mane flying and snapping in the wind. "Gonna need gentling. Gill said he's not halter broke yet, so that'd be your place to start, Eli."

The boy turned to face him, eyes nearly as wide as the colt's were a minute ago. He seemed to be waiting for something, and when Duck didn't say anything more, he shook himself, like he was trying to wake up, then breathed the disbelieving question, "What?"

"Gill's got the final say, but I'm thinking this is a good chance for you to put leather to your learning." He shrugged, watching Eli's face as his bright and excited gaze flicked between Gill and him.

"You got good ideas, boss," Gill said laconically and Eli's face lit up in a grin as he turned to watch the colt again.

***

"Tellin' you, Mason, she's got a strut that won't quit. Doesn't surprise me he's holed up with that fender bunny." Watcher chuckled. "Brenda works for him, but you can tell she means a fuckuva lot more. Climbed down from the cab of the truck and, Jesus, you could tell at a glance from a hundred yards away she was pissed right the fuck off at him. Still made her way to where we were standing. Fear pouring off her in waves at the boys between her and her old man even as she rocked that strut. Respectful, not pushy. Ignorance of club was clear, though. 'Reuben' her call instead of Duck."

Mason shook his head, cutting his gaze to where Fury sat on the couch in the office, listening to the conversation on speaker. He would give a little here, and then wait to see where the man took the knowledge. How he handled it would be telling in the long run. Mason told Watcher, "Duck asked for time, then called and asked for more. His family's business is there in town, and he didn't go home after his brother took a dirt nap, so it is entirely reasonable he needs time."

Watcher started to say something, and Mason talked over him, "I'll pull him home for a couple of days, see where his head's at."

Angling his chin towards the door in a silent directive that got Fury on the move, Mason then reached out and picked up the handset, waiting until the door closed behind Fury to speak again. "Now, brother. Tell me the real reason you called me about my man."

"Duck wasn't wearing his colors." Anger and an edge of suspicion trailed through his words, and Mason knew this right here was the trigger for the call today. "I sat on the info for a few days, thinking and stewing why you'd send a man my way without a call. Send him in without a patch."

Watcher paused, and Mason waited, giving him ample time to say what he needed. Watcher growled, "Fucking anon, in my fucking town, walking towards me on my fucking lot at my fucking bar. Mason,"—he sucked in a breath—"I greeted him like a brother, no reserve. Found blank denim underneath my fist. Blind and empty, as if he owed no allegiance. Feels like I'm treading a fine line here, brother. You know that kind of shit looks disrespectful. Fuck, it *is* disrespectful. Makes men look at me, gives them something to gab about, takes their focus off what I need it to be, which is fucking *Diamante*. Wiping that goddamned club out of my territory. I don't need my men thinking...fuck me, maybe even *believing* my strongest ally is looking to backstab me. Maybe think you're the type to slide a man in under the radar until he's found out. To be strong, you have to believe strong. That's what I need right now. I need my men to believe strong."

Silence bled into the airwaves lying between them for a few moments as Mason waited to see if Watcher was finished. Mason let it go on until the quiet was uncomfortable, then, his voice hard and rough, said, "You. Out of everyone in my life, you know what it means when I call you *brother*. I would not fuck you like that, Watch. No way. No how. You know how it is between us. Duck said West Texas. Digger said Midland. Fuck, man. I called and asked you if you carried a charter in

Midland and you told me no. I did not know to ask Lamesa, but you could have volunteered that shit, knowing how close the two are. He was not anon as an insult, but rather out of respect. And you fucking know it, you know you do.

Without giving Watcher time to respond, he continued, "If you have shit in your house, brother, then you need to clean it out. Can't nobody make that shit right but you, and it's something else you fucking know. If a patch brother don't trust you, don't believe in you, then drop the motherfucker's center. He don't straighten his ass out, check himself, then you cut his fucking rockers. Wrecked himself. Let him go find a pussy outfit to ride at the back of instead of giving him a chance to start crap with you.

"Now, if my man...if Duck didn't show you proper respect, then we can have a different conversation. But I know him, and Watch, dammit, you know him, and we both know he fucking did respect. Stopped as soon as he saw you, pulled in and pissed off his pussy so he could pay that respect. He's a good man, been solid for years. One of my *most* trusted. You fucking know that, too.

"So here we have a decision. A fork in the road, and...*fuck,* man, I think everything depends on how you answer. Your answer is gonna drive our relationship from here out. What kind of man do you believe I am? Do *you* believe strong? Are you strong in what stands between us? Do you believe me? You're my brother, my *true* brother, and you know it's how I feel.

"But, if you believe for one second, one mother*fucking, god*damned breath, if you really believed I was running one of my own down into your house without making it right, then it is crystal we have a burned bridge somewhere between us instead of what I thought we had. So what'll it be, brother? Tell me what you believe."

"Mason," Watcher said instantly, "respect, brother. We've had us a misunderstanding. You called, that's truth. I didn't put two and two

166

together. That shit's on me. Saw Duck's face, pleased me down to my bones. Felt it. Then when I felt that naked back? Fucked me up, brother. Felt that, too. Diamante keeps creeping along the edges, man, got me twisted inside out these days. I don't know what Lalo's got planned, but I know from chatter he's got something churning. He's playin' and layin' low, hiding his face. Laying along the edges of the wind, sure as I'm a bastard. Just can't get a handle on what it is, but I know...know in my goddamned belly it is going to fuck. With. Me."

Mason let the silence sit for a minute, but not as long as before, then he said, "Respect, brother. Belief, too. Know you didn't track that shit, so it's not on you. We'll set this aside. Never happened."

Watcher asked, his confident voice sounding certain of the answer, and Mason appreciated him asking just to make sure. "We good, brother?"

"Fuck, yeah. We're good. I'll pull Duck back up here, figure out what's up about his old lady, make sure he's not falling into a Diamante trap over pussy. That would be a shame. Never seen the brother with anyone more than once. He's never struck me as the long-term type. Will be fun to ring his bell over this shit, seeing as he hasn't come clean to me about it. So, thanks for that. I'll let you know how the entertainment plays out, yeah?"

"Yeah, you do that, fucker," Watcher said with a chuckle. "Shiny side, brother."

"Shiny side, man."

Have it sweet

"Brenda, you got a minute?" He called the question up the stairs to where she was getting dressed. Tonight was the final visit with the rodeo sponsors, reviewing the placement of banners and promotional material in and around the set-up at the fairgrounds. "Need to talk to you, honey."

When he had come back into the house from working in the barn office and checked his phone, there had been a message from Mason asking him to phone in. The man himself wasn't available when he made the call, but Red told him Mason wanted him back in Chicago for a day and Digger had already gotten him a ticket, leaving tonight. He had called and left a message for Digger, making sure the man knew the ticket needed to be round trip because he would not be staying in Chicago. It was sudden, but if the club needed him, he would go, no questions. He just wouldn't stay.

Bee called, "Coming," a moment before he heard her feet on the stairs. He shook his head. The woman managed to hit every squeaky board every single time she traversed the staircase. He watched as she used her grip on the post to swing around and head to the kitchen where he stood, grinning at the expression on her face. Equal parts pleasure and amusement, her smile stretched her lips, curving them up at the corners.

Opening his arms wide, there was a rush of satisfaction when she walked into them without pause, no questions in her eyes. Not yesterday. Not today. And, he prayed, not tomorrow. *A gift*, he thought, *having her trust me like this.* Wrapping himself around her, he held still for a moment just soaking in the feel of her, and then said, "There isn't any way I can say this that won't make you wonder for at least a minute, so let me say up front, the tickets are round trip and I'm back here tomorrow night." She jerked, making a noise and trying to pull back, but he tightened his arms, holding her close. "I got a call a couple of minutes ago. My boss in Chicago needs me back there tonight. I fly out of Midland in about four hours. I'll be right back here tomorrow night. Back in our bed tomorrow night. Home." He kissed the side of her head. "Home, with you, my Bee."

Slowly, she relaxed and her chest expanded with a long, soundless breath. Then, without argument or hesitation, simply giving him what he needed, she quietly said, "Okay." With that single word, he knew he held her trust, fully and without question. She believed what he said, that he wasn't leaving, that he would be back here with her just as soon as he could make it happen and he found himself again thinking, *a gift*. Softly, he pressed his mouth to the side of her head, kissing her temple. When she tipped her chin up, wordlessly asking for more, he dipped and captured her mouth with his. Duck worked hard to give her what she needed, kissing her deeply, tenderly stroking against her tongue with his.

***

CHICAGO, ILLINOIS

Duck had worked his way into a very foul mood by the time he stalked into Jackson's that evening. The flight into O'Hare on his one-fucking-way ticket had been unpleasant, his neighbors on the plane loud and obnoxious. That was followed by a trip from the airport to the bar that was less than pleasing.

Letting the door swing shut behind him, he looked around, seeing the typical group of patrons and members in the bar, with the exception of a clearly missing Mason. *Dammit*, he thought. Lifting his chin to his brothers, he acknowledged the welcoming chorus of greetings as he turned to where Merry stood behind the cash register. Catching sight of the look on his face, she laughed aloud and he frowned more deeply. "The fuck you laughin' at, woman?"

"You look like somebody stole your last piece of candy, shit on it, and put it back in the box," she responded, eyes on him but her hands in constant movement, making change for a customer. "Lookin' for Mason?"

"Yeah, he called me up here for something, but now he isn't answering his phone. Didn't have a brother meet me, and he isn't at the clubhouse. Took the train in because I was told he was here, but now I don't fucking see him. You know where he is?" A woman's laugh floated through the room and with a lightening of his mood, he recognized Mica. He watched as Merry's eyes flicked over his shoulder, then back to his face. "Fucker's right behind me, ain't he?" She nodded with a grin.

A hand fell on his shoulder, pulling and swinging him around before Mason's hand clasped his wrist, his grip in return an automatic response. "Duck," Mason said warmly, tugging him forwards for a thumping one-shoulder clench. Not giving him a chance to respond, Mason said, "Come sit with us." Motioning with his other hand, he indicated a crowded booth along the wall.

"Boss." Duck shook his head and pulled back on the grip, feet firmly planted. "I didn't come all the way back to Chicago in order to socialize with citizens." Since he found her, since he took on the privilege of protecting her, spending time around Mica had always twisted a knife in his heart, and he waited for the pain to grip him. Waited for a pain that did not materialize. For the first time. He pushed back at what he was feeling, trying to decide the difference, realizing that for once, seeing her wasn't tied to his shame and guilt, but circled around with pure pleasure at her happiness.

Mica was listening to Molly talk, broad smile in place, her head leaned against Daniel's shoulder, her ever-classic look as out of place as her comfort in this rough biker's bar should be. J.J.'s wheelchair positioned at the end of the table, Molly perched on the end of the bench, near his knees.

The other occupant of the booth surprised him, and he frowned slightly when he recognized Fury, a former Diamante officer who had folded his chapter into the Rebels in Fort Wayne.

Turning to face Mason, he said, "You called me back for business. I'm only here for a few hours, brother, and I'm exhausted. Been up way too fucking long at this point. We need to talk now, before I pass out."

"This is the business," Mason said cryptically, laying a hand on his shoulder, and steering him towards the booth.

He held up a hand in greeting as they approached the group and wasn't surprised when Mica climbed to her feet to hug him. They had known each other for decades, and from her perspective, he was ever a welcome sight, reminding her of the best parts of home and growing up on the circuit. With a grin at Molly, he reached out and shook first J.J. and then Daniel's hands before he rocked back on his heels, dipping his thumbs into the corners of his back pockets, giving Fury a nod.

Mason stood beside him through that, then snorted, telling an again-seated Mica, "Scoot yer ass over, woman." He slid in next to her and Duck waited for Molly to stand before he slid in on her side, moving down to give her ample room. This put him side-by-side with Fury and he grumbled, "Coulda moved to a fuckin' table, boss."

"Ten minutes," Mason said and Duck nodded. He could give him ten minutes. The conversation turned from hockey to trucking, to Mica's business, back to trucking, then over to a start-up catering business Molly was working in conjunction with Road Runner, another Rebel member, this one a highly trained chef.

Duck had wondered about Mason's 'ten minutes' comment, but sure enough, within that timeframe, Red walked in with two boys in tow. It looked as if the older Rebel had been on babysitting duty this afternoon. The success of that duty was clear, as both Molly's son, Tomas, and Mica's son, Jon, were covered head-to-toe with dirt, smiles shining out of their filthy faces, sweat-stained circles around their eyes showing where goggles had been.

"What in the world, Red?" Mica called. "Did you boys leave any dirt outside?" She scooted Mason out of the booth and stood, inspecting her son a little closer, swiping at the grime with a dampened thumb.

"We wode a dirt bwike," Jon reported happily, submitting to his mother's attempts to clean him up without complaint. "Unka Wed said we was bwadwassas." He grinned broadly, tipping his head to look around his mom to his dad. "Unka Wed said we was Webels. I fwell down. A wot."

Duck laughed as Mica's head angled up, her unsmiling features focused on Red who stood with his hands palm-up in front of him, his grin as wide and bright as Jon's. "Now, Princess. You know the boys were safe with me."

"Not fussin' about the dirt bike, Red," she said. "Fussin' about the language, and you know it." He laughed again, reaching out with one hand to ruffle Jon's hair, earning himself a tipped-back boy head and an upside-down grin.

Molly laughed, swinging her son into J.J.'s lap, ignoring the dirt that smeared onto their clothing. "Tomas, did you ride a motorcycle?"

"Nawp, was a itty dirt bike, Mom." A year older than Jon, he tried to sound bored with the activity, but looking at his face, it had obviously been exciting, even at the advanced age of four years old.

Daniel stood, reaching back into the booth to gather Mica's purse. "Time to take these baby Rebels home, I suspect." Turning, he glanced at Duck and Fury, gave them a nod and then his gaze landed on Mason. With a grin he said, "Bikes." He chuckled. "Boys and their toys. See ya around, old man."

With a snort, Mason nodded. "Chase wants a bike in the worst way. I've staved it off so far with the truck, but it's comin', I think." Chase was his son, just turned seventeen and nearly ready to leave home for college...or a musical career, depending on the boy's mood of the day.

Goodbyes done, Mica, Molly, and J.J. all headed for the exit, but Daniel hovered at the end of the table, gaze fixed on Mason. "How's Hoss doing?" Duck tipped his chin down, not wanting to look at Mason's face, but as he shifted, he realized Fury had gone absolutely still next to him, frozen in place. From the corner of his eye, Duck saw a profound pain wash over the man's features, heard him take in a shallow, unsteady breath as Mason said, "Doin' about as well as you'd expect, glad as fuck he got his boy back like he did, whole and safe. But he's still holdin' onto fear it happened that easy."

Hoss, veep of the Fort Wayne chapter, was living with a woman who had brought her son into his life. Hope and Sammy. Two months earlier, the boy's daddy had kidnapped him, and it had been a hard and frightening two days before Hoss and Hope got him back.

"Give him my best," Daniel said and waited for Mason's nod. "See ya around." With a hand lifted in farewell, he turned and walked to his wife, wrapping his arm around her and their son, escorting his family out the door.

Twisting his neck, Fury reached up a hand, smoothing the long strands of his trademark red hair back from his face. He looked up at Mason, then over at Duck and said, "Business here, or private room?"

***

Mason watched Duck's face as Fury spoke. Smooth and still, his features were expressionless, hiding everything. This was one of the smartest men he knew, able to look at a problem and suss it out without any fucking clues other than what was in front of him. Duck was important to him in many ways, only one of which was a key member of the club. According to Watcher, the man had a woman in Lamesa, a serious someone he hadn't shared knowledge about with Mason, even when he asked for permission to head out of town for a few days. Those few days had turned into weeks, still with no end in sight if his comment earlier about heading right back out was true.

He needed to get a read on Duck about the girl and how things sat with Watcher's boys. Not something to be talked about over the phone, or even via video chat, he had wanted the man in his house and in front of his face when he asked the questions, determined to talk it through until things were answered to his satisfaction. Not that he would ever worry about Duck's loyalty, but there were a lot of clubs out west who were not friendly to the Rebels and every nuance of his insight would be valuable.

"Here is good," he said smoothly and Fury nodded.

Turning back to Duck, Mason decided to get the hardest questions out there on the table. "Watcher called," he said, and then paused. With a sigh, he said, "Told me you weren't covered, brother. Said it chilled his bones to see you without your colors, man. Wanna talk me through the situation he found you inside? Tell me how he handled himself? Man called, pissed as hell, until I talked it through with him. I need your take on it, brother."

Fury, having heard only the parts about the woman, jerked back in the seat next to Duck, physically reacting to the words, twisting his torso to look at Duck, eyebrows raised.

Duck snorted a laugh and Mason tensed, knowing the tension in his stance would be a clear response to what some would count a deadly insult. "Prez. Brother. Watcher was cool. He got we didn't know he had a charter in town. His boys were cool, too."

Mason frowned and shook his head. "No, he fucking was not."

"Yeah, he was, Prez. I told you I'd be wearing on the plane, but once I hit the ground, I'd pack them away. Respect, man. We vetted my visit with him and he didn't raise any questions. We did not vet my visit with other local clubs. I saw him, stopped and paid my respects. Met some of his men, put faces to names with some we've dealt with long distance. There is no shit that's going to come back to roost on my brothers, my club. He was cool, totally."

Duck shook his head, reading into the silence this was serious and Mason watched the muscles in his forearms and hands bulge, fisted balls at the end of his arms. "I would not fucking disrespect him that way, Mason. Soldiers are allies, a club we depend on when in need. To fuck with them is to fuck with our club, which is not something I would do." He thumped his chest with one of those balled fists, grinding out the words, "Rebel Wayfarers forever," and Mason and Fury both repeated the answering phrase, the words ringing out as if they sat in church with a half-hundred brothers, "Rebels forever."

"Hand to my patch, Prez. It wasn't until I realized it was the Southern Soldiers who held the town that I knew I'd be cool with my vest on. I didn't go to Lamesa for club business, so for what I needed to take care of, I did not need the push or sway of the club. But knowing Watch's men were in town, I slipped my cut back on and been wearing it ever since."

Mason frowned. He wanted to move the conversation forward, but there was still the question of the woman. With Duck gone, Mason had been working with Fury and Tater, a displaced chapter president now in Chicago. They were concentrating on business, trying to track down the name of a person Deacon had sent to Lalo for mentoring. Deacon was the former president of Mason's first club, a brotherhood Mason had killed, much as Fury had his. He and Fury had more in common than most people knew at first glance, or even after prolonged study.

Lalo was now a gypsy member of the Diamantes, stripped of both his chapter and his office by war with the Southern Soldiers and the Rebels. The same club Fury had left in his dust. Mason knew Lalo and Fury had a long history of mutual hatred but did not yet know all the ins-and-outs of their relationship. He wanted that knowledge, needed it if he were going to trust Fury with any parts of his Rebels. Patience would bring him what was necessary, but with the way things were headed across the country, Mason wasn't certain they'd bought enough time to be patient.

"So, no issues from their side? No disrespect?" It sounded like it was what Watcher had said at the end of their conversation, a misunderstanding. Still, he was glad to have brought Duck home. If he admitted it, he was relieved the man came without argument, given the length of time he had been gone, and his elusive responses about the woman.

"Not a chance, Prez. Club comes first, man. I wouldn't have sat on anything like that. Woulda brought it back to you immediately, brother." Duck's voice rang with conviction.

Time to pressure him, see what the truth was behind his trip. *Here we go.*

"And your Brenda don't hold any place in that line?" Mason's unexpected question jarred Duck, seemed to take the wind out of the man's sails, but then he straightened, looking Mason in the face. Fearless, not seeming to hide anything, this was what Mason expected from his men. *My brothers.* "A woman who's met Soldiers standing on their lot, but I learned her fucking name from Watcher, not you? Pussy getting in the way of your thinking, Duck? She don't hold point on that waving line?"

"Different conversation, boss. I need to talk to you about making some adjustments in my place within the club, but it's not for today." Fury made a noise and they both swung to glance at him, then back at each other and their gazes locked. "And, brother…Mason, you know how I feel about you, but you talk about her like that again and we will have a problem." *Fuck*, Mason thought.

"That still don't sound like club comes first, brother. Might want to wrap your mind around today being the right time." Mason's tone was cautionary, telling Duck without words his next comments needed to be better considered than his last.

Their gazes stayed locked and Mason felt the full force of Duck's stare, his eyes darkening with passion or anger. After a long moment, Duck barked out, *"Fuck.* Okay, now it is. Let's talk." He sighed heavily and leaned back, lifting one hand, palm up, a supplicant's gesture. "Brother. I've never hated a conversation more than this, never had dread for anything like I have these past hours. You know the club is my life, tied around my soul in a way it can't be untangled without killing me, Prez. You know the club comes first for me. Always has, always will.

"But you, out of all men who wear our patch, know how family counts in the balance of our lives. Unbalanced we will fail and fall, every time. Brenda is a woman from my past, and I've unearthed some hard truths these past weeks, not the least of which is a ten-year-old boy." Mason jolted, shocked, feeling an instant of anger and panic at the quiet declaration. Fear and wrath on his brother's behalf, knowing what those words might mean. Ignoring his reaction, Duck forged on, "Elias, a son hidden from me by circumstances. Not deception, thank God, but it's still a decade with the boy I'll never get back." He looked up at Mason, fear and sorrow on his features, tension in his pose as he leaned forward, forearms to the edge of the table.

This clearly was hard for him to say, pain-filled because the rawness was so new. "Elias is my blood, Brenda his mother, now my old lady. My heart is in West Texas, brother. It's pounding, beating in my chest right now, but yearning west."

Mason's head tipped back involuntarily, chin raising in response because Duck was right. He did know about things like this. His own boy had been kept from him for twelve years. Chase was nearly a teenager before Mason ever laid eyes on him, that happy event orchestrated by none other than Watcher, a man he still knew without any doubt would always have his back. Now knowing Watcher was in Duck's hometown at the same time this kind of fuckery happened, it all struck him somewhat strange.

Duck leaned back and kept talking, not realizing where Mason's thoughts had gone. "I'm Rebel to the core, but with what I've found out about Ray and his shit, and then finding out about Eli...I'm torn. I was thinking...hadn't really planned on asking you for some time. But it seems right, so I guess, since you called me back, here I am."

Duck sucked in a deep breath, blowing it out slowly through pursed lips. "*Fuck*, this is hard." His mouth twisted with sorrow and he slowly nodded before looking up at Mason, fingers curling in to his palms, fists pressed to the table, fighting his own emotions. "Prez, I'm here, formally asking permission to step away from where you've had me for years. It's never been an official office, so unless you say so, I don't expect I'll need to speak up in church. You've needed me, and I've done everything asked. Every time."

Duck dropped his eyes and Mason clenched his jaw tight, holding in his words with effort. This had to be Duck's ask, and hard as it was, he had to give the man time to get to the end. "I found out some things about my family, about myself, Prez. I can't sort my shit from way up here, and some of what I found might not be able to leave Lamesa.

His voice dropped to a hoarse whisper, "Boss, I don't know when I can come back." He shifted his weight, glancing up and then looking back down again. "Might be years." Bringing his head up, he stared at Mason. Accepting the weight of that intent look, Mason locked eyes with this man who meant so much to him. Voice gaining strength, he went on, "Might cost me my patch, and I fully recognize that. So, here we fucking go. I need some time, boss. And, however you tell me I have to take it, I will. You drop me to nomad status, I'm good with that. I understand I can't have the privileges of a chapter without supporting that chapter, and charter."

He sucked in a breath, and gave words to the fear Mason could see dancing across his face. "You tell me gypsy is my only option, and you have to cut me…" His voice trailed off and he looked down at the table, then back up at Mason, his words ringing true and real, offering everything. "Then that's the way it is. Love the club, you know that is fucking truth spoken. But, Mason…*brother*. Patch on my back don't matter for what's between us, brother. You'll always be my president, my brother, my friend."

"Fuck you." Mason said this immediately, automatically, the words rolling easily off his tongue, granting some measure of peace to his brother at the instant rejection of the idea. And, as he spoke, he watched the fear and tension flee from Duck's face, relief and surprise taking root. *Fuck, he actually expected I'd cut him*, Mason thought, intensely glad he had pushed to bring his brother home for this. Duck's fisted hands pushed flat on the table, corded muscles jerking under the skin of his arms. An ease spread through the man and Mason watched him gulp in breath after breath, deep and shuddering, chest expanding with each, wordlessly releasing the pent-up anxiety.

"Ain't cuttin' you, Duck. Nomad is an honor, and you fucking know it. Means we…means *I* trust you to hold the club close, even without folks to help you keep your footing. Nomad is a trust from me to you that you'll do right, be right, no matter the pressures. Risky for you, because you fuck up out of territory, or even within it, you ain't got anyone to cover your back. Nomad roaming sound like what you need? You got it. No question in my mind, I'll keep you however I can have you, brother. Watcher won't have a problem with it, but there's more than just Soldiers in the west, Duck."

With a nod, Duck got out, "I know, Prez. Same reason I was runnin' anon before seeing Watch. Need to keep one eye in front, see what's comin' at ya, and one eye in back, see what's sneaking up on your ass."

"Yeah, well, for a couple weeks you'll have a brother with you, so we'll sort out negotiated visits. Take the sting out of their skin when they learn you're in town. Lay the reality out for anyone wanting to know what Rebels are doing in West Texas." Mason leaned back in his chair, even Fury didn't know the play, and this secret knowledge made Mason grin. "You ain't flyin' back, Duck. Roll your iron, brother. You can make a fast trip of it, and then you'll have your scoot there so you at least ain't got shit in your head to deal with from being caged all the time."

Duck stared at him, eyes narrowed. "Why's it matter if I got my ride there? Won't lie to you. There were a dozen times over the past week alone I wanted my fucking scoot like a son of a bitch. Not having it was like a toothache, throbbing and aching. Didn't want to poke at it too hard, make it flare wide and hot 'cause I know it tweaks me. Makes me a bear to live with sometimes. It's a good idea, and I'm all for it. Hell, my Bee would probably appreciate not having *that* in her bed."

Mason leaned forward, putting his forearms on the edge of the table, cutting a glance around the bar. There was no one near, no one to hear. It was as safe as anything could be out in the open like this. "Because Watcher is looking to bring his club into the Rebels. We rolled a charter in Oklahoma City six months ago, and West Texas makes sense. It's a good stretch between charters, but gets me...us a little closer to SoCal."

At the surprised looks on the men's faces, he nodded. "Soldiers are already wearing support patches. They got a RW square on their shoulder, brothers."

Duck shook his head, "Fuck, Mason. Saw that, didn't click. That's a good thing."

"Hell, yeah it's good. That was the first logical step, and this will be the next. Gives Watch the backing he needs...gives us men I would trust with my life. All our lives. So for respect, to keep it and give it, I need you on your iron, brother." Leaning back, he said, "Shift ain't happening today. Nor tomorrow. But sometime in the next year, I expect to expand again."

Fury asked, "What does that mean for us, boss? What do you need from me and Duck?"

"Good fucking question, man. One, I need *you* to ride to Lamesa with your brother here. Take his six, man. You're his ridealong on his way home." He cut his gaze at Duck, pleased to see a small, satisfied smile at the word 'home.' For a man who had held pain and shame on his features for so long, this was a new look. A good one.

Mason nodded and continued, "Mica and Molly are flying down in a couple days for the rodeo. Since their cousin's gonna compete, they wanna be there for her. With everything we know is swirling around, we ain't gonna advertise their presence, not at fucking all, but I want to have Rebels there, because no matter her citizen status, Mica is ours. Rebel Princess. Our fucking treasure."

Duck blew out a breath, pounding his chest twice with a closed fist while Fury looked between them. "Story for another day," Mason said softly, waiting until he got a nod from Fury, surprised the man didn't already know Mica's standing in the club, but he had first patched in over in Fort Wayne, hadn't been immersed in the culture of Mother as he came along. *That's a fucking mistake,* Mason thought. Protocol was one thing, knowing the history another. *We need to have a fucking entrance exam these days.*

He shook his head, putting aside those thoughts and continued, "What we will advertise is I'll be there." At the look on Duck's face, Mason laughed. "He don't know it yet, but my boy will be travelin' down, too. Benny's opening the rodeo with a performance of Occupy Yourself, and I've worked it so Chase'll be playin' with him."

Benny was Ben Jones, the baby brother of Slate, Rebel's Fort Wayne president, and had taught Mason's son to play guitar. Occupy Yourself was Ben's band, recently picked up for representation by Iron Indian Records, Mason's record label. "Hold onto your dicks, there's more, brothers. My Bethy will be there, too." Bethany was Mason's sister, who worked for the record label.

"Jesus wept," Duck whispered under his breath. "All the Rebel royalty in one place. Our king, prince, princesses. Willa not going? Is the queen at least staying home, where she's protected?"

Mason shook his head, ignoring the bar's door opening. "She's staying home. She ain't happy about it, but she'll do it for me. We're near the end with the baby, and the pregnancy means I don't want her to stress. And she would stress with seeing Mica and Bethy together. She just ain't far enough past what happened, brother." The last time Willa had seen Mica had been right after Utah. He had worked hard to get her head to a good place, to move her to where they could look forwards and not back, and he wasn't about to let anything trip her up, send her tumbling. *My blood*, he thought, *my blood did that to her, made it so I have to skate around so many fucking holes.*

Shaking his head, he looked up and continued, "So yeah, need y'all rolling down. Watcher's going to have a scoot for me to straddle while I'm in town, but I'll want you there day after tomorrow. Twelve hundred miles, means you gotta drop at least four today yet to make it there."

"Fuck," hissed Fury. "When we leaving?"

"Right the fuck now," Mason said, gesturing towards a group of members who had just walked in. "Boys should have all the shit I asked 'em to pick up, so you can pack, crack, and roll."

"My bike's in the garage across town, boss." Duck was watching the faces of their brothers as the men crossed the room towards their table, broad smiles in place on every face. He seemed to like what he saw, easing back into his seat, some of the tension leaving him.

Mason never stopped grinning as he said, "Naw. Trailered it here yesterday soon as I had the ticket sent. Knew you'd need to get in the wind pretty fast, seein' as you been cage-bound for weeks. We'll need to pause for some tailoring,"—he pulled a new black and white bottom rocker from the inside pocket of his vest, flattening it on the table, the word Nomad brilliant against the dark background—"and then you can get in the wind."

Surprise flared in Duck's eyes, his mouth falling open. Mason enjoyed the sight of catching him off guard like this, able to give his brother a good thing, something that mattered so much. "Fucking shit. You knew. All along, and you already knew. I sweated bullets for hours, trying to decide how to tell you...how to ask you. And, you fucking knew. And now, you're..." His voice trailed off, and he squeezed his eyes shut, shaking his head again.

Leaning across the table, Mason reached out and gripped Duck's arm, feeling the bones and muscles under his hand move to return the gesture. A warrior's shake, respect and support between brothers. A promise of honesty and shared knowledge of a deep abiding affection that anchored so much. Their friendship. The club.

"Rebel Wayfarers forever," Mason muttered, feeling his throat closing around the words.

Duck's eyes flashed open and he nodded, saying slowly, "Forever Rebels."

They sat like that for a moment, then Mason leaned back, breaking their grip, knowing each would continue to feel the connection for a long time.

Duck leaned back too, and then dipped his chin, shaking his head again. "Lemme piss first, Prez," Duck said, looking up with a grin. "Need to call Bee, too. Let her know I'll be a tad late." Shaking his head, he muttered, "Fuck, Mason. You're an asshole."

"Yup. I own that shit," Mason said, joking as he stood to make room for the men to come up and greet the two members he had been talking with. "Fucking own it."

Keeping secrets

Oh, yeah, Duck thought, *this is* exactly *where I'm supposed to be.* Standing in the doorway of Brenda's bedroom, he had stopped in his tracks as soon as his gaze landed on her. She was sleeping, lying on her side facing him, sheet to her chest, bare shoulder thrown back, arm draped across her side and stomach. The moonlight gilded her face and hair with silver and he had a moment where he could see what waited in his future, where he knew what she would look like in his bed forty years from now. *Cannot fucking wait*, he thought, breaking free from his stillness, exhaustion fleeing as he stalked towards her, shedding clothing as he did so.

Three days was too long to be away, and he had scarcely pointed Fury towards the guest room before abandoning him with a brusque, "There's food in the kitchen. Help yourself. Don't scare the boy in the morning." Then, his long strides brought him here, to her room...their room from here on out. Folding his cut, he glanced for a long moment at the new, barely broken-in bottom rocker spelling out 'Nomad,' telling everyone who saw him he had permission to roam.

Looking back over at the bed, he saw the glint of Brenda's eyes and knew she was awake, watching him. When he had called to tell her he would be late, in response to the news he was riding his bike back, she had simply told him, "Come home to me." Now, as he undressed in the darkness, he smiled at the memory because her saying those words had fattened his cock, made him swell with desire. Something he hadn't tried to hide from his brothers there in the bar, knowing the want each man would have inside him for something like what Duck had. The want for a woman in their bed like the one warming his mattress right now. *Mine*, he thought, as he slid in between the sheets beside her.

"Hey, Duck," she whispered, and he thrilled again at her instinctive use of his name, pleasure coiling deep inside his chest. He reached out, running his hand up from her hip and realized the concealing covers were the only thing on her.

"Little Bee. My beautiful, bare darlin', did ya miss me?" He leaned in and brushed his lips across hers, gratified when she shifted closer to him, her hand sliding up his bicep to curl around his shoulder, pulling him in. He slipped his hand down her side, over her bottom, tucking in between her legs to find a wash of wetness there. Curling his fingers around her pussy, he pushed with his thigh, feeling her legs part with willing swiftness. "Aw, yeah," he whispered against her lips, eating down her moan before deepening the kiss. "I can tell you did."

***

Sitting with Watcher at a table in the Soldiers' bar the next afternoon, Duck was waiting for Fury to show so he could introduce them. He and Watcher had spent the last half hour talking about the increasing issues with coyotes Brenda had noted; their mutual hatred of slavers giving them a reason to want to stop any trafficking running through the area.

There was a noise in the bar behind Duck and he stilled, his eyes fixed on Watcher. The Soldiers didn't have any mirrors on the wall and his position at this table placed him with his back squarely to the room, leaving him blind for all intents and purposes. Entirely dependent on his friend to warn him of any incoming trouble. The trust implied when he accepted the offered seat had been acknowledged by an approving nod; that nod recognizing the burden of faith in its own way.

"What the fuck?" Watcher muttered, but the corners of his mouth turned up so Duck knew it was friend and not foe approaching. Twisting in his chair, he draped his arm across the back of it and then pushed off it, standing with a grin on his face.

"Fuck, yeah. Fury showed, finally," he muttered, taking a single step back to allow Watcher to greet the new arrival first. Protocol demanded he give way in the Soldiers' bar, even if the man walking their way was one of his own patch brothers.

"You're Fury? Fuckin' kidding me?" Watcher called his questions, holding out a welcoming hand. Duck looked at the extended palm, frowning. If Fury wasn't known to Watcher then the gesture was odd. Very odd. And if Fury was known, then why was he here to conduct introductions in a way to give respect to both men? The redheaded biker stopped in front of Watcher and stood for a minute ignoring the offering, stood silent before he shook his head and laughed, reaching instead to pull the big man into a hug, stepping back after a moment with one arm still slung over his shoulders. Turning to grin at Duck, Fury nodded as he tightened his arm powerfully, pulling and trapping Watcher's head to his side. With rough knuckles, he scrubbed Watcher's scalp to the accompaniment of cussing and writhing. Watcher snarled, "Goddammit, Gabe, let me the fuck go." *Gabe?*

With a grin, Fury released his captive who stood upright, slowly rubbing the top of his head. Glancing around the bar, Fury seemed unconcerned for any offense he might have caused with his behavior and Duck held his breath, waiting for the response because this could go very badly for both of them. "Cuz," Fury said, drawling out the word. "Nice place." He nodded and grinned at Duck, warmly calling, "Brother, good fucking mattress, man. I slept like a baby."

Stepping away from Watcher, Fury gave the man his back as he extended a hand towards Duck. *Gave the man his back* as if they were patch brothers standing around a fucking bonfire. Every action shouted trust and comfort built from long association, but he was beyond pushing the boundaries of what was acceptable between clubs.

Reaching out to grasp the offered palm, Duck used the grip to yank Fury close. As he fisted his fingers in the cut on the man's back, he muttered into his ear, "This would appear the exact opposite to fostering good relations, *brother*. Wanna explain what the *fuck* you think you're doing?"

Shouted laughter gusted past his ear and Fury pulled back, turning to face a grinning Watcher. *What. The. Fuck.*

"Watch...Michael," Fury called, "you keepin' secrets, cuz?"

***

"Tell me about your folks," Duck said, giving Brenda a squeeze with the arm he had draped around her shoulders. They were reclining on the couch in the living room, TV on but neither was watching it, more interested in each other than anything the talking heads had to say. Fury was in a chair to one side, eyes to his phone but Duck saw his chin lift at the question and knew he was listening.

"My aunt and uncle? You knew them. You spent as much time at our place as you could." She reached up, linking her fingers through his where they wrapped around, holding his arm in place.

"Not them, your mom and dad. You didn't talk about them much growing up. Where did you live before you came to Texas?" She had been young when she moved in with her aunt and uncle, and he had always assumed a tragedy brought her here, but wasn't sure.

"Mom and Dad died in a car wreck. I was just little. I came to live with Mom's sister here. She had left Kentucky before I was born, so the first time I ever saw my aunt was in the hospital." Brenda had gone still, locked into her head and he shook her slightly.

He asked, "Hospital?"

"Yeah, I was in the car. It went off the side of a mountain, into the trees." She gave a heavy sigh, followed by a softer one. These thoughts held sadness for her. "I have some memories of the wreck. Not much, mostly just noise and smells. They don't know who found me, the nurses at the hospital wrote out reports that one minute the hallway was empty, and then the next, I was lying there on a gurney with a note pinned to my coat telling the police where to find the car."

"Where in Kentucky?" The question surprised both of them, and Duck swung his gaze to see a suddenly attentive Fury completely focused on Brenda.

"Eastern, I was born in Cynthania. My folks are buried on Mom's family's place in Lair. My aunt married a military man, moved out here." She cocked her head to one side, asking, "Why?"

"I'm Kentucky raised and bred. Born in Louisiana, but I lay strongest claim to my mountain roots," Fury responded. "You were Harrison County. I grew up just over the mountain in Robertson. So did Watcher. What year was the accident?"

"Nineteen eighty-four," she responded quietly and Duck squeezed her tight for a moment.

"I was twelve," he said, his tone musing. "You would have been what, three...four?"

"Six. I was six," she whispered and Fury's gaze sharpened, taking in whatever he saw on Brenda's face.

"I've lost folks too, gal. Close ones; early. Sucks, but you got through it, found a good life." Turning his head, he swung his gaze around the room before coming back to Brenda to say, "Good for you." The mood in the room shifted, becoming oppressive as Fury looked away. "Need to call Watch." Moving abruptly, Fury slapped his knees before he stood and turned to walk towards the mudroom. Duck and Brenda sat there silently as the echo of the door slamming behind him rolled through the house.

Within a day, Fury seemed to settle into a comfortable routine, communicating through contacts provided by the Soldiers' to set post-rodeo meetings with various clubs in the area. Duck let him deal with that while he worked, laboring side-by-side with Brenda, getting final details into place for the rodeo. In the evening, both men sat in the barn office, organizing the guard duties it would take to safeguard the Rebel visitors headed into town, ensuring everyone was covered. Fury talked to Watcher to lock down the assistance his Soldiers were comfortable providing. Time was ticking forwards, the measurement of hours and minutes passing unrelenting in its movement.

Everything was falling into place. Smooth and sweet, slotting together like a puzzle that wanted to be solved.

***

Mason chuckled as he disconnected the call from Duck, thinking to himself that his choice of men to send with his brother was fortunate. *How in the hell did I not know Gabe was one of the Robertson County Ledbetter boys?* From talking to Duck, it didn't sound as if Watcher had been aware of Fury's identity either. Not until the man walked through the doorway and into the Soldiers' bar. Blood to one of his closest friends. The knowledge sat easy on his shoulders, making it seem as if fate had pulled the man's chapter into the fold, bringing Fury to the Rebels.

Watcher's girl

LAS CRUCES, NEW MEXICO. THREE O'CLOCK IN THE AFTERNOON, MOUNTAIN TIME ZONE

"Where the hell could she be?" Duck muttered the question into the stillness of the truck cab, turning the wheel to steer around another corner. "A-fucking-lone out here, no backup, nobody around. Club calls, you deal, man." He scanned up the street, noting the make and model of the vehicles parked along the curb. *Fury'll have your six,* he thought. *Sure, he will. He's got to fucking be present to win that position, for sure.* He shook his head at his thoughts, twisting in the truck seat to look between buildings as he passed by another alley, rolling slowly so as not to miss anything.

Isabella Otey, Watcher's daughter, was missing. Nearly an adult, she wasn't a risk as a runaway, so the unspoken fear was business. The kind of business that sucked in innocents. From the look of things, she had been plucked from her off-campus apartment, her bedroom undisturbed by any violence. Reports said the space was devoid of any clues, silent except for a song left playing on repeat. That song seeming to be a message, a familiar tune by Occupy Yourself about how family could poison and hurt you called, "Is It The Blood."

Her disappearance wasn't found, so much as reported. Watch got a call from Estavez, president of the Machos, who had gotten a call from a gypsy Outriders member, who had received a call from who the fuck knew. It was like a sick game of telephone, with the end result being the knowledge that Isabella was gone, and their most likely suspect was Lalo.

A Diamante nomad, he was a man well known for his brutality, who seemed to have sucked at the teat of the devil himself, absorbing lessons of cruelty while he developed a taste for blood. Watcher's first call had been to Mason, who sent texts to Duck and Fury while still on the phone with his friend. They were the only Rebels within hailing distance of the Soldiers' stomping grounds and had the best chance of helping until Mason could get here. Clubs all over the region had rolled out, looking for Isabella.

As Duck drove from Lamesa, Myron called, having picked up electronic chatter from two sources. Those leads pulled the club's assistance in different directions. One was Memphis, where some dirty business had been conducted not long ago. Rebel members headed there as fast as their wheels could take them. Other brothers had been dispatched out of Little Rock, the intent to back up and support the Memphis chapter, and also to keep an eye on the men patched into that house. Memphis shit was dark these days, and there was damn little trust going their direction.

Fury remained in Lamesa, his orders clear: Protect the prince. Chase was already in the air at the time, far too late to turn him around, so he would be met in Midland and taken to where he could be secured in Lamesa.

Duck was in Las Cruces, having driven the 350 miles as fast as possible, making the trip in just under four hours from when he left. Now he was circling the area Myron had directed him towards, looking for anything out of place.

Brenda had been with him when he got the text, and stared at him with wide eyes while, on the move, he explained what was going on and why he had to leave. She had told him, "Of course, go. Go, baby. God, how scared she must be. Find her." Pressing a hard kiss to her mouth, he had jumped into the truck and headed off, earpiece in place so Myron, who was organizing the Rebel rollout, could talk to him.

Which lead his thoughts back to here, now, where he wasn't finding anything to indicate the girl was close. "You're sure you got a ping from here?" For what seemed the hundredth time, he asked the question, hearing background chatter over the line for a moment before Myron responded.

"Yes, her phone records show it logged towers in that area at least three hours before the first anonymous call came in." Patient with the repeated questions, Myron repeated himself, then said, "Hold on, I got Pinto." The line buzzed and hummed, on hold.

Twisting in the other direction, Duck looked up a street, seeing more fences, more metal buildings, more loading docks, and a fucking lot of more nothing. Circling the block again, he instinctively slowed when he approached and passed a parked police car, and then shook himself when he remembered it had been there on his last circuit, too. Looking at it in the rearview mirror, he braked gently, gliding the truck to a stop while he stared, trying to decide what had caught his attention. The noise in his ear stopped, and he noted distractedly that, like it had on his last circuit of this block, his call with Myron must have dropped. *Dead zone*, he thought.

Parked halfway between two buildings, the car looked relatively clean and free of the ever present dust blown in by the desert winds. But, now that the sun had shifted, shadows sliding backwards into the artificial crevasse between the structures, he could see only half the car was clean. Subject to some bizarre cleaning process, the front half looked to have been dusted. Perhaps in an attempt to make it look like the car hadn't been sitting for long, the illusion destroyed by the thick layer of grime and dirt covering the back window and trunk. He wondered, *Why in the hell would anyone clean an abandoned car?*

Pulling away from the curb, he glanced one more time at the car in the mirror. *Why would anyone clean an abandoned* cop *car?* To make it look like this was a protected area, maybe. To keep unwanted eyes away from the buildings it was set to guard? Whipping the steering wheel to the left, he turned the truck around, the passenger side wheels careening up and down as he ran over the curb and braked hard, springs rocking as the chassis shifted. *Something isn't right*, he thought, sitting in the stopped truck, staring at the car.

Easing ahead, he drove until he stopped directly in front of the car. Studying it, he saw the lights on top weren't attached, just laid up there for looks. Something to make the façade more believable. *Someone is definitely hiding something*, he thought, opening his door and stepping out into the arid heat of Las Cruces, thumb tapping the screen on his phone. He frowned and shoved it in his pocket when the beep-beep-beep tones of no service sounded in his ear.

***

LAMESA, TEXAS. FOUR O'CLOCK IN THE AFTERNOON, CENTRAL TIME ZONE

Brenda sat on the top rail of the corral, attempting to take her mind off where Duck had gone by watching her son working with the young stud colt entrusted to him. Movements slow and self-assured, he approached the skittish horse, soft words flowing from his mouth like water in a river. The patter was instinctive and probably not something he was even aware of, but she watched, amused as the horse's attention remained focused on the young boy edging into his space.

The colt wore nothing but a halter. Eli's intent for today's lesson made clear by the lead rope he held loosely coiled in his hands. She grinned as he slipped one hand into the front pocket of his jeans, coming out with what looked like a piece of candy. She briefly wondered if he had pulled this trick before, but the colt's focused attention at the crinkle of the plastic wrapper answered her question.

She smiled when the horse zeroed in on Eli's palm, neck stretching out and nose pointing to where the red-and-white sweet balanced, cupped slightly as proof against fumbling lips. When the colt pulled back, teeth clacking together as it enthusiastically crunched the candy, she saw the lead rope now dangled from beneath the horse's jaw, attached to the halter without the animal's knowledge. *Ninja boy*, she thought.

Eli turned slightly and stepped back, hand going into his pocket again, the movement of his mouth never slowing as he talked sweet and low to the colt. The lead rope went taut between the horse and boy just as the next piece of candy made its appearance, the tug of the rope barely noticed by the colt in its efforts to get to the sweet part of the exercise again.

***

FORT WAYNE, INDIANA. FIVE O'CLOCK IN THE AFTERNOON, EASTERN TIME ZONE

Mason's bike skidded to a stop in the parking lot of the hospital, the rear wheel barking as it locked and slid, leaving black marks in its wake. He parked and dismounted at a run, heart thudding in his chest, choking the breath in his throat. Willa's water had broken. He was at the clubhouse with Chase, then on the phone with Watcher then Myron, and he had missed her calls. Three hours she had been here by herself while he was taking care of club business. *Fuck.*

Stopping his headlong run just outside the entrance, he took in two deep breaths, blowing them out and trying to compose himself. "Fuck," he hissed, shaking his head hard. Then chin up, shoulders back, he strode into the lobby of the hospital and over to the elevators, steps still quick but controlled. Stifling a laugh when a nurse scurried out of the car, opting for the stairs rather than ride with him, he glanced at the only other occupant, a doctor. Clad in a white coat, the man looked familiar. *Fuck*, Mason thought, *could be anybody. I ain't no stranger to the med units in any city where I have a charter.*

Then the doc opened his mouth and Mason knew for sure he knew him.

"How's your man going?"

Aussie accents weren't something often heard in northern Indiana, and pair that with him being a physician and it was an even rarer combination. This was the doc who had treated Bear when they brought the man home from California with a punctured and deflated lung; an injury made worse by two flights, a significant change in altitude, and a delay in real treatment. The man had saved his brother's life and given Mason respect while doing it.

"Well. He's doing well. Nice of you to remember us." Mason nodded at him in the reflection of the inside doors.

"What's brought you back our way today?"

"Wife's in labor." Mason shivered silently, the phrase didn't come close to illustrating the terror running through his veins right now, but taciturn was the way to go with any authorities, even the medical ones.

"Devil you say?" His face split into a broad smile. "First tyke?"

"For her." He shrugged. "For me, too, in some ways."

The elevator stopped and the doors opened, Mason and the doc both stepping off. Lifting a hand in farewell, Mason turned to the right and stopped dead. The corridor was filled with men, every back bearing his patch. Fear struck him hard at that moment, clutching tight around his heart, causing it to stutter and stop until the expression on the faces registered. Laughter and quiet conversations rolled up the hallway towards him, and he heard the doc behind him ask on a mutter, "Bloody hell, you always bring a crew of bikies?"

Making his way down the crowded hall, he didn't respond. Didn't stop to talk to anyone either, his steps falling faster as he got closer to what was clearly Willa's room. The door opened and two men walked out, but after a single glance, he ignored them to stare at the woman standing upright and supported between them.

Leaning lightly on Gunny's arm, Willa was shuffling on socked feet into the hallway, her other hand clutching the edges of her robe together in the front. Her eyes were closed, but he could hear her muttering a slow singsong cadence, "Left-o, right-o, lefty, mighty, here we go and, keep up tidy," in time to her steps.

From behind him, he heard a loud, "How're you going?" Twisting to see the doc crowding him, he realized the white coat had addressed Bear, the other man standing beside his Willa. "You look a damn sight betta than I last seen ya." Bear nodded at the doc noncommittally, and Mason stared at them both for a moment until he saw the doc's features flash white in the light of the hall.

"Bloody hell," the doc whispered, eyes now fixed on Gunny's face. "I fucking know you. Never met a man survived worse. Bloody...Holy Mackerel. Never thought I'd see you again." Reaching around Mason, he shoved out a hand and Gunny silently gripped it. "I'm bloody glad to, though."

"Mason," he heard Willa's whispered call and moved to her side, replacing Gunny's support of her with his own, placing his arms around her. They stood there silently, him wrapped around her, surrounded by two dozen men he trusted with his life. He held her without care for his own safety because he knew every member in the room had his back. He breathed in her scent, the light vanilla musk she preferred, and closed his eyes, resting his cheek on top of her head. "I was afraid you wouldn't make it." Her whisper cut at him, the wound unintentional, because she would have understood, did understand so much more than she ever should have to.

Instead of telling her it was a near thing, or telling her Watcher's Bella was missing, he reassured her, "Of course I made it, babe. Ain't gonna miss this one's entrance to the world. I'm here."

That became the theme of the night, just his quietly voiced reminder, often spoken, reassuring her. "I'm here." Even in the controlled chaos of the delivery room, a place he had visited once before, but this the first time for a child of his own, he told her with each touch, each caress, and each tender kiss that he was there with her. Body and soul.

Later, after her hard work was done and he had been assured everyone was healthy, he stood holding his son and gazing down at Willa as she lay exhausted, sound asleep. Staring for a long time, he allowed his eyes to trace her serene features; her face, so well-known by now, relaxed and peaceful as she rested. Then, he looked back down at the babe in his arms. Eyes more infant blue than gray stared up at him, and the lips of his child pursed and moved in imitation of the nursing he would be doing again soon. *My child. My son.*

With a soft smile curling the corners of his mouth, Mason stared down at his son, his gaze going to his wife as she stirred in the bed. A woman he had fought to hold, had struggled to bring back to herself, encouraging her, reassuring her with every step that he was in this with her, side-by-side. *Mine. Worth every moment, every effort. My Willa*, he thought and found himself easily able to define the feeling flooding him. Love.

Three hours

Something doesn't add up, Duck thought, pacing off the dimensions of the room again. The cop car had been the first clue, and then he'd found the building next to it filled with a dozen other puzzles he had to piece together. False trails, red herrings to pick through to find the ones with real importance. The ones that didn't scream 'Look At Me.' The office for the storage facility, which on the surface seemed unremarkable, but once he was inside, things felt...off. Nothing obvious. Just *off* in a way he couldn't define, but which set his nerves on edge, so he *had* to pay attention.

The room looked like it had recently been occupied by a tidy squatter, which was an oxymoron in his book. Dirty towels were neatly folded in one corner of the room, laid on top of a cushion taken from the couch. Newspapers disassembled, the parts reassembled into piles of similar assortments. Section ones, section twos, and advertising sections, all piled into squares. The papers, torn but tidy, arranged randomly on the floor along one long wall. Ripped and sagging furniture squared with the straight lines of the walls, impotent lamps precisely lined up with the center of the tables, electric cords stretched out on the floor, ends plugged into nothing.

Pegboards on one wall held row upon row of keys, at first glance giving the impression of random arrangement. Upon closer inspection, if paying attention, it was possible to see the groupings matched the furniture in this room and the adjacent one.

Duck was paying close attention. Absolute attention.

Three keys together represented a couch, another similar set stood for the desk. Even the towels were accounted for, the jumbled piles of paper. Everything just right, even the things which should be wrong...too much so to be randomly arranged.

Empty lines of pegs were the walls, straight and in place. All but one. One of them was misplaced. So, he paced off the distance, counting, pacing, and repeating.

He stood, first looking at the peg wall, then swinging to look at the room. If the arrangement of the keys matched the contents of the room, with the groupings arranged to scale, and those empty lines of pegs were walls...then one of the walls he was looking at in the room didn't exist, and there were about eight missing feet from that side of the room.

Making his way along the wall, he thumped with his fist, feeling stupid. This wasn't a fucking TV show where he would miraculously find a hidden door leading to the evil mastermind's torture chamber. It was a fucking storage unit rental place in fucking Las Cruces, and he was an unemployed enforcer for a fucking motorcycle club, not a goddamned detective.

He paused his advance, thumping hard against the same place on the wall, then moved his hand down a foot and thumped again. It sounded different, hollow. Running his fingers along the surface, he found a ripple, an unevenness in the drywall. Bending over, he looked closely, fingers and eyes working together to find a seam, a well-hidden join in the surface he could trace with his thumbnail. Reaching down further, he trailed his fingers across the bottom of the wall where it stood on the floor. There was a cool draft there, blowing outward across his skin. *What the fuck?*

Down on his knees now, feeling like time was stretching around him as his blood ran cold, he realized the wall was not for support. No, not this wall. It was hiding something, he just had to find out how to get into the space behind it, find out what it was sheltering. Fingernails scrabbling along the floor, finding no purchase, but that draft of air remained fresh and steady, taunting him with the sure knowledge that *something* was there. Remembering the kitchen cabinets in his grandmother's house, he found one edge of the wall section and used the tips of all four fingers and his thumb to push in. *Click.* The top corner sagged out, and he quickly repeated the motion on the bottom corner. *Click.*

Shuffling backwards, he rocked back over his heels, still on his knees as he stared at the opening. It was small, only about three-foot square. Small enough you would have to crawl through it, small enough to feel tight in ways that were uncomfortable. Constricting access, it would expose you as you entered, seemingly a contradiction. It gaped open a few inches on its own, the dark sliver appearing along the vertical edge beckoning to him. *I feel like Alice, only I don't have any fucking dope to make me smart*, he thought, reaching out with one shaking hand and easing the door open. Heavy; his hands and arms felt like they weighed a thousand pounds and he was filled with heart-pounding terror at what he would find. *I've got to be smart. Something isn't right. I need to find it, figure it out.*

No doubt now this was a door, and—*thank God*—the smell rolling through the opening was sweet, not a stench to roll your stomach. No, this smelled of rich earth, dug deep, well-watered and fertile. Vaguely chemical laden, but not overwhelming. Glancing around behind him one last time at what he now realized was a waiting room—a holding cell for would-be rescuers—from this new angle he saw there was a medium-sized something shoved underneath the couch.

He scrambled, making his way quickly over there, dragging out a worn and weathered canvas bag. Not locked, not zipped, just the placket folded over the open top. Easy entry. Without thinking, he reached blindly inside the bag, fingers fumbling, finding a cold, metal cylinder and another object, warmer wood. He gaped the mouth of the bag open, gripped the metal and pulled out a flashlight, and then looked inside to see a small tool, like a child's garden spade. Wood and steel pretending to be a useful thing, more of an excuse to spend time with someone who loved gardening. Someone who loved to dig in the dirt, running fingers through loamy soil, finding treasures to share with a little one in the form of wiggling worms and tightly curled grubs.

Reaching in for the tiny spade, he heard a crinkle and stretched the opening of the bag wider, looking inside again. A piece of paper. He was unfolding it when his phone rang, the sound inside his head startling because he had forgotten about the earpiece. Reaching up to tap the button, he straightened the last fold to read the words just as he heard Myron's voice say, "Pinto's got squat. You find anything, Duck?"

Eyes fixed on the paper in his hand, he didn't answer for a moment, pulse jolting erratically, his breathing coming faster the longer he knelt there, reading and rereading the oh-so-brief message written in bold stripes of black ink. Absence scrawled in loops and swirls; lack as promise. He could feel the words' weight through the paper, the pen having impressed deeply on the material, nearly punching through in some places. Unreadable Braille. Handwriting, small and cramped, even and unhurried. The author took their time with no fear of discovery, no need to rush. One more piece of the riddle to toss down, clues gobbled up by Duck's brain like bread on the shore of a pond.

As if from far away, he heard Myron's voice barking a question, "Duck, you there, brother?" Duck sucked in a harsh breath, then another, Myron evidently hearing that because he shouted, "Brother, talk to me. Tell me. What the fuck's going on?"

"I got her." There was a sudden increase of noise on the phone but he couldn't focus on that. It didn't come close to hitting the scale for attention. "I got her." He sucked in a breath. "Jesus." Another breath, urgency pounding through his veins. "I don't got her, but I got her. I gotta go. I gotta get her, brother. Get someone here, Myron. *Fuck*, get them here. I gotta get to work. She ain't gonna die, man. Not like that. Not alone, not like this." He didn't wait for Myron's response, disconnecting the call. He knew the man could track the device within a three-foot radius, and also knew his brother would spin up help just as fast as he could fucking dial it in.

Looking down at the joke of a spade in his hand, he stared at it for a moment as panic and adrenaline fought for dominance within his chest, and then he worked hard to stifle it. Successfully forced it all down, shoving it deep as he shifted his gaze back to the paper.

You coming in shut down her air. She's got three hours.

Taped to the paper below the message was a picture of a young Mexican woman with light blonde hair. She lay contorted, legs curved tight to her body, curled up on a rag of a blanket. Taken through a pane of reinforced glass dividing the area in the picture into two spaces, the photo showed her position was reminiscent of the human remains in Pompeii, mummified by the volcanic eruption of Vesuvius. Lying on her side, arms tucked in front of her face, hands wedged underneath her head. With dark bruising on her jaw and cheek, she was isolated in a glass cage, waiting.

Fuck.

Spade clutched tightly in one hand, he took a picture of the paper with his phone, then texted it to Myron. He took another picture of the doorway, then one of the room in general, sending those on their electronic way as well. He set a timer, and then shoved the phone deep into his pocket and crawled towards the opening, dragging the canvas bag behind him.

Flipping on the flashlight, he shone it into the dark recesses of the area hidden by the false wall to find his nose hadn't misled him. The floor behind the wall was dirt, loose and dark, damp with water, it spread evenly from wall to wall, the space about eight-feet wide and fifteen-feet long. On the far end, a pipe stuck up from the dirt, pale and bone white in the glow cast by the flashlight. Vent. Air. Silent. **You coming in shut down her air.**

Before going another inch, he impatiently scanned the area for traps, not trusting his senses which were telling him nothing was waiting. His muscles screamed for him to move, to get started, but he had to be sure there weren't any more pieces to unravel. That there weren't things lying along the path to trip him up, because he couldn't make a misstep here. This was coloring within the lines, faced with an unthinkable consequence if he got it wrong. Scanning one last time, he knew there was nothing. No snares. This wasn't a ruse. There was nothing to be found except the one thing he couldn't wrap his head around. Nothing except a girl who would die if he didn't dig her up in time. *Think*, he raged at himself. *Think, you bastard*.

He knew the vent wouldn't be by the entrance to the buried cell, it would be in the room with the girl. His brain shifted into a higher gear, thoughts racing as he tracked down the facts, lining them up like the pegs on that goddamned board in the waiting room. Jumping from clue to clue, leapfrogging past only to circle back to be certain.

The girl will be behind the glass and away from the door, contained so the motherfucker can come and go without worrying about her escaping. The door will be behind the glass from the girl. Farthest end from the vent. Nearest the crawl through.

Bringing the paper up again, he shone the light on it, looking at the picture, studying it.

She's got three hours.

Isabella was young. Not yet twenty, she stood five foot six, weighed about a hundred forty. *Look at the space she takes up*, he thought, *look at the space around her.* From what he could see in the image, that made her end of the room about five-foot square, because while she had curled into a tight ball, trying hard to protect herself by presenting a smaller target, him knowing her stats meant he could gauge the room size.

He glanced back at the peg wall, studying the just-right way things were lined up. Precisely arranged. Organized. Controlled. *Motherfucker likes things symmetrical.* Knowing that about her abductor, looking at the picture, knowing how big her space was, he knew the whole set-up would be a rectangle, knew it would be five by ten, or there about. Broken cement showed where the foundation had been removed, and he looked around at the dirt floor then up at the grooved, metal walls, gauging the size of the empty, barren space between the four walls in front of him.

Eight foot by fifteen foot.

The math was easy, easiest part of this whole fucking puzzle. Give it five square for the prison, five square for observation. The still-silent vent was set out about two feet from the far wall. That would put the front of the room at least three feet from the crawl through on this end. He drew a mental line.

Foot and a half out from either side to find the edges of the space, dropping into the middle would put him four feet from the long wall nearest him. Then, checking the angle, he looked at a spot three feet from the end nearest him, noting where it intersected the other line. That was where he would start, and fuck him if he was wrong. Fuck him. If he got it wrong and killed her with his stupidity. *Fuck.* If he was wrong.

Think.

Go over it again. She couldn't afford for him to be wrong. He couldn't be wrong, so he wouldn't be.

Spend two minutes of her three hours to make sure you don't fuck this up.

He looked down at the ridiculous fucking spade nearly swallowed in his hand, and then back out over the expanse of dirt. Seeing, but not seeing, instead, he saw her bruised face, eyes closed in a mockery of rest, curled up protectively, fending off her demons. The demon who'd brought her here and laid hands on her. Made her life a fucking puzzle to be solved. Her survival a fucking game. He saw Watcher's face as he looked when talking about his family, lines softening, and voice taking on an indulgent tone when he spoke about his girl. She was loved. Smart, sassy, cute, and loved. Watcher's princess, his treasure. And someone was trying to steal that away.

Please, God, don't let me be wrong.

If he was wrong, she would pay the price. If he got any part of it wrong, Watcher would pay, too. He couldn't get it wrong.

Don't fuck this up.

***

"What the fuck is he doing just sitting there?" The clearly frustrated question hit the quiet air of the cheap motel room and Lalo jerked, frowning at his cousin seated on the foot of the bed. They had both been staring at the screen of the small laptop, the image dark and grainy because the quality of the cameras he could get on short notice wasn't great. Still unmoving, the video looked frozen, and his companion reached out, thumping the side of the computer.

I need you to shut it, hermano. Don't wake me up.

"He read the letter. Don't he realize he's killin' the bitch?"

The window unit kicked on, noise of the air conditioner's compressor rattling and loud. Lalo shook his head, his own frustration rising, and not just with the half-breed man stuck in place on the screen. "Chismoso, *hermano.* Do me a favor. Shut the fuck up." Noise came from the computer and he turned, seeing the man was on the move, putting the bag and paper down inside the room with the furniture.

"About fucking time." Chismoso's mutter was quiet, but even quiet, it still was not what he had asked for so Lalo's arm shot out, the back of his hand connecting hard with the back of the man's head. "Ow, fucker." Chismoso reached up, rubbing hard as he twisted his neck to glare at Lalo.

Lalo bared his teeth as he looked back at the computer, watching as Reuben Nelms, otherwise known as Duck, got up on the soles of his feet, creeping into the space Lalo privately called the graveyard. *Duck walking, ha.* If the man dug in the wrong places, he would find more than the box, but Lalo suspected Duck's focus would be solely on getting to the girl, meaning he would be unlikely to go investigating the corners and shadows.

Edwardo Suches, Lalo, was in the middle of a war he had not wanted. He'd tried hard as fuck to avoid it, but it dogged his heels across the states. He had always been good at puzzles, good at working through challenges of growing up in the *barrio*. Watching and learning from the men who fell around him, not making their deadly mistakes. Navigating club politics was child's play compared to what he and Chismoso grew up with. Forced to adult roles early, they learned to dissect actions and intent in order to survive.

Lalo liked order, liked things to be the way he wanted them to lay out, so not being able to derail events of the past months fucked with him, fucked with his head until it was all he could think about. Fucked with his gut until he couldn't eat for trying to find a way out. Find a way he couldn't lay hand to, fucking assholes all wanted their piece of him. *Want their piece of me.* Only until they were done, and then they would be throwing him against the wall, pointing *their* piece at his head. Unless he drew on them first, then it would be his party again. *My piece, my party. Make it my party, fuck yeah.*

"Fuck them. All I wanted, needed was a small slice of the pie, but to get what I want means it had to be taken from someone. You know I'm right, cuz. You know." Lalo shook his head. "That someone was the Southern Soldiers, fucking short timer's MC that hasn't held this territory but for only a few years." Only a few years, not long at all in the life cycle of a club and he knew that well. *Some clubs have been in existence for decades, so Soldiers are short timers, hell yeah.* "Jumped-up upstarts, those motherfuckers in a fucking start-up club. Some of those clubs, the real ones, the ones we talk to, they've been around for longer than you and me have been *alive*." *Fuck them all.*

Vaguely he knew his fractured words couldn't make sense so he turned and, seeing Chismoso's eyes on him, nodded, assuming loyal agreement. "But the Soldiers won't give. They hold onto fucking everything with a fucking tight grip, like the idiots they are, thinking they can best me. *Me*. Lalo, president of the Las Cruces Diamante."

He frowned, studying the impassive face in front of him, again making an assumption of the thoughts rolling through his cousin's head. "Sure, I know what you're thinking, *cabron*. You're thinking the Diamante are another young club, birthed after the Soldiers, even. But, brother, we are strong. Strong with a long reach, each of our chapters boasts hundreds of members. And I'm proud to be part of this, part of everything. Proud of having expanded so fast most of the goddamned members didn't even know how many chapters there are from week to week." He fell silent, eyeing his blood cousin, watching as he turned away, attention back to the computer.

Chismoso was president of the Chicago chapter. His cousin was stupid but so fucking loyal, when Lalo wanted him pushed to the top, it was easy to convince the nationals it was a good move. Well, he had been president until not long ago, but that changed because the fucking chapter was no more. Folded. Shut down, just like the one in Las Cruces. Sorrow filled him as he thought, *My chapter.*

That led them here, because he needed to understand what the Soldiers had on him, on his club. He wanted to understand why they would collaborate with other clubs, but not his. No partnership extended, and the one he offered, not accepted. Thrown back like trash, a slap in the face. He knew his experience was limited. It was the only club he had ever known, but still, the Diamante were the shit. *We party like nobody's business.* His proud voice filled the room, "With pussy and blow in quantities to boggle the mind." They were strong, and there were a fucking lot of them. Every chapter a fucking arsenal. The club could roll a thousand from a single region, thousands from the entirety of the membership in the states.

But they couldn't fucking hold territory. They sat on some of the most lucrative places in the country and would spin up a charter piece, sit and ride that shit for a time, then it all fell to shit around them. Las Cruces, Chicago, Dallas, Kansas City, Memphis. "Memphis," he muttered, gaze glued to the screen, watching Duck easily maintain his balance even on the loosely packed dirt. Rebels had fucked his play there, hard.

In Memphis, he had backed a drug dealer, Ling, into a corner, knowing the man couldn't hold his own against the Diamante. Then, before he could make his final move, had to stand in place and watch as the fucking Rebels rode into town and, "Fucked my play. Forget the fact they had a chapter there and didn't dare fuck with me. Wasn't until that man rode in from the Fort my shit got hot." He heard Chismoso make a sound of agreement, and closed his eyes, remembering the aftermath of the war Hoss had raged against Ling. "*Dios*, the smell. So much blood, I could have bathed in it."

That was his first real understanding how far the Rebels were willing to go. Their boundaries. "Everybody's got a weakness." They would kill foot soldiers, members who fought against them, even kill those in the know, but families? *Oh, hell no.* That particular collateral damage was to be avoided at all costs. "Righteous motherfuckers, thinking their shit don't stink." Families were in the know. They supplied the next generation of fighters, so victors in a war between clubs couldn't afford to leave anything behind. "Scorched earth." Not the Rebels, though. Even if it left enemies behind. *And the Rebels have enemies.* "They are my enemy." *So do I.* "Soldiers are my enemy." He needed information on the Southern Soldiers, needed to find out what made them tick in their heads. So, he looked for and found the weak link in the Soldiers' world. Daughter of the president. *Isabella.*

"Weak. So fucking weak." Lifting his chin, he reached out, tapping at the keyboard to change the view of the camera. "Broken in four days." The screen showcased the box where she lay along one wall, silent and still.

"Fucking waste," he muttered, cycling back through the views and then laughed aloud when he saw Duck's frustration with the tiny shovel they left him escalate in such a way he threw it hard against one wall of the open space. Tongue protruding from his mouth, lips pulled back from his teeth, Lalo laughed gutturally as he elbowed Chismoso hard, hearing a pained grunt, gaze fixed on Duck beginning to scoop dirt with his bare hands. "Told you he'd do it. Man's in the dirt now. Told you he'd take the bait and fuck-up hard. *Aaiieeee!* Sumbitch's gonna hurt in the mornin'. Dig for that gold, motherfucker. Dig in that dirt."

Chismoso rubbed his ribs and scoffed, saying, "Supposing he lives that long."

"Truth." He cycled through the views again, stopping on the girl.

Isabella. Useless bitch, she didn't know anything. Even after he broke her, getting her to talk freely, it wasn't long, not but a few minutes before he knew she didn't know shit. "Waste." Nothing at all about the club, her *papá* kept her clear of any questionable shit. "Wanted a different life for his baby girl, no doubt. Club's not good enough." Then after a while, she just...shut down. Empty eyes, he knew from the look that she had vacated her own fucking head. *Useless waste of my time, all of it.*

Then he got the call telling him the Soldiers had enlisted Rebel help. Fucking *Mason*. "Fucking asshole," he muttered, gaze still glued to the screen. Rebels were the club the Soldiers wouldn't abandon, the support line they held tight to, even when Diamante pressured them hard. "Duck's a fucking *Rebel*, *güey*. What the fuck is he doing in Lamesa?" Soldiers had a chapter in Lamesa. Stood to reason the Rebels were looking towards what would always be his patch of dirt. *Las Cruces. My fucking chapter.* "Time to teach them a lesson."

So he'd made a plan. Put that plan into play, and waited. Took fucking forever for them to get a clue, and when they did, it took another fucking forever for them to find the right location. Half the club was east, half the club was north, and he got one fucking guy who had a fucking brain and found his puzzles...solvable. One fucking guy, and it was goddamned fucked-up the one guy was Duck. Fucking Rebel, the only one with his head outta his ass. Soldiers were worse than useless; they had all left the fucking country as far as he could tell, crawling up the cartel's ass down in Juarez.

"He's too far out," Chismoso said. "Wanna call him and tell him he's fucking up? Tell him she gonna die if he don't get himself straightened out?"

Lalo laughed, the shrill sound echoing off the walls. "Rich, brother." Holding thumb and pinky to his head he pretended to talk into a phone, affecting a high-pitched, mocking voice. "Uh, yeah. Duck? Yeah. Hey man, uh, uh, hey...how you doin'?" He paused, then said, "Good, good. That's real good. Here's the deal. Uh, yeah. You're in the wrong spot, man. Shift two feet west and then a foot north. That should do it. Got it? Oh, yeah, you betcha. Happy to help." His voice changed back to normal and he dropped his hand as he continued, "Fucking rich, 'mano. Sure, call him up and help him solve it. Fuck you."

Chismoso twisted, looking at him. "You want the girl to die?" He seemed shocked by this, but he hadn't been there for hours upon hours. Stalled for days, waiting for the right time to talk to her. Putting his own life on hold only to find out she wasn't worth the air he had pumped into her cell.

Lalo sucked his bottom lip into his mouth and bit down hard, mouth stretching into a smile around the pain as he shrugged. "No skin, brother. My give a fuck done got up and gone. I just wanna watch the show now." He leaned close to the man, knowing his breath would be touching skin when he hissed, "So you wanna shut...the fuck...up...so I can fucking watch the fucking show?" Eyes rolling in his head, Chismoso nodded, and Lalo returned the motion, leaning back and looking at the screen.

Knuckles rapped hard on the wooden frame of the door and the bed moved as Chismoso got to his feet. Lalo didn't turn from the scene playing out on the computer screen as he called loudly, his intended audience on the other side of a thin wooden door. "Zip your fucking lip this time. Talk to me and die, maggot."

He heard his cousin's laughter as Chismoso opened the door for their guest.

***

Straining to pull his burden up the sloping wall of dirt, he heard a shout. "Duck, where the fuck are you?" Arms wrapped around the lax body, he dug his heels into the loose dirt, shoving hard with his legs, gaining another six inches of progress.

"Here," he shouted, his voice stronger than he expected, ringing noisily off the enclosed space. "I'm here." The loudest sound he had heard for a while, hours. Four of them. Longest hours of his life. "Here!" he shouted again, hearing running feet approaching, then the scrape of someone falling to their knees and he knew they were in the opening to the office he had left standing wide behind him as he entered the false space.

"Need a rope," he called up, shifting and digging his feet in again, a little higher, using his thigh muscles to shove his way up towards the light coming in through the opening. "I got her, but can't get her out."

"*Bella*," Duck heard and clenched his eyes shut tight against the raw pain in her father's voice. "My Bella, Duck. Is she...my Bella."

"I got her, Watch. Get me a rope—" His shouted words interrupted by a body sliding feet first down the slope towards where they were wedged into place, then Watcher was beside them, reaching out to touch the chilled face of his daughter. "She's alive, Watch." He tried to reassure him but knew what the man was seeing, what he had seen when he finally broke through the locked and sealed prison, because just finding the hatch hadn't given him access. No, the sick fuck who set this up had made every step a fucking puzzle, one his exhausted brain nearly hadn't finished in time, her lips purple with cyanosis when the first hissing crack finally appeared in the glass.

Pale, too pale, even with smears of dirt staining her cheeks. She was badly dehydrated and in desperate need of fluids. He had run the timeline through his head so many times, trying to find her another hour...another minute. He knew everything by heart. Gone at least two days before she was reported, but he now expected they would find it was longer. Then another two days before he found her. Drove like a bat out of hell to get here, and then he'd circled this area of town for more than a day before he realized the cop car was a decoy, a ruse to keep intruders at bay. No food, no water—she was in a bad way.

Still breathing, the thought ran through his head and he began the process of handing her off to Watcher. "She's alive."

A rope snaked down and he caught it with one hand, tugging another few feet of slack from it before he told Watcher, "Hold still. Let me tie this around her shoulders. You can steady her while we pull her out, brother." Matching actions to words, he wove the rope between the bodies of father and daughter, bringing it underneath her arms and efficiently tying it off between her shoulder blades.

Without her body weighing him down, Duck quickly scrambled up the slope, trying to minimize the dirt scattered down onto Watcher and Bella. When he slid at one point, dirt disappearing from underneath his boot, his heart pounded in terror as he prayed for the thousandth time the walls would hold, wouldn't collapse. He reached the top and his gaze followed the rope to a dozen men he didn't know. *Don't matter*, he thought, turning to shout back down, "We're pulling now, you shout out if you need us to stop, Watcher. Got me?"

There was an assenting noise and he turned back to the men, saw the rope held loosely in several pairs of hands. In a low tone, he told them, "We pull slow and steady. I've got it tied snug, but not too tight. If he loses hold of her, it could slip off. Make sure he doesn't lose her." More men moved into place, readying themselves. Pulling the flashlight from his hip pocket, he tossed it to an older man wearing a VP patch, the other side of his vest bearing a name patch reading, 'Pops.' With a nod, Pops caught the light, and then wordlessly stepped over to an area of undisturbed dirt, shining the light into the hole.

Nearly ten feet deep, it was only about a yard wide and angled steeply down to where there was metal showing. The container had a hatch on the top, and Duck's first contact had been a couple of feet away from that hatch. His first attempt at a course correction had been a misjudgment in the wrong direction, but he had found it finally. Found it in time.

Taking a wrap around his bleeding and blistered hands with the rope, he grunted when the pain hit and then took a step backwards. One step and then another, leaning with all his strength against the pull as they dragged Isabella free from what could have been her grave. *Still breathing.*

Hands reaching far

Duck waved off the bottle of water someone tried to pass to him, only to have it shoved in his face again by the Soldiers' veep. Accepting it, he immediately dropped it to his lap, hissing at the pain in his hand. The Soldiers' medic was here, but Duck had refused treatment until the man could assure him Isabella was going to be okay.

Glancing across the room to where she lay on the couch, he watched as she stirred, her hands jerking in uncoordinated movements. *Bad way,* he thought. *She's in a bad fucking way.* His imagination superimposed Brenda's face on the girl, then Essa's, and then in rapid succession Lisa, Molly, Mica… Shaking his head hard, he forced those thoughts away, focusing on the single goodness. "I got her."

"Yeah, you did. Every man here thanks you, Duck. Big fucking marker. Anything. Anything you need, brother. Rest of your life." This came from Pops, his ass seated on the floor next to Duck, the false wall propping them both up. "How'd you see this place?"

"Things that didn't belong. Took me a while to see it, too fucking long. Too fucking long to scope it out, too long to figure it out, too fucking long to dig her out. Every step along the way, nearly too fucking long." He shifted, pulling his feet in, propping wrists on top of his bent knees so his ruined hands didn't touch anything.

"We were in Mexico." Pops offered this with a bleak fear threading through his voice like the sour smell from an abandoned freezer. Bitter and nasty and ruined. "Nothing here. Not her apartment. Not the compound. Not the ranch. Nothing. Not a damn thing, so we figured cartel. It's been a hard road cleaning them up these past years. Prez figured slippery as they are the cartel had grown another head, like a demon snake. Find it, chop it off, save Bella." He stopped to suck in a hard breath. "We weren't even here. Not even *here*, Duck. Nowhere close when Myron called. We'd committed every damn asset to Mexico."

One of the other men pointed to the ruins of a chair across the room. "What was that?"

"A tool." Duck shook his head, remembering his pounding terror as he worked with shaking hands to unthread nuts and screws, fingertips slick with blood. Black boots stomping and kicking, vicious and wild. "No fucking tools in the place. I didn't have time to look far, had nothing except a two-inch by four-inch piece of flat, thin metal in my hand. Every step a puzzle. From the outside, where the cop car was the first tell, to this room, where I found the dimensions didn't fit. The door, the bag, the prison. Everything a puzzle. Had to get it right, because *'You coming in shut down her air. She's got three hours.'* Had to get it right." His voice trailed off, and then he began again, needing to purge this, needing someone to know he had tried his hardest.

"I ran the numbers in my head, ran them again, and again. Fast as I could calculate, I tried to plot where the door would be. Then digging, I had to figure the degree of angle in my head, too, make sure I cleared the walls so they wouldn't collapse because I didn't have time to dig anything twice." He gestured with his hands, showing how he had moved the earth covering her prison. "Dirt loose enough so scooping it with my hands and arms was easier, then I realized it had some kind of shit mixed in. That's why it was wet. Fucking burned, but it didn't matter because she only had three hours."

He sucked a breath, blowing it out in a shaky wheeze. "Then two. Then one." He looked at the knees of his jeans, eaten through by whatever had been mixed with the dirt, the skin behind them eaten away, too, blood, dirt, and fabric mixing to a broken, crusted horror. He glanced over at Pops. "Make sure your man cleans her off, Pops. Watcher, too. This shit burns."

The steady pat-pat-pat of dripping blood caught his attention and he turned his hands over, frowning as he examined his knuckles, blood running across them freely, streaming from places where they were split to the bone. Purple and swollen, the fingers of his left hand were twisted in unnatural ways and he figured at least two of them were broken. Everywhere that didn't hurt or wasn't burning was soaked through with sweat. He shivered, a chill moving down his spine "Note said, *You coming in shut down her air.*' I had to keep going, keep digging. Had to get it right." *Fuck.*

"Found the hatch. Couldn't be so easy as to just walk in. No. But, I've seen this shit before, it's fucking Deacon's influence, man. A fucking slidey puzzle locked it. Like a puzzle box, only deadly instead of pretty. Once in the room, my phone wasn't any good, no signal at all and I didn't have time to truck up and down the hole to get in and out to call Myron. Nothing spare, not a moment, not even a movement. Just me. *You coming in shut down her air. She's got three hours.'* Just me."

He realized the room was silent and looked up to see nearly every face turned in his direction, Watcher's eyes fixed on him, medic still working on Isabella, one hand reaching upwards holding a saline bag, waiting on a willing hand to take it. "Help him," Duck demanded, motioning to the man and his words seemed to startle the Soldiers, two sets of quick hands colliding as they reached to take the IV bag from the medic. Duck nodded, satisfied, for now.

"Got that. One lock at a time, got it, opened the hatch and it fucking popped." He made a noise like pulling a cork out of a bottle. "Like I'd broken a vacuum seal. Two hours and forty-two minutes. Eighteen minutes left. The final door looked to be just that, a door, but it wasn't. The edges had been welded into place, the glass wall firmly built into the sides of the container. More of Deacon's influence, stretching far. Man's hands spanning so far to touch shit he should never have sight of."

He gestured towards the broken chair, remembering the question that had started his mouth working, the words spilling out like an unstoppable tide. He needed them to know he'd tried. Tried so fucking hard. "Heard the pump kick on at three hours, and I realized what he had done. Needed a tool, so I made one. Busted a leg off, busted the glass. Air rushed in. Five minutes over. Five *goddamned*, *fucking* minutes over the deadline."

He scoffed, the grating sound painful to his own ears. "*Dead*line. *Fuck*. The air pump had shut off when I opened the door up here." He pointed towards the crawl through. "At three hours, the pump kicked back on but in reverse, sucking out the remaining air in her cell. Needed a tool." He shrugged and every man looked at his hands when he held them out. "Made one."

He looked at Watcher. "I got her. Deacon didn't win, brother. I got her." Watcher nodded, staring at him, eyes haunted by the alternatives.

***

"I don't fucking care if you want to do this or not, Tater. Watch is a long-time friend of the Rebels, and if he needs us, we'll help out where we can." Mason was annoyed and he knew it showed. He wasn't accustomed to having his members or officers second-guess him on things like this, and while this was one of the reasons he liked Tater so much, he didn't need it today. The man wasn't afraid to call him on things, even little shit if it needed closer inspection. He was just wrong this time was all.

"Yeah, boss. You know I will. But babysitting a club's princess isn't something most of the members will understand." He stopped talking at Mason's ringing laughter, bitter with memories, and then asked, "What?"

They stood in the kitchen of the Chicago clubhouse, empty mugs in hand, waiting for the coffee maker to finish spitting into the pot. Mason would be headed back to the Fort in a couple hours, his trip to Lamesa canceled, his only desire to be with Willa and Garrett. *My woman*, he thought, *my boy*. "You weren't around back in the day, but if you ask any of the Chicago guys from even a couple of years ago, they will know exactly what is involved with babysitting a fucking princess, believe me." He shook his head, leaning close.

"Mica wasn't the easiest chick to sit on, but the situation was very different. She was older, for one, and had time to develop her own brand of stubborn. Ask Slate sometime what kind of shit she caused on a regular basis. I suspect Isabella will be easier to control."

At Tater's look of confusion, he continued. "Soldiers' princess. You know Watcher is the president of the Southern Soldiers. Well, Isabella is his daughter. She's the gal Duck pulled out of that trap in the desert." Dawning comprehension showed on Tater's face now, and Mason nodded. "Yeah, she got fucked over by Lalo. Fucked right the hell over. Damn near dead by the time Duck dug her up."

"Dug her up? I thought he found her in a closed compartment?" Tater leaned one hip on the countertop behind him, twisting to set his still-empty mug down.

"Dug her up," Mason nodded, reaching to grab the handle of the pot and pouring coffee into their mugs. "Container was buried. Ventilated, but air don't count for much when you got nothing to drink or eat. She'd stopped pissin' the day before he found her. Three days alone in a hell hole, locked up in a glassed-in cage. Damn near dead."

"Fuuucck," Tater drew the word out softly, and Mason nodded again.

"Yeah. So when Watcher calls to say he's sending her up here so we can keep her safe, my only response is 'yes.' And we *will* keep her safe. Our lives on it, brother."

Sipping his coffee, Mason pulled out his phone to check the time. "Fury'll have her here sometime tomorrow. I expect him to roll in before lunchtime. I got to get in the wind soon. Need to get back to the Fort."

"Fury's bringing her back? I thought he was helping Duck with the Diamante shit there in West Texas. Why's he coming back so soon?" A pause, then the man's brain kicked in. "Do we need to send anyone else down there to have Duck's back?"

More questions from Tater, but like always, these were good ones. "Gal's got a thing about being closed in now, as you can imagine, so flying her up here was out of the question unless Watch was willing to sedate her. He was not. Her state of mind wasn't conducive to alteration, so we compromised. Quickest way to get her here, since Fury was already there, was to drop her on the back of his bike."

Back to you

Duck pulled up beside the ranch house, hands reaching automatically to shut off the engine. He winced as the pain hit him. *Even normal, easy things are difficult with broken fingers, burns, and blisters,* he thought. The porch light was on, and before he could step out of the truck, the front door had slammed open and Brenda was running towards him, arms pumping, head up to look at him. He stood up quickly, seeing fear on her face just before she hit his chest, driving him back against the bed of the truck.

"Jesus." He gave a pained grunt, arms coming up to wrap around her. "Bee, baby. Little Bee, what's wrong?"

"The man on the phone said you found her." She was gasping, sounding near tears and he cradled her to him, wrapping her up, reassuring her with the strength of his hold that he was here, with her. "He said your phone wasn't working, so he called. Said you were okay."

"Yeah, I am. Baby, hush now. I'm here." Nuzzling the side of her head, he breathed her scent, filling his lungs with the freshness that was Brenda, soothed in ways he didn't even understand just by holding her. "I'm okay. Myron called you, he told you the truth, baby. My phone got

221

fried, so I had to get someone to ask him. I didn't want to take the time and stop to replace it on the way because I wanted to be here, not listening to you on the phone. I wanted to be here, with you."

"You're okay?" The question was a whisper, her lips moving against his neck, her arms tightening around him, holding him close.

"Couple broke fingers, some surface damage, but nothing big. Nothing bad." When she would have pulled back, he tightened his grip, keeping her in place, molded against him. "Be still, baby. Let me just...I wanted this. Let me have this for a minute."

At his words, she subsided, melting back into him, her head resting on his shoulder. "You're okay." Said now with more confidence, he still reassured her.

"Yeah, baby. I'm okay. Gal's okay, too. She's on her way to my friends in Chicago. They'll keep her safe."

***

Twenty minutes later, Brenda walked beside him into the kitchen and when she saw him underneath the bright light, it felt like the room tilted, her stomach pitching in dismay. He had what looked like burns across his chin, cheeks, and forehead, blisters in the shape of fingerprints on his throat. And his hands...she sucked in a shocked breath.

His poor hands. Three fingers of one hand were taped together, probably the broken ones he had referred to. Scabs crisscrossed the knuckles on both hands, black lines of stitches drawn across the hills and valleys in between. The burns, though, they were the worst, the skin of his palms looking like it had been peeled back. Raw and seeping flesh showed through the cracked and broken surface.

It looked like he had put them through a meat grinder, and she winced at the thought of him driving himself home, not wanting to take time for proper treatment so he could return to her. The man on the phone was clearly upset by his insistence on leaving right away and made her promise to take him to the clinic if she thought it was needed.

She pointed to a chair beside the table and said, "Sit." With a grunt, he started to drag the chair out with the toe of his boot and she helped, adjusting it to give him room to seat himself. Frowning, she realized he wasn't wearing his own pants. These were too big, held up by a belt, but bagging around his hips and thighs. "Where are your pants, Reu— Duck?" Barely catching herself, she changed her words at the last moment.

"Trashed," he said, sitting with a huffed sigh. "Fuck me, I'm tired." He paused, the corners of his mouth curling the slightest amount. "Home, though. Home feels good." Tipping his head backwards, he rolled his neck with a groan, blowing out a heavy breath. "Feels like I could sleep a week."

"Let me get your hands cleaned up," she said and frowned when he shook his head.

"Doc got me before I left. Shot me up with antibiotics. Had to guess, but he smeared all kinds of shit on me to neutralize the compounds. Covered all the burns. I'm good, baby." Eyes closed, he didn't see her shock at his confirmation of what his wounds looked like. Chemical burns. He continued, "I'm just fucking tired, Bee. Made it home, my goal. Hadn't thought past that, just wanted you. Wanted to be with you." He lifted his head with a weary effort, eyelids opening halfway, gaze locked on her face. A crooked half-smile preceded his next words. "Wanted you."

"Then let's get you to bed," she said, reaching out to tug at his elbow. When he winced, she frowned. "Where are you hurt, Duck?"

"All over, baby," he muttered, struggling to stand, swaying on his feet once he made it there. "Fucking everything hurts. My whole fucking body feels like one crispy, strained muscle. But, it's worth everything to get Isabella back for her daddy, her family. Worth everything to get that girl out of the hole she was in. Worth anything."

Her arm around his waist, they walked up the stairs. Once in the bedroom, he toed off his boots while she worked the buckle of his belt. She unfastened the unfamiliar pants, letting them sag to the floor, gasping again as it revealed even more damage to his body. He had what looked like the worst case of road rash she had ever seen. Skin raw and oozing from mid-thigh to mid-shin, front and sides. His flanks hadn't avoided damage, with scrapes and burns on his hips and ass. "Jesus," she whispered, squatting to pull his socks off, thankful his feet appeared to have escaped unscathed.

Grunting, he tried to unbutton his shirt, and she scowled up at him, silently rebuking until he dropped his arms to his sides, lifting his chin to give her easy access once she stood. Draping his leather vest on top of her dresser, she peeled the shirt off where it had plastered to his shoulders only to find more burns on his arms, elbows and forearms, and shoulders. Across his back burned down in places to what looked like the second layer of skin. "Duck," she whispered, finally seeing the full breadth of the damage. "Baby. *Jesus.* What in the world happened to you?"

"Let me get into bed. Just…" He sighed, rolling his shoulders with a pained twist of his mouth. "I'll tell you anything, baby. Answer any question. Just let me…" He turned and kicked his pants, uttering a groan and wincing at the jolt when he connected. "Got some pain pills in there. Can you get me a couple out? I was supposed to take 'em hours ago, but couldn't open the bottle."

She rushed to get the pills, then back downstairs for water. He was seated on the edge of the bed when she returned, head bent far forward, exhaustion written in every line of his body. Shaking two of the purple tablets from the unmarked bottle, she put them in his mouth and then held the bottle of water for him so he didn't have to try to grip it with his hands. "Jesus," she whispered again.

"Looks worse than it is," he tried to reassure her, but then groaned when the burns on his back stuck to the sheet as he tried to slide into bed.

"No, it's bad, Duck. This is really bad, baby. I'm so sorry." She laid down next to him, carefully not touching him, propped up on her bent elbow, gaze roaming his face.

"I'm not," he said, staring at her. "No hesitation. Knowing the cost, I'd still do it again. No question."

"I know you would, hero man." She tried for levity and felt it fall flat, Duck's eyes staring at her. "No, really. I know you would, Duck." She swallowed, thinking of the voice of the man on the phone tonight, telling her Duck was coming home to her. That he was okay; he had saved the girl.

She thought of the care in Myron's tone, his words claiming this man next to her in a way she barely understood. Calling him brother with a meaning running deep and rock-solid; the truth an anchor against the currents of the world that could unmoor a lesser bond and she said again, "I know you would."

He nodded, his eyes never leaving hers as he raised a hand to her cheek, stroking her skin with the backs of his fingers. Then he began to talk, telling her what happened, and she listened, taking it in. In the end, she did understand the man on the phone, because this one in front of her—her man—Duck was worth everything. Worthy of the care and affection she felt for him, worth everything she had heard in Myron's voice on the phone.

With what he had been taught as a child, the examples laid for him by his family, the fact he had turned into this strong, caring man was a miracle. That this man, after everything he had seen, all he had endured, that he had come out the other side with this kind of empathy and love for people... For her. That was amazing. *He* was amazing. *My*

Duck, she thought, watching as his eyes gradually sagged closed, the pain medication finally dragging him down into sleep.

***

"Why you runnin', bro?"

The voice echoed down the hallway, empty walls stretching off into the distance, space narrowing down small, sound growing large.

"Rue?"

Fresh echoes, red pain painting the walls this time, the voice uneasy.

"Reuben?"

Frightened.

"I never wanted this, bubba."

Heavy footsteps pounding up the stairs, leather soles hissing, sibilant noise in their wake as they slid on the bare wood. Boots meant to be durable, delivering lessons lasting far longer. Deep grunts mixed with meaty thuds. Reuben's body jerked sideways, slamming into the wall, the back of his head connecting with the bedroom doorframe.

"Goddamned kids." Words bursting from his father's lips as he breathed through his exertions. *"Nose where it don't belong. What'd you see?"* Something gripped his shirt, lifting his torso from the floor as it twisted him, slamming him into the wall once, twice, three times, his head flopping loosely on his neck, warmth flowing down his back. *"Shed is off limits, boy. You mind your beeswax."*

"Rue, I never meant to be his kind."

I won't be, *he thought, finally recognizing his baby brother's voice.*

"I couldn't let him hurt you. Not anymore."

226

Crusted eyes opening, he squinted down the long hallway, fifty times its normal length, seeing a glow coming through the window at the end. Flickering lights, red and yellow, sound of sirens in the distance.

"I did it for you, bubba."

You didn't do anything for me. You were his, through and through.

"Not always." Boots thundering down the stairs, shouting in the distance. "Not always, Rue."

"Boy, you think that'll stop me?" Dark muttering in the shadows, his father's door opening and closing on a scream. "Burned down my play shed, think it'll stop me?"

Not me, *Reuben thought.*

"Not him," Ray said.

"Make you sorry, boy. Break everything that matters to you." Shrill shouts from the bedroom, voice one he knew. The pretty math teacher who tutored him, told him he was smart, made him promise to make something of himself. Get out of Lamesa, see the world. "Break it all."

Everything fuzzed out for a minute, then the lines of the hallway snapped back into place and he saw Ray standing there. "He hurt Lessa, bubba. Hurt her so bad she was gonna leave. Leave me. I didn't know what to do. I lost Mica, lost you. She stayed, but he was there, always there. Forever in my head."

You killed your wife, Ray. Killed Lessa dead, her carrying your baby.

"I didn't know. Never knew. Only good thing came of it, killing the bloodline." Ray's laughter spiraled high, twisting in a wind suddenly rushing down the funnel created by the hallway, spilling out through the window, chilling and insane. Broken.

You killed our father.

"Had to. He was out of control. He'd go to El Paso, come home exhausted and covered in blood, bubba. Had to. I'd stuffed it into a box, closed the lid. The crazy. Boxed up tight. Put the box in a hole, covered it up. Tried to fake normal. Faked it hard. Kept the monster in the box. Taped, tied, chained...didn't matter. He wanted me to go. Wanted to dig up that box." Ray leaned close, lips barely moving as he told the secrets staining his soul. "Dug it up. Made me, bubba. Made. Me. Had to."

You tried to kill Mica.

"She was the key. My key. My beacon. Started it all for me in earnest. If she was gone, I could put it back in the box. Stop. Stop being what I was. She was the start, and would be the end. She could be the new box." Head tipped to the wall, Ray stared at the ceiling and Reuben stared at him, mesmerized by what was playing out in front of him.

"Tried to stop. Couldn't. Every time I said it was the last. Promised myself. Then it would start to build again. It built and built. Swelling in me like a sick infection, you think I didn't know it was sick? I did, Rue. It was sick, seeds planted by our old man. I couldn't cut it out. That shit was too deep. Rooted inside me, all I knew. So fucking deep. Infested.

"So I'd lance it, let the pus leak out. Find relief. Things would be better so I'd let that hole heal up, seal over. But it didn't work. I needed a box because the stinking shit would start to build again, festering inside me. She was the first who made it better. In between times, I mean. She made it better, made it not so hard." He brought his chin down, staring at Reuben seated on the hallway floor. "That's how it lasted so long with her. Because in between, she made it better. She was the strongest I found, the strongest box. I wanted that back. She wouldn't give it back to me, Rue. I couldn't find it again, and I looked. God, how I looked. Went through a hundred boxes, none of them her. So she would have been the end."

Ray, so fucking sorry.

"Me, too, bro." Ray raised a hand, bringing an enormous pistol to his head, the barrel and grip painted black and white, and Reuben could see the outline of a skull in the lines of color. The Rebel patch made into a weapon. Destruction in an emblem of honor. "Mason fixed it, though. Ended it for good. Put it all in the box in the end."

Reuben surged to his feet, lifting his hands to grab at the gun, hearing the tendons in his brother's hands creak as they tightened, applying pressure to the metal bar underneath his forefinger. There was a blast, so loud it flung him violently backwards against the wall and he groaned as the pain exploded in his body, not able to hear his own voice over the ringing in his head.

***

Brenda jerked awake at Duck's shouted, "NO!" She twisted off the bed, standing beside it, knees and thighs pressed against the mattress as it bucked and pitched with his movements. It looked like he was fighting the very air around him, sheets winding around his arms as they stuck to the salve covering his wounds.

"Baby," she called, "be still. You're going to hurt yourself." Leaning in, she rested her hand at the base of his throat, sucking in a shocked breath when he snatched at her wrist, flinging her hand away as if the touch burned. "Duck." Using a firm tone, trying to break through what was an obvious nightmare, she said, "Stop it. Duck, stop it."

"NO!" His shout this time was garbled and she realized he had begun sobbing in his sleep, tears streaming from his closed eyes, lips slanted downward. "Don't let him win." Those words were another shout, and she stared at him for a moment, finally making a decision.

Reaching towards the nightstand, she grabbed her phone, going straight to her recent calls and dialing the number Myron told her to save into her contacts, one he said would ring directly to him. She had texted after Duck got home, received back a single word, **Good**. Now she would call him, because he had assured her he was available to her or Duck twenty-four/seven. Had even said so, verbalizing the slash. One ring later, she found he was truthful when he answered the call, "Brenda, what's wrong?"

"He's…" She trailed off because her chest seized tight, holding her breath hostage and suddenly she wasn't sure what to say or even why she had called this man. A stranger who was sitting somewhere in the dark, a thousand miles away. What did she expect him to do? It wasn't like he could drive across the road and help her hold Duck down.

"Is he having trouble? Brenda, talk to me." Myron's voice was low, deliberately calming, and it worked because she sucked in a breath, then another, convincing her body it was able to breathe again.

"He's having a nightmare. I can't wake him up." She knew she was whispering when she said, "He's shouting."

"*NO!*" Duck twisted in the bed, nearly rolling off the edge and she rushed to stand where she could brace him if he started to fall, knowing she couldn't catch him, but only make it easier when he hit the floor. "Don't do it, brother."

Myron spoke in her ear, asking, "He take the pain pills?"

She nodded, knowing he couldn't see her but unable to stop the movement. "Uh, yeah. But, not until he got here. He couldn't open the bottle—"

She hadn't finished talking when Myron broke in with a guttural, "Fuck. Didn't think of that."

He continued, "He seem coherent when he got there? Making sense when he talked?"

"Uh…yeah. He talked for a while, told me what happened. Myron,"— she pulled in a slow breath, trying hard to stay calm as Duck shouted again—"he's…the burns are *bad*."

"I know, honey. I saw pictures, talked to him on video before he climbed in that truck to get back to you." *Back to me?* The thought struck her with wonder, because it sounded like something she would do, want to get back to Duck if she were in a strange city and hurt. "He eat before he take the pills?"

"No, he was so tired. I got him undressed and in bed, got the pills down him and then let him talk himself to sleep. Shit, I should have known he shouldn't take them on an empty stomach. *Shit.*" Teeth clenched, her hand tightened around the phone in anger at herself.

"Okay. Makes sense, honey. He's drugged, so his dreams are going to be jacked up, and because he is, he's gonna be harder to wake. I suspect in twenty or thirty minutes, he'll slide back into a deeper sleep, and your house will quieten down again." Myron's voice dropped to a soothing, calm tone, and she drew strength from his certainty. "He just needs to know you're there, and that you're okay. After what he saw today, that's going to be his worst fear, the chance something happened to you. Just let him know you're okay."

He stayed on the phone with her until Duck began to settle down, then a little longer until she had reassured Myron she was okay, too. They finally disconnected, and she crawled back into bed beside Duck, where she watched over him until he woke, ensuring his remaining sleep was deep and dreamless. The few times he stirred, she quickly lulled him back to sleep as she murmured to him how much she loved him.

Twisted justice

"Tommy said that to him?" Brenda's voice was small and sad, breaking on the words. Last night they laid in bed, him talking for hours before falling asleep out of exhaustion. Each time he woke from his dreams, she was there, her presence in the room soothing and letting him rest. He was where he belonged, where he wanted to be. With her. Duck had slept most of the day away, too, rousing to eat food Brenda brought to him before collapsing back into the rest his body demanded.

Now it was nighttime again, and they lay side-by-side, his gaze trained on her face as he finally shared what Eli had confessed. Unshaven, the stubble on his jaw scratched against the pillowcase as he nodded. "He'd carried it for a while, Bee. Our boy trusted me, and I'm glad he did. Glad he trusted me enough to let it go, to let me help him bear it."

"God, I hate Tommy more now than I thought possible," she cried, rolling to her back and covering her face with both palms. "If he knew, then why wouldn't he talk to me? Why would he do something so heinous? Dump it on a child like that. He knew how Eli idolized him."

"Idolized might be a bit much, Bee." The tension he carried transferred to his voice, and he knew this when she turned her head to look at him, an agonized question on her face.

"He came to me that morning because he was worried. Wanted to know if I had fixed things with you. Boy lookin' out for his mama, but he did it in a way which told me it wasn't the first time he tried to look out for you, baby." *No secrets in this bed, Little Bee*, he thought, forging ahead. "What he said suggested perhaps things between you and Tommy weren't always as good behind closed doors as they might seem from the outside."

Immediately, she shut down, features freezing into an impassive, neutral expression that was so automatic, it told him exactly how often she had to wear it over the years. "What do you mean?"

"I promised Eli I'd cut my tongue out before I hurt you like that again." His frank admission drew a hissing gasp from her, and he watched as realization tore through her that her son knew how much pain she'd suffered during the fracture in their relationship. "You thought you shielded him from that, but Eli's smart and he's got a good eye. He sees a lot. He saw what I did to you. Knew when I fixed it...when *we* fixed it." Duck wished his hands weren't still so tender; he wanted to hold her close, but he made do with a gentle brush of the back of his hand across her cheek. "He knew what kind of man Tommy was, knew it by his friendship with Ray."

"I should have found you." Her whisper filled the room with regret and he met it with a shake of his head.

"No, Bee. I never shoulda left." Pursing his lips in a silent demand, he held the pose, waiting and she slid closer, pressing her mouth to his in a soft kiss. When she pulled back, he launched in again, saying, "We could round robin this game for a decade and no one would come out the winner. Go back and forth with the blame we have, the guilt. That's a non-productive activity. Things happened the way they did, and

233

everything is for a reason. If I hadn't left, I wouldn't be the man lying here in bed with you, worthy of you."

She made a small sound, dismissive, and he shifted, kissing her again, wrapping his hand around the back of her head, ignoring the pain stabbing through him at the movement and pressure. "Best thing I ever did for us was leave Lamesa. Hate missing the time with Eli, with you. But, the good news is I came back, and now we have time. We still have so much time, Brenda. Time to build memories. Things Tommy and Ray can't ever take from us, because they aren't walking the earth any longer. The main thing I'm happy about is being here with you. You and Eli, because the three of us can make this whatever we need."

"I love you, Duck." Firmly spoken, the affirmation of her feelings struck a chord within him, that resonance rising to fill him with emotion.

"I know you do, Little Bee. I love you, too," he whispered and then pressed his lips to hers again.

He shifted to his back, letting her snuggle into his side, her head on his shoulder. In a determined voice, filled with an echoing timbre leaving no room for doubt, he told her, "Love you, and *God*...how I love Eli. I thank God Ray never knew Eli was mine. It's a twisted justice, but if he had known, he would not have hesitated to fuck with you. So, as sick as it might sound, I'm glad Ray died before I found you again. Before I found Elias. My son." He squeezed her, bending his elbow to tighten his arm around her. "My treasure."

"You're my dad?" The quiet question cut through the room and Brenda went rigid at his side. Eli's voice shook with what Duck hoped was surprise and not anger or sadness, but the kid was so guarded it was hard to tell from the tone alone. He had moved closer to the bed from the sound of it before he asked again, "Duck, are you my dad?"

Without hesitation, not missing a beat, Duck held out his other arm invitingly and said, "Yeah, Elias. I am."

When he dozed off this time, it was with warm bodies pressed into him from both sides, his family wrapped up in his arms.

***

"How long have you known?" Eli's question was understandable, but the undercurrent of hurt in his voice ripped at Brenda's heart. When she rose from the bed, he was already gone and she came downstairs to find the morning's chores completed and General's tack gone from the barn, which meant he was out riding. Such a smart boy, taking time to think things through. He had walked in the door a few minutes ago and because she needed to know where his head was at, she didn't lose any time pinning him to a stool so they could have a talk.

She took a moment, studying his face, reading his mood and instead of answering right away, she changed the topic, saying, "You name that colt yet? Horse needs a name. Just sayin'."

His head tipped back and she watched as his brows drew together. Just before he was going to say something to urge her on, she sighed, circling back. "Elias, I'm going to be straight with you. You can ask any question and if I can, I'll answer it. If I say it's not something I can talk about, then that's just what it means. That's not me trying to hide anything, but if it's not pertinent, then I won't always answer."

"I can live with that," he said, sounding very adult as he shifted on the stool to face her. "How long, Mom?"

"Not quite five months." At her answer, his body moved back as if she had hit him, and she asked, "What?"

Voice quiet and low, he asked, "Not before he died?" His head angled down and he stared fixedly at his knees.

"No, baby. It was after. Remember the cheek swab deal we did for the gene test?" She paused and he nodded. "Remember I told you it said you didn't have the ALS gene?" He nodded again, cutting his eyes up to her face, then back down to his knees. "They tested for the gene, but part of that was looking at how your genes differed from your...from Tommy."

At her stumbling recovery, she saw the muscles in his legs tense, saw the toes of his boots curling around the stool legs, holding him in place. "And the test told you he wasn't my dad?"

"Yes, baby. That told me." She reached out, threading her fingers through his hair. "Things were...complicated when I got pregnant. I'd known Duck forever, it seemed, and then we dated one night. Just one night, and then he had to leave town. By the time I knew I was going to have a baby, have you, he had been gone for nearly three months, and I'd been dating Tommy for about two."

"So when you knew, when the test told you, what did you do?" Lifting his head, he pressed back against her hand, not to push her away but to be closer to her.

"Well, first I cried, because it meant I had done a good man wrong. Duck's a good man, and he would have wanted to be there for you. But, there it is. I got it wrong, so he didn't know. And he wasn't around to experience the everything that is you." She forced a smile, but dropped it when Eli's face remained serious. "It felt like I had stolen something important from him. My second thought at the time, was how glad I was Tommy never knew." He opened his mouth to interrupt but she shook her head, resting two fingers against his lips. "I know what he said to you. Duck told me. Tommy never spoke to me about that, and baby,"— she cupped his cheek, thumb grazing across his cheekbone—"I hate that he said those things to you. Hate even more you lived with it for so long, baby."

"When did you tell Duck?" He seemed frozen in place, eyes locked on hers as he waited, still and silent, breath suspended.

"Just before he went back to Chicago," she responded immediately, watching as the lines of tension eased in his face. "He hasn't known for much longer than you have, Eli."

"Why didn't you tell him sooner?" Now he was frowning at her, seemingly angry about the delay.

"I called to talk to him right away, but got voicemail. Not something I wanted him to learn from a message, so I asked him to come home." She frowned at the painful memory. "So he did. But then it was hard to find the right time. Remember the night you came to the drive-in movie? I was working up to telling him, but then it didn't...wasn't the time." He tipped his head to one side, then nodded. "There were a lot of those kind of moments leading up to me finally having the conversation with him. I'd work myself up to tell him and open my mouth and the phone would ring, or Gill would walk in, or God's chariot would descend from the Heavens. For a while, it seemed like it was fated he not know." She cupped her hand behind his head, pulling him close for a minute so she could kiss his forehead.

"Then I found the right time and I told him, and you want to know what his first words were?" Eli nodded, shining eyes staring up at her. This was going to be a good thing for him to hold onto and know, that his father wanted him and hadn't been afraid to say it, straight away.

"He said, 'Thank God, Elias is mine.' First thing out of his mouth, baby." She grinned as he sucked in a deep breath, pupils dilating, an expression of hope on his features. "Yeah, I know. First thing, right off the bat, he was pleased. No bull, baby. He never got mad about not knowing, either. Do we both wish things had been different? Sure we do." Now it was her turn to look at her knees. "But we all know now. And now is what we've got, so we're just going to have to roll with it." She turned her neck, looking at her son, noting not for the first time how much like Duck he looked, now that she knew. *He should know this, too*, she thought, and whispered, "You look so much like him. I don't know why I never saw it, baby. Next time you're in front of a mirror, you look and you'll see."

"Is it bad—" his voice cracked in the middle of his question but he pushed past it, "I'm glad? Not just that you think I look like him, but that he is who he is and we all know it now?"

Reaching out an arm, she tugged until Eli rested against her side, cuddling in like he would when he was younger. "No, baby. He's a good man, and I have the feeling he's going to be a great father if you let him in. He's a beautiful man, and I don't mean the outside parts. You and me, we've talked about the importance of picking the right friends. Friends who will help you make good decisions. Who you can help to become better people." He nodded, no surprise, because she had talked to him about things like that until she was blue in the face, hoping with sheer quantity something would soak through. Seemed something had, and it was a good lesson.

"He is good, through and through, has good men for friends, who hold him in high esteem. The people he's surrounded himself with really tell the tale of how good he is. You let him in...if you give him the green light to be a father to you, to help you with whatever is needed, he is going to tie himself up in knots so he can be all over that."

She gave him a squeeze and he twisted his neck to look up at her. "Shoot, Elly-belly," she used Essa's nickname for him to pull a grin on his face, "since he's been here, you're already picking up some of his habits. In these past weeks, you've gone from a lumbering lumberjack, thumping around the house, to being what he is." She leaned close, putting them nose-to-nose as she dramatically whispered, "A Ninjacan. A 'creep on silent feet until you sneak up behind her and scare your momma' Ninjacan."

The shouted laughter of her son rang through the house and she smiled, grateful for the joy in his voice. He hadn't sounded like that in far too long.

Things are different

ONE WEEK LATER

"Boss," he said, phone to this ear as he tipped his head back to look at the ceiling. "I didn't make the show. I heard Mica and Molly already went back home, too. I didn't even get to lay eyes on them this trip."

"You did good, Duck," Mason reassured him and Duck heard pride in his voice. "You were exactly where you needed to be, when you needed to be there. Watcher and Juanita send their thanks, again. You have a big fucking marker with the Soldiers. That alone makes it easier to turn you loose the way I have, knowing they have your back down there."

"Chase do well?" Duck had been present at Marie's the first night Benny let Chase take the stage at the club's main bar in Fort Wayne. The duo had been accompanied by Bear, and together, the three of them had rocked the joint. A surprise to no one, because like his old man, Chase was stubborn to a fault when it came to mastering something, so once he had set his mind on playing on stage with Benny, it wasn't long until it came to pass. Bear was so fucking talented, been playing for years. He could hear a song and within minutes, have it picked out in his head, expertise and skill translating down his hands to the strings of his guitar. Brilliant. And Benny? Not only was he good on the guitar, but his vocals were outstanding. *For a dude.*

Pride rang in Mason's voice again, stronger and closer to the surface since he was talking about his oldest son. "Yeah, he did well. Myron hooked up a live feed for me and Willa. We watched the whole thing just like we were there. Just like we had box seats. Kid's got something going on there, and with the group Benny put together, they might have some legs. We'll see, but they might have something going on." He took in a breath and Duck could hear the grin on his face when he said, "Bethy has a dozen gigs already set up for them back up here. Chase'll get a chance to see if he likes this for himself. But, yeah, he's solid onstage, and did good."

"Damn straight he's good," Duck reaffirmed, glancing out the front window of the ranch house, seeing Eli walking out of the shadows by the barn and into the sunlight splashed across the driveway and yard separating the buildings. "Mason, got a question for you."

"Hit me, brother," Mason said immediately, as Duck knew he would.

"I told you about Elias, about how his mom didn't know until a few months ago he wasn't fathered by her old man. What I didn't tell you is her old man knew this same fact for a while and dropped that on the little man in a way that did damage. I can see it. I just can't figure how to fix it. Same day me and her got our shit straight, Eli gave it to me, laid it on me, letting me carry it for him. I shared this with Brenda when I got back from Las Cruces, without knowing he was listening."

"Fuck," Mason breathed, and Duck could picture his head shaking back and forth.

"Yeah, but he's more a man than a lotta men I know. He didn't slink away with his questions stuck in his head. He asked right out if he belonged to me. Straight out, pushing through his fears." Duck looked out the window again, seeing Eli was closer to the house.

"What'd you say?" Mason's tone was light, but it sounded as if he were thinking about something other than what they were discussing, so Duck brought it back to topic.

"Told him he had the right of it. He didn't even hesitate, just crawled up into bed with Bee and me. Stayed there 'til morning." The memory of the moment had burned into his brain, how comfortable Eli had been with the knowledge he had a daddy who was here, who loved him.

"So what's your question, brother?"

"With how things were with Sosa, with Chase, I know you lost a lot of time with him. How do you make it up? How did you figure out where you stood in his life when you hadn't been there for anything along the way?" He desperately wanted to know this, to see how his mentor had managed to come out ahead with his boy.

"Different circumstances, brother. Chase's mother was an all-around bitch on wheels. Only good thing Carrie ever did for my boy was birth him. Next best thing was to bring him to me, but it took us a long fucking time to get to where he would agree with that statement." Mason's voice was wry, and Duck remembered the night Sosa had dumped Chase at the bar, remembered the panic in the boy's eyes when he scanned Jackson's, seeing a lot of what were probably scary biker faces, damn few of them familiar.

Mason continued, "Sounds like your woman did right by the boy, even if her old man was a jackass about things. You seriously give a shit about her, so that's different, too. Sosa was a weight around my neck until the day she died, and even afterwards, when all I could think about was how she'd been used by my blood. Sounds like things are different, brother. Also sounds like Elias has his head screwed on straight and isn't afraid to question the important things."

Even looking at the door, he didn't hear it open, didn't hear Eli's boots on the floor as he walked across to where Duck was standing. *Kid's light on his feet*, he thought with a grin, reaching out to run a hand gingerly through Eli's hair, something easing in his chest with the boy leaned into his touch. *My boy. My son.*

"Yeah," he said softly. "He's a good'un, for sure." Clearing his throat, he looked down at the brown eyes so like his own staring up at him. "I'll touch base with you in a couple days. Let me know when Fury starts back down, so I'll know when to expect him."

"He's already on his way," Mason said curtly, the change in tone so unexpected Duck froze for a moment.

"All right. I'll watch for him. Any ideas why he's in such a hardass hurry to get back to Lamesa? Missin' his cuz already?"

"He called my sister twice on the road, then once after he got Bella up here. Then he rolled again fast as he could turn it." Now the cold in Mason's voice made sense, because in no way would he want a brother for his sister.

"She still here in town?" This was a simple question, and when it was met with a low growl, he already knew the answer.

"Yes."

***

THREE DAYS LATER

Brenda sighed and leaned back in the chair, closing her eyes as she lifted her beer to her lips, the condensation on the outside of the bottle cool on her fingers. "Ahhhhh," she made the sound only half-jokingly, because after a day like today, the first drink of an ice-cold beer was just about that good. Essa laughed softly from beside her, her own bottle of soda no doubt just as satisfying after the day they had put in.

"We did it. Show's over for another year," Gill announced, and Brenda and all the hands in the room lifted their drinks in salute, shouts of 'hear, hear' and 'fuck, yeah' filling the air around them. It was nearly midnight, and the last of the official week-long festivities had ended about two hours ago. The day had been filled with parades and the awarding of prizes and trophies, buckles and ribbons. From the various competitions to the judging of pies and jellies, it seemed all their hard work had paid off, and everything had come off without a hitch.

The heat from Duck's body hit her before his touch did and she turned her head, looking up, caught off guard when he brushed his lips across hers. Eyes open, she watched his lids sink closed, loving the look of concentration on his face when he deepened the kiss. "Mmmm," she hummed against his mouth, feeling the teasing flicks of his tongue across her bottom lip. Before she was ready, he had pulled back. After the kiss his chin lifted, gaze sweeping the room.

Mouth to her ear, he quietly asked, "Fury and Bethy?"

Brenda ducked her chin and smiled. The two had circled each other all day, the intense attraction between them obvious to anyone who cared to look. Softly, she replied, "She said she was tired, going to head back to the hotel. He was about three steps behind her. Has been since he got back from Chicago. I can't decide if it annoys her, or if she likes it."

Duck pressed a kiss to the side of her head and she leaned into him. His voice was barely audible as he spoke, his words not for her, "You go on, brother. Find your happy."

Full home, full life

Duck leaned on one arm on the bed, propped over Brenda. He was staring at her as she slept, her mouth closed, lips softly pursed. He had never realized what a gargantuan effort it took to organize the whole show. The rodeo by itself was a lot, but she managed the entire thing; with help, sure, but every decision still came down to her. Thank God, Essa had stuck around because he hadn't been much help at all, only able to field calls over the last few days of the event.

Their lovemaking tonight had been soft and slow, hands roaming in intimate touch across flesh already memorized, mouths coming together in passionate kisses. With the burns on his knees healing, but still painful, they had begun lying on their sides, her leg over his hip, hands free to roam, stroking and pinching, mouth following the trail his fingertips blazed across her skin.

Tongues tangling sensuously, he kept his mouth on her the whole time he was inside her, thrusting in a slow, deep gliding rhythm that was exquisite, holding onto his control so hard it was like walking a bladed edge between pleasure and pain. His hand skimmed down her side, fingers brushing across the curve of her breast, and then curling around her hip as her movements became more urgent, seeking. His thumb found and pressed hard on her clit, rolling and tugging, helping her find release. Then, hips bucking she took him deep as her eyes sank closed and she called his name, lips against his mouth giving him each panted breath, her pussy rippling around him when she came beautifully.

Duck performed a slow roll to his back, all while keeping the connection with her, staying inside her, draping her limp form across him as her breathing slowed. Hands on her ass, heels to the mattress, he set a new rhythm, pushing and pulling. Belly muscles tight, he thrust up, stroking into her, feeling her entire body jolt with each long plunge.

Her hand curled around his shoulders and he experienced the loss of her heat when she pushed up and off his chest, legs straddling his hips, head tilted down as she looked at him. "Love you, Bee," he whispered, and at his words, she started to move, thighs, muscled from years of riding horses, effortlessly lifting and letting her weight fall, burying his cock inside her.

Her head tipped back, and he watched her mouth open and close on a silent gasp, felt her clenching down on him again and again as she circled her hips, chasing close after another climax. He filled his palms with the soft globes of her breasts, softly caressing, allowing their weight to set them swaying in his hands as he gently touched her. Then, thumb to her clit again, he brought her with him when he came, hips thrusting up and pressing deep to hold there as he filled her with his semen, the heat of their combined orgasms surrounding him.

He pulled her down on top of him, arranging her head on his shoulder, feeling the silk of her hair dragging across his arm. He grumbled when she roused to go clean up, but then nestled her close as soon as she got back into bed, stretching her out alongside his body.

Which is where he found himself now, thinking about the changes in his life over the past few days, marveling at how differently things had turned out than he had expected. How much better than he had ever hoped they could be.

When he finally dragged himself out of bed and made it downtown and then out to the grounds to watch the last few events, he found things had changed around town for him. No longer were the residents shunning him, keeping track of him out of the corners of their eyes like he was a vicious dog they were afraid would attack at any moment.

When he drove to the feed store yesterday with Gill, expecting to sit in the truck as usual while he sent the manager in with the order, he hadn't been parked at the loading docks two minutes before old man Kennwort was there, talking his ear off. He suspected Transom had passed on parts of their conversation, making it clear Duck didn't have any part of what Ray had done. That, combined with the widely spread knowledge of what happened to Bella, and his part in her rescue, was changing the path of the Nelms name in town. His kind of man very different from what his father had brought to the table. Another set of skeletons brought into the light of day, stripped of any power to wound once they became known.

Things were good for him and Brenda. *Great, actually*, he thought, smiling down at her as her nose wrinkled in her sleep. She had meant what she said about taking their problems in stride, and with both of them focused on moving forward, there wasn't any energy left over to look backwards and hold a grudge.

He understood her fears so much better now, could see on her face the emotions when she talked about how broken she felt when she realized he had left after their night together. Her words, 'Not worth a goodbye,' shining a different light on what he had believed was a graceful exit, leaving her to pursue what he saw as her desires, not knowing he had taken her dreams with him when he left.

She had been embarrassed, cheeks reddened when she told him how quickly she had fallen into bed with Tommy, but bravely met his eyes as they talked about it, determined to have everything out into the open. He could even see how the immediate assumption the pregnancy was from their new relationship made the most sense, not the single night with him.

She told him about her talk with Elias, and then they talked to him together. Taking the time to explain their childhood infatuation while downplaying the years of hurt caused by the misunderstandings between them. What he told Eli was the truth: he had loved Brenda since he was fourteen, and they both emphasized to him that had his parentage been known, Duck would have been involved his whole life. *So much time lost*, he thought. Reaching out to trail a fingertip across Brenda's forehead, he smoothed the dark blonde hair off her face and leaned in to place a soft kiss there.

He scooted down in bed beside her, resting his head on her pillow. As his eyes slowly closed, his last thoughts were of how different this house was now. A home, complete with a family he loved, his life full— filled up with joy and happiness. It had never been a happy place before, but now these walls weren't caging him. Instead, they protected something that was so much more than just a place to live. "Home," he muttered, his voice thick with sleep, "I came home."

***

"I'm serious," she said, leveling a look at him over the edge of her coffee cup. "What do you want for yourself?"

With a wry smile, he asked, "What does that even mean?"

"You said you're staying here, right? In Lamesa?" He recognized uncertainty in her tone, hesitation threaded through with fear.

"Yeah, baby. I'm staying here. I have Mason's approval, so I'm here for the duration. In it for the long haul." He stepped close, plucking the mug from her hands and set it on the countertop before he turned back to her. Cupping her cheeks in his palms, he lifted, pulling her to her tiptoes for a kiss. "I'm here, with you and Elias, for as long as you want me." He paused, looking down at her, and then amended his statement. "Actually, for as long as...well...ever. I'm not going anywhere, baby. Even if you decide you don't want me anymore, I'm still gonna be here."

She flashed him a quick smile, but he still saw the worry in her eyes. "So, then, tell me. What do you want for yourself here in Lamesa?"

Tipping his head to one side, he considered her words. The meaning behind the question seemed to point to what would keep him happy, which was her and Eli. Flat out, that was all he needed. Everything. But, he remembered Essa told him Brenda only stayed in town because she felt he needed her to, so he turned it around, asking her, "What do you want for you, Bee?" He tipped his head to the other side. "What do you want for us?"

When she sucked in a surprised breath, he knew he had hit on the real question. He slid his hands down her neck and across her shoulders, wrapping his arms around and pressing into her. Body to body, she wasn't going anywhere until they hashed this out. "Brenda, baby, what would you think about making a change? Moving away, starting over? Or maybe we start looking at us splitting time between here and Chicago? We can do whatever you want, baby. I'm not picky. As long as I get you and Eli, I'll be good." He paused, then twisted his lips to one side. "And a chance to get in the wind frequently. Need my scoot like I need to breathe. Need to introduce you to the road, Bee. Get you bit by the bug."

She laughed, leaning forwards to rest one cheek against his chest. Laughter now colored her voice when she said, "Silly man. I don't want to...I don't know. I've...me and Eli have been here so long, it's hard to imagine being elsewhere. And he's gonna hit those teenage years sooner or later." She sighed. "We need to make sure he's settled because friends are harder to make as you get older." She lifted her head, looking up at him. "But, I'm not tied to the ranch. Eli would miss Tony and—"

He interrupted her, "And General."

She grinned. "And General," she agreed, adding, "and the colt. But, the only good memories I have of this place are tied up in just these past few weeks. Tied up in you. So, wherever you need to be, that's where I want to be. I don't want to hold you back from doing what you need to do, and really don't want you to stay here out of some sense of loyalty."

"It would be a big decision to leave, baby." Tightening his arms around her, he pulled her against his chest, feeling her heart beating fast and strong. "Not a decision to make quickly, and not one we have to make today. Feel Eli out, see what the boy thinks. Gill could run the ranch without us easily, but the contracting business and rodeo are different beasts. Let's consider everything, but know nothing is off the table. We can make this what we both want, baby."

Soft and sweet, her lips moved against him as she whispered, "All right, Duck. I love you."

"I love you, too, Little Bee," he whispered, pressing a kiss to the top of her head. "I love you, too."

Finding our way

"Like where you're livin' these days, brother. Got visitors headed your way." He heard the grin in Slate's voice over the phone as he talked over Duck's attempt to question who. "My man, Blackie, and his woman, Peaches. Lottie. Good people. They're coming through on their way west; told them they would be assured of a welcome at your place."

"Always, brother," he responded, shaking his head. "And you know them from…"

"My pre-Rebels travels." With loud laughter, Slate hooted in his ear. "Hooked those two up in a good way. They'll have all five kiddos with them so you can expect chaos for a few days. Be nice to my goddaughter, Randi. Do what you want with the rest of the hoodlums. I won't vouch for Tater, Possum, Punkin, or Little Bit, but you be nice to my baby girl."

"Jesus, Slate. What the hell were they smokin' when they named their kids?" Now the laughter was shouted, and he saw Brenda's head lift as she heard it ringing from the phone all the way across the room.

"I gave Blackie your number, man. He'll call when they get close. It'll be a couple days yet. They're taking the scenic route."

"Sounds good, brother." Duck grinned, responding to Slate's sign-off of "Later" with his own.

He looked up to see Brenda studying him, a questioning look on her face. "We're gonna have visitors, baby. Some friends of a brother. A man named Blackie, his woman Peaches, and get this, their five kids." He watched her mouth drop open and grinned. "Yeah, need to figure out where we're gonna put them all. Kids might like to bunk out in the barn, depends on the age. We'll sort it out once they get here, okay?"

She nodded and then seemed to hesitate so he asked, "What, baby?"

"Does this happen a lot? People dropping in because they know someone you know?"

Even before she finished asking, he was nodding. "It's part of it, Bee. They need a place to stay that won't cost them an arm and a leg, and the knowledge that place is safe for them and their kids. Yeah, that's something we can give them. Slate wouldn't have asked if they didn't matter to him, and since they matter to him, then they matter to me. It's just part of it, part of being in the club. We look out for each other, and if it's in our power to grant an ask from a brother, we will do it."

"What if they're not nice people?" She was trying to work this through in her head, he could tell, rolling around the pros and cons of being that kind of support system for someone. "What if they get up in your face?"

"There're only here for a day, two at the most. I can reel it in for that long, even if they are assholes." He laughed. "Or I make it clear they are being assholes and need to move along in a slightly expedited fashion."

He sobered, looking at her. "If I believed there was danger to you or Elias, I'd kick them to the curb so fast you wouldn't even see them go, Brenda. But, that's part of trusting my brother, Slate. He vouched for them, which means if they abuse the welcome we extend, then they're shitting on him. He wouldn't put himself out there for just anyone, which means it's unlikely they're gonna be assholes. Brotherhood and honor mean everything in my world."

"In your world," she repeated his words with a slight shake of her head. "It sounds like you think you exist on a different planet."

"Might as well," he said, walking towards her. "I'm patched into a club where we pride ourselves on being our own men within the rules set down for the club. We don't necessarily answer to government rules, except where it benefits us, and even then...shit, baby, even then we work it as needed. The club laws, the protocol we follow for our meetings and to control the membership, those things matter so much more than anything Uncle Sam could tell us."

He pointed to the diamond on the front of his vest. "This means I hold myself above 99-percent of all men. That I'm in the one-percent group who isn't afraid to make my own way. Who isn't dependent on someone telling me what to think, or how to hold my mouth when I chew. I'm not a sheep, needing a shepherd to keep me safe. I'm a one-percenter, and I'm proud of that."

She looked up at him, gaze trained on his face. "What part of your world will I live in?"

Frowning, he thought for a moment, remembering a conversation he had with Hoss not long ago about where Hope fit into things. "Language lesson, baby." Pausing until she nodded at him, then he continued, "In my world, and I don't use those words in any way other than exactly as you've already taken them. In my world, you're my old lady." At the flash of indignation in her eyes, he grinned. "Don't mean you're old, just means you are mine and you can have every expectation I'm yours, too.

A partnership the whole club gets behind and protects. You own me, and I claim you." Pausing again, he looked down at her. "With me so far, baby?"

There was a slight hesitation and she wrinkled her nose, but said, "Old lady, check."

"Okay. So, I don't have an official role in the club, but up to now, Mason, he's the national president of the Rebels, moved me around as needed. Mostly because I didn't have anything tying me down, not after we had eliminated the threat to Mica." *How bizarre,* he thought, *to talk about the death of my own brother in such a detached way.* "But, my voice carries weight in the club. I carry weight. I'm a respected member, and without tooting my own horn, I can say I'm one of the men Mason trusts enough to bounce ideas around with. Means I know about shit before it goes down, and nine times out of ten, he makes it so I'm positioned in a way that best benefits the club."

"I've never had an old lady before you." Her eyes grew wide and he grinned, dipping down to lightly kiss the tip of her nose. "So this is fresh ground for both of us. But my old lady has responsibilities. If I need her to roll up a support run, organizing the grocery-getters and cages, then all I'd want to have to do is say is what's needed. Give her…you, a rundown on where and when, so I can focus on my shit knowing you'll have all of that in order." He took a breath, because this was edging into complicated club territory, and he didn't want to scare her off, but he also wanted her to understand how things were. While he might be Nomad right now, it didn't mean the status would stick forever, which meant it was inevitable she would be around club.

"Club business is handled by the men. No exceptions, only if it touches on needing support for the families. If we have problems with other clubs, like the shit Bella ran into with her dad's enemies, it's up to the members to sort the shit. But, we can't do it without the support and knowledge our families are safe and cared for." He ran a hand over her cheek, tracing her lips with his thumb. "Sounds archaic, I know, but it's my world, baby."

"I get it," she said immediately, pressing into his touch. "I do. And I know more than most that the support work can be just as hard as anything else." She swept out a hand, indicating the ranch. "I can run a tractor, ride herd on the cattle, throw bales of hay, or fix fence with the best of the men we have. But even I can't do everything. I know my limitations, and even more important, I believe I know my strengths. I'm much better at the organization than I am the execution of physical tasks like that. Doesn't mean I can't do it, just means I know where I can be most effective." Shaking her head, she said, "I doubt all women feel that way, and it wouldn't be true for a lot of them, but I get it. I'm not so hardheaded to argue things I know not to be true."

Leaning forward, she said, "Doesn't mean we won't butt heads over stuff. But as long as the description doesn't have me barefoot and pregnant in the kitchen, I'm good with it."

"How in the hell did I get so lucky?" Shaking his head, he stared down at her for a moment, thinking about some of the women he had known through the club, how some of them had been associated with a member for a decade and didn't get things like his Bee did right off the bat. "Easy and beautiful. Makes me laugh...loves me." Her lips parted, looking up at him.

"Barefoot is a personal choice," he said, trailing his nose along hers, pressing his lips to her mouth in a brief, hard kiss he hoped conveyed how fucking proud he was of her. "In the kitchen, well you're a hell of a cook, woman." He kissed her again, hands slipping up to grasp her waist, pulling her closer. "And pregnant, that would be as soon, and as often as possible."

"Duck," she cried, laughing and slapping his shoulder, laughing again when he growled at her.

"Not kidding around here, baby. Already told you what I wanted, not backing down from that." He snapped his teeth, playfully threatening her, his head coming up when he heard Eli's clear laughter ringing brightly through the room. "Gonna eat your momma up, boy," he growled, snapping his teeth again, feeling Brenda's hands pushing at his chest, her uncontrolled laughter undermining her efforts. "Better save her while you can."

"No, sir," Eli said through his laughter. "She's on her own in this."

"Baby." He leaned in, snapping his teeth again, pulling her tight against him, laughing as she collapsed against his chest. "Your boy ain't gonna help you. You better work on—"

His words cut off when fingers dug into his side, poking and pulling along his ribs. He looked down to find Eli plastered to his side, hands tugging at his shirt, trying to get to skin. "Boy," he warned on a growl, then found himself laughing helplessly when Brenda's fingers joined their son's in the tickle attack.

Five minutes later, they were all collapsed, wheezing on the kitchen floor, having laughed themselves breathless. Brenda was on one side, his arm around her waist still. Eli was on the other, draped half over his chest and Duck grinned at the ceiling as Eli shook with mirth, quaking giggles still bubbling from the boy's lips. Yeah, this life was far from sucking.

***

He stood on the porch and watched the huge pickup truck roll up the driveway, pulling to a smooth stop in front of the house as he lifted a hand in welcome. About half a second after it halted, the front doors flew open and shouts and laughter flowed out, the sound ringing through the yard. A large, dark-complexioned man was the first to exit, leaning back into the truck to shout, "I heard every word, woman. Bathroom, food, and sleep, in that order." He reached to open the back door on his side and his hand disappeared into the backseat, pulling out a bag with a small child holding tight to the handle, dangling the bag until the child found its feet, draping the strap over their shoulder.

Lifting a hand, he shouted, "Duck, pleased to meet you. Got an outhouse this crew can destroy?" Leaning back into the truck, hands under their armpits, he brought out a slightly older child, also accompanied by a bag. Setting child and bag on the ground, he bent into the vehicle again, repeating the process with yet another child, this one a couple of years older than the two already extricated from the vehicle.

On the other side, a woman climbed out, ducking into the backseat on her side of the truck to emerge a few moments later, babe in one arm. She lifted one hand in a wave to Duck before leaning back into the truck. As a girl about Eli's age climbed out on the driver's side using Blackie's arm as a launch pad, the woman straightened up with a bag in her other hand. Duck leaned back, calling into the house, "Brenda, Elias, they're here. Eli, come help with bags, son."

Walking towards the family, he nodded at Blackie first, reaching out to grip his wrist. "Good to meet you, Blackie. I hear good things about you from Slate."

"Fucking Andy," the man said, gripping Duck's arm firmly. "He's a good man." Tipping his head to indicate the woman, he introduced her. "This is Peaches, my old lady. These are my kiddos. And it seems everybody needs to piss. Like...yesterday."

"I'm sure he already got that, baby," the woman said, smiling at Duck. "That your woman?"

He turned to see Brenda standing on the porch, uncertainty clouding her face. At his smile, she moved towards them. "Yeah," he said, eyes never leaving Brenda as she walked down the steps. "My woman. Brenda. That's my boy, too, Elias." He let go Blackie's hand, bending to take the bags from the kids. "Eli for short."

Blackie rested a hand on his oldest daughter's head and then touched the other three in turn as he said their names. "Randi, Tater, Possum, Punkin. Peaches is holding Little Bit." He ruffled Randi's hair, saying, "Manners, beasts. Mind all your manners. This is Duck, Brenda, and Eli, beasts."

In a clearly rehearsed, just out-of-sync chorus, the kids all sounded off, "Pleased to meet you, Duck."

Laughing, Duck rounded Brenda's waist with his arm, turning to lead the way into the house, twisting his head to look at the family as they followed them. "Bathrooms times two on the main floor. Off the mudroom as you go out the back door of the kitchen, and off the main hallway. One bath upstairs, if we need some overflow for immediate needs."

"Thank Jesus," Peaches muttered, shifting the baby to her other arm as Eli took the bag out of her hand.

With a grin, Eli didn't miss a beat as he replied, "You're welcome, but you can just call me Eli, ma'am."

Blackie's roaring laughter overpowered the sounds of nine sets of footsteps as they made it to the house.

***

Brenda glanced up from slicing tomatoes for the salad and found Peaches looking at her with a considering expression on her face. Last night, their guests had all been so tired from their road trip that once everyone was fed and clean, the whole clan had fallen into bed. This morning, Brenda had to go to town early, so everyone except Duck and Eli was still in bed when she left.

Things had taken longer than she expected in town and she had only been back for a short time so this was the first time she and Peaches had any kind of real chance to talk. Duck had holed up with Blackie in the barn, and Eli had taken the two oldest out, Randi and Tater, intending to show them the calves and chickens. The other two kids were busily amusing themselves with toys on the living room floor, and the baby was doing what babies did best, eating and sleeping in turns.

Brenda watched as, without being asked, Peaches got up and began gathering the things needed to set the table, opening and closing cabinets until she found everything. Then she set about pulling plates from one cabinet, cups for the kids from another. Tomatoes done, Brenda moved on to the next prep item, turning the chickens out of the slow cookers they had been in all day.

Peaches cleared her throat and then asked, "You've known Duck for a while?"

"My whole life," she responded easily. "We grew up together here in Lamesa."

"What he did for Watcher's girl..." Peaches shook her head. "That was something else, what I heard."

Brenda drew an unsteady breath, closing her eyes to try and block out the memories of Duck's skin, his fingers. Him following her with his eyes for days, tightly controlled dread on his features. After a moment, she nodded and said, "Yeah. I'm glad he found her. Glad things went the way they did and she's okay."

"Watch will be laying the world at that man's feet. Saved his little girl. Duck talked about that?" Peaches kept her head down, avoiding eye contact as she straightened already neatly aligned plates.

Brenda shook her head. "No, but he got a bunch of calls right after. Each one ended with a variation from him of 'you'd do the same,' and he met some of the New Mexico people at the bar in town, too. I figured those were all gratitude calls."

"What do you think about his club?" *What an interesting question. How do you meet an entity*, she wondered and shook her head.

"I don't know. I haven't really given it any thought. He talked about some things the other night, but I didn't understand a lot of it." Pulling out a knife, she began cutting up the chickens, placing the serving sized portions into a dish she had set out for that purpose. "I think I've only met one other person who belongs to the same group."

"Club, not group," Peaches corrected her absently, and Brenda noted there must be a difference. "So you don't know any of the women?"

"No. There were a couple of women who came down from Chicago, but the way Duck talked, neither of them were involved with the club, really. Just on the outskirts because of things that happened a long time ago." She shrugged, glancing up at Peaches. "Is Blackie in a club?"

"Yeah, he's not wearing his colors because we're in the truck, but he's president of the Freed Riders in Longview." This was said with pride, and Brenda paused a minute to look at her.

"President. Does that mean he has control over the club?"

"Kinda. It's a responsibility, more than anything. Most of the offices are voted in. Back when I was carrying Randi, he was the SAA, not the prez. A couple of years later the old president needed to step down, and the members all voted him in." Looking around the kitchen, Peaches settled her gaze on Brenda. "Forks?"

"Middle drawer in the hutch." She gestured with her chin, eyes on the last pieces of chicken in the pot. "SAA?"

"Sargent at Arms, the person who enforces protocol within the club, keeps things under control during meetings, that kind of thing. The first line of defense against outside threats, so when they went to war with another club, he was the first one into the mix." She filed away the word 'war' as Peaches looked around. "I think that's everything. You want rolls or bread on the table?"

"There's a loaf of bread in the pantry." She pointed with her chin again, grinning this time. "Duck said he didn't have a title, but the national president moved him around a lot."

"Go-to guy." Peaches nodded knowledgeably, closing the pantry door, bread in hand. "Every club needs *that* guy who can drop into any situation and sort things out. I saw his rocker says Nomad, but Blackie thought he was based out of the Mother chapter in Chicago. Is he okay with the change?"

"Rocker?"

"Yeah, the top and bottom patches on the back of his cut—his vest. The top one is the name of the club, the bottom one can be one of several things, but is usually a region or territory where the member lives. Nomad means he's on his own, no set territory or charter, but welcome into any of the club's businesses or houses." She came towards Brenda, cocking a hip to lean against the countertop. "Earned badges go on the front of the vest, the back is typically reserved for club."

"Nomad is new," Brenda said softly, remembering the crisp colors of the thread-covered fabric when he came home from his visit to Chicago. "It did say Mother before." She looked up, frowning. "What does that mean? He went home for a visit but then rode his motorcycle down instead of flying back as he'd originally planned. His friend Fury made the trip, too, came back with him."

"His brother, riding at his back, no doubt."

"He said something similar." Brenda shook her head. "I don't understand a lot of it. He talked about the club as if it were a living thing, and the men in it closer than family."

"They are," Peaches told her, smiling. "You have family here?"

"No. My parents died when I was little. I moved here to live with my aunt and uncle, but they passed years ago. There was Tommy, my husband, but really it's just been Eli and me for a long time." Peaches' smile faded with Brenda's words, sympathy plain on her face.

"So sorry, hon. You have friends here then, a good support system?"

"Not really." She wrinkled her nose. "I've been busy running things. Not a lot of time to socialize, you know?"

"So when you need something, you just manage, right?"

"Pretty much." She picked up the two pans of chicken, carrying them to the table.

"So here's old lady class one-oh-one. You ready to listen and learn?"

Twisting, Brenda turned to look at Peaches. "He said that. That an old lady was a title of respect."

"Title, yeah, but the position is more important. Check it." Peaches put her hands on the countertop, and gave a little jump. Scooting back to sit on the surface, she swung her legs as she looked over at Brenda. "Old lady is like being married, but more, because it's a relationship recognized by the entire club. You marry into a family, taking a husband, and out of that you sometimes get a new mother or father, siblings. You marry into a club by being a member's old lady and you gain every member. Every single member becomes part of your life. You don't even have to meet them. They can be from a chapter three states away and they'll still be something to you.

"Our old men are members, and we can't ever be that, but you let someone try to jack with us and the whole entire club will land on 'em, crawling up their asses. Any member will defend us with their lives if needed, same with our kids. Think hyper-protective big brothers, always on the lookout for things that might bring us to harm." She grinned. "It gets even better, swear.

"Other old ladies will also have your back. You got troubles—family, community, random assholes, party dolls—anyone gives you grief and it doesn't fall under the member's role, then with the old ladies you have a built-in group of women to support you. Shit starts getting to you? They will circle the wagons and make sure whatever is eating at you doesn't get its hooks in deep. Someone comes up sick? They'll run a fundraiser for medical bills. Holidays? They'll organize a poker run to raise money for charities. All kinds of shit, but the most important thing is they always have your back. Family to the max."

"I've never had that." Brenda wasn't aware she was going to say that aloud, but when her whisper hit the air, she saw a determination bloom in Peaches' eyes.

"You have it now. Right here and right now we start your circle with me, because my old man and your old man might not wear the same club colors, but they are brothers. Makes you my sister, woman." She pulled up her sleeve, showing Brenda a tattoo high on her shoulder, elegant script spelling out the phrase, 'My sister's keeper.'

"Got this after Randi was born. Slate, I know you haven't met him yet, but he's a good man. He showed me caring for someone wasn't just doing what they wanted, but sometimes what they needed instead. Keeping the faith, the friendship, sometimes means making hard choices and then enforcing unpopular decisions." She grinned. "Don't tell him, but he's like a brother to me now."

Brenda twisted to look at the door when Blackie's laughter filled the room, watching as his face lit up with humor from what was clearly an inside joke. Through the rolling sound of his joy, he was able to say, "Oh, I'll make sure to tell him, baby. Damn good thing the man caught a clue and moved the fuck on. Caught you, made sure you were good, and then he cut you loose and moved on. Now, we both know his Ruby is as precious to him as my Peaches is sweet to me." He held out his arms, demanding, "Come here, baby. Give your man a big ole liplock. Smoochies to me, woman." He grinned, shaking his head dramatically and sticking out his tongue as he lisped, "Kith me."

Duck's spot

Duck stood in the center of the round pen, rope held behind him low on his hips, one hand loose on the line where it stood straight out from his body, the horse on the end of it moving smoothly today. Every time he worked a horse in this fashion it reminded him of a night long ago, watching as little Brenda McCoy climbed the side of a wooden pen to keep an eye on him with her uncle's horse. That was the first time he'd noticed how cute she was, hair tousled, sweatshirt bagging on her frame, but that beautiful face peering over the top rail of the corral, lit by moonlight and filled with wonder.

I loved her even then, he realized with a smile.

He heard the slap of the screen door in the frame, so when the voice came a few minutes later it wasn't a surprise.

Blackie said, "She's pretty. Nice confirmation."

He grunted in response, his focus still on the filly, watching her ears twitch forwards and backwards as she tried to decide if she could get away with being afraid of this stranger. He urged her on, slapping the end of the rope against his thigh, tongue clucking, encouraging her, taking away the option of refusing. "Yeap, she's a nice one. A keeper."

"Brenda's nice, too."

"More than nice, brother," he responded, concentrating on the horse, the respectful title coming out naturally because he trusted Blackie as much as he would a patched brother and knew it showed.

"Nice and sweet. Woman makes a mean meal, too. Keeper, brother." Even without looking, he heard the smile in Blackie's voice.

"Plan on it, man." He eased the mare in, took a minute to run his hands over her neck and shoulders, then turned her to travel the other direction. Once he had her pelting along again, a glance around caught Eli standing by the barn, watching. *Time to reassure him, make him believe*. "She's everything, Blackie." He pitched his voice to carry, not wanting any missteps with the boy. *My son*. "Gonna keep her, that's for sure. Love her, love that boy, too. Proud of the man he's becoming."

"He's a good'un, too," Blackie agreed. "Randi likes him, and she doesn't take to most people. Said she felt safe with him today, felt like he could take care of her, Tater, and Possum, no matter what. She asked if she could stay here while we head on out to Cali." Blackie barked a laugh. "I teased her with thoughts of princesses and parades, but she's set on hanging here. You got something she likes, the family you've built here, man."

"She's welcome," Duck said shortly, clucking gently to the filly again to increase her speed until she was moving at a fast and easy lope around the circle. She responded well to careful handling, reacted to the positive encouragement she received from him. "Welcome to stay as long as she needs. You and yours will always have a place set at our table. No questions."

"Good to know," Blackie said, and Duck heard him moving. "Gonna go find my old lady, see what she says." There was a pause, and then he said, "You found your spot, brother."

"Yeah, I did," Duck agreed readily. Speaking softly to the horse, he eased her down to a trot, watching her attentively as he repeated, "I sure did."

Things that matter most

Standing in the mudroom, Duck called, "Brenda, have you seen Eli and Randi this morning?" It was nearly noon and Gill had just told Duck that Eli hadn't shown for his mid-morning chores. He suspected the kids had hooked out early, something not unheard of for Eli, but certainly more frequent during Randi's visit these past two weeks. It was unlike him to bail on his responsibilities, though.

From upstairs he heard her response, "No, they were gone right after breakfast. Horses missing from the barn?" Randi had proven herself a natural rider and General quickly became her favorite, Eli gladly giving up the patient horse to his friend, opting to ride Brenda's mount instead.

"Nope, first thing Gill checked."

"Then they can't have gone far," she called, and he heard her footsteps clattering down the stairs. Looking up, he saw her appear, jeans shorts hugging her hips, the tails of one of his button-down shirts tied at her waist. He grinned at the sound of her sock feet still managing to clump and thump on the steps. "Swimming hole, probably."

"Wanna come in the truck with me? Won't take long to go and remind Eli his chores are still waiting for him." He reached out, wrapping his palm around her waist, pulling her towards him. "We could stop on the way and neck a little."

She grinned, laughing up at him and he smiled back as she rolled up on her toes, pressing her lips to his. "I'll slip on some shoes. Ride with you." She reached up, lifting the hair off the back of her neck. "Stir some air around. This Indian summer is killing me."

They climbed into the truck, hands immediately going to the window controls, rolling them down to release the heated air from the cab. Laughing, he looked over at Brenda where she had leaned against the passenger door, feet in the seat to keep the backs of her bare legs off the scorching upholstery. "It's a hot one, for sure," he said and she nodded as he pulled out, headed up the dirt track leading to the upper pasture where the creek ran.

Ten minutes later, he pulled up alongside the bank of the creek. Gaze sweeping the sandbar at the bottom of the bank, he said, "They're not here."

"Towels and what looks like their lunch is there." He glanced over to see her pointing and followed her finger, seeing the pile of belongings near the foot of a sycamore tree rooted near the bend of the creek where the erosion had scooped out a large, shallow area, taming the water flowing through so it swirled in lazy, slow circles, perfect for swimming.

An unexpected thrill of fear flooded through him when he stepped out of the truck, his skin prickling in apprehension. "Brenda, baby, wait in the truck." Her door slammed before the words cleared his mouth and he knew she hadn't heard him. Turning to face her, he opened his mouth to repeat himself when the flat *crack* of a rifle shattered the air, the muted thud of a bullet striking the tree nearly lost in the ringing echoes. "Brenda, get down," he shouted, turning in place even as he crouched behind the fender of the truck, reaching to the small of his back to pull his pistol, thanking God he hadn't left it behind today. The words ripped from him again, fear thick in his throat. "Get down."

He heard the high-pitched, thin cry of Randi's scream and his gut clenched hard, lurching sickeningly because she sounded terrified, which scared the shit out of him. And, he knew Brenda wouldn't stay where she was if the kids were in trouble. Sure enough, her feet pelted around the front of the truck and she launched herself off the edge of the bank just as another shot came, this one punching through the metal only inches from his head. "*Fuck*," he growled, throwing himself onto his back, twisting and rolling across the sand to reach the creek as Brenda had done.

A metallic ping sounded, signaling another shot ricocheting off the truck. Randi and Eli were shouting now, yelling at Brenda from where they were crouched between two beached logs. "The man," he heard Eli scream and Duck's gaze jerked up to see his son pointing over his head. He turned and what he saw pulled the breath from his lungs, but caused him to slide to a stop in the sand and stand straight, making himself the largest target in the riverbed as he stared down the barrel of the rifle pointed at him to focus on the face of the shooter.

"Get the kids out of here, now," Duck shouted. "Fast as you can, baby." Lifting his arm, with a steady hand, he aimed his own pistol, and knew the look on the man's face mirrored the determination on his own. "Go, baby. Go." Short and thick, the Mexican man was muscled in a way that spoke to genetics, not workouts. There was an old bruise showing through the bronze skin on his cheek and temple, and his lip lifted in what looked like an unconscious snarl. *Coyote*, Duck thought, the word frightening in his own head.

"*No mames*," the man spat, his thick accent revealing his linguistic roots, "gonna need you to carry a message, *estás pero si bien pendejo*. Don't be stupid, Duck."

"Don't think so, fucker," Duck ground out, calculations flying through his mind as he noted the distance to the shooter. Factoring in the angle, also marking the gusts of wind lifting dust swirls at the surface level where the man stood.

"Tell Mason I got something he wants. He's got one of mine, and I want the *puto* back." *Fuck.* He realized this wasn't a flesh trafficker. It was someone who knew him, knew his associations, which meant it could only be...Club. *Who the fuck is this? Knows my name, knows Mason's. Fuck me. Brenda and Eli. He targeted Eli and Randi, the kids.*

Duck's finger tensed, beginning a smooth pull on the trigger. Licking his lips, the man shook his head. "*Mira que carbón*, don't do it. I read you like a book. Don't take the shot, *güey*. If I wanted to kill you, you'd already be dead. I need for you to carry the message."

"That's the message? That you wanna be a titty baby about club business? Planning on going even-steven next? Gonna whine about life's not fair? Grow a fuckin' pair, man." He gestured with the hand not holding the pistol, hearing Brenda's voice as she moved away, down the creek bed. Her words urging the kids to a faster pace, getting them to safety. He opened his mouth again, not trying to provoke but he wanted to keep the focus on him, so he pushed. "Damn, man, you're more stupid than I thought. Fuck, sounds like you'd struggle to pour water out of a boot with instructions on the heel."

"Fuck you. He's got one of mine. I want him. I want my man back, gotta get my own from his skin." The barrel of the rifle dipped slightly as the man took a step backwards. "I left you enough with the girl. Made you the hero. You got to be the man of the hour. *Tu gilipollas estúpido*, Duck, the big fucking deal."

"Lalo," Duck said softly, finally putting things together and realizing who this was. He watched the man's chin dip in acknowledgment. "Heard you were DEA'ed in Florida. Locked up, wrapped up, sealed and delivered. Government's problem now. RICO, chico, man."

"You heard wrong, *ya valió verga*. You gonna call Mason? Gonna tell him I got something he's going to want to know about?"

"Phone's in the truck," Duck said, his breathing evening out when he realized he could no longer hear Brenda. She had gotten the kids away. They were safe. Not that he was looking to die today, but he would gladly take it on if it meant she stayed upright and safe. *Love you, Little Bee.*

He sucked in another deep breath and took a steady stride towards the bank. Climbing up and out of the creek bed he snarled when his head hit the level of the ground and he saw the fluid leaking out from underneath the truck. Fucker had somehow hit the radiator, which meant the truck was out of commission. It wasn't far to the house and on any normal day, the walk would be easy, but it was scorching hot and he knew the kids probably were in their swimsuits, which meant they would be at the mercy of the sun.

Reaching through the open window he plucked the phone from the seat, hissing as the metal of the door touched the underside of his arm. He unlocked the screen and tapped a button, then another, placing the dialed call on speaker. They listened to the ringing for a moment, and then Mason answered, humor ringing rich through his voice. "Brother, save me. Hope like hell you need me. My boy's been cryin' for three days straight, I'm about outta my—"

He cut Mason off hard, saying, "On speaker, Prez. I got *Lalo* here. Diamante."

The difference in his tone distinctive, edges now hard and rigid as Mason ground out his words. "The fuck you say?"

"Got Lalo standing ten feet away, Prez. Rifle aimed my way." Mason made a noise and he cut him off again. "My piece is leveled, too, boss." He snorted, and then laughed aloud, surprising himself. "A real Mexican standoff."

"The fuck you want, Lalo. You got balls, man, walking into my man's place like that. Watcher wants you in the worst way and he ain't a bit particular about the condition your carcass might be in when it arrives." Mason's voice hadn't softened at Duck's words. If anything, danger rang through even more pronounced. "Gutted. Flayed. Upright and wheezin'? All the same to him."

"You got one of mine. I got one you want. Give me mine, and I'll do the same." Lalo called the words across the space separating them. Duck noted his language changed as he spoke to Mason. He was no longer using the North Mexico patois of casual insults, not angling for any comradery. "Trade, straight up."

"I got one of yours?" Duck could almost see Mason looking side to side, face as puzzled as the words sounded. "I ain't got nobody. Who the fuck you think I got?"

"*Fury*." Drawn out, the single word rang with hatred and Duck's grip on his pistol tightened. That level of anger and frustration didn't leave a lot of room for sane, and he knew from Lalo's previous work that while the man could be scary smart, he tripped up trying to walk that line on a good day.

"Fury's mine now," Mason clipped the words, but there was movement and sound in the background from his side of the call now. Duck squinted, thinking about the layout of Mason's house. He was in the office, probably, and there would be Rebels on the premises, no doubt. "You got nothing of mine, fucker. I haven't lost anyone."

"Yeah, you have. You just don't know it yet." Duck's attention split between the phone and Lalo, listening attentively as he tried to interpret the man's body language.

"Who you got? Who the fuck do you think—"

There was another flat crack of a rifle and Lalo spun in place, staggering as blood sprayed from his shoulder. Duck jumped backwards, rushing to put the bed of the truck between him and Lalo as another shot came. He heard a grunt from behind him, then running footsteps receding. A moment later, he heard a bike start nearby, engine barely audible over fast approaching hoofbeats. Gill rode into sight, rifle balanced across the horn of the saddle in front of him.

"You okay, boss?" Gaze scanning the area, Gill turned the horse in a circle. "He get away?"

He nodded as noise from his hand registered and he looked down to see the call to Mason was still connected. Lifting the phone, he took it off the speaker and put it to his ear in time to hear Mason ordering, voice low and threatening, rising to a roar on the last four words, "—takes, you get someone out there *right the fuck now.*"

"Prez," he called, and Mason must have put the call on speaker when things went down because a dozen voices answered him, shouted questions loud in his ear. "Lalo's gone, man. He's in the wind." Shaking his head, he watched Gill slowly riding a circuit around the clearing, rifle at the ready. "Winged, but in the wind."

"Need you to tell me what the fuck just happened, Duck." Mason sucked in breath, then asked, "You okay, brother?"

"Foreman rode up, clipped him twice. He got to his bike and scooted, boss."

"Jesus Christ," Mason said in disbelief. "Did the fucker tell you who he had?"

"Nope, he wanted to talk to you. Just told me he had one of ours." He paused, then said, "Actually he said he had someone you'd want, one of yours, boss. Not ours." He swallowed hard, his mouth suddenly dry as the dust beneath his boots. "Mason, brother. Your family. They all accounted for?"

***

"You sure?" Mason reached up, rubbing his fingers across his forehead. When the voice on the phone gave an affirmative answer, he disconnected the call, lifting his head and looking at Slate, seated across the room on a couch. With a headshake, he said, "Nothing. No one is missing. Even Willa's folks are safe. I don't know what Lalo was talking about, brother."

"Okay, so not family. Back it the fuck up. Let's see what we can find." Slate leaned back, stretching his arms out and hooking his elbows over the top of the couch. "Not family, that leaves the club. I've asked for check-ins from all fucking chapters. They've been rolling in for the last hour. But, my take? From what we have so far, it looks like everyone's covered, Mason."

"Lalo doesn't bluff." Mason rested his elbows on the desk as he told Slate something they both knew. "If he said he had someone he wanted to trade, then it's someone I want…" His voice trailed off and he lifted his chin, looking up where the corner of the room met the ceiling. "Someone I want," he repeated. Without shifting position, he raised his voice, roaring, "Gunny, office."

A moment later, the door opened, and the big biker stood in the opening, one arm braced on the top of the frame. "Yeah, Prez?"

"Enemies," Mason said softly. "Name 'em."

Taking hardly a moment to think, Gunny started reciting, "Individuals, we got the normal lineup in Deacon, Morgan, Shooter, Lalo, Chismoso…there's only a couple of clubs that qualify. Sins of the Brother, Outriders, Diamante. Anyone still hanging around from the Fiends, which is unlikely, might be old River Riders if they have a hard-on for your brother, and Devil's Sins holdouts who didn't fall for Rogue's bullshit. Any of the bad outs we've had over the past years." Gunny stepped inside the office, swinging the door shut and leaning against the wooden surface. "What's up?"

"We have credible intel Lalo has someone we want."

Slate lifted his gaze to Gunny's face and then dropped it back to Mason.

"How credible?" Gunny's voice held a low hum of anger, and the door creaked as he shifted against it restlessly.

Mason's lip curled as he growled out, "From his lips to my ears."

"Fuck. Let me think a minute. Make some calls." Gunny turned without waiting for a response and walked out, shutting the door behind him.

"You agree with his list?"

"Yeah. And, I'm with you. I think enemies are a good place to look. Fuck knows we'd pay a hell of a lot to get our hands on Deacon or anyone from the Sins." Slate shrugged. "Ear to the wind on the other side of things, too. I'll wait for the rest of the chapters to check-in, let you know what we find out." He paused a moment, then said, "I don't know him, but Lalo doesn't strike me as someone who makes impulsive decisions. Him going on Duck's land, takin' potshots at him and his old lady with kids there...Mason, that sounds about half crazy. Which don't sound like Lalo to me."

"Agreed," Mason said, clenching his teeth shut on the word. "Now, you wanna give me a fucking clue why Fury would be in my fucking sister's hotel room when I called?"

Can't we have easy

Mason wrapped his arms tightly around his brother, holding a sitting Hoss upright as he sagged against him. Raw, painful sounding sobs racked the man, grief almost tearing him in two. The doc had just walked out of the room after delivering news that stripped Hoss of nearly everything he loved. Mason had been one of the first men to reach the couple when Hope crumpled to the floor, taking Hoss down with her. The man's hands latched onto his wife so desperately, they had to unravel his hold finger by finger until the medical staff could lift Hope to a gurney.

Mason had stood behind his brother, hand to his shoulder to grip the leather of his cut and hold Hoss upright. They remained like that, Mason standing and Hoss kneeling as the nurses and doctors worked on her. Mason's eyes continuously flicking between the huddle of frantic activity around the too-pale woman and the clock on the wall, watching the seconds and minutes tick past. He knew it was bad; recognized expressions of agony and hurt in the despairing faces of the professionals as they glanced over their shoulders. Futility glazed darkness in their eyes when they looked towards the grieving man kneeling on the floor, knees wide to hold his weight, chin tipped to the ceiling, raw and hopeless howls of pain pouring from his mouth.

A Rebel appeared beside Mason, and the two of them had manhandled Hoss up, off the floor, taking him through a doorway to an empty room nearby. Falling silent as he gained his feet, Hoss hadn't looked at the gurney surrounded by circles of useless medical equipment and helpless attendants. Hadn't acknowledged anything. Simply shuffled between his friends, blank stare fixed on the floor. Once they got him inside and sitting, he hadn't even picked up his head until Mason touched him a moment ago.

Now Hoss was holding on with despairing strength, Mason trying everything in his power to keep the man anchored in the now.

Mason knew in addition to the newborn girlchild in the hospital's nursery, there was a young boy whose spirit had bonded with Hoss. He also knew both of those precious lives needed the man, their dad, to keep it together. To be the strong one, even if he couldn't see his way there right now. Mason and the club would help him, be there every step of the way. Ready to lend their shoulders, strength, their deep belief in the family and connections they'd created within the club. Their brothers.

Even as grief for what Hoss was feeling tore through Mason, his imagination was running wild with the knowledge his Willa had been in Hope's position not long ago, smiling up at him in exhausted pride after pushing new life into the world. Now Hope was gone, and he prayed to God his Willa would never fall.

Deacon
FORT WAYNE, INDIANA

For a bitch who hadn't been associated with the club for long, there are a fucking lot of Rebels who came to pay respects to Hoss' old lady, he thought, watching the steady stream of bikes and black leather heading towards the funeral home. The crowd was big, likely more than anticipated, if the waves of men and women moving into and out of the building were to be believed.

And not a fucking one is a face I recognize, he thought bitterly. There was a time when anything to do with the Rebel club had to be conducted under his stamp of approval, or it didn't happen. A time when every fucking face that held a center patch would be one he knew. Now there were so many fucking chapters and charters, he couldn't keep track of who was what. Old clubs, respected clubs, closing their doors and burning their papers, joining ranks with his traitorous son.

"Mason," he hissed, unable to kill his reaction at seeing the grey-eyed bastard walk out the door, gaze sweeping the crowd. Those eyes passed over him, and he wasn't surprised. He had put some thought into his appearance today, wanting to get close without being recognized. In this gathering, he was just one of a couple hundred men with bandanas on their heads, beards or mustaches on their faces, and sunglasses in place against the glaring of an Indiana evening sun. It worked in his favor that enough rival and friendly clubs had sent representatives, too, so his Utah patch wouldn't raise any eyebrows.

Even as he took a breath, thinking Mason's attention had been safely avoided, he registered the snap of the man's head and knew those eyes were staring back at him. Turning to the side, he presented his old prodigy with a view of his back, tracking the responses of the men and women around him to gauge the weight of Mason's continued interest.

"Fucking beauty," a man nearby muttered, his arms wrapped around a petite brunette, one arm banded above her tits, one across her softly rounded belly. "Hope was just gorgeous. Never seen Hoss as happy."

"I know," a woman's voice answered from beside Deacon, and he slowly turned to look at her. Shocked. Shocked, and thrilled.

He knew that voice. Had heard it in his dreams after listening to a recording of it for hours. "Sweet and generous. She was fierce, too. I only met her a couple of times, but she impressed me a lot." Her voice was softer in person, less shrill, and he watched as she tipped her chin down to press soft lips to her infant son's head. "Mason was there in the hospital. He said Hoss lost it. He loved her so much."

"Yeah," the man said, and Deacon watched his arms tighten around the brunette who had begun to sob, twisting her face to press against his chest, planting her cheek next to his nametag. "We had Sammy, were supposed to be there, but I ran late from the shop." He turned the woman so she faced him, pulling her close, hand sliding up her back and into her hair as he whispered, "Shhhhhh, baby. I got you." He lifted his eyes, gaze cutting across Deacon and to Willa standing there with what the math indicated must surely be the product of one of the longest plays he had ever engineered, silently asking the woman for help.

With a smile he hoped reached his eyes, masking his glee, because this was absolutely fucking perfect, Deacon held out his arms to Willa, telling her, "Let me hold your boy, Mason's boy. You help Deke here with his woman." She nodded and was reaching out, lifting the child to him when Mason's voice lashed across the crowd.

"Deke, bring Mercy on inside. They're ready to start." At those words, the brunette sobbed again, her hands curling into the shirt under Deke's cut, pulling herself tighter against him. At the same time, Willa's arms withdrew, taking his prize with them, her son cradled to her chest once more. "Thanks,"—she looked at the nametag on his vest, a stolen mockery of Mason's past—"...Ripper. Sounds like we need to head inside." Looping one arm through Mercy's, she wedged the woman between her and Deke and the three of them began the slow procession into the building.

He looked up and sucked in a hard breath when he saw Mason still looking at him. Stares locked across the heads between them, he waited for Mason to call him out. Waited for Mason to roar his name, for the masses of men to fall upon him and beat him to death with boots and bare fists. The moment passed when the trio's path crossed between the men and their gaze was broken. Deacon took that chance to duck his head, turning and moving against the flow of men, headed to his bike parked on the fringes of the lot. He had seen what he came to see, found more than he expected. Mason's little family was vulnerable.

War looms

Duck stood next to Fury, listening as Watcher gave instructions to his men. There had been unfamiliar cuts rolling through town for the past two days, and the Soldiers wanted to get shit locked down. He agreed it was a good idea, best done before some randoms decided to try and stake a claim, mistakenly thinking the club was weakened by what had gone down with Isabella. As often happened, the risk to one of their own had drawn various factions within the Soldiers together, solidifying the club.

"I want a three-a-day check on Bella," Watcher told Pops, who nodded gravely in response, accepting the responsibility of ensuring the lines of communication stayed open between Chicago and Lamesa.

"Buy me some peace of mind, brother," Watcher then told Spider, who also nodded in response. But that man did it while a crazy-ass grin split his face, hand already going to his phone before he had even turned away.

"Bammers." His greeting was audible, but Duck didn't comprehend the one-sided conversation he heard following. *"Háblame. Necesito que traigas un cuerno de chivo para el que desea a la venta."*

279

Turning to Fury, Duck lifted one eyebrow in question. With a fierce smile that showed all teeth, more a snarl than anything, Fury sucked in air through his nose and quietly said, "Goat horn. Crazy man is buying AKs over the fucking phone. Banana clips, brother, he's buying us some weight, in case we need to run ourselves out there for Watcher."

"Fucking shit," Duck muttered, eyes on the tattooed man who was now nodding and grinning, if anything, even wider. Since Lalo showed in town, the sense of danger had ratcheted to levels so high it was possible to taste the emotion. They still didn't know who Lalo believed he had. All the chapters had checked in and there weren't any leads at all, nothing any of them could put their hands to, nothing to wrap minds around. Knowing it was Fury that Lalo wanted, they were not fucking around making a show of force. Even if Lalo hadn't known Fury was in town, that ignorance evidenced by his extreme play to get word to Mason, nobody was taking any chances. Fury being kin to Watcher was now common knowledge. Clubs who had watched as Fury worked hard to foster a trust with Mason knew it meant he would be protected by both clubs.

For Duck, if he had a chance to get his hands on the fucking Diamante member again, he would explain to the man, at painful length, how fucking wrong what he did was. He hadn't shot at the kids, *thank fuck*, but they had been scared out of their mind when a rifle-toting stranger wanted to talk to them. Eli'd gotten Randi down the bank, hustling her between the two logs, covering and protecting her with his own body while he looked for a way to get them clear and safe.

Scared as fuck himself, he had still watched out for the girl, earning him hero status in her eyes. Randi had stuck to Eli like glue in the days since that visit went down, but not because she was still afraid. She wasn't. That girlchild seemed fearless. Even Eli had worry written on his face every time he walked to the door, but not Randi. She was so unafraid she had told her dad and mom to not be in any particular hurry to come pick her up.

Once assured his girl was okay, Blackie spoke to Peaches and the two of them decided to do what Randi asked, so they were taking their time driving cross-country. When he told Brenda, she shook her head, and then, wrapping her arms around his waist, softly said, "Blackie is your brother. He and Peaches trust you. They trust you to do everything you can to keep her safe."

"Us," he had told her, just as softly, "they trust us."

Now, standing in the large back room of the Soldiers' bar in town, he felt the same trust coming at him from every man in the room. He was still considering what this meant when his phone buzzed in his pocket, and he saw Fury jerk, pulling out his phone, too. *Fuck*. Thumbing the screen open, he saw the message and glanced over at Fury, knowing he had the same set of instructions.

"What. The. *Fuck?*" Fury's clipped question held a considerable measure of anger and Duck froze in place because it seemed way out of proportion to the request. They were always being moved around, pulled here by one club need, pushed there for a different one. Fuck, Fury had been back up to Chicago once already this trip, being called to the Fort wasn't out of the norm. Pulling him solo with an active threat against him was interesting, but Fury, like Duck, could handle himself.

"Looks like you're in the wind, brother," Duck said, frowning.

Lips thinning, Fury turned to look at him. "Yeah," was all he said, then he whistled and Watcher's head came up. "Recalled," was the only word Fury said and Duck knew the puzzlement on Watcher's face was mirrored on his own. Thumb moving over his screen, Fury typed a response, and Duck's phone buzzed again, then again, the two near-soundless vibrations coming so close together it nearly seemed like a single notification.

He looked down to see two messages, one from Fury, and one from Mason. *In the wind*, was what Fury had sent, and just below it in the window, ***Make sure he leaves alone***, was from Mason.

***

Duck heard the shouting through the big, double doors of the barn and he sprinted from the office, pelting across the open space to the porch, only slowing when he recognized the voices as Brenda and Elias. He paused for a moment beside the door, listening closely.

"I'm not a baby, Mom," Eli screamed and there was a metallic crash. "I can do things without you crawling up my butt all the time. I do my chores," his voice went from a scream to a screech and Duck winced, "every single day."

"I know you do, Eli." In contrast, Brenda's voice was even and as normal as she could make it, given her anger rang through loud and clear. "And, I know you aren't a baby."

"Then stop calling me one." Voice cracking, Eli gave a wordless shout and there was another crash, this time sounding like breaking glass.

Brenda barked, "Stop it."

"You don't care. You don't care." Duck squeezed his eyes closed tightly at the sorrow Eli shared in his tone. "I can't be your little boy forever, Mom." He was whispering now, but even lower, his voice was just as intense. "I'm not a baby, and I can take care of things without you hovering. You don't have to remind me a dozen times to feed the chickens, because I do it. Every. Single. Day. I do things. I make sure what I can do, I do. It's what you taught me, Mom. Make other people's lives easier by carrying your own weight. So, that's what I do. Every. Single. Day."

"Elly-belly." Essa spoke from further in the house. "Let's you and me go for a walk, yeah?" Footsteps sounded, moving into the kitchen. "I find myself in desperate need of a walk. Wanna give me one?"

"Yeah." Tears were thick in Eli's voice when he responded and Duck moved quickly. He stepped off the porch and walked around to the side entrance of the kitchen, not wanting the boy to know he had overheard this most recent blowup. When the backdoor slammed shut, he moved inside, already knowing what he would find, what he had found the last half a dozen times Eli had gone at his mother.

"Bee," he called, pulling her tear-filled eyes to him and then he waited as she ran across the room to bury her face in his neck. "He's just going through a lot, baby."

"He hates me," she sobbed, voice breaking between every word. "Hates me so much."

"He doesn't hate you." Arms tight around her, he reminded her of what she already knew. "He's been through a lot in a short time. Tommy dying, and the shit he pulled on Eli before he passed. Then trying hard to keep things together for you. I bet you never knew how much you leaned on him in the weeks leading up to the rodeo. Now that's behind you, and the pressure's off, and he might feel like you don't need him as much now. Only now, you've added me in the mix. His father, who's never been around, suddenly holed up every night in the bedroom with his mother. Then throw in the shit by the creek with Lalo? Jesus, baby, it's a wonder he's not drooling in the corner."

"That is a lot," she admitted, trying to pull away but his arms tightened, holding her close.

"Yeah. Consider it an understatement, Bee. He made a friend, too, got to hang with her for a couple of weeks, and they got tight. They went through that shit together, got *real* tight. Now Randi's gone, which means one more loss for him." Her head moved, hair brushing his cheek and neck as she nodded. "Let's cut him some slack, give him time to sort through his head. Essa's good for him. They're tight, too. Why don't you see how he is when they get back, and then adjust your approach as needed, yeah?"

She nodded again, and he smiled, tipping his chin down so he could kiss the side of her head, lips pressing into her hair. "Now, baby. Kith me." Smiling, he waited for her reaction and she didn't disappoint.

When she tried to pull back this time, he gave her a few inches, looking down as she looked up at him, eyebrows raised nearly to her hairline as she said, "Seriously?"

Perfect for me

"How do I help make things right with Eli?" Duck asked the air in the empty office, not expecting an answer. Which was good, because no guiding spirits spoke from the ceiling, giving him parenting advice. He snorted, thinking, *Even advice from the other side would be welcomed about now*.

In the beginning of their 'we are a family' exploration, from the first night when the boy crawled into bed with them, things had been easy, the two of them falling into a comfortable relationship which existed separate from what either of them had with Brenda. The bonds Duck had been careful to tend when he met the boy had smoothed the way, making them feel like a family from the start. Eli settled in, still the boy Duck first met, sociable and respectful, outgoing and hardworking. It was good to see, and both he and Brenda had drawn more than one breath of relief, sharing proud looks over the boy's head when he went out of his way to do things for Duck or his mother.

Even when Blackie showed with his family, when Eli met Randi and the other kids, he had still come to Duck for reassurances he was welcome, that what they had was real. He didn't ask right out, of course, but he put himself into Duck's path often enough and in ways which let everyone see his unease, making his mom note where he lacked confidence. Knowing what Eli had told him about Tommy, and putting that alongside the bits Bee had been comfortable sharing, he suspected the brutal truth-telling Eli had offered was the tip of the iceberg for a dysfunctional father/son relationship.

So, he suspected this was Eli testing him. Every time he turned around Eli was pushing and pulling, trying to rip reactions from Duck, hitting him from all sides. First with careful hero worship, to see if Duck would puff up, get a big head, or let down his guard and be whatever Eli thought he was really like underneath everything. Since the shit went down by the creek, he hadn't been able to break through with the boy, not like he had before. They hadn't been able to get back to where they were before Eli knew he belonged to Duck.

After the scene at the creek, it had been nothing but attitude and none of it good, directed both at him and at Bee. Eli acting out, turning a rough tongue to everyone around him except Randi, who he treated like glass. With what he was doing, the only reaction Eli received in return was a resigned disappointment from Duck, and his mom's patient responses. Duck let Bee deal with the barbs sent her way, but it killed him to see Eli trying to find a soft spot like he did. Things had seemed to be slowly settling down until after Blackie and Peaches picked up Randi on their way home.

That's when things fell to shit. Duck thought it had to be anger driving him. Anger he could have lost his mother or Randi. Anger the place which should be safe, always, wasn't. He just didn't know how to go about making the boy understand it would be okay.

Picking up his cell from the desktop, he dialed and waited through two rings, then heard his friend's voice. "Mason," he said, hearing the relief in his own voice. "Got a question for you."

"Hit me," came the quick response, and he smiled.

"When you found out about Chase, and you went down to visit for all those years, how did you keep him from...I don't know, being pissed at you for not being there before?" The laughter that came through the phone startled him, and he looked at the phone, pulling it away from his head to scowl at the device. "I'm serious, brother. How did you deal?"

"Well, first off, don't ever think you can do one damn thing to change how your boy feels about finding out about you being his dad. He feels it, it's his emotion. He can own that. Doesn't matter if it's joy or hate, it is *his*, brother. You don't get to tell him how to feel." Mason's voice still carried a thread of humor, but the tone was now serious. This was an important question from Duck and he knew it. "He feels it, you feel it differently, and I bet your woman feels it different yet again. You can try and guide him to a place where your viewpoints intersect, but that's a crapshoot at best. Tell me what's up, brother."

"He's acting out. Right after he found out, everything was cool for a while. He was glad, it seemed, but then he started up. Didn't take long, we got a handle on it."

"How did you get a handle on it, exactly?" At Mason's question, his brows snapped together because he didn't know.

Admitting this lack of knowledge wasn't hard. Mason knew everything there was to know about Duck, so letting him in on this secret wasn't a big deal. "I don't really know. He just pushed until he hit a boundary Brenda and I didn't back away from, and then he settled."

"So he pushed and pushed, found a wall, backed off because he knew the lay of the land. Structured boundaries. Felt you out, probably trying to piss you the fuck off, see how you dealt with anger or frustration. Then he found a place where you and his mom stood side by side, liked what he found, and he was good. You were a match for his mom, who he knows and trusts." Mason cleared his throat, and then asked, "Pains me to ask, but what's changed since then?"

"Lalo," was Duck's direct answer, knowing Mason heard every nuance of anger and hate he held inside.

"Man comes at the kids, takes potshots at his mother, but they got away safe. She didn't stick around, you told me that much. So she, what, took the kids back to the ranch, right?"

"Yeah. Took them up the creek bed until she believed they were far enough away, and then angled through the scrub to the house. They met the foreman along the way and she sent him to where I was." Duck shook his head, remembering how good it had been to see Gill ride up, knowing the man had his back. He might not be a fan of the man's lifestyle, meaning it wasn't for him, but Gill had proven his worth that day, fearlessly riding to the clearing in order to make sure the man Brenda had described as 'armed and goddamned dangerous' wouldn't get to Duck's woman or kids. Or Duck. "Had my back, brother. I owe him huge."

"Good you got that, man. Trust is hard earned, but that's surely a trial by fire. So, back to your Brenda. She took the boy with her when she headed out of the fray?"

"Uh, yeah, she got him and Randi out, Randi being Blackie's little girl." The girl had bounced back fast, treating the whole thing as just another facet of her summer adventure.

"Leaving you behind. The man he barely knew, but liked. The man he just learned was his real dad, the man who had stood up to his tests, earning his...respect? Maybe affection?" Mason scoffed, and then laughed softly, a thread of derision in his voice. "While his momma totes him off with a little girl. Totes him off, taking them home like they were babies been out playin' in the sun too long. A little girl that—until you and his momma showed up—he had been protecting." There was silence on the phone for a beat as he turned over what Mason said, considering everything his friend pointed out. *Dammit, he has the right of it.*

Then Mason spoke again, that derision turning to a soft strength, "He's scared, but he don't know how to show it, so he's trying to pretend he ain't afraid out of his fucking mind that he nearly lost you. I bet he also thinks he lost your regard, his momma treating him like a kid. Boy that age, treated like a little girl and he knows it because there was a little girl there and she got the exact same as him. He's not going to see how precious he is to his momma...to you. Won't know what went through your head when you saw Lalo, heard the gunfire, knew your boy was vulnerable to that shit.

"Brother, his head is full of ageing panic, fresh shame, and not a little bit of misplaced anger. You gotta talk to him, Duck. Show him your fear. Teach him to embrace the feeling, rise above it, and become better on the other side. You know how this shit works, brother. You've done it yourself, seen many of our brothers deal. Help your boy learn how to be a man. Help him, so when he needs the lesson most, he can reach back, bring it out and look it over. Help him turn that fear into courage, brother."

***

"Bee," he called as he stepped into the house, hearing a muffled response from upstairs. Dropping his boots in the mudroom, he headed up the stairs two at a time, walked directly to the bath off the master bedroom and stopped in his tracks, rocking in place at what greeted him when he opened the door. Brenda was in the tub, head back, reclining in the water lapping softly around the sides of her breasts. Candles were lit, scattered around the room, the one on the inside edge of the tub casting a flickering glow over her features.

Startled, she looked up, arms instinctively folding to cover her chest in response, the movement setting the water rocking, pressure on her breasts pushing them together, creating a vision of plump, delectable cleavage. Glistening, wet skin, her softly flushed cheeks, the slow smile that curled her lips...all for him. Just him. *Mine*, he thought, stepping into the room and gently pushing the door closed.

"Bath time?" His fingers flew down the buttons of his shirt and he shrugged it off, and then reached over his head to grip the collar of his tee, pulling that off and discarding it on the floor, too. "You didn't tell me it was bath time, Bee." He scolded her as he worked the tail of his belt loose, unbuttoning his jeans and pushing them down his hips. "I'm the new bath time inspector, didn't you know?" Shoving his socks down, he let them fall inside the legs of his jeans onto the floor.

"Oh, yeah?" A soft, amused, tender look suffused her features and he halted in place again, shocked at how much he liked seeing that expression on her face, wanting to preserve the moment. "New rules, bossman?"

God, I love her. Duck went to his knees beside the tub, rested an elbow on the edge and lifted his hand to brush her hair off her cheek, unable to go another moment without touching her. Not another breath. "Yeah," he said softly, and she must have seen the emotion overwhelming him because she reached up, cupping his hand to her face and then turned to place a gentle kiss on his palm. Thoughts of Watcher flashed through his head, an image of Bella, purple lips. Slate and Ruby, her body jerking as Goose's hands thrust hard against her chest, breathing life back into her again and again. Still and cold. *Never miss a moment*, he thought and breathed out his love. "God, I love you, Brenda."

"I know, baby. I know you do." She moved his hand, placing it palm-down on her chest, gaze locked with his. Her skin was heated under his hand, pulse thudding, flesh soft and yielding. *God.* "I feel it here, every time you look at me. I don't question it, never have to wonder, because you show me a dozen times a day...a hundred. Giving and giving to me; giving and making sure I know." Lifting his hand, she brought it to her mouth again, grazing her lips across his knuckles, her breath dancing across his skin. "And I don't. Wonder, that is. I know. And, I love you, too. So much, Duck."

Pushing up on his knees, he angled his torso close, tilting his head, pressing his lips against hers. "Love you," he repeated, murmuring, tracing his tongue across her bottom lip, cupping his hand behind her neck, cradling the back of her head, pulling her into him. "Let me in, Bee."

Her mouth opened for him, their tongues sliding and tangling as he angled his head more, deepening the kiss. He mapped the column of her neck with his hand, curved his fingers over her shoulder. Holding on tight, the fragility of her flesh and bone impressing itself under the strength of his hand. He wrapped his palm around her arm and caressed her slowly, easing his hand down into the water, and his thumb grazed the curve of her breast. Breathing faster, he flattened his hand on her ribs, moving up, gathering and cupping her breast in his palm.

"God, I love your tits," he whispered in between pants, their mouths still pressed together. He plumped and squeezed gently, drawing a whimper from her so he dragged the pad of his thumb across her nipple. Palming her breast, he plumped and caressed her again. "Pretty, so fucking pretty. Perfect for me. Nips perched on the tips, waiting for my lips." Thumb and fingertip met there and he rolled and pinched lightly, pulling another whimper from her. "Pretty little nips." He tugged and rolled, stretching her nipple, cupping his palm underneath and lifting her breast as he shifted, drawing back, seeing her eyes closed, brows drawn together in cute concentration.

Bending his neck, he brought her breast to his mouth, latching on and sucking deep, groaning in his throat. Rolling her nipple with his tongue, he trapped it, guiding it between his front teeth and flicking the tip relentlessly for a few moments before drawing her deep into his mouth again.

His hand moved, gliding into the water along her hip. Then he skimmed across her belly before pushing between her tightly clenched thighs. Sucking hard on her breast, he lifted his other hand to her face, cupping her cheek. Groaning as she turned her head, she captured his thumb between her lips and mouthed it, using her teeth on the pad. He mimicked her motions with his mouth on her breast and Brenda moaned softly.

Cupping her pussy with his palm, he pressed firmly, feeling her legs fall apart, opening without him having to ask. Thrusting his thumb in and out of her mouth, the suction she gave him grew stronger and he groaned, rolling her nipple in his mouth before drawing her deep again. He focused on his hand in the water. Shifting on his knees, he moved, getting closer so he could rock the heel of his hand against the top of her mound. Grinding into her clit he smiled at the cool air caressing his thumb as her mouth opened in a gasp, and then she closed around him again, sucking and nibbling harder, more frantically.

He worked his fingers, moving up and down, drawing his fingertips between the lips of her pussy, then pushing down past her opening, feeling the slickness of her wet even in the water of the tub. Leaning back, he looked at her. Face even more flushed, her mouth locked around his thumb in a tight 'O,' cheeks hollowing as she sucked on him. "Love you, Bee," he murmured, pushing two fingers deep inside her, bringing the heel of his hand down on her clit again and moving it firmly side-to-side.

He worked her, in and out, drawing his thumb from her mouth and tracing across her now-slack lips, feeling the puffs of her panting breaths on his hand. "Fuck yeah, feel me inside you. Hot and tight, so fucking good." She moaned, her head rolling to one side, neck extending in an unconscious invitation and he lunged forward, planting his teeth in the side, sucking hard while he stroked into her.

He drew back, mouth open with hard pants. "Mine, Bee. Marked you. Mine." He stared at the love bite on her neck, his cock tight and throbbing, feeling his pulse pounding there, the need for her driving him forward. "Tight, God, Bee. Hungry, fucking pussy. God, love touching you, fingering you, watching you, baby. Love your pussy." Plunging deep, he gripped hard, pulling and tugging, grinding into her pussy again, his arm moving back and forth rapidly. The water sloshed high on the sides of the tub, the noises of the waves and the water nearly as frantic as the ones pouring from Brenda's mouth.

"You're gonna come for me, Bee. Come on my hand, like this, letting me look my fill. Pretty tits, beautiful face, that look in your eyes just for me, because I'm fucking you so hard with my fingers." She cried out, hands flying down to grip his wrist, not trying to still his movements, just holding on as she fell apart, the climax roaring through her. He watched the muscles all over her body tense and clench while her pussy clamped down on his fingers. "Fuck, yeah, baby. Come for me. Come just like that."

His name echoed off the tile in the bathroom, her voice fearless in her claiming of him. "Duck!"

Moving, shifting, he slipped his arms underneath her and lifted. Bringing her dripping body over the edge of the tub and into his lap, he positioned her with one arm, the other going between their bodies to angle his cock. Then he pulled her down while surging inside, driving to the root and staying planted, her cry ringing off the walls again.

Duck threaded a hand into the hair at the back of her head and angled her face towards his, capturing her lips in a brutal kiss. Wet hair curling around her shoulders, she took him with soft cries, his hands at her waist lifting and pulling her back onto his cock. He tugged and pushed, thrusting up and into her, building to a steady, fierce rhythm as he stared into her eyes, seeing everything he ever wanted reflected there.

"Gimme a titty, Bee," he panted, feeling her hands moving at his demand. He kept the connection with her, never losing her eyes as he dipped his chin, sucking her offered nipple deep, powering through the feeling of her fingers on his face, feeding him like he needed, his cock deep, the walls of her pussy hot and tight around him; greedy.

"Duck," she breathed, mouth falling open on a gasp as the walls of her pussy started pulsing and contracting again, carried on the wave he'd started in the tub. Mouth to hers, their hard and heavy breaths mingling, he used his grip on her waist to slam her down, sliding her ass high on his thighs and grinding, a groan escaping him. Angling his knees out, the slick wetness of her making every stroke brilliant, he told her, "Fuckin' close, baby. Deep inside you. Home."

Leaning in, he brushed his mouth across the angle of her jaw, watching her eyes sink closed. "My Bee." He roared and thrust hard, his arms crushing her to him, mouth covering hers, tongue delving deep as he came, feeling her heat all around him.

Her hands lifted, eyes opening as she cupped his face, bringing their foreheads together. Her walls clamping down, milking him, the look on her face intense when she told him, "Love you." Chin lifting, lips parting, tongue swiping across. "My Duck."

Slowly his breathing returned to normal and he cradled her, holding tight as she shook in his arms, still lost in the sensations assailing her. "God, Bee," he said, pressing a kiss to the side of her head. "So fucking beautiful. You give that to me and I'll take it. Want it. Need it, baby. Love it. Love you."

On shaking legs he rose with her in his arms, carrying her to their bed and gently laid her down, stretching out beside her. Reaching for the folded blanket from the foot of the bed, he flipped it over their naked forms. She roused enough to roll her head, looking up at him as he lay propped over her on an elbow. With a grin, he leaned in and kissed her lips, dragging the tip of his nose along her cheek until his mouth was near her ear. "Sleep, Bee. We'll play in a bit." Sucking her earlobe in between his lips, he nipped gently and heard her soft giggle. "Sleep."

***

"Hey, Mica," he said, surprised to hear her voice on the call. "What's up, honey?"

"Hello to you, too, Duckmeister." Her laughter sounded, bringing a grin to his face. "I have some news, honey. I wanted you to hear it from me, first."

He finished entering a receipt into the software, clicked to save his work and leaned back into the office chair, resting one foot on the edge of an opened drawer. "Hear what, hon?" he asked absently, still somewhat focused on the rest of his to-do list for the day. *Generate invoices, stuff envelopes, call in the feed order, talk to Watcher to see if there were any new leads...*

"I'm expecting." His thoughts derailed at her response and he sat up, setting his boots on the floor. This was good news. She and Daniel made a handsome couple, and their young son, Jon, was a smart kid. Not earth shattering news, but good to hear nonetheless. He started to respond, but she spoke over him, "Molly's preggers, too."

In his mind, he saw the beautiful young woman as she had looked the first time he'd laid eyes on her. Afraid of her own shadow, never quite meeting anyone's gaze, standing along the wall so she could stay on the fringes of the group in the backroom at Jackson's. With them, but separate. Cautious. Fearful. Nearly broken by his brother's treatment of her.

"Duck, are you there?" Mica called and he grunted, which was all the response he could generate at the moment. "Honey, she wanted me to call you." *What the fuck for?* he wondered, pulling up an image of her boy, Tomas, the one she loved beyond all belief, no matter his beginning had been violent and hateful. She loved that little boy in spite of what Ray had done to her. Now she would have a child created with love, a child to share with her husband, J.J., the two sisters having married the older two Rupert brothers. "She said you needed to hear this from someone you'd listen to, and she didn't think you'd listen to her." *What would this mean for Tomas?*

"Duck, she said to tell you that you have to help her out." *Fuck, she wants me to take her boy.* His nephew, even if he could never say that word aloud, not wanting to rub her face into the memories of his connection to the asshole who had shared his blood. "Said when the time comes, you'll need to explain things."

He thought about Lisa, how she had shrunk from him in the beginning. Alternating emotions of fear and hatred. Those gone now, and her able to stay in the room without wanting to kill him. She could look at him and carry on a conversation. Moved past his association and found peace with who he was. Accepted he was his own man, not tied to his family. He had thought Molly was well past that long ago. Had hoped. She had told him so, more than once, back when she was urging him to do the same.

"She wants you to promise to love this child the same. She knows it will be hard because it's J.J.'s, but she doesn't want her children to know there're any differences between them. She asked if you could find it in your heart to love them the same."

Now he couldn't talk because his chest was heaving. *Wrong, I was wrong.* Lips pressed tightly together to hold back the sobs, he was shocked at the emotions surging through him. *Him*, she wanted to make sure he was okay with this. A moment in time where Molly should be caught up in experiencing joy and goodness, and she was orchestrating someone to share it with him in a way that would make sure he was good with it all. Giving, when she could be taking, that was all Molly. No matter what his brother had done, it hadn't broken her.

Strong. Fierce. Good.

"Duck?" That was all Mica, too, trying to make sure he was okay. Raw, harsh sound burst from his lips, and he reached up to cover his mouth, trying to keep the pain inside. Her voice was soft, filled with love when she called, "Duck, *honey.*"

The door to the office opened and Brenda was there, her face white, fear stark on her features as she looked at him, scanning to see what was wrong, eyes locked on him because she had found him sitting, sobbing helplessly, phone to his ear. "Baby," she called, rushing to his side, wrapping her arms around his shoulders and head, cradling him to her body. "What's wrong?"

"Duck?" Mica's voice was still coming through the phone, and he could hear the tears she was shedding, too. "Duck, honey, it's okay." That was all Mica, too. Always trying to make things better anywhere she could. His brother hadn't broken her, either, even if he had tried so fucking hard.

"I tried," he said, anguish thick in his voice. "I tried to keep you safe. So fucking hard." Brenda's body jerked, her arms clamped around him, holding him tight. He could hear her shushing him softly, but his focus was on communicating his grief at his failures to Mica. "I ran. I know I ran, but God, I tried. I couldn't live with myself so I came back and tried, then I found you, and I wanted you to have a good life. A *good* life. You deserved everything, got so much shit from him. Wanted you to be safe, to find love, to get on with your life so he couldn't...wouldn't win. Wanted you safe, tried, Mica. Tried so hard."

"Oh, honey," Mica cooed. "You did. You kept me safe. As much as anyone could, you did it. You always did good, honey. Hush up, now. You kept me safe. Hush."

Brenda held him, hands stroking his face, sweeping the tears from his cheeks.

"I tried. God, it hurt to find out what he had done. Ripped me to pieces. What he did. To you, to Molly, to all the women and girls he hurt. Hated him. My own brother. My blood. I hated him so much, even while I loved him. But, God, he was a monster, like my daddy." Now he was hiccupping like a baby, tears still pouring from his eyes. "I wanted to make it better. That's all. I just wanted it to be better. Wanted you better, and then our Molly. God, this kills. Tell her I'm sorry she had to ask. I'm sorry she had this happen."

"Duck." Mica's voice was firm, filled with rebuke, and he hiccupped again, pressing his face into Brenda's belly, holding on. "We've had this conversation. You. Are. Not. Your. Family." Still firm, she continued, "You are a good man. A good friend. Someone both Molly and I cherish in our lives. We love you. *You.*"

"I know," he choked out, feeling Brenda's arms secure around him. "I know, Mica. I love you, too. Both of you." Drawing in a hard, hitching breath, he tried to steady himself, calming from the rush of emotions, pulling strength from Brenda's unfaltering hold on him. "You tell Molly I can do that. Whatever she needs. Those are her kids, hers. That makes them special, both of them. Tell her congratulations."

"I will, honey." She was cooing again, her voice soft and understanding. Then she laughed and he sucked in a rush of air, the music of her joy suddenly making him so fucking glad she was still in the world, glad he had a hand in making sure that happened. Then he was laughing along with her at her next words, which were so typically Mica. "About time you gave me some love, too, big man. Did you not hear me telling you I'm giving Daniel another baby to spoil?"

"Yeah, Mica. Congratulations to you, too. I'm so happy for you, sweetheart. You make pretty babies." He grinned, listening to her rattle on about the pregnancy and her husband, waiting until she wound down, realizing she'd continued talking to fill the space until his breathing evened out, until he was okay. Until she felt comfortable letting her friend off the phone. Him. Her friend. Forgiven long ago for what his brother had done. They finally signed off the call and he pressed his lips to Brenda's belly, cutting his eyes up at her when he said, "Thank you, Bee."

Tipping his forehead, he pressed it against her chest when she whispered, "Anything, baby."

***

Duck rolled to his side, wedging one arm underneath his head so he could look at Brenda sleeping. She was stretched out in the bed beside him, having held him until he dozed off earlier. After the call with Mica, she had taken his hand and led him to their bedroom, undressing him like a child, touching and stroking him, comforting him.

She got him into the bed, and then crawled up alongside him, wrapping herself around him and holding on with everything she had. It had been so freeing to talk to Mica, to hear the fears they shared, fears made moot because of the love and respect between the sisters and himself. The exhaustion that accompanied the cleansing conversation had surprised him, but he hadn't expected to fall asleep. Had wanted to talk to Bee about what she heard, what he had learned, and what he wanted...needed from her.

Tomorrow. Tomorrow would be soon enough. They had the rest of their tomorrows together.

She wanted more kids, and he was no longer afraid of the idea. Knew in his heart the Nelms blood wasn't a curse. There were no buried monsters inside him waiting to dig free. Seeing Eli, getting to know the boy—his son—had split something wide open inside him, and now he couldn't wait to build on that with Brenda, with Eli, with any children God saw fit to bless them with.

The rest of their lives.

"Love you, Bee," he murmured, stroking her face with a fingertip. Down over her forehead and along the edge of her nose, tracing the ridges of her lips, then across her chin. He cupped her throat, then pressed his hand against her chest, feeling the gentle, regular thudding of her heart underneath his palm. "Mine," he whispered, leaning in to press his lips to hers. "Mine."

Love like a rock

"What do you want me to call you?"

The question from Elias surprised Duck. Surprised him so much, the horse he rode nearly broke into a canter, responding to the sudden tightening of his legs. He controlled his mount easily, but he knew Eli had caught the reaction. He had learned the boy didn't miss much. Should he give him the answer Duck wanted, needed? Tell him the title would be an honor to bear? Or, turn the question back around on the boy, find out where he was headed?

Duck decided to do a bit of both, providing Eli with an unasked-for give-and-take that would, hopefully, give him courage to ask whatever he was building up to. It was unlikely he would have led with the most important question, so Duck would have to be ready for anything after this.

"I'd like it if you wanted to call me your dad. Father, not so much, but that's my hangup, not yours. You could call me Duck, like you've been doing, but I think it matters more what you want to do, Eli. What do you want to call me?" Turning his head, he saw the muscles in Eli's shoulders relax slightly. This was the answer he'd wanted, which meant he really wouldn't be making any changes. *Hmmm. I'm right, this was not the main show, then.*

"So Dad would be okay?" If Duck had been standing, he would have rocked back on his heels. That wasn't what he expected, which meant he wasn't reading something right. "I...you wouldn't mind?"

"Nope," he said, tipping his chin down, using pressure from the reins and his outside leg to sidle his horse closer to General, who Eli was riding. "But, I'd like to know what you want." General lifted his head, pranced slightly and snorted, giving away Eli's involuntary tightening of the reins. "That part of it matters to me." General tossed his head, bit pulling at the corners of his mouth. "A lot." Eli's eyes moved to him, then away.

"Tommy told me..." His voice trailed off and Duck was filled with fury, knowing exactly what Tommy had said. The bastard had not only told the boy he wasn't his, he had also pulled back the parts of him Eli had always known, the things the boy never expected to have to give up.

"Got it." He spoke the words softly, but even that soft was harsh with overflowing anger. "Eli, you call me whatever you want, whenever you want. Not something you have to clear with me, and if you pick a word now, that don't mean you gotta stay with it forever. Words are just that, sounds to put a name to something we need to talk about, a concept that can change over time, so different words might be needed. A man bears many names or titles in a lifetime, beginning with son, or brother, friend. Then husband, and father, grandfather. All the same blood and bone, but changing with life." He paused and took a breath, pushing down his frustration about how Tommy had fucked with his boy's head.

"What we don't gotta talk about is how I feel about you, because that is not gonna change. Loved you nearly since I met you, standing in your momma's kitchen hat in hand, asking to ride that old gelding you're sittin' on now. Smart, respectful, funny—boy, you're awful easy to love. Loved you more when I got to know you, because everything you do builds the respect you're gonna get from those around you. Loved you even more when your mom told me I was the luckiest man in the world, when I found out about you. You're a good kid, a strong young man, and one I'd be proud to have call me Dad."

"He was gonna go to the courthouse." These words came out strained and thick and Duck looked to see Eli staring forward, his focus far beyond the attentive points of General's ears. "Take his name off the paper."

"What the fuck?" The question slipped out without his permission and Eli's face got tight, chin tucking tight to his chest. "Man." *Jesus*, the bastard was going to take it as far as possible, strip Elias of the name he had been born with. *Shit*. "Not meanin' to speak ill of the dead, but Tommy was one stupid motherfucker."

That brought Eli's sweet face towards him, relieved shock written on his features. "I mean...Jesus. He was going to voluntarily do that shit? Stupid to not want to hold onto whatever thread or connection he could. Stupid to give you any space, because a man would be proud to be connected with you, Eli. Any man, any good man would see that and be pleased." He snorted a laugh, startling his gelding when he slapped the reins against his thigh. "Damn, Tommy," he muttered, "you were one *stupid* motherfucker."

He looked over to catch Eli relaxing, which made him smile.

They rode in silence for a time, gazes sweeping up and down the fencerow, verifying everything was in place before they turned the freshly-calved heifers into this pasture with their bright-faced babies.

"We're here at home, folks might wonder if I started calling you Dad." Eli's voice was soft, but he heard the regret in it, deep and profound. The boy wanted it, but was astute enough to know there would be repercussions to that kind of a change. "If it's okay, I'll stick with Duck here."

"Sounds like a plan." He tried not to give away his disappointment, but wasn't sure he hid it entirely, because Eli's next words left them both open and raw.

"People here can be closed-minded. They wouldn't understand how none of us knew until now." Eli paused, hesitating, cutting his eyes to Duck, then away, something like fear flashing across his face before he firmed his jaw, pushing through to say, "Some of the folks still talk about Mister Nelms. I don't want to give them reason to remember him at our expense."

Duck sucked in a breath at that. Not what the boy had said, because it was true. Undeniably so. But because of the courage it took to say what Eli was thinking. That was something, and spoke to the way Brenda had raised her son, giving him enough strength so when he saw the tough coming, he could find it in himself to power through anyway, flinching but steadfast. Without thinking about it, Duck pressed into the horse again, stepping him sideways until he jostled against General. Reaching out, he wrapped a hand around Eli's waist and tugged him, catching him off guard so the boy's toes slipped out of the stirrups and he pulled him out of the saddle and into his lap, drawing back on the reins, stopping the horses.

"Proud of you, Eli. So fuckin' proud. You are your mama's boy, through and through. She just shines from you in a way I hope someday I will shine from you." He laid his cheek on top of Eli's head, resting there, eyes closed, feeling the boy slump into him, muscles finally losing the tension the boy had carried into this conversation. "Every good thing inside you is only going to become more, and I want to be the one to help you grow that, make it bigger, better. I hope, when you're older, you look back and recognize the gift you're offering me right here, right now. And I hope in that moment, when you see what you gave me, you can see how proud I am to take it. You want my name? You got it.

Anything you need. You call me whatever you want, Elias. I'll always call you son."

***

"He's pretty amazing." Duck whispered these words to Brenda, mouth to her ear as they stood in the bedroom doorway watching Eli sleep. She leaned into him and he smelled the fragrance of her light perfume, still lingering and even more *her* after a day working in the barns. Her hands squeezed where they gripped his wrists, holding tight. He stood, his arms across her middle, his front pressed to her back. He had shared the conversation Eli had initiated, letting her feel the same amazing pride at how their son—*their son*—wanted to protect Duck against the wagging tongues of long-memoried townsfolk.

He released one hand from its hold on her side and reached out, tugging the door to Eli's bedroom shut. Turning her in his arms, he looked down at her face, lifting one hand to sweep the hair from her forehead, bending slightly to press a kiss there. "You raised an amazing young man. Doesn't matter his age, he's definitely not a child. A child wouldn't think the way he does, measuring and weighing his words. You have an amazing son, Bee. You should be proud."

"I hate he had to learn that." Spoken quietly, this showed she understood the cost to Eli to gather that kind of knowledge, because it was something Tommy had forced on him. "But you're right, I'm proud of him. He loves you, even if he hasn't said it, and he showed it today with the caution he had. Love like a rock, solid and firm. " She paused, and he didn't understand when she folded herself into him tighter, holding on with both hands, like she was about to lose him. She wasn't losing him. She was giving him something, and he got it when she said, "*Our* son is amazing."

He froze at her words, locked in place for a moment. Then he nodded jerkily before leaning down to capture her mouth in a hard, hot kiss that deepened the instant her lips parted, giving him the chance to slip his tongue in to stroke alongside hers.

303

She gave that to him, too.

***

Gill reached a hand out but Duck slapped it away, leaning a shoulder to the wall of the barn office, knees weak at the news just delivered. Gill, his expression twisted with anguish and fear got out, "Duck, man, come on. We need to—"

He interrupted whatever Gill thought it was they needed to do when he roared, "Tell me she's okay."

Face blanching white, Gill stood there in front of him, between him and the door, shaking his head. "I told you all I know. Every word the dispatcher said, you got." He sucked in a breath, then shook his head again. "They're enroute now, and if we leave now, we'll get to the ER about the same time. That's the only way we'll know anything, Duck."

His feet were already moving, taking him to the door and he watched as Gill swung it open, stepping out of the way just in time to prevent being knocked down by Duck's mass as he ran towards one of the trucks. Gill shoved him so he diverted to the passenger side, then the men slammed their doors shut at the same time, Gill's shaking hands shoving the keys into the ignition and firing up the engine.

Twenty minutes later, they passed the accident site, twisted metal crumpled into the ditch. One tarp-covered mound nearby. Doc Winters' rig parked just beyond it, him and his assistant working to load a horse into the trailer. The chestnut stood with its head down, obviously in pain, bloody slashes in the horse's hide visible even at the speed Gill was driving. *Breezy.* Everything flew past so quickly Duck could only see flashes of the wrecked vehicles and he twisted in the seat, craning his head to try and see more.

There was a broad swath of disturbed dirt leading up to where the rig lay on its side. Metal guardrail crumpled around the passenger's side of the truck where it was wedged into the ground, wrapped up and around the hood. Windows broken out and use of the fire department's metal saw apparent in the gaping hole on the battered driver's side, dark, empty space aimed up at the cloudless sky. More darkness staining the dirt under the vehicle. Huge ribbons of darkness Duck prayed were from the engine, or the transmission, or even, *fuck him*, from the horses that had been traveling inside the trailer. *Not from her, please God, not from her*.

Highway patrol and city cop cars parked on either side of the road, interspersed with other random cars and farm trucks. People, so many people, standing around in clots and groups, heads down, toeing small pieces of debris scattered along the length of the wound in the earth. Larger pieces were scattered, too, the back axle from the truck stood on end, one set of flattened and twisted tires pointed to the heavens.

All of this rapidly receding into the distance as Gill drove them, as they sped past and beyond. Single vehicle accident, only the one truck and trailer. Anything could have caused the crash, but it wasn't lost on him that he was *club*. It also wasn't hard to pull up the memories of the tapouts the club had seen recently, trucks and cars coming up alongside a lone or pair of bikes and gently, so gently there would be no scratches or dents to either vehicle, pushing bikes off the road and riders to their deaths. All this, while the truck or car drove on, leaving destruction in their wake. Club business. Bloody.

Breath clogged in his chest, he twisted back around to face front. Fists clenched, bloodless fingers lying helplessly on top of his thighs, he waited silently for Gill to get them to the hospital. The hospital where the ambulance was headed. The ambulance that picked up Brenda and Essa at the accident. The accident he feared was because of him.

Learn the history

"Tell me again, *güey*."

Lalo found himself immune to the pleas dripping off the *pinche estúpido gringo's* lips. Words falling into the air that had zero information needed, just sounds to distract and capture his attention, taking it away from where it needed to be. *Retribution was to have been mine*, he thought.

Without conscious direction, his leg moved backwards and forwards again, the toe of the black motorcycle boot connecting with the hip of the man on the floor, dragging a screaming howl from his throat as the bullet wounds in his shoulder tore apart again. It had been like this for hours. Him asking and getting nowhere. He clamped his teeth against the pain. "No fucking answers I wanna hear gonna come outta the cave your lying tongue inhabits, are they?"

The man on the floor groaned, sucked in breath through the blood in his mouth, and said in a voice thick with red, "I saw the chance." He sucked in breath. "Saw the chance." Groaning, he rolled slightly, "Took it."

He wheezed, the sound coming from deep inside his lungs and a bubble worked its way out of his mouth, dark red film stretching and thinning, going from opaque to transparent. Bursting finally, it covered his bottom lip and one side of his jaw in a new layer of gore. The split skin of his cheek sagging sideways where gravity tugged on it as he laid his head down. Matted hair resting in a dark puddle, his eyes slipped closed as his chest rattled again. "Bitch needed to pay."

Head tilted, Lalo froze in place, leaning sideways, one hand pressed against the wall, teasing at a memory in his head. Not his memory, but one shared with him over booze and blow. "Manzino had so much blow. A snowstorm." A dealer who sought to heal a breach with the Rebels, Manzino had been confined to a room in their bar and treated to an experience much like he was giving to the man on the floor.

"Laid there on the floor, spitting my blood on the toes of his boots as he drilled into me. His brother screwed the pooch and Slate beat me." Even years later, when telling Lalo the story there had been incredulity in the man's voice, because he still didn't understand. Didn't know that was honor's way, to strip all options from the person threatening you, threatening family. Honor's way to make abso-fucking-lutely certain there were no lasting misunderstandings. Honor, something all clubs understood. Not all men, not even all members, but clubs grasped the need.

His toe connected again, muscles in his leg and back ensuring power drove it in deep. A howl testified to the success of the action. "My choice." *Rebels took from me. Las Cruces was mine.* "Fury tipped the scales." *Defecting. Closing the chapter.* "Burned his papers. Motherfucker burned his *papers*." *Mason waiting at the end of the tunnel with open arms, every person watching understanding he had just birthed his successor. When a man like Mason took in a man like Fury, you had to know it was to the benefit of both.*

"Mason gained a second. Fury gets an entire *fucking club*." *Could have been mine. Should have been.* "Mine."

"Yeah, naw. We have all the support clubs we need right now, Lalo." Bear's voice boomed in his head, words once whispered at a sit-down between their clubs, now shouting loud, memories muffling the noises around him. *"Diamante needs to get some age on them, man. Grasp tight to protocol, learn the history. Figure out where you want to take the club, then take it there. But, take your time and grow it right. We'll talk then, yeah?"* And the look on the man's face. *Puto.* Chin up, eyes angled down his fucking Anglo nose.

"Looked down his nose at me." Lalo bent at the waist, throat burning as he screamed, "*ME!*"

Legs moving, first one then the other, hands braced on the wall, he didn't notice when his kicks began landing on the wall instead of the slackly rolling body.

***

Chismoso waited across the room, head up, watching Lalo like a hawk. Still bent double, he gripped the leather of Scorch's vest, ready to drag him out of the way again if needed. As soon as the asshole sauntered through the door all puffed up about what the boy saw as a coup, he knew this was going to go badly. It didn't take much to wind his cousin up on a good day, and they hadn't seen a good day in so long, he didn't know if Lalo would recognize one at this point.

Oscar Ibarra released his hold on the unconscious man, letting the body slide down the front of his shins to rest on the floor. He then reached up to swipe his long, black hair back from his face. Lalo had finally stopped attacking the wall and stood still, red seeping through his shirt. Hands pressed flat against the surface, his shoulders heaved with breaths that whistled in and out of his open, slack mouth.

All his life, Edwardo had been subject to outbursts of anger like this. Insanely intelligent, his cousin had plotted their course since either of them could remember. But, Edwardo would occasionally go down a wrong path, losing himself in his own rage. Oscar's mama called them an attack of a crazy kind of rabies, likening Edwardo's behavior to a dog struck with the fits that came with the deadly disease. Sometimes they burned themselves out fast, sweeping in and out within a few minutes, leaving his cousin drained and weak, but ready to listen to reason, mind clear of the whispers that tormented him. Oscar's mama said in these moments her nephew was destroyed by his mind, *El hombre estaba destrozado por la locura.*

"Chismoso." He heard the rasping whisper and knew his cousin had reached that quiet place in his head, a few brief moments of rational thought between the crazy. He might hate the name Edwardo had saddled him with back when they were dirty bastards running the streets of their village, accusing him of being a tattletale, not realizing it was his own behavior that most often told the tale, but he loved his cousin. Closer than brothers, they were. "Can we hold?"

Oscar's brain slipped into high gear, running through the limited information Scorch gave them before Lalo ignited. Glancing down, he took in the broken, unrecognizable face, ripping splits in the skin swollen so the edges nearly turned inside out. On his way to Midland to catch a ride with a Diamante caging it across country, Scorch recognized a truck and trailer traveling the same direction and took advantage of what he saw as a boon. An opportunity.

He admitted both women survived the wreck on the isolated country road. He also admitted only one woman got loaded into a bus by EMTs alive. Boasting of looking into the bitch's eyes when he pulled the trigger, watched the light leak out of them alongside the blood leaking from her body. Oscar glanced across the room, to the handgun resting next to the wall, kicked there by Lalo when Scorch pulled it from the back waistband of his pants.

The other woman was out, never saw him. Wouldn't recognize him if she did see him, if she survived, so that wasn't a path the Rebels could tread, trying to pin down the shooter. In Las Cruces, they kept Scorch restricted to the motel, never letting him be near the warehouse or storage unit. No eyes on him anywhere, no one to know him. Even Duck, smart as the man was, wouldn't have a scent to follow. Which meant it was a fifty-fifty chance any trail could lead them to Lalo, or take them so far astray they'd never see their way back.

Chismoso tipped his head and met Lalo's gaze, telling him, "We can hold."

Waking up

Twisting in the darkness, she jerked when a gentle, warm hand fell on her shoulder. Unable to resist, she moved as directed when it urged her into the center of an open space, staggering when the supportive hand vanished, leaving her standing there unmoored and alone. Into the strict silence pressing in on her, a man's soft voice spoke from beside her head, so close she scented an illusively familiar aftershave. "Time to open your eyes."

With a wrench she tried, and even thought she opened them, but nothing changed. Her fingers scrabbled over her face to rip off whatever blinding cloth she assumed was there, only to find nothing. Horrified, a weak wail filled her head when her fingertips confirmed her eyes were already open.

The voice came again, only now imbued with so much sadness tears pricked her eyes in sympathy as it spoke beside her ear. "Time to wake up, Brenda Bug."

Lurching to the side in a bed, she did, and immediately wished for the swaddling darkness again as pain rained down on her, stealing her ability to breathe. In opposition to the darkness from before, brilliant light now filled her vision. "She's awake," a voice said, and even pushed so far under the swells of pain as she was, she knew it was not the voice from her sleep.

Far less than awake, she thought irritably, and then tried lifting her hand. Only partly successful, she managed to scrape it along the side of her head, in an eerie facsimile of the dream, able at least to move them into view and assure herself she could see. Darkness encroached on her vision, gradually resolving into a face. A face she knew, but barely recognized.

Reuben.

No, that isn't right.

She remembered.

Duck.

"Hey, babe." He whispered the words as if she might have the world's worst hangover. If that was why he was speaking so softly, a night on the town might indeed be why she hurt so badly. He looked terrible. Ragged. That would be the word selected to describe his features today because he looked as if he had been through the wringer of an old-fashioned clothes washer, then left to dry with all the folds and creases left in place. Awkward and stiff, those clothes would never be comfortable worn like that and he was about as uncomfortable as he could be, she gauged, staring at him.

"Welcome back," he said, still whispering. Glancing away from him, she took in her surroundings, not surprised to find everything looked highly technical and entirely medical. As she brought her gaze back to him, he confirmed, "You're in the hospital in Midland."

She moved her head up in the start of a nod but then froze and gasped when the movement woke a fierce pain radiating down her back and into her arms. "There was an accident," he continued and a sarcastic *well duh* rolled through her head. "Do you remember anything?"

He was treading cautiously, prodding at the sliver of darkness underneath that particular rock with care, in case there was a viper waiting for a carelessly thrust-in hand. Pressing eyes and lips closed, she tried to remember, thinking. Hard. Digging for the last thing in her memory, finding meals and conversations, but no shadowing of an accident cast across anything. She dug more, deeper, finding happiness and fear spread out over the past weeks. Thinking.

Then, in the very instant, just before she would have given up, just before she would have opened her eyes to look up at Duck with sorrowful negation in her eyes, just before she could have gone on breathing easy, she remembered.

Essa driving the rig as she always did, fast but with competence, her handling of the truck showing a care for the animals secured in the trailer pulled behind. Stereo volume turned up loud, she sang along with the Occupy Yourself song on the radio, off-tune but enthusiastically, making a joke of her talentless rendition. Breaking off when she glanced behind them in the side mirror, muttering something Brenda didn't catch, but after a moment, Essa was back singing, eyes flicking between the mirror and the road ahead.

The roar of a truck coming up beside them, a big dually-wheeled pickup, mud crusting nearly every visible surface. Brenda stared as the truck pulled up even with Essa's door, watching the passenger window lower. A man inside, not old, not young. Wraparound sunglasses in place, a bandanna tied around his head. He had on a leather vest like the one Duck wore, like she had seen on Fury and the other bikers.

"He rolled down the window and shouted something," she said softly, Duck's features tensing. "Diamonds." His flinch caught her attention, pulling her out of the memory, but he made a motion with one hand for her to continue. She lowered her chin, feeling tightness from what had to be stitches in her back, the ache keeping her from immersing as deeply into the memories.

"Mica, the bitch. She took it all," he shouted, whipping his steering wheel to the right, smashing against the side of the truck Essa drove. The jarring crash pushed them sideways in the lane, towards the shoulder, the pickup reacting dramatically to their trailer slamming back and forth. Essa tried to maintain control, braking hard, her hands clutching desperately at the wheel, muscles standing out in sharp relief in her arms as she wrestled the vehicle.

More shouting, barely heard over squealing tires. "Tell Mica, it's time for the bitch to pay. That's right, bitch. You're gonna pay." Brenda braced herself against the roof of the cab, her other hand holding tight to the seatbelt as he jerked his wheel again, using his momentum to crash against them a second time, then a third, Essa countering the hits with all the strength she had.

There was a bump, the truck bouncing up and down when the trailer's passenger side wheels dropped off the road, running on the soft gravel shoulder. The trailer dragged the pickup farther and farther off the paved surface, the entire rig sliding at an angle that quickly grew more acute.

A tattoo on the man's shoulder drew her attention for a moment, a grotesquely yawning skull spitting out a huge, lunging spider.

Then the trailer began its inevitable slow tip sideways, the high quality steel of the hitch holding, lifting the rear of their pickup, removing any semblance of control from Essa's hands. Slow, but incredibly fast all at the same time. One minute they were driving, the next moment, the weight of the trailer was pushing them around like pebbles in a sandbox, shoving the vehicle this way and that.

Horses screaming, the sound excruciating to hear, the animals' stark fear dominating the noise.

Essa screaming, pain filled and raw, echoing as if her head were thrown back, howling at the sky.

Sounds of metal bending and tearing around them, the grinding sound of the vehicle sliding on its side coming to a halt. Relief when the noises from the horses stopped, too. New sliding sounds, boots in gravel, maneuvering down the steep incline to where they had come to rest. A man shouting, "Fuck walkin' away. Fuck Slate. I got you this time, bitch. You'll feel this cut. Feel this fire burning in you. Losin' to me, bitch. You ask her. Ask her. It feel good? How's it feel, bitch?"

Breaking glass. Grunting.

Blackness. Sounds. Horrible sounds of pain, which seemed to continue on forever, trailing off only to swell again to deafening pitch.

The blast of a gun.

Blackness. Silence.

Blackness.

***

"Mason, here's what I got. Late twenties maybe early thirties. Man has a hard-on for Mica, same for Slate. Skull tattoo on right shoulder, tarantula crawling out of it. Shouted something about Diamante before he ran them off the road." Duck sucked in a hard breath, blowing it out slowly, shaking, trying fruitlessly to control his fury. "I think we just found out who Lalo's prodigy is, boss."

"Tucker." With only one word from Mason, Duck remembered the scene in the backyard of Mason's house. Remembered the stories of Slate using fire and iron to remove the man's club tattoo. Branding him on the floor of a wetwork room in a St. Louis clubhouse.

"Yeah."

***

The cell rang once and he glanced at the screen before touching it, answering the call and bringing it to his ear. "Yeah?"

"Brother." Slate's voice carried so much emotion Duck straightened in the chair where he sat, looking over at Brenda sleeping in the hospital bed, afraid for a moment something had happened with him unaware. "Got the news."

"Yeah." His answer this time was full of anger, because he had just been reminded there was nothing he could do to make this better for Bee.

"*Fuck me.*" Slate was silent a moment, then asked, "She okay? Gonna be okay?"

Trembling with barely controlled rage but careful of Brenda's rest, Duck stood and stalked out through the door, turning and leaning his shoulders against the hallway wall opposite, keeping her in view. He couldn't stand to be far from her right now. "Yeah," he answered somewhat belatedly. "She's gonna be fine. Nothing broken, no deep damage. She took a hard knock on the head, and got cut up by the guardrail slicing through the cab, but she's gonna be fine." Pulling in a breath through his nose, he let it trickle out through his lips. "Feels like my fault, brother."

"Fuck that noise," Slate exclaimed. "Not at all, man."

"You sure? If I wasn't here in fucking Lamesa, the man wouldn't have looked this way. Not a chance. Guarantee it." Duck fisted the hand hanging at his hip, pushing it deep into the front pocket of his jeans. "She's sure as fuck not at fault."

"No, brother. This is on me. Anything you need, you tell me. I owe you." Quiet and low, Slate's voice was pained. "Got a history with Essa, and that's weighing on me hard and tight. Then there's the fact if I had done what a dozen brothers urged on me back in the day, Tucker wouldn't be upright and mobile to pull this shit. I fucked up. Hard and deep, fucked to hell and back. You and me both know Essa's death is on me. Brenda's wounds are on me. Any other shit he pulls, also on me."

"Jesus, Slate." He paused, unsure how to convince his brother of his mistake. "That isn't right, and you know it. You didn't patch him in, and you didn't do the fucked-up shit he did to be out bad. Then you didn't continue to do fucked-up shit, including not covering up his club tat. That's on him, not you. Not me, either." Duck closed his eyes, infusing certainty into his voice as he said, "Not on you, brother. You did what your gut called you to do. Looked at the man, looked at his history, then made a call based on what you knew and how you felt. It's not on you that he's hooked his wagon to a psychopath. Not you."

"You suppose for one moment you can sit there and tell me you won't cuss my name every time you look at the scars on your woman's body? Are you that sure you can set this aside?" He wasn't certain if Slate was looking for reassurance, or condemnation, but Duck knew what he felt and Slate was wrong.

"Standing, not sitting." At his words, harsh laughter rang through the phone. "And yeah, I can be absolutely certain I won't be thinking of you when I look at Bee. Ever. She's soft and sweet, especially when she's giving it to me, and you're a hard motherfucker with a dick." The smile that had eased the strain in his muscles crawled away, leaving only tension behind. "It's club business, brother. If there's anyone to claim the guilt, it's me, because I knew. Club. Our found family. Fuck, man. I stood in the Soldiers' house not long ago watching them gear up for war, and I let my woman traipse off in the fucking truck like we're living a citizen's life."

Slate started to say something, but Duck talked over him, "But, you know what? She's livin', brother. So, I'd do it again. Because fuckers like Tucker? They don't get to win. They don't get to tear the safe from my woman's head, giving her fear and limiting her life. We have one shot at this, brother. Sometimes, if we're lucky, we get two. That's where I am right now. I'm a lucky motherfucker." He looked down at his hands, scarred and mottled with almost-healed wounds. "Watcher, he's a lucky motherfucker, too."

"Yeah," Slate breathed his agreement and Duck nodded.

"Yeah, you know it and so do I. Brenda's my second chance, man. Scars don't bother me. Her knowing what happened does, but I won't shield her from it, because she is that. Fucking. Strong. Strongest person I know, bar none, brother. I won't tell her everything, but she'll know what she needs to know. Found family, a made life. Second chances. Your Ruby, same deal. So fucking strong. My scars, the wounds I took digging up Bella, badges of honor. Bee's scars, those are fucking war wounds, brother. I look at them, and I see only strength."

***

Mason leaned against the edge of the desk, elbow bent, holding the phone to the side of his head. Staring out the window at an office building in the distance, he was too far to see the name in the granite. But, he knew well the look of those letters etched into the stone. Mason Corp. Set in stone. Solid. A foundation for everything he had built for his brothers. After three rings, he heard the call connect and drew a quick breath, tensing.

"Hello?" He had called their house phone instead of one of their cells, using a burner to make the call, because he needed to keep this connection understated. He hoped like hell he was the first call, so he could help control the response, knowing if he wasn't, there were no guarantees of clean lines. The question in the male voice answering the call said he would be the first contact. Good for him, but also bad, because sometimes the bearer of bad news was remembered for that act, rather than anything else. She had known him long enough, and well enough, he suspected he would be immune to the hazard, but still, bad for him. Pitfall-filled moments ahead.

"Daniel." He spoke the man's name quietly. They were not friends, but friendly, having a connection through Mica that was unbreakable. Before Daniel could respond, knowing he would recognize the voice even without a greeting, he continued, "I need to talk to Mica, but need you hanging close because she's about to get bad news."

Silence from the phone for a moment, then a soft question. "How bad?"

Right to it, no bullshitting around. Straight at the problem, just as he knew the man would. Taking care of his wife in whatever way she needed. One of the things he liked best about Daniel was the man's devotion to Mica. In every way. Not many men would be cool with their woman being friends with an old lover, and that was exactly what Mason and Mica were to each other in the days before Daniel laid his claim. But because it was what Mica wanted, Daniel found a way to be okay with it. "Bad."

"Give me an idea of what I'm going to be dealing with, Mason." The sounds around Daniel changed and Mason thought he was probably moving through their house, going to wherever Mica was, taking it to her so he could control the situation by staying in her space while Mason talked to her.

"Essa's dead." He wasn't there to see it, but knowing Daniel for this many years, when he heard the man suck in air, he knew the sick look that would be sitting uneasily on the man's features. "It wasn't pretty, it wasn't easy, and it was club."

"Fuck." Daniel gritted the word out and asked, hesitation in his tone, "You're sure?"

"Yeah. There's no doubt about this. She was in a wreck, but that wasn't what killed her. She was hurt, and hurt bad, but every injury was survivable." His gaze lowered to the floor, then tracked up to the wall where a picture of Mica was displayed near one of Willa. Next to that was a group picture of Mica, Molly, Essa, and a bunch of the other

319

women associated with the club. Arms around necks and waists, they were all laughing hard, standing in front of a bonfire. DeeDee bent in half with her laughter, carefully holding out her cup of beer so it wouldn't get spilled. "It won't be in the official report, but she took one to the head, man. That part was fast, at least."

"You can't tell her that." Daniel sounded so certain, so sure, for a moment Mason's resolve rocked, but then he remembered how he had underestimated Mica before, so he shook his head.

"I ain't gonna lie to her. I need her to be vigilant, because the man who did this has a vendetta against not only the Rebels, but Mica, too. She can't be heedful of the situation without the information, man. I'd rather her be sad, but alert and have that vigilance leading to her stayin' alive, instead of lost in sadness and not looking over her shoulder." He shifted, resting both feet on the floor, turning away from the window. "Need her alive."

"She's expecting again." Daniel spoke the words like he thought they'd be a surprise, which meant he didn't know Mica had called Mason weeks ago, as soon as she knew for sure.

"Molly's knocked up, too. Both of the Rupert boys got it goin' on." Mason knew there was no humor in his voice, but he wanted Daniel to know there were no secrets between him and Mica, and the flow of information went both ways.

"She loves Essa." The sound coming through the phone changed again, and he knew Daniel was back on the move. He also knew the man had given up the quest to derail the delivery of information when he said, "Break it to her fast. Just the fact Essa's gone. She's gonna fall apart, and I'll be here to help her deal. She can call you back for the details."

"Agreed," Mason gave him the promise immediately.

Phone away from his face, Daniel's voice was muted when he spoke next. Mason heard him say, "Baby, Mason's on the phone for you." More noise, Mica's voice lifted questioningly, because he always called her cell to chat. Then Mica on the phone, his name in her mouth now meaning his heart warmed, but did it in a way which was true friendship. They had found their way to this place a long time ago, and every time he had occasion to see her, he was glad again they had made it. Worth every bit of work it took to get here.

"Mica, got something to tell you."

My fears

FOUR WEEKS LATER

Duck looked up as Brenda walked into the kitchen. She had just come in from the barn, stopping in the mudroom only long enough to toe off her boots, padding gracefully across the room towards him in her sock feet. He took in the gleam of sweat on her face, how her hair was half out of her ponytail, the dust on her jeans, and he shook his head in wonder, thinking she had never looked more beautiful. *I love her so much*, he thought.

"Hey, baby," she called casually, and just her voice caused him to suck in a breath in amazement. That he had this, her, all of her, with him... *Luckiest fucking man in the entire goddamned world*. Walking past him, she reached out, slipping her palm up his arm and gripping his bicep for a second before he lost the heat of her hand. The thrill of her touch caused his cock to wake up, thickening and fattening behind the buttons of his jeans.

He turned, watching her move, reaching out for the refrigerator door, the muscles of her arm and back shifting, visible through the worn tee she wore. Visible, too, were the long, red, angry scars, and he ignored them, not giving a fuck about what they looked like, except how they troubled her, undermining her confidence. A month out from the accident, she was well physically, but he worried about where her head was.

Gritting his teeth, the muscles in his jaw flexed and popped when she bent over to grab a bottle of water from the bottom drawer. Jeans fabric stretching across her ass, molding to every curve, accenting the sweet roundness of her cheeks. Scars didn't matter at all, not to him. Like he'd told Slate, he saw them as a mark of her strength. Survival, against all odds. Against the designs of a man who, once upon a time, was a brother. She lived, and that was all that mattered. Her sucking air in and out, lying in his bed at night, loving him, even if she was afraid to say it now.

Mine.

His own socks slid soundlessly across the slick floor. Her surprised gasp was audible in the quiet house when he gripped her hips—*those fucking gorgeous hips*—and pulled her back against him. The heat of her body hit him, the dip between her cheeks the perfect place to press his rigid cock, the thump and thud of blood pounding in his dick. Not grinding in, just holding her there, and letting his body tell the story of what he wanted to do to her.

"Duck?" That lift at the end of his name gave him an idea of the uncertainty she had, and he knew part was fear the scarring she now bore would be a turnoff for him. That the experience of seeing her hurt and lying in a hospital bed would cause him to pull back.

Any withdrawing he had done wasn't about the scars, however. It had everything to do with the shit swirling around him, around the club.

Days of working angles with the Soldiers and other clubs, trying to find Tucker. Coming up with nothing, which pushed far beyond frustrating and deep into rage territory. He couldn't keep his family safe if he couldn't find the fucker, and there was no satisfaction in knowing he wasn't the only one looking and coming up blank. He had to believe someone would find a clue soon, and then he could start putting the puzzle together.

First he had to keep his family together.

The first time Gill brought Eli to the hospital, the boy's anguished face tore at Duck's heart. Eli had flown across the waiting room and latched on, arms wrapped around Duck's hips, head pressed against his body. Eli stayed like that for a long time, holding on so tight Duck thought the boy would split in two.

Duck held on in his own way, trying to find a path to help Eli deal with his terror and anger about the accident, even some guilt that with school back in session he hadn't been with the women. When they went into Brenda's room, Eli's fear at seeing his momma helpless in a hospital bed was palpable, waves of it filling the room until Duck wrapped him up in a hug again.

Together with Brenda, they grieved over the loss of Essa, Brenda's wisdom bringing them through to tears of joy as they told story after story of the spirited young woman. He and Brenda had both held their breath, waiting and watching for a return of the attitude but, thank God, Eli had gotten past that. Duck knew it helped that Eli had Breezy to nurse back to health, and Doc Winters had moved the horse to their barn as fast as he could. Duck and Gill set up cots for Eli and Tony in the next stall and the boys slept there for days, until they were sure Breezy would fully recover.

Then there was her near-hysteria when told she wouldn't be released in time to travel to East Texas for Essa's funeral. Driving her across the state, drugging the pain away. Then pushing her to the church in a wheelchair so she wouldn't pull her stitches trying to walk that far. Finally, hauling her angry ass right back to the hospital, part of his deal with her doctor so she could attend the memorial, which pissed her off because by then, she simply wanted to be home. Home with him and Eli.

While he had been dealing with that, Brenda had been laid up in a bed, wound up in the thoughts in her aching head. Now, no shock, he suspected she was afraid. Lost in sorrow at Essa's death, her memories of the accident, and a late-blooming fear something could happen to Elias.

And, hell, he couldn't blame her.

Who the fuck wouldn't, he thought, *when you know the pain suffered by someone you love is because of you? A fucking club cut, reaching out across the years to pull shit like this. On my woman.*

Without thinking, he said the words aloud, the growl in his voice surprisingly loud in the room. "My woman." She gasped, and he realized his hands had tightened on her hips to the point of pain, his fingers complaining about the grip he knew would leave bruises on her body. "Mine. Motherfucker hurt *my* woman."

"Baby," she whispered, twisting to look over her shoulder at him. "I'm okay. Standing right here in the kitchen. I'm with you, honey." Leaning backwards, she pressed into him, her arm crossing her chest so she could cup his cheek with her palm. She lifted to her toes, touching her lips to the corner of his mouth and he watched as her eyes fluttered closed, felt the sweep of her tongue as she moved along the edge of his jaw towards his ear. Still in a whisper, she said, "I'm right here with you, baby."

He bent his head, breath coming quicker as she nipped at his earlobe, her palm still cradling his cheek, holding him in place for a moment. She told him again, "I'm okay."

Could be it wasn't her fear holding him back, but his own. She was his, and hurt, because of him. But, she was his.

"Mine," he said once more and groaned when her lips moved across his skin in a smile before she responded.

"Yes. Yours."

With that statement, her acknowledgement of what he felt in his bones, he broke from the frozen position, grabbed her hand and pulled her with him as he turned. Every other step up the stairs, he paused to look at her, the unfailing smile aimed up at him catching at his heart every time. *My fear.*

In their bedroom, he took his time undressing her, covering every exposed inch with strokes and touches, relishing the heat of her, the slide of skin-on-skin. Standing close, he reached up, teasing the ponytail tie out of her hair and threading his fingers through the heavy fall once freed.

Cupping his palm around the back of her neck, he pulled her in and up, their mouths meeting in a demanding, hot kiss filled with the tangle of his tongue sliding along hers. Eating down the soft gasps she made, he deepened the kiss, feeling her touch on his shoulders and the thrill of that was enough to push him to respond even more, biting and pulling at her bottom lip, sucking it into his mouth with a hard draw, the sting of her nails incentive to continue.

Lifting her, he put a knee to the bed and stretched out with her underneath him, her body cushioning his, legs parting to cradle his hips intimately. "I love you," he said, voice vibrating with passion, pressing his lips to the side of her neck, hoping she understood everything he tried to convey in those three words.

***

"I love you," Duck told her, and those three words echoed down to her bones. Those words meant she was his, owned in a way she never expected to want, his guttural claims of *'mine'* from earlier echoing through these few syllables.

Instead of responding, she reached up, and gripping the sides of his head brought their mouths into alignment. She allowed her eyes to track back and forth across his face before lifting those last centimeters and kissing him. Eyes open, their gazes locked as they came together, soft and slow, mouths opening and working against the other.

His elbows caged her in and when he transferred his weight, she felt it, gasping against his lips as he pinned her beneath him. He arched his back, breaking the kiss and moved to grip her sides, the heat from his touch scorching against her skin. Arms shifting and changing position, fingers slipping up across her ribs, he palmed her breasts, teasing the nipples of each with the coarse pad of his thumbs, sliding up and across her collarbones, curving over the arch of her shoulders.

He tugged her arms, stretching them up and over her head, his palms stroking the sensitive skin of her inside elbow, tracing along her forearms and then his fingers braceleted her wrists. He gripped tightly there for a moment before he moved again to press their hands together, palm to palm, roughened fingers threading between hers. He neither concentrated on the scars, nor ignored them, instead telling her with each touch that they didn't matter. They didn't factor in his desire for her. They were there, inescapable, proof of how fragile life could be, and his gentle hold showed her he wouldn't allow them to change how he felt for her. The scars were part of her, and she was part of him. Claimed. *His.*

Twining their fingers together, he pulled, bending her arms so their clasped hands were beside her head and he took some of his weight off, pressing into the bed with their combined grip. He moved and she shifted with him, eyes closing as her hips arched up, seeking, and then he came down, the tip of his cock poised at her entrance.

His body locked into place for a moment, every muscle becoming rigid and unyielding. Her eyes flew open as her breath caught in sudden fear; a fear she knew was irrational but still her chest tightened painfully at what felt like rejection. Then she watched, rapt, as his eyes darkened with desire, mouth falling open in a groan as he eased forwards. "Little Bee," he called softly and she marveled at the intense look on his face. His back rounded, hips stroking slowly, thrusting his length inside inch-by-inch, and as the width of his cock stretched her, he spoke, the ardent tone in his voice a promise, drawing a surprised gasp from her. "I love you."

Rocking into her, he sustained that same focus, his body moving powerfully over hers, their fluid movements in tune with each other. Present in the moment, concentrating on loving and being loved. The glide of his belly across hers a touch that felt like a caress. Every deep, penetrating stroke inside her ended with the same softly spoken words, until she anticipated each indrawn breath preceding them. "I still love you."

Every utterance of the words pushed back the fear he wouldn't want her, didn't need her any longer. "I love you." Every touch branding her in a way that let her believe again. "I'll always love you."

Later, much later, cradled to his side, her breathing beginning to even out and she reveled in how his arms tightened fiercely, protectively circling around her as she told him, "I love you, too. Always, Duck. Always."

Epilogue
FIFTEEN MONTHS LATER

Elias watched their progress avidly on his phone, the green dot advancing slowly, oh so slowly on the map. Brenda flipped down the sunshade on her side of the truck and used the mirror to watch him for a moment. She felt the heat and pressure on her leg at the same time and smiling, glanced over at Duck, behind the wheel in the driver's seat, one hand on the top curve of the steering wheel, his other resting on her leg just above the knee, fingers curling possessively as he squeezed lightly.

"You okay, Bee?" She knew his question had many layers to it and she reached up to flip the sunshade back into place.

"Right now, this minute? Yes, I'm okay." She paused, and then gave him more. "And I'm not nervous about visiting Blackie and Peaches." She twisted her neck, looking over her shoulder at Eli who had raised his head from the phone for a moment to grin at her. "I know I'm not as excited as Eli is about seeing Randi after being forced into months and months without her. It's been too long since her last visit, I know." She sighed in mock grievance. "It's just that summer only comes once a year." Eli shook his head side to side, tongue stuck out roguishly. "As does Christmas." Duck laughed. "And Easter." Then Eli grinned at her again. "But they are good people, good friends, and I'll be glad to see them again."

"You sure you're okay, baby? That was something to see back there." They had passed an accident scene about ten miles back, cop cars and ambulances lining both sides of the road. A pickup pulling a trailer full of cattle had flipped on the shoulder of the highway, pained and panicked sounds from the cows in the crumpled trailer shockingly loud as they drove past.

"I'm okay, Duck," she said quietly, reassuring him. She knew from the tight squeeze on her thigh he had seen the sadness in her face as she thought again of Essa. The Lamesa cops still didn't have any leads on who had run them off the road that day, even though she knew Duck had pulled a telling description from her that both the Rebels and Soldiers used to identify the man responsible. "I'm fine."

That last was a lie and he tilted his head, scowling at her from underneath his brows. "Okay, maybe not fine," she muttered, twisting in the seat to look out the window on her side of the truck, "but good enough." She sighed, tipping her head back on the seat, relaxing for a moment, eyes closed.

Duck moved to clasp her hand, threading their fingers together then tugged, bringing their joined hands to his leg, pressing the back of hers against his thigh. "Love you, Bee," he said softly, his tone thick, intense with emotion and she looked up to find he was watching her closely.

"Love you, too, Duck," she responded, seeing his eyes flick forwards and then back to her and she stiffened, swallowing against a sudden lump in her throat.

"We're here," Eli crowed from the backseat as Duck steered the truck off the road and onto a long, winding driveway, their arrival announced loudly by the brindle dog standing on the edge of the wide, welcoming porch wrapped around a two-story ranch house. She heard his door open just before the truck rocked to a stop and grinned as

Randi pelted from beside the house, feet unerringly finding the beaten path running along the edge of the grass.

Before he was even completely out of the truck, the two kids were talking, yelling and then jumping around, so excited to see each other their little bodies couldn't contain all the joy. "What's your dog's name?" Eli asked, and she heard Randi respond, her voice trailing off as they ran back the way she had come, towards the backyard. "Dee Two. It's got like three meanings, because Pops is like that. Two Dee's, because the real name is Dammit Dog Two, because Mom had a dog named Dammit Dog so when we got this one, she was telling the story and it stuck, so Dee times two, but, she's also Dammit Dog the second, so there's that..."

The front door of the house opened and Peaches stepped out, baby on one hip and a wide smile stretching her lips. A shadow appeared behind her and Brenda watched as a large hand curved around Peaches' waist, urging her out of the house as Blackie moved behind her, lifting one hand in a brief wave Brenda quickly returned.

Twisting in the seat, she looked at Duck, cupping his jaw in her hand. "I love you, Duck." She grinned, hearing the snuffling noises from the backseat, the sound familiar enough so she knew if she looked in the strategically placed mirror, she'd see an open mouth, hunting and rooting, balled fist pressed tightly to bowed lips. "Someone's hungry."

He smiled back at her, the look on his face stealing her breath because it was filled with so much love. "I got her." Twisting his head, he planted a firm kiss into her palm, and then folded out of the truck, opening the passenger door behind his seat. "Who's my ladybug?" He crooned the question and she watched as he unbuckled, then lifted their daughter from the car seat, pulling an infectious giggle from her when he pressed his face into her neck, pretending to eat her up.

"Who's my Ellie-belly?" Brenda's smile faded slightly at Duck's innocent use of Essa's pet name for Elias, but then Elizabeth giggled again, squealing as her father cradled her carefully in his arms. With effort, she let the feeling go, allowing joy and happiness to flood back in as she set her grief aside. She would never forget, didn't want to forget. But, today was for the living and her life, finally, was filled to overflowing with love.

Watcher
LAS CRUCES, NEW MEXICO

Watcher looked down at the papers he held, the charter for the Las Cruces Southern Soldiers. When he could be assured his hands were steady, he rose to his feet, locking gazes with the man in front of him as he folded the charter and tucked it safe inside his vest, rejecting with his actions what he had been about to do. "I can't, brother." All he needed to say echoed within those three words, and with a steady gaze, Mason looked at him and nodded. "Not yet. But we need to plan." Mason nodded again.

Looking at the men surrounding him, he leaned forward and the intensity in the room jumped a thousandfold when he said, "I promise you, brothers. Six go in. Six will come out." Mason gripped his shoulder, fingers tight around the leather and shook him slightly in silent agreement.

The end (of this story)

THANK YOU FOR READING *DUCK*!

Thank you for reading *Duck*, book #8 in the **Rebel Wayfarers MC** series. I grooved on writing his story and seeing things come full circle for him in so many ways. Liked watching, tagging along in his head as he figured out how a broken life can fit back together, puzzle piece by piece, even if it looks impossible. He never gave up, and I love that about him. I hope you enjoyed reading his story half as much as I liked writing it!

DUCK'S PLAYLIST

I put together playlists of music both mentioned in the book, and used during writing and editing. Want a peek into the mind of me? Be sure of your decision, it's not always normal here!

Duck's playlist: bit.ly/duck-playlist

ABOUT THE AUTHOR

Raised in the south, MariaLisa learned about the magic of books at an early age. Every summer, she would spend hours in the local library, devouring books of every genre. Self-described as a book-a-holic, she says "I've always loved to read, but then I discovered writing, and found I adored that, too. For reading...if nothing else is available, I've been known to read the back of the cereal box."

Also by MariaLisa deMora

Alace Sweets

A dark thriller, this book is not a light read. Filled with edge-of-your-seat suspense, this intense story commands the reader's attention as it drives towards the explosive ending. Alace Sweets is a vigilante serial killer, with everything that implies and is sure to trip all your triggers. Be ready.

At seventeen, Alace Sweets turned a corner in her life, taking the wrong shortcut home from school.

Resisting the harsh knowledge her attackers will never be made to pay for their actions, Alace takes a stand. Justice must be served, and if fate's scales are out of balance, she's determined to set things right as best she can.

When the laws of men fail, the rules of Alace prevail.

5-Star Reviews for Alace Sweets

"deMora has a superb story-line and exceptional character development. All of her characters have such depth that will intrigue the reader..."
~Turning Another Page

"Hot, sweet, dark thriller."
~Beth D

"It will keep you on the edge of your seat and give you chills."
~Escape Reality Book Blog

"Disturbing, haunting, sickly; yet hot, sexy and heart racing!"
~Amanda L

"From the first page [deMora] pulls you into the world she has created and you do not even try to escape..."
~Little Shop of Readers Blog

"A must read for all those dark, gritty romance fans out there."
~Sweet & Spicy Reads

"You will find yourself so drawn into the story that the outside world is blocked out and your locking the doors and turning on all the lights."
~Danena F

"Don't judge me for bonding with a vigilante serial killer, she's more than what she does."
~iScream Books

"Thrilling...chilling...full of suspense, nail biting edge of your seat excitement."
~Tracey H

"Every time MariaLisa deMora picks up her pen (or opens her computer), she creates characters you want to believe in."
~Gail S

"Intriguing dark storyline, beautiful love story and nail-biting conclusion, what more could a reader ask for?"
~Manda M

"This book takes you a dark and twisted ride that is gripping..."
~Renee Entress' Blog

"This book is dark and gritty and I literally had to take a day off from reading it because it's that intense."
~My Girlfriend's Couch

"This is my favourite book so far from this author ... I recommend this book if you enjoy dark romantic thrillers."
~Cheekypee Reads and Reviews

"There's not enough stars to give this book and 5 just doesn't really do it justice!"
~DeLane C

"I couldn't put this book down from page one! Tried to stop & go to bed but couldn't sleep thinking about Alace and got up & finished the book."
~Debbie M

"MariaLisa DeMora, wordsmith that she is, made this a story of the enlightenment of a woman and finding love in a life where she has had none."
~Kat W

"Whatever deep dark trench [deMora] pulled a character like Alace from should be revisited again and often."
~Confessions of a Serial Reader

ADDITIONAL SERIES AND BOOKS

Please note that books in a series frequently feature characters from additional books within that series. If series books are read out of order, readers will twig to spoilers for the other books, so going back to read the skipped titles won't have the same angsty reveals.

Rebel Wayfarers MC series:

Mica, #1
A Sweet & Merry Christmas, short story #1.5
Slate, #2
Bear, #3
Jase, #4
Gunny, #5
Mason, #6
Hoss, #7
Harddrive Holidays, short story #7.5
Duck, #8
Biker Chick Campout, short story #8.5
Watcher, #9

A Kiss to Keep You, novella #9.25
Gun Totin' Annie, short story #9.5
Secret Santa, short story #9.75
Bones, #10
Gunny's Pups, novella #10.25
Never Settle, short story #10.5
Not Even A Mouse, short story #10.75
Fury, #11
Christmas Doings, #11.25
Gypsy's Lady, #11.5
Cassie, #12
Road Runner's Ride, novella #12.5

Occupy Yourself band series:

Born Into Trouble, #1
Grace In Motion, #2 (TBD)
What They Say, #3 (TBD)

Neither This, Nor That series:

This Is the Route Of Twisted Pain, #1
Treading the Traitor's Path: Out Bad, #2
Trapped by Fate on Reckless Roads, #3 (TBD)

Other Books:

With My Whole Heart
Alace Sweets
Hard Focus

More information available at mldemora.com.

www.ingramcontent.com/pod-product-compliance
Lightning Source LLC
Chambersburg PA
CBHW071519260626
47170CB00002B/429